A demon in the house

The demon was in the middle of my living room, stepping over the wreckage of my shattered front door and carrying a Browning Hi-Power semiautomatic.

He was bald, with pale skin and dark, almost black, eyes. I knew he was powerful because I could feel his genetic imprint even standing this far away. It was like the stink of sulfur, assaulting, making my eyes water.

"What do you want?" I asked.

"What do you think?" He smiled, revealing two separate rows of fangs and a flexible mandible . . . He had the grin of a homicidal shark.

Well, Dad, I thought, as usual, you were right. I should have gone into real estate.

The Vailoid demon laughed—a horrific, burbling sound.

Then he pointed the gun at me and fired.

Night Child

Jes Battis

ACE BOOKS, NEW YORK

THE BERKLEY PUBLISHING GROUP
Published by the Penguin Group
Penguin Group (USA) Inc.
375 Hudson Street, New York, New York 10014, USA
Penguin Group (Canada), 90 Eglinton Avenue East, Suite 700, Toronto, Ontario M4P 2Y3, Canada
(a division of Pearson Penguin Canada Inc.)
Penguin Books Ltd., 80 Strand, London WC2R 0RL, England
Penguin Group Ireland, 25 St. Stephen's Green, Dublin 2, Ireland (a division of Penguin Books Ltd.)
Penguin Group (Australia), 250 Camberwell Road, Camberwell, Victoria 3124, Australia
(a division of Pearson Australia Group Pty. Ltd.)
Penguin Books India Pvt. Ltd., 11 Community Centre, Panchsheel Park, New Delhi—110 017, India
Penguin Group (NZ), 67 Apollo Drive, Rosedale, North Shore 0632, New Zealand
(a division of Pearson New Zealand Ltd.)
Penguin Books (South Africa) (Pty.) Ltd., 24 Sturdee Avenue, Rosebank, Johannesburg 2196,
South Africa

Penguin Books Ltd., Registered Offices: 80 Strand, London WC2R 0RL, England

This is a work of fiction. Names, characters, places, and incidents either are the product of the author's imagination or are used fictitiously, and any resemblance to actual persons, living or dead, business establishments, events, or locales is entirely coincidental. The publisher does not have any control over and does not assume any responsibility for author or third-party websites or their content.

NIGHT CHILD

An Ace Book / published by arrangement with the author

PRINTING HISTORY
Ace mass-market edition / June 2008

Copyright © 2008 by Jes Battis.
Cover art by Timothy Lantz.
Cover design by Lesley Worrell.
Interior text design by Laura K. Corless.

ISBN: 978-0-441-01602-0

ACE
Ace Books are published by The Berkley Publishing Group,
a division of Penguin Group (USA) Inc.,
375 Hudson Street, New York, New York 10014.
ACE and the "A" design are trademarks belonging to Penguin Group (USA) Inc.

PRINTED IN THE UNITED STATES OF AMERICA

10 9 8 7 6 5 4 3 2 1

Acknowledgments

This book owes its existence to a number of brilliant, generous, and patient souls. My editor, Ginjer Buchanan, has offered valuable input throughout and done her best to guide this first-time novelist through the sometimes scary process of publication. My agent, Lauren Abramo, first saw potential in the book and helped me revise it into something much better than it was before. She consistently deflects my anxiety (including late-night e-mails asking impossible questions) with composure and kindness. Lynn Flewelling and Chaz Brenchley both offered encouragement and advice about publishing this book, and were also kind enough to participate in my doctoral research on fantasy literature (which is a whole other story). The folks at *Fangs, Fur & Fey* welcomed me as a first-time novelist and gave me great tips.

My friends and colleagues in the English department at Simon Fraser University have all, at one time or another, offered perceptive suggestions and encouragement about this book. My New York friends Marty and ej (and their dogs, Mabel and Buckley) have soothed me with hospitality, hockey games, and tofurkey. And my roommates in Greenpoint—Myka, Christine, Katy, and Dave—have all done their part to keep me fed and sheltered, especially when I was too swamped to deal with the business of being a human being. My students at Hunter College, with all of their amazing stories and perspectives, reminded me why I loved being a teacher as well as a writer. Thanks to the forensic teachers and writers whose work intrigued and astonished me: Vincent Di Maio, Henry Lee, Bill Bass, Michael Baden, Tom Bevel, M. Lee Goff, and John Douglas. Also, thanks to Gail Anderson, professor of forensic entomology at SFU, who answered some bizarre e-mails from this author and even let me take her advanced forensics class.

Brooklyn Label supplied me endlessly with coffee and delicious scrambles, while the Ashbox Café gave me comfortable chairs and nonstop bagels, and Champion Coffee was the first café I went to in Brooklyn (their outdoor patio and wireless connection were lifesavers in those first few weeks). Strand never failed to deliver when I required an obscure title, and when I needed some Canadian love, I could always hop across the border to the Toronto Women's Bookstore, Glad Day Bookshop, and the Robarts Library at the University of Toronto, as well as Little Sister's and Spartacus in Vancouver. I also want to say thank you to the customs agent at the Winnipeg International Airport who asked me if I was "one of those subversive academics." I hope the answer is yes, although I lied at the time and said that I studied grammar. Thank you to the Social Sciences and Humanities Research Council of Canada, whose funding for my postdoctoral fellowship in New York also gave me the living wage necessary to complete this book—and thanks to Robert Fulford, whose spirited article in the *National Post* attacking my research (and my sexuality) only encouraged me to keep stirring up shit as a writer and an academic. Thanks to every independent-bookstore owner who might shelve this novel, even as she's fighting to stay in business: Bluestockings, 12th Street Books, Mercer Street Books, St. Mark's Bookshop, Oscar Wilde, Giovanni's Room, This Ain't the Rosedale Library, Books of Wonder, BakkaPhoenix, Revolution, and The Book Man (where I practically lived as a teenager). Thanks to all the underpaid and overtired employees working for chain bookstores who love reading books but hate selling them.

Finally, I hope this book finds its way into the hands of queer and questioning youth around the world and that they find characters within it who matter to them. You are never alone.

1

"That's a dead vampire."

Selena Ward, my boss, raised an eyebrow. "Uh-huh."

"You dragged me out of bed, to a disgusting alley on Granville Street—at two in the morning—to see a dead vampire?"

She handed me the clipboard with the MCS entry log. Anyone entering a mystical crime scene has to sign in first, just like a regular crime scene. The only difference is that some of our responding officers aren't human. The scene was divided into three zones with a base of operations, or staging area, near the far end of the alley where extra photographic equipment, evidence bundles, and chemical reagents could be stored in portable kits. The perimeter around the vampire's body was taped off as the primary focal point, with access far more restricted than the outer edges of the scene. It all seems orderly until you have to explain to a high-ranking investigator that she should really get the hell out of your way. I'll admit it—I did get a secret pleasure out of that sometimes. There weren't any doors or fire escapes at the back of the alley, so the only natural point of entry and exit was the street.

"Take a closer look," Selena said. "Make sure to put on gloves."

Tasha Lieu, our medical examiner, gave me a wink as she passed by. "Just released the scene, so it's all yours."

"Thanks, Tash." Selena looked tired.

I was already fishing the gloves out of my purse. "Sorry to call you out so late," I said sheepishly. I'd always assumed that Tasha had some type of normal human life outside of the CORE, unlike the rest of us. She was an intensely private person, and all I really knew about her was that she lived in Richmond and had a Calvin and Hobbes cartoon strip taped on the wall above the autopsy sink.

"No worries, I'm a night owl. See you at the morgue, bright and early tomorrow morning. I should have the post done by the time you get there."

I swallowed. "Yeah, great. See you there." It was just like a trip to the dentist, only the dentist was a vivisected corpse. Not my idea of a sweet morning. Tasha waved and left the scene, stepping carefully over the caution tape.

"Where's Siegel?" Selena's frown had deepened. Shit.

"Parking. The strip is packed, as usual, so I sent him down to the seedier part of Nelson Street. He may have to fend off some goth-chicks, but he'll survive."

West Granville was Vancouver's nightclub district, and its irregular streets were an explosion of noise and neon light. Hipsters danced the night away at Aquarius and The Plaza, while underage kids drank pitchers of cheap Molson at The Roxy. After last call, the strip became a drunken labyrinth of kids eating hot dogs and fries from late-night vendors, taxi cabs dodging each other, and police cars wailing their sirens. Just another night in Terminal City, as Vancouver was often called, since the only thing beyond it to the west was ocean. Like Shangri-La. The end of everything. No wonder demons liked it here so much.

"Funny lady." Derrick Siegel emerged from behind the yellow tape, smiling apologetically. "Right here, Selena. Sorry—I had to—"

"Park the car, yes, I heard." She rolled her eyes. "Just put some gloves on and follow us. Apparently there are four different concert venues spilling out drunken teenagers onto Granville right now, and I'd like to avoid a security leak."

Neither of us looked like we belonged at a crime scene. Derrick was wearing a pajama top and rumpled blue jeans with a jacket hastily thrown over. The jacket was probably Kenneth Cole: Derrick was the only person I knew who would wear designer clothes to a crime scene. He'd learned some tricks over the years, though, and he was wearing old shoes this time. Black runners—the kind that he'd normally never be caught dead in. I was wearing the same. Try scrubbing blood out of a new pair of Charles David boots. I learned that lesson quickly, and now I always brought sneakers.

A black cat was wandering about the scene, delicately avoiding a tripod stand as she surveyed the walls of the alley. This was no random stray, but rather Sophie, one of the trained forensic animals that the CORE employed for sniffing out magical scenes. Cats didn't have quite as broad a sense of smell as dogs, but their olfactory nerves were more refined, which allowed them to detect a variety of demonic and nonhuman scents that lingered in the air long after a kill. Unlike dogs, alley cats like Sophie didn't need to be trained with a scent pad—she simply roamed about the alley, did her thing, and let her trainer know if she found anything interesting. Cats don't exactly work on the clock, but they're more valuable to the CORE because their close proximity to magic allows them to sense the residual chemicals left over by strong materia flows. Why do you think they always followed witches around? Cats are strongly attracted to the smell of materia leftovers, or "frass," as they're known. Like mystical catnip.

Sophie, however, didn't appear to be turning up anything tonight. She sniffed the air around the body disinterestedly, then flicked her tail and retreated. A handler returned her gently to the cat carrier, and she immediately curled up and fell asleep. She was used to being around mystical crime scenes.

Selena had paged me around 1:30 a.m., which was actually a pretty decent time, all things considered. I'd gotten calls a lot later than that. As an Occult Special Investigator, it was my job to do the preliminary investigation around any mystical crime scene in the Greater Vancouver Regional District and follow up on leads. Selena gave the orders, and I followed them. Most of the time. I used to be scared shitless of her, but three years of working together had softened our relationship.

Derrick and I were both junior employees for the Mystical Crime Lab unit of CORE, the Central Occult Regulation Enterprise. CORE was a transnational blanket organization that controlled just about everything mystical within North America and Europe. The City of Vancouver's crime lab was one of the best in Canada, with a fully equipped DNA testing site and separate pathology departments that included a standalone morgue. Vancouver may have had the reputation for being a quiet city when it came to violent crime, but as far as mystical disturbances were concerned, it was a hot spot.

Since I was only an OSI-1, the crime lab tended to give me probationary assignments—that is, the back-alley jobs like this one that nobody else would take. Derrick was on probation as well, but as a telepath he had a different union. I think. Office politics get kind of hairy when you're dealing with demons and mages.

We slipped on our Tyvek suits, which were modified to protect us from mystical as well as organic contamination, and then Selena led us to the body. It was a male vampire, lying almost peacefully near the back of the alley. His head was propped up slightly against the corner of a Dumpster, and his shirt had been unbuttoned, revealing a smooth white chest that was unmarked. He was wearing a pair of dress pants and black shoes. Cheap stuff—the kind you could pick up at an Eaton's sale. The guy looked like he'd just come from an accounting firm. His blond hair was neatly trimmed, and he was clean shaven.

"Have a look," Selena said.

I knelt down beside the body. The photo techs were milling around me, snapping pictures from every conceivable angle with different filters for contrast in the dark. One photographer was taking reference shots of the alley with a 28mm lens, while the other snapped shots of various artifacts around the alley with a 55mm macro lens for close-ups, placing evidence placards next to them to establish scale. A third technician was furiously scribbling notes in the photo log, trying to keep up with the others. All of the flashes gave the scene an even more macabre feel.

An occlusion, or perimeter field, had already been set up at the entrance to the alley. In order to work unhindered, we have to seal off the area from bystanders. The occlusion is a kind of mystical envelope that alters light wavelengths around the area. It has something to do with quantum packets, but I never really get the explanation. With mystical crime scenes, you have to preserve all the evidence while simultaneously hiding it from the general public, and that includes the VPD. Not always a simple matter in this city.

Vampires decompose a lot more slowly than human bodies, so it was impossible to tell how long he'd been lying here. No insect activity, no temperature change, and no postmortem interval to establish. But I was trained to detect even more subtle alterations. Einstein told us that energy can't be destroyed—only transformed. Every organism has an energy signature, an aura. Even the undead.

I passed my fingertips through the air a few inches above the vampire's chest. I could feel a faint differential in the energy flows—a trickle of something, like spider silk against my face. It made me want to sneeze.

"Feels sketchy. Maybe forty-eight hours ago, but I can't be certain. You know how tough it is to establish time of death with vamps."

"Derrick?" Selena gestured to the body. "You want to give it a try?"

It wasn't really a question. Derrick sighed.

"One of these days," he said, "I'd like to read the dying thoughts of a really happy person. Someone who expired in a bed full of puppies and bunny rabbits."

"I'll see what I can do," Selena said flatly.

Derrick knelt down beside me. He placed his gloved fingertips on the vampire's forehead, and closed his eyes.

I didn't really understand how Derrick's powers worked, since I wasn't a telepath myself. All I knew was that, just like I could sense auras, Derrick could sense faint neurological impressions—like letters pressed into wax, or soft slate. He couldn't always make sense of what he saw.

Derrick's body tensed up. He was trying to read the vampire's last thoughts, just like a laser would read a compact disc. When we die and our brains collapse, they send a myriad of electrical spasms throughout our bodies. Organic memory, it's called. Telepaths can try to access that memory and reconstruct it. Sometimes a victim's last few seconds, or perimortem interval, can be recovered.

Derrick was starting to sweat. I put a hand on his shoulder, tentatively, and his eyes flicked open. He lurched away from me, as if my touch had burned him.

"You okay, hon?"

"Tess." He said my name like it was unfamiliar. His pupils were huge and black. Then he blinked, shaking his head as if to clear it. "Sorry. That was intense."

"Did you see anything?" Selena asked. "Anything that makes sense?"

"A lot of it was a blur." He closed his eyes again. "There was a girl, though."

Selena leaned in closer. "A girl?"

He nodded. "I can't really make out her features. I think she's a teenager. Thirteen, maybe fourteen years old. She seems young."

"What else?" Selena was writing notes on a pad.

"Fire." Derrick swallowed again. "Some kind of fire. Something burning, but I can't tell what." He nearly gagged. "A horrible smell."

I flinched at the word "fire." Memories I didn't want to deal with. Screams I couldn't bring myself to hear again. I looked away to hide my stricken expression. I don't think Selena noticed.

Only things and people burn—not the past. I heard my old teacher's voice, sighed, pushed it down. You can't bring people back. It's not like in the movies.

Mostly, magic is just a bitch.

"I could feel intense fear," Derrick said. "Not of the fire, but—something else. Whatever killed him must have been extremely powerful."

"Not necessarily," I said. "I think he was newly minted. Inexperienced. A lot of higher demons might have been able to scare him."

One of the photographers was leaning close to me, peering at the vampire's body. I pushed his camera away.

"Something we can help you with?"

He grinned sheepishly. He was just a kid—barely twenty, at best—with one of those spiky faux-hawk cuts that was currently popular, hair sticking out every which way. He looked like he should be at a rave, not at a mystical crime scene.

"Sorry, Miss Corday." Points for knowing my name, at least. "I just don't get it—shouldn't he be dust?"

"Vampires only dessicate when they're exposed to direct sunlight," Selena explained. "And even that takes a while. But this guy doesn't have a mark on him. No beheading, no heart trauma. Under optimal conditions, a vampire body like this could avoid decomp for a few days, maybe even a week."

"He looks so peaceful," Derrick said.

"I know. Almost like he's been posed this way." I turned to Selena. "Any way for us to tell if the body's been moved?"

She shrugged. "Hard to say with a vampire. No lividity marks, and you know how weird their blood chemistry is—blood and plasma don't separate in the same way. I think we'd just be guessing."

Most bodies decomposed in a uniform fashion. As the process of cell death, or autolysis, went to work, the body was devoured from the inside. All of the bacteria, the intestinal flora, that protected us in life now began eating away at the vital organs. Without any cardiac momentum to pump it through the arterial system, blood separated into plasma and serum, producing a marble effect as it settled throughout the flesh. But none of this was evident on the body of a vampire. Their rate of decay was too bizarre for even CORE pathologists to determine any kind of pattern.

Two investigators were probing the area around the body with long, black-handled daggers that shone like snowflakes in the dim light of the alley. The athame was a ritual dagger used for channeling mystical energy, or materia, from a variety of sources, usually geothermic. Our bodies are like transistors that can absorb materia without the help of ritual tools like the athame, but the energy—especially the type used in combat—can be as harmful as radiation to the body. The athame works as a kind of circuit for the materia, breaking it down into a palatable stream that the body can absorb.

At the moment, the two investigators were using their blades as alternate light sources, manipulating the radiant-energy spectrum in order to produce more penetrative types of illumination within the darkness of the alley. One athame was calibrated to emit clear blue light, which would cause any stray fiber to flare up like a tendril of orange flame against the cone of blue. The second investigator was moving her athame in a slow arc like a flashlight, bathing the walls and floor of the alley with the purple glow of longwave ultraviolet light. She flicked the dagger momentarily, and the cone of purple narrowed to an intense line of burning mauve—shortwave UV light, a new technology that could be used with a reflecting UV imaging system, or RUVIS, to reveal latent fingerprints. They fluoresced under the purple glow like writhing bruises, their loops, whorls, and tented arches glimmering like bright tattoos against porous wood and stone.

Derrick kept looking nervously at the vampire. "You're sure he's dead?"

"Yep. Again." I chuckled. "Sorry, I don't know why that's funny."

"Seems like a lot of expensive technology out here for a dead vampire," I said, noting one investigator as he began to carefully snap together the sighting rods for a total-station mapping device, which would be used to download 360-degree infrared pictures to a scene-reconstruction program like AIMS. That piece of equipment alone was worth far more than I made in a year.

"Marcus says we have to be thorough, given the delicate political situation," Selena replied. "We've got a vampire body with no visible wounds, which means that something must have killed him from the inside. We'll have to do an autopsy."

"Shit." I rubbed my hands to keep warm. "The vampire community won't be happy to hear that we're cutting up one of their own."

"We can do damage control later. We'll put a spin on it. For now, the body's in public view. It's fair game, and we found it first."

"That's kind of cold-blooded, don't you think?"

She blinked. "You want to send his family a card?"

I sighed. "Fine. Just trying to be politic for once."

"Leave that to me. Your job is to follow up."

"I know what my job is."

She handed me two evidence bags. There was a small, yellowed square of paper, folded up, inside the first bag, and a crumpled photograph in the second.

"From his pocket?"

Selena nodded. "The note is written in vampire script. I'll send it to questioned documents for analysis."

"And the picture?" I peered at it. One of the subjects was the dead vampire—he was grinning, eyes bright, arm wrapped around a woman's shoulder. I didn't recognize the woman, though. She had blond hair and sharp blue eyes. She was smiling as well, but there seemed to be a hardness to the expression—almost a hint of cruelty.

"What do you think?" I asked Selena. "Vampire sweethearts?"

"Could be. Audiovisual should be able to pull something out of it."

"So other than this picture, and the note, we've got nothing?"

"Nada." Selena cast another look at the body. "We've already been over every inch of the alley with UV and IR lights. We sprayed every surface with luminol and swabbed his clothes with phenolphthalein. Not a drop of blood. Anywhere."

Luminol was a chemical reagent that reacted to the iron in hemoglobin. Spray it on a surface, turn the lights out, and it fluoresces. UV light works particularly well for that. Phenolphthalein was a bit trickier—generally it was used for swabbing fabrics. Just add a drop of hydrogen peroxide, and if there's blood present, the swab turns purple. Our solutions were modified to detect the unique plasmids in demon blood, so our presumptive tests were species-specific. Goblin blood was pink. Like Klingon.

"A vampire dies without a mark on him, and there's no trace of blood. Seems unlikely. What about fibers?"

"None that we could find."

"There must be a print somewhere," Derrick said. "Nobody's that clean. Not even a trained killer. They always leave something behind, right? Locard's exchange principle: Every interaction leaves a trace."

"Depends if it was another vamp. Prints come from a mixture of oil and amino acids, right? But vampires don't sweat or produce oil. They're ghosts." Selena drew out a pack of smokes from her pocket. She stared at it ruefully for a moment, then sighed and put it back. I'd forgotten that she used to be a smoker. "If another vamp did this, we might never find prints. Aura traces, maybe, but getting a match will be impossible. And auras don't hold up in court."

A photographer's flash lit up her face momentarily, and I was struck by what a surprisingly beautiful woman she was. At nearly six-one, she was tall enough to be considered statuesque. Lean and lithe, she had the kind of body that most women would kill for, although she made every effort to conceal it with gray pantsuits and men's shirts. She was wearing a tan jacket that made her brown skin look even darker, and her hair was tied up tightly. Selena wasn't the kind of black woman who let her hair down in public. I'd have killed to see what it looked like.

"What?" she asked. She'd caught me staring.

I looked away. "Nothing. Just wondering if the victim's own prints will pan out. We can run them through D-CODIS."

D-CODIS, our own version of the Combined DNA Indexing System, had all sorts of interesting DNA profiles that would have knocked the Vancouver Police lab techs right out of their chairs. Fortunately, our records were restricted.

I signed the tag on the evidence bag, then put it in my pocket. "I'll swing this by the lab on my way home. Anything else?"

"You leaving already?" Selena asked. "Why don't you stick around? There's still lots of work to be done here."

"I've got a meeting with Marcus at six thirty a.m.—something to do with my upcoming performance review." I exhaled. "I'd rather chew on napalm than deal with him so early in the morning, but I guess I don't have a choice."

"He does outrank both of us." Selena's grin was sympathetic. "Don't worry about the meeting. I'm sure it'll go fine."

"That's probably what they said to Napoleon. And Custer."

"C'mon." Derrick fished the car keys out of his pocket. "You have to drop me off in Kits, and I don't want you taking any of your rage out on the late-night joggers."

"Right. Let's go." I took the keys from him. "Maybe we'll stop at Denny's for an ice cream sundae. I'm craving sugar."

"You just saw a dead body."

"What's your point?"

He sighed. "None whatsoever."

2

They're going to kill the girl.

That's what I heard in my dream. Except, in the dream, everything was black. Everything around me, everything above me—but not *me*. I was a flaming red shadow, leaving fiery vermillion footprints wherever I walked, trailing clouds of light. I was moving across a smooth black surface, cold like a starless night sky, or a universe made entirely of black velvet.

A tongue of flame, the shock of heat on my face, and then—

—and then it was the more familiar dream, the one I knew so well. It was a different girl, but she was burning, screaming. The house was collapsing around her, crumbling in like a nightmarish sand castle, and she kept calling, calling:

Tess! Oh God Tess help me help God—

The flames were so high, the smoke was everywhere, in my eyes and lungs, filling every part of me like a mass of killing shadow. I'd always hated fire. Magic kept most of the heat away from me, but I was too young, inexperienced—I couldn't banish the smoke. I didn't know the proper shields and procedures, the correct rituals. I couldn't say the right words. I couldn't. I just—

A wall of flame struck me full on the face, and I woke up screaming. I could still feel the heat all over my body, the house collapsing like a burnt and calcined skeleton around me, and what I saw—in the living room—what I saw—

I closed my eyes, hands curling around the bedsheets. As always, her name was on my lips.

Eve.

Marcus Tremblay's office was hidden in the labyrinthine depths of the CORE crime lab, at the very center of a world of sliding doors, glass partitions, locked vaults, and security checks. You had to walk through two just to get into the foyer of the building, and they weren't only looking for guns and contraband. Those machines were calibrated to detect a fraction of a change in a human's energy signature, an aura fluctuation, a spike in temperature, the slightest residue of a spell or charm clinging like toilet paper to the bottom of your shoe.

I stopped at the front desk, waving to one of the ubiquitous security guards who never waved back. It was 6 a.m. and my cheeriness was bullshit, but there was no sense in taking my mood out on everyone else.

"ID," she said simply, adjusting her sunglasses. They were CORE special-issue, designed to pick up changes in body chemistry, along with otherworldly auras. They reminded me of those shades from *The Matrix*.

I produced my laminated card, and she swiped it through the desk-scanner.

"Name and designation, please."

"Tess Corday," I said, slowly and clearly. "OSI-1." The last bit held, perhaps, a trace of bitterness. I almost thought I saw the security guard smirk.

Then the light on the console turned green, and the sliding glass door opened.

"Have a pleasant day, Miss Corday."

I grunted and walked forward.

The main foyer narrowed down to a long hallway, equipped with evenly spaced cameras, along with other surveillance devices that I could sense without seeing. I came to the second security check, which was unmanned, though far from unmonitored. Just a pedestal set into the floor with a small console, and beyond that, another sliding glass door just like the first one. I wasn't fooled. That innocent-looking glass door could fry you like tofu in a wok.

I placed my hand on the console. There was a brief tingle as five blue lights appeared around my thumb and fingers, and I felt the familiar pinch of scanning-magic as my DNA was thoughtfully perused by the computer. The blue lights turned green, and a voice chimed: "Tessa Isobel Corday, born May 21, 1982, probationary clearance."

That "probationary clearance" made me want to grind my teeth.

The second door slid open, and I proceeded down another long hallway that opened up into the reception area of our lab proper. Kaylee, our newest intern, waved to me from behind the desk. I smiled. She wouldn't last much longer.

I walked past the various training rooms, where agents were being put through a battery of different field exercises. In one room, I saw Selena, dressed in jeans and a T-shirt, holding a long, slim dagger above her head.

"This is your athame," she was telling the line of fresh-faced recruits, who all stared at her in a mixture of awe and terror. "It's your primary tool for combat-magic. It focuses primordial energies and filters them, just like a living organ, so that your body can handle the power. Without the athame, those same energies could burn a hole through your chest. Got it?"

They all nodded in unison. None of them was a day over thirteen.

I often wished I'd failed that particular test.

"Can anyone tell me what materia is?" Selena pointed to a serious-looking girl with tawny hair. "Nadine?"

"Materia is the energy produced by organic and electrical

forces around the world," Nadine replied with textbook precision. "It includes electricity, magnetism, combustion, photosynthesis, and other chemical interactions. We can channel materia currents by using our athame."

"And what is the danger of using materia?"

"The physical energies can harm our bodies, shorten our lifespan, and even kill us." Nadine seemed only marginally conscious of what she was saying. "Materia can be as dangerous as nuclear radiation, earthquakes, thunderstorms, and mass floods."

"Good," Selena said. "That's why we have to maintain complete control. Point your athame at the target—make sure it's level—and then reach out with your senses. Feel along the length of the blade, and try to balance the energies as they flow through your hand, up your arm. It doesn't hurt, but it *does* feel a bit odd at first, like a low-voltage shock."

She leveled her blade at a steel target placed against the wall.

"Where am I drawing this materia from?"

"Seismic tremors in the ground," another girl piped up. "And thermal materia from all of the fluorescent lights."

"Exactly. The trick is to separate the materia currents and focus only on the energy that you need. Let the tension build as the materia interacts with your body. And once you can feel it buzzing in the back of your head—release the energy."

A line of incandescent white flame burst from the tip of the dagger, striking the center of the target. It was like staring at a thread of holy light—only I knew exactly what that power could do to a human body, and there was nothing spiritual about it.

Selena lowered her athame. "Now, everyone have a try."

It was all about physics. When astrophysicists discovered that a good chunk of the matter that made up the universe was actually invisible—even as it exerted an enormous gravitational pull on distant galaxies—they called it "dark matter." But at times, there's very little difference between physics and magic, and even pictures from the Hubble telescope can't quite convince the majority of people that the universe is composed of, for lack of a better term, shadowy stuff that we can feel without seeing. Mages had known of its existence for centuries.

Science didn't catch up to magic officially until Stephen Hawking suggested that *everything* produced energy, including black holes. It was around this time that astrophysicists dropped an even bigger bombshell on the scientific community: that galaxies at the farthest edges of the universe were actually moving *faster* than they had during the Big Bang. In essence, all of this dark matter had somehow picked up velocity, thereby violating just about everything that Netwon had said about inertia and momentum. The only explanation was that some type of unseen energy had entered into the closed-system universe and was actually speeding things up. So they called it "dark energy." Of course, mages had known about that for even longer than dark matter, but we called it materia instead. Telling a witch about dark matter was about as illuminating as telling her that mandrake should be soaked in a bowl of sour milk in order to cure birth pains. It was folk knowledge.

"I'm a spark!"

I looked down and saw a black girl in pigtails—she couldn't have been older than eleven. She held her practice athame easily, almost casually, in one hand. I looked at her matching green frog barrettes.

"Are you, now?" I smiled. "And what does that mean?"

She rolled her eyes. "*You* should know." Then she snapped her fingers—I felt a rush of inflowing materia, and a tongue of flame burst to life in her hand. She snapped it on and off like a Zippo, looking delighted.

"Don't be showy, Lil." Selena placed her hand briefly over the little girl's, and her flame vanished. She sighed and looked at me. "Trust this new generation of kids to start talking street and messing up all our definitions. Now we've got 'sparks' who manipulate fire, 'glides' who manipulate air, 'subs' for water—"

"And I'm a miner," I said, grinning at Lil. "'Cause I'm all earthy."

"Sparks are better," she said flatly, then turned back to the crowd.

Selena shrugged. I just laughed and walked past the training rooms, remembering acutely what it felt like to be so young and inexperienced. Thirteen and smiling, with my pigtails and *Animaniacs* T-shirt, wondering why everyone else seemed so terrified. An empty vessel just waiting to be filled. Back then, it hadn't been Selena teaching me, though—she was still an OSI-2 and mostly away on fieldwork.

Marcus's office was in a hive of similar rooms, tucked away behind a maze of hallways and generally inaccessible unless you really knew the layout of the lab. My first week here, I'd gotten lost four times trying to find my day supervisor, and somehow kept ending up in the underground parking.

I walked in without knocking. Marcus was on the phone, but he waved vaguely toward a nearby chair. He had those iconic middle-aged looks—trim, graying hair, pleated khakis, nicely ironed shirts, all a variation of the same boring color—that made you feel oddly at ease with him. Until he opened his mouth.

Marcus hung up the phone, but he didn't smile. "Hello, Tess. What was this meeting about again?"

Fuck—was it *this* game? I hate when authority figures try to appear all bumbling and Mr. Magoo-like—"Oh, dear, I've misplaced my memo"—it was all an act. He knew exactly why I was here, since he'd scheduled the damn meeting.

"You wanted to talk about my upcoming performance review." I ventured a weak smile. "Got any tips on how I might ace it?"

Marcus was expressionless. "Huh. Right." He shuffled through some papers, all color-coded. God help you if you submitted the improper cover page.

Finally, he withdrew my file from the stack and looked it over. His frown wasn't precisely encouraging. "We may have a problem, Tess."

I looked him in the eye. "Who's got the problem? You or me?"

"Don't get fresh." He leaned across the desk. "Your file is colorful, to say the least. You've been written up half a dozen times already for various procedural infractions, and I've had to sign each report. They're starting to add up."

I rolled my eyes. "Oh, right. What are these big infractions?"

He scanned the file. "Three warnings for insubordination, two notes on tardiness, a reprimand for some evidence that you claim to have 'misplaced'—"

"It got torched in a firefight!" I glared at him. "You were there, Marcus, and if memory serves, you set fire to a couple of things as well. You know how paperwork gets compromised sometimes in a situation as volatile as that. What was I supposed to do—collect the ashes in a bundle and bring them back?"

"It would have been a start."

I sighed. "Okay. So I've got a few notes in my file—nothing major, though. And I could ace this performance review—"

"*Could* isn't a word that I'd use. Try *must*."

I stared at him. "What are you saying?"

He shuffled some more papers, maddeningly refusing to look at me. "I'm saying that there's a lot riding on this case, and you can't afford to get sloppy. People are watching you, Tess—not just me. You can't afford another reprimand."

"Great." I really wanted a cigarette now.

"Everyone has to submit to quality control, Tess."

"So if I don't crack open this case—what—you're dismissing me? Just like that?" I shook my head. "I'll file a grievance—"

"You're not a teamster. It doesn't work that way." He held my gaze. "All I'm saying is, this is your test. Don't blow it. Follow procedure to the letter on this one, or this will be your last assignment. And there's no easy exit from this place. You know that as well as I do."

He was right. People don't walk away from this job.

I swallowed, trying hard not to lunge across the desk. Marcus could be coldly robotic when he wanted to, but he was still a competent supervisor, and he had the welfare of the entire lab to think about. Still, I was afraid that a part of him might have been enjoying this. He'd always been critical of my work.

"Any advice?" I asked.

"Sure." He returned the file to his desk. "Just be a good OSI. Document everything, keep the chain of evidence in line, and follow protocol."

Marcus always followed protocol. That's why his shirt was pressed, his tie was crisp, and his watch was set to go off exactly four minutes before lunch. His office was arranged for maximum efficiency, and his walls weren't cluttered with photos or paintings—just memos. I secretly hoped that the backseat of his car was a mess.

"All right," I said, trying not to clench my teeth. "What would you like me to do first? I can stop by trace—"

"Go to the morgue. Tasha's opening up the vampire, and you can take notes." He smiled faintly. "If you manage not to pass out."

I blanched slightly. Nine times out of ten, watching a demon autopsy still made me violently ill. Marcus always enjoyed sending me there.

"The morgue." I smiled like a stewardess. "Right. And then?"

He shrugged. "I'll let you know. Just stay out of trouble." He picked up the phone. "And relax. Siegel can help you. I'm sure he'd like some extra fieldwork."

Great. Not that I didn't appreciate Derrick's company, but he wasn't exactly a combat specialist.

"Thank you," I said slowly. "I'll—"

He pointed to the phone. "Sorry, Tess. You'll have to excuse me."

I gave him my best dutiful daughter smile, then walked out of the office. I kept walking, through another hallway, down a flight of steps, through an emergency exit, until I was standing on the outside terrace.

Then I screamed.

3

There's nothing quite like the smell of formalde-hyde and antiseptic at 7 a.m.

I paused outside the entrance to the CORE morgue facility.

Okay. I'm fine. This is fine. Everything is—I closed my eyes. *Look, Corday, just get through this without throwing up. Tasha would never forgive you, and Marcus is just waiting for something like that to happen.*

The examination room was cold, with dark cement floors that constantly smelled of industrial-grade antiseptic. You could hear the hiss of the vents, and the clicking of stainless-steel surgical instruments. There was an X-ray station against the far wall, and a small, neat desk adjacent to it. Every file-folder and notebook was tidily squared away on its proper shelf, and beside the desktop computer sat a black ceramic coffee mug and a Tupperware container. There was a small metal plaque on her desk, with the Latin phrase: *Hic locus est ubi mors gaudet succurrere vitae.* "This is the place where death rejoices to teach those who live."

In the center of the room was a stainless-steel operating table, with a smaller steel tray for holding instruments. Next to that was a scale for weighing organs, and beside that, a large sink with a detachable spigot for washing down the bodies. There was an ominously large metal drain in the floor next to the sink.

The vampire's body lay on the operating table, and Tasha Lieu, our chief medical examiner, was leaning over it, closing up the Y-incision. I could see the first cut running from shoulder to shoulder, and the second, longer cut running from the chest down to the pubis. I knew he couldn't feel it, but it still made me shiver. Being *opened up* like that, vivisected, your organs all weighed and measured. It was a private terror of mine.

Well—one of them.

"Come on over," Tasha said, putting down the needle and coarse thread.

"Great." I concentrated on keeping my breakfast down. "Have you identified the cause of death yet?"

"Nope—we might find something when we open up the skull, though." Tasha chuckled. "Always seems ironic when we get a vamp on the table. Only demons I know of who actually die twice."

"Can we get on with this?"

Tasha looked up. "Feeling twitchy today?"

I sighed. "Sorry. Guess I just haven't been sleeping all that well." My eyes darkened. "Lots of bad dreams."

"If you want to sleep soundly," she said, laying the scalpel against the vampire's forehead, "you picked the wrong business, baby." Then she began to cut.

She made an incision just behind the vamp's left ear, then cut deeply with the scalpel, across the crown of the head and all the way to the bottom of the right ear.

"This is usually where the medical students throw up or faint."

Once, I'd actually seen Tasha make a newly minted OSI scream and run out of the room. She'd handed him a seedless grape when he wasn't looking, and told him that it was a victim's eyeball that he would have to withdraw vitreous fluid from using a massive needle. Oldest trick in the book.

"I'll bet," I said, resisting the urge to look away. I wanted Tasha to respect me. And I could do this. I'd watched a demon's head explode like grapefruit; I'd seen what a mystical vortex could do to a human chest cavity at close range. I could certainly handle a bit of—

—oh fuck—

Reaching into the incision with her gloved hand, Tasha peeled back the scalp, revealing the skull that lay beneath. She picked up a Stryker saw from the steel tray, and flashed me a look.

"This is kinda loud."

"No worries," I said weakly.

The saw made a high-pitched *bzzzzzz* whine as it cut into the vampire's skull. The bone dust was stale, and oddly warm. I turned away to keep from sneezing. Tasha made two precise cuts. As she lifted off the top of skull, there was a distinct sucking sound. Once she'd removed the dura covering the brain, Tasha put down the Stryker saw and leaned forward for a closer look.

"Huh," was all she said.

I blinked. "Is that your expert medical opinion?"

She beckoned me over. "Come look at this."

I peered at the gray matter. "Is that blood?"

Tasha nodded. "There's visible bleeding within the subarachnoid space. We'd need an angiography to pinpoint the source, but I'd say that it probably started somewhere in the cerebral ventricles. Looks like there's some malformation there."

"So that's like hemorrhaging, right?"

Tasha nodded. "Just like a subdural hematoma, except it's deeper in the brain—harder to detect."

I finally had to look away from the bloody gray mess that had once been this vampire's brain. "What normally causes that kind of trauma? Blunt force?"

Tasha made a face. "Could be, but then you'd find

evidence of fractures in the skull. This guy's skull is clean. Judging from the striae in the bone, I'd say that his human life ended when he was still pretty young—twenty-five, thirty, tops. Since then, he hasn't sustained any kind of head trauma."

"Vampires don't just drop dead from a brain aneurysm."

I must have had an edge to my voice, because Tasha peered at me. "A little impatient to solve this one, Tess?"

I sighed. "Sorry. It's just—" I tried to look at *her* rather than the mess of blood and brains on the table. "Marcus has decided that the future of my career, or lack of said career, all depends on how I conduct myself in this case. It's a test."

She nodded sympathetically. "That's a bitch. So you're worried that you're gonna screw the pooch."

I scowled at her. "Doesn't *anyone* have confidence in me?"

"It kind of starts on the inside, Tess—or hadn't you heard?" Unexpectedly, Tasha put her hand on my shoulder. "Look, don't worry about it, okay? You may be the lead on this case, but you can't be expected to control every little detail. As soon as I know something, you'll know it."

The door to the morgue swung open, and Selena walked in. Behind her was Marcus. Great.

"Tess—" He glanced at his pager, then back at me. "I'd like a moment-by-moment report of how this turns out. Every move you make, I want documented."

"Of course," I said, gritting my teeth.

"Good. I want you to speak with our liaison to the vampire community. Lucian Agrado. Young, but dangerous. He might be able to ID the vamp that we found in the alley, as well as the mystery woman in the photo he was carrying."

"Great," Tasha mumbled. "A goddamn necro."

Marcus leveled his gaze at her. "What's that, Dr. Lieu? Something discriminatory to add?"

She shook her head.

"Lucian Agrado is a necromancer, yes—but he's still on our side."

"Not entirely convinced of that, sir." Tasha gave him a

dark look, then continued with her postmortem exam. "His kind cause me a whole world of trouble."

"I know that." Marcus almost sounded patient for a moment. "Undead politics aside, if we want access to the vamps, we have to deal with him."

Necromancers were like the drug pushers of the mystical community—everyone hated them, but there they were, patiently working their corners, knowing that you'd have to call on their services eventually. The CORE didn't like to admit that "necros," as Tasha called them, were really just the nonlegitimate brothers and sisters of practicing mages. Back in the day, they were called warlocks. Dante was convinced that they spent eternity in the middle ring of hell, trapped headfirst in impenetrable rock for all of their gross betrayals in life. Given the soaring real estate prices in this city, suburban *inferno* didn't seem all that bad anymore.

"We couldn't get any prints?" I asked hopefully. Being alone with a necro, even one who was ostensibly on our side, rated at least a nine on my one to ten scale of things that were really, really stupid and potentially fatal. Merging onto Highway 1 at the Port Mann Bridge was a four.

"None from the photo, and none from the vic either," Selena said. "D-AFIS didn't come back with a match. Nil for D-CODIS as well. The vamp had no priors."

"Well," Tasha interjected, "judging by his stomach contents, he didn't feed on humans—or even animals. Unless he was fasting. So maybe he's just an all-around nice guy with nothing to hide." She grinned.

"Right," Selena said simply.

"Um . . ." I stared at Marcus. "Can we get back to the part where you want me to interview a necromancer? Alone?"

Marcus looked preoccupied, as usual. "You can bring Siegel along," he said, still scanning paperwork.

"At least give me some backup! Another OSI. Even some rookies—they're always in need of field training—"

"We can't spare anyone." He finally met my gaze. "Don't worry, Tess. I'm sure you'll be able to handle this."

"Just keep your head up, and stay smart," Selena said,

giving me a knowing look. "The vampire community can't afford to show hostility against the CORE. They aren't willing to violate our nonaggression pact, and a single OSI asking a few questions shouldn't pose too much of a threat to them. Lucian is their politician, and as long as we go through him, everything should be fine."

"He's a mortal in bed with demons," Tasha said distastefully. "He's not just their politician—he's their twink."

Marcus started to retaliate, but I positioned myself between them—the last thing I wanted was to spend the rest of my day filling out an intradepartmental fatality report.

"Remember," I joked, "my life insurance policy covers dismemberment."

"Actually," Tasha clarified, "if your body is completely disarticulated, you get quadruple the payout." She grinned. "Not that it'll help you much."

"Can I have a raise?" I asked.

Marcus ignored this. "Keep me posted. I'm supervising four other cases right now, but this one is high-priority."

Selena raised an eyebrow. "A dead vampire?"

Marcus shrugged, but the motion didn't seem innocent. "I just do what my superiors tell me."

He left the morgue, and I breathed a sigh of relief.

Selena gave me a reassuring look. "He's just edgy because he's getting reviewed by CORE management. I hear he's in line to become some kind of occult director for the entire West Coast—if he makes the cut."

I rolled my eyes. "Whatever. Did the QD lab at least manage to decrypt that vampiric script on our dead vampire's note?"

"They did, actually." She checked her notebook. "It was an address—878 Crescent Road. House belongs to a Cassandra Polanski—you can stop by there before you visit the vampire patrician. It's somewhere in Elder Heights, I think. Isn't that where your parents live?"

"God, *yes.* Selena, don't send me there, please—"

"A job's a job, Tess. Besides, you can stop in for a visit—daughter's duty, you know. We all have to do it."

"Orphans don't," I muttered.

Selena ignored that. "Bring a photo of the dead vamp when you talk to the necromancer," she said. "Hopefully, someone will know who he is. If the vampires don't want to cooperate, be firm, but don't push things. Let them know that the CORE wants to investigate the death, and that we're prepared to offer all of our resources to help the vampire community. We don't want this to become a publicity nightmare."

Tasha laughed, still holding the Stryker saw. "Fat chance! A dead vampire, a human's address, and an assassination attempt. You'll have to spin this story so hard, it'll practically go into orbit."

Selena glared at her. "This is why we don't let you out of the morgue."

I was already heading for the door.

4

I found Derrick in the Psionic Training Facility, or the "Psi-Tank," as the initiated called it. Kind of like the drunk tank, only a lot more dangerous. Speaking of which, never, *ever* get a telepath drunk. It's a bad scene—trust me.

Derrick's powers weren't kinetic, at least not normally, so he didn't do a lot of combat training. The Tank had a separate facility for that, with gymnastic-style floors and padded walls, perfect for bouncing around on a telekinetic slipstream. You'd often see random objects flying around, followed by swearing. The Reading Room was separated by a Plexiglas partition (mystically tempered to keep anything on the inside from getting out, and vice versa), and that was where Derrick spent most of his mornings, practicing thought-exercises and trying to see through walls. I wasn't sure how, but staring at cubes-within-cubes and ten-dimensional space was supposed to polish his abilities. It just gave me a headache. Derrick showed me a representation of something called "Calabi-Yau Space" once, a torque-shaped mass that had been folded into itself and was somehow crucial to string theory. I think it existed only as a mathematical abstraction—although to be fair, so did mages. I told him it looked like a lima bean.

Currently, he was staring at a series of holographic shapes projected from a black console, frowning as he tried to puzzle out—well—whatever. Sometimes telepaths all seemed like Mensa geeks, obsessed with getting the highest possible IQ scores.

Derrick looked up from the console and asked simply: "Coffee?"

I handed him a Styrofoam cup. "No-foam-extra-hot sissy-boy latte, just like you asked, hon."

He stuck his tongue out at me. "We can't all drink it black. Some of us would like to keep a working relationship with our digestive systems."

"Slow this morning?"

He rolled his eyes. "Pretty much. It's fine, though. Gives me a chance to work on my reading exercises. I am so down with Venn diagrams."

"God, I love it when you talk dirty." I leaned against the edge of the console. I wasn't going to tell him about the dream—the old nightmare that I'd been having for years. He didn't need to hear about my neuroses, especially when they probably had nothing to do with the case. And besides—nobody knew about Eve.

Nobody remembered her either.

"Earth to Tess." Derrick looked at me oddly. "You still here?"

He held my hand for a moment, but his expression didn't change. I couldn't feel anything. I could hardly ever feel him digging around in my mind, and that thought scared me a little.

"Stop that." I yanked my hand away.

"You *seem* okay, but something's wiggy."

"I'm just not sleeping very well." I looked away.

He leaned back in his chair. Derrick was one of those gay men who had once been unattractive and out-of-shape, but had managed to earn a pretty decent physique for himself through exercise (possibly) and dancing to house music (probably). But he still had that boyish uncertainty about his body that only comes when you remember what it was like to be the one picked last for the volleyball team, the one that nobody wanted to go to the prom with. That hesitation, that little flicker of discomfort and sheepishness, was damn attractive, and he knew it.

"What are you grinning about?" He'd noticed my lapse in concentration.

"Oh—I was just remembering junior year. That party we went to at Patty Hornburger's house."

"The night where you drank B-52s and barfed out your retainer?"

"Yeah. We were so *cute* back then."

"Seriously, Tess." His brown eyes narrowed. "You've been working yourself into the ground lately. You're not a cyborg. You have to sleep, and I know you've been staying late at the lab, hogging all the good microscopes."

I thought of telling him about my "conversation" with Marcus—more of an ultimatum, really—but decided not to. No sense in worrying him.

"Well, someone's got to do it," I mumbled.

"There are lots of other OSIs out there."

"You mean younger ones."

He sighed. "I didn't say that."

"You didn't have to. I know the drill, Derrick. I've been getting the speech for the last three years now. Tess, you're too old for this sort of work. Tess, you've got to move up in the world. You can't work the front line forever."

"Well, you can't."

"And why not? It's ageism. It's discrimination."

"Tess, those guidelines are in place for practicality's sake, not to make you feel oppressed. You know as well as I do that young mages have more power."

"But I've got more experience! I can run circles around those little Michelle-Jessica-Parker girls with their goddamn Hello Kitty cell phones."

"Your cell phone has a Morrissey dial tone."

"That's not the point!" I smoothed my hair as a reflexive calming action. It was getting short, so there wasn't much to smooth. "I'm getting old and embarrassing, and nobody wants to patrol with me anymore, and *why* did you let me get this haircut?"

"You said you wanted to look like Julianne Moore."

"But she's got that translucent Irish skin, and I've just got"—I scowled—"frizzy red hair. I look like Peppermint Patty with a hangover."

"No you don't—"

"I do! I look"—I stared at him—"oh God, Derrick, I look *twenty-four*."

He put his arm around me. "You *are* twenty-four, sweetie. And that's okay. There are all kinds of support groups."

"I just don't want to be told what I can't do. I don't want to be told that I'm getting long in the tooth, like some horse—"

He groaned. "I don't see why you're always complaining anyway. You've got your whole career ahead of you. Nowhere to go but up. You've got good friends, a great family, a job that's pretty much everything you ever dreamed of."

"So why can't I sleep at night?"

"Ha." He smiled bitterly. "Join the club. That's one thing the CORE never promised us, right? A clear conscience."

I closed my eyes. "I have to go home."

"Why, did you forget something at your apartment?"

"No, I mean *home*—to Elder."

He winced. "Bring a cross and stake. And sensible shoes."

"I'm bringing you. Marcus said."

His grin faded.

"How much do you hate me right now?"

Derrick glared at me. "It would be one of those google-plex numbers."

I smiled. "Thought so."

I stared at the WELCOME TO ELDER: THE SUNSHINE TOWN! sign, and felt my stomach beginning to lurch. "Great. Just great."

We began to pass familiar landmarks. The tourism center, which looked suspiciously like a red barn. The Cherry Lane mall, whose parking lot was now deserted, which gave it a strangely haunted look. The Greyhound depot, where every bus was always late, and the coffee could actually bore a hole through your intestines.

Derrick turned left onto Yale Street, and we headed into the residential neighborhoods. We drove past the satellite campus of Valley College, which was actually an old converted motel that seemed—I remembered—to require constant fumigation. Past the Lighthouse Inn, which was nowhere near a lighthouse (or a body of water, for that matter), and whose suites looked out onto the scenic Vedder Bypass Road. Past the abandoned gas station on the corner of Yale and Hocking, which had been mysteriously boarded up due to some zoning conflict for the last two years. Past the Schnitzel House restaurant, where my dad had almost choked to death on a scallop when I was eight years old.

"God," Derrick said. His voice was almost a whisper. "The streets are almost completely empty. It's like an episode of *The Twilight Zone.*"

"It's after seven thirty," I explained. "Everybody's home from work by now, sitting in front of the television."

"Holy Stepford."

"Just drive, city boy." I scowled. "You know, just once, I'd like evil to take root in some nice seaside town, or on the beaches of Santa Barbara. Why is it always in the suburbs? Is a sweet vacation too much to ask?"

"Well, if it's any consolation, we may get killed on the job soon," Derrick replied. "That's sort of like a vacation. In whatever heaven-dimension we're both destined for."

"I'm not going to heaven," I said glumly. "I'm staying here. For eternity. Eating at the Dairy Queen with my parents."

"That's funny. My private version of hell is being stuck at the Water Street Café with my parents, eating crab bisque and talking about how I should have gone to an Ivy League school."

"I'll trade you any day."

We drove down First Avenue, then turned onto Crescent, which was one of those tiny cul-de-sac streets with manicured lawns and puppies playing around sprinklers. The houses were three-story colonials, with balconies and bay windows. They made my parents' town house look like a pita shack. Cassandra Polanski, it seemed, came from money. Or at least from a family trying to look like they had money. I saw plenty of that in the city, but it still existed in the suburbs as well. Oh, *sure* we can afford that big house with the pool on our teaching salary. No problem! Maybe that was the case here.

I sucked in my breath. "Ready for the sweep?"

"As ready as I'll ever be."

We both got out of the car, and I took another look at Cassandra's house. I could see the glow of the television set through one of the living room windows. And the sound of laughter. Was it coming from the TV, or was there really a happy family in there, laughing and talking with each other?

"So," I asked, "spiral or grid?"

"Spiral." Derrick grinned. "I'm feeling kind of twisted right now."

"Your puns always suck."

"Oh yeah? So does your face."

I stuck my tongue out at him. "Okay, let's actually try to be serious for once."

I began the sweep by walking in concentric, expanding circles—widdershins for the traditionalist, spiral search pattern for the OSI—scanning the grounds for any hint of material psychic power. Like prints, which could be visible or latent depending on the nature of the transference, mystical and psychic energy might be lying in plain view, or buried deep underground. I didn't sense anything in the driveway, but most people laid complex materia down closest to their front door.

As I got closer to the porch, something dark and immense brushed against my psychic boundaries, and I instinctively took a step backward. It wasn't a defensive spell per se— more like a declaration of power, a rune drawn in blood on the very surface of the air. For anyone mage-trained, it was the equivalent of waving a flag, or setting off a flare gun: *Keep away*.

Great. Necromancers, vampires, and psionics—we almost had a musical.

5

"Well." Derrick appeared behind me. "I can certainly feel that. Someone's put out the BEWARE OF DOG sign."

"Selena didn't say anything about mages being involved in this." Derrick was fidgeting. He always fretted and fussed like a bird when he was nervous. "I thought it was strictly a vampire thing."

"We don't know specifically that it's a 'mage thing' either. For now, all I'm sensing is power, and that comes in a lot of packages."

"So knock and find out."

Shooting him a look, I walked up the short flight of steps and found myself facing the door. It was one of those huge black doors you see in the movies, with a brass knocker and a little stained-glass window at the top. My parents' door had a macramé woodpecker attached to it. I had definitely crossed a class boundary somewhere.

"Very Dickensian," Derrick supplied.

"Very creepy, you mean. What if they're reclusive millionaires or something? Doing illegal experiments?"

"Evil geniuses living in the sweet-corn capital of the Fraser Valley?" He rolled his eyes. "Come on, Tess."

I took a deep breath, and knocked once. Loudly.

The door swung open. A short women, a bit plumpish, probably in her midforties, was staring at me. She had steely blond hair cropped into an unfortunate bob, and a pair of glasses hanging from a string around her neck. She was wearing a flower-print skirt that probably came from Sears, and a sleeveless denim top. Something that my mom would have worn. She was also carrying what looked suspiciously like a cookbook. Suddenly, I was the one who felt like a freak. She might have been a necromancer, but if so, she was a necro who knew how to make spetzle, and that was better than me.

"Yes?" The woman blinked at me. "Can I help you?"

"Cassandra Polanski?" I suddenly felt like I was twelve years old again, knocking on my best friend's door. This was why I hated doing interviews. When it was strictly a human affair, we just announced ourselves as "Van Criminalistics" and took everyone's statement. You'd be amazed what an ID badge can do for you, especially if it's been enspelled with a charm of complacency. We monitored the police lines twenty-four hours a day for any calls that might relate to paranormal activity. Kind of like how the USA's Patriot Act monitors alleged terrorism—only less evil. Instead of listening for keywords like "bomb," we paid attention to phases like "ectoplasm" and "my grandmother just summoned an evil djinn."

Somehow, I didn't think it was going to be easy this time.

"Yes, that's me." Her eyes narrowed. "What's this regarding?"

I resisted the urge to clear my throat. "I'm Tess Corday, and this is Derrick Siegel—we're from the Vancouver Crime Lab, MCD. We're investigating a death that occurred last night in the city—"

Cassandra raised a hand to stop me. "I commute to Vancouver during the day, but I don't spend my evenings there."

"Well, I didn't say that the crime occurred during the evening."

Cassandra gave me a sour look. "Is there something you're trying to insinuate? Because I don't really have time to stand here trading semantics—I'm in the middle of making dinner for my niece."

"What's her name?" Derrick asked.

Her expression didn't improve. "Mia. I'm her legal guardian."

"What happened to her parents?"

"They died. A long time ago." Her frown deepened to a scowl. "If you'd like the details, I can refer you to the law offices that handled their estate. I'm sure that the paperwork is all in order."

Okay, different tactic. Appeal to her maternal vibe.

"Miss Polanski," I said, "the reason we're here is that we found a note in the decedent's pocket—a note with your address on it. Now, for the sake of your safety, as well as Mia's, we'll need to investigate this further. Unless"—I gave her a level look—"you think it's just a remarkable coincidence."

"There are all sorts of coincidences, Miss Corday—remarkable or otherwise." She leaned against the door frame. "Maybe this person of yours had the wrong address. Or maybe it was a robbery attempt gone bad—there are scads of wealthy homes in this area, ours notwithstanding, but perhaps we appear to be rich by association."

"If it was a 'robbery gone bad,' as you say"—I smiled thinly—"well, Miss Polanski, that would make you a suspect, wouldn't it? If you were only defending your home, the safety of your niece—"

Something glittered in her eyes. "I am not a killer. I don't know what happened to this person, whomever they might be, but I surely didn't touch them. As you can see"—she gestured wearily to her apron—"I'm not exactly a trained assassin."

"Aunt Cassie?" I could see, over Cassandra's shoulder, that a girl was standing at the top of the stairs. "Who's there? I thought I heard my name."

"Tess Corday is here," Cassandra replied thoughtfully, as if she was trying out my name to see if it fit. "She says there's been a murder, and we're connected to it somehow. Although"—her eyes returned to me—"I'm still not quite certain how that could be."

Mia was about thirteen or so, wearing a baggy black sweater, ripped blue jeans, and brown Converse sneakers. The high-tops were back in again, unfortunately. She had thin black hair, glasses, and that awkward kind of prettiness that some girls can manage without expensive clothes and makeup.

And I recognized her.

I didn't know her, but I'd seen her around Elder—it's a small town, and whenever I was trying to get away from my parents' neurotic wonderland, I tended to go for long walks around the neighborhood. I remembered seeing her a couple times, maybe a few months ago—just walking around, aimlessly, like me. I hadn't thought anything of it at the time. She'd always dimly reminded me of someone, but I could never figure it out. Now, I could feel the answer burning like a rune before my eyes. Burning.

Eve.

She looked just like Eve. And Eve had been thirteen, too—back then—when it happened—when—

"A murder?" Mia's voice brought me out of the memory. *"Shit."*

"*Language*, Mia."

The girl managed to look embarrassed. "Sorry."

"Mia," I said, "we found a body last night, in an alley between Granville and Nelson Street. Do you ever go to that area of town?"

She stared at me. "Hey, I *know* you. Or I've seen you around—didn't you buy something at the Rosemblatts' yard sale a few months ago?"

I had, in fact—a vintage hip flask, which I was desperately wishing for right about now. I just smiled. "Yeah, that was probably me. I think I've seen you around, too—go for a lot of walks?"

She nodded enthusiastically. "Yeah, especially by the duck park—"

"This is all very scintillating," Cassandra cut in, "but could you just answer Miss Corday's questions so that we can get back to having dinner?"

Mia gave her a strange look, then nodded. "Right—um—Granville. No, I'd never go walking down there at night—it's a total crack-den."

"Well, your aunt mentioned that she commutes to work—maybe you come into the city with her sometimes to do some shopping?"

"Mia does come with me often," Cassandra supplied, "but if you knew her at all, you wouldn't look for her in a shopping mall. She's usually at the library."

"It's true," Mia said. "I'm like the empress of dorks."

I pulled out the vampire's picture from my pocket.

"Have you ever seen him?"

Mia squinted at the photo. I saw a brief flash of something in her eyes, possibly recognition. Then she shook her head. "Never. He's kind of cute, though."

Bullshit. It didn't take a mage to tell that she was lying, and I'm sure that Derrick's empathy was practically bristling from the deception.

"If I understand correctly," Cassandra said, "he's also kind of dead."

"*Ew.*" Mia made a face. "I mean, um—that sucks. For him. But what does it have to do with us?"

"I'm wondering the same thing." Cassandra stared at me. "Perhaps Miss Corday has a few more pertinent questions for us. Otherwise, supper is getting cold, and I don't have the patience to make guesses about our role in this murder—which, I should remind you, took place last night, a hundred kilometers away, probably while we were asleep."

There was something about her eyes. They were cold and a bit threatening. But there was something else as well. I looked closely at Cassandra, and although the prim smile never left her face, her eyes seemed to change. They flashed violet, just for a moment, and then returned to their normal shade of blue. I felt my cheeks flush suddenly and looked away.

"Tess?" Derrick put a hand on my shoulder.

"It's nothing. Just"—I looked at Cassandra again—"felt like someone walked over my grave for a second."

I knew then. Sweat trickled along my arms, and I could feel that sickening sensation in the pit of my stomach. I shivered, like someone stepping into an air-conditioned room. My hands clenched in my pockets.

Cassandra was a demon.

I didn't know what kind of demon she was, or what she might be capable of. But I did know that she was powerful enough to conceal her nature from me until now—and that was something to be scared of.

Cassandra understood my recognition. Her lip curled, but she said nothing. All of this happened within the space of three seconds. Okay—now, the goal was to get out of here as fast as we could, and call Selena. I wasn't about to engage a mysterious demon on her own front lawn.

"Could we possibly have a look around your house?" I asked. It sounded lame—even to me. "We don't have a warrant, but it would help our investigation if we could at least eliminate any connection you might have to the decedent."

"You're not entering this house without a court order," Cassandra replied. "Not to be rude about it, but I have to insist."

"Oh, come on, Aunt Cassie." Mia gave her a long-suffering look. "They're only doing their jobs. I'm sure they won't mess up the place."

"No," she repeated. "If it's important, I'm sure they'll return—with the proper documents in hand."

"Right." I tried to keep my voice polite, even though a dozen questions were screaming in my brain. *Who are you? Why is there a power-mark on your door? Why is a demon living in the suburbs with an adopted niece?*

"Another time, then," I said.

"Yes. I look forward to it." Cassandra smiled.

"Okay, well"—Mia looked at me, then at Cassandra—"thanks for your concern, I guess. It was nice meeting you."

"Let me give you my card." I handed her the card with the MCD extension on the back, as well as our e-mail. The square of paper was enspelled, too: they couldn't destroy or misplace it. Like a boomerang, it would always reappear. Cassandra might be able to break the spell, but not without a lot of effort, and I was willing to bet that she had more important things on her mind. Like blood sacrifices, or destroying the world, or whatever else demons thought about.

"If you think of anything," I said, still smiling, "or if you need to talk, please call the crime lab and ask for either Derrick or myself."

Cassandra reached for the card, but I made sure to put it in Mia's hand. She would be more impressionable to the trace of materia.

"Thanks." She slipped it into her pocket.

"It was a pleasure meeting you, too, Cassandra," I said. I couldn't help it. I was always inching too close to the flame.

"And you, Tess." Her expression was indecipherable. "We part well, and may the ways remain open for you."

I blinked. That was a traditional salutation: what a demon said to a mage when they were parting on good terms and no blood had been shed. The gesture of an ally.

Mia seemed confused by the archaism as well, but she said nothing.

"Travel the ways in peace," I replied, keeping my voice level.

Cassandra smiled, and closed the door.

Derrick was silent until we got back into the car. Then he stared at me, and I could see that he was white as a sheet. "What's going on, Tess? She's a demon, the girl's lying like a rug, and nobody's talking. And I *felt* something between the two of you. She was challenging you, wasn't she?"

I nodded. "Her turf, her rules—we were bound to lose. Like she said, we'll have to come back with a warrant—"

"And how are we going to get that? We don't have a scrap

of physical evidence connecting either of them to the crime scene."

"We'll just have to check their records. If the tiniest blemish shows up, we can use it as leverage to get a court order. I can name half a dozen judges who would write paper for us, just because they like pissing off demons."

"This town is full of demophobes."

I rolled my eyes. "It's not like we don't have good reason to be afraid of them."

He looked at me pointedly. *"Them?"*

I bit down on my reply.

"Well, what if they're clean?" Derrick pressed. "What if we can't find anything that will justify a search? The CORE isn't a mercenary organization, Tess. We have to work through the proper legal channels, even if some of those channels happen to lead to other dimensions. We still have to do this properly."

I leaned back in the seat as he started up the car. "It won't be a problem."

"You're so sure?"

I shrugged. "Everyone's got something to hide."

6

The flames were everywhere, licking across my skin, my hair, like snakes crawling all over my body. The magic kept them from burning me, but I could still feel the heat, and the smoke was making me dizzy.

"Eve! Where are you? *Eve!*"

I crawled on my hands and knees through the remains of the living room, where fire streamed along the mutilated couch, pooling in spots on the floor. It curled across the ceiling, spreading out tongues like hungry animals, searching for anything combustible, anything that could be destroyed. Including me. I poured everything that I had into the shield, and kept screaming.

"Eve! Where *are* you?"

The kitchen was ablaze—the linoleum curled and melted under my knees, and almost nothing was recognizable. This was the heart of hell. This was what it felt like to burn eternally, to suffer for all of your sins and mistakes. All of the people you couldn't save, or the souls that you just didn't care about until it was too late.

Still, it didn't matter. I was thirteen. I was strong, flush with power—nothing but a raw skein full of glowing possibilities. I could do anything. I could save my friend—and she'd never have to know. I'd never have to tell her how I managed to crawl inside the house, how I kept us both from dying. She'd never know, but she'd always be grateful, and then—finally—I'd have a friend who wouldn't leave. Someone who didn't think I was strange.

Eve was the first real friend I'd ever had, and I wasn't going to lose her.

"I'm here!" I screamed. "Eve, I'm here, just say something! Say something, so that I know where you are, and I'll come get you!"

I crawled up the stairs, holding a wet cloth to my mouth, silently feeding energy into the fire shield. Her room was the first door on the landing. The door was open.

"Eve?" I crawled into the room. "Are you here? Are you—"

I woke up curled on the break-room couch, my back aching from being tied into a pretzel. I was alone, but some kind soul had thrown a blanket over me—probably Derrick. God, I hadn't fallen asleep here since—

Pushing the dream away—as well as its uncomfortable association with Mia—I smoothed the wrinkles out of my shirt. I may have dozed off, but I sure as hell wasn't going to let anyone know.

That's your problem, a familiar voice said. *You never let anyone know—never let anyone in. You're like a locked tower. Problem is, Tess, eventually they're just going to slap a condemned sign on you, and you'll be a vacant building.*

Meredith Silver—my old teacher. Even now, I could see her waist-length hair that, ironically, had come to match her surname—like a sheet of silver cascading down her back, so curious and wonderful that I used to always stare at it. Her warm blue eyes. Her small hands—small, but *strong.* I'd seen her snap a quarterstaff in half with just the power of her own will and a quick, graceful gesture of those hands.

Meredith—God, had it really been two years already? It didn't seem like it. Most days, I thought she was still here.

Maybe I just wished it.

Brushing the thought away, I headed for the computer lab. As expected, I found Rebecca, our resident computer genius, sitting at the photo manipulation PC; she was frowning as she chewed on a piece of vibrant blue hair. Rebecca was barely eighteen, but if she ever called in sick, the entire crime lab would probably implode and cease to exist. Although we had other computer mavens who dealt with various hardware and software maintenance, Rebecca was the one whom everyone called. She would calmly say things like, "Oh, the problem with this hard drive is that 347 has a null boot sector," in her sweet British accent, then watch as the other lab techs shifted uncomfortably.

"Hey, Becka," I said. "Any luck with that photo that we recovered from the vampire's body?"

She looked up, nearly choking on the lock of hair in her mouth. Then she smiled sheepishly. "Tess. You startled me."

"I can see that."

She chuckled. "We need to put a bell around your neck or something."

"I promise to wear squeaky shoes next time."

Rebecca gestured to the screen, and I saw a digitized version of the photograph. The young vampire looked so happy. He'd obviously loved this woman, whoever she was, and it was strange to think that a vampire would be capable of such a free, easy kind of affection. He was standing there, grinning like an idiot in love, wearing a pale gray sweater and casually leaning against her—the woman whose smile, I realized now, was not so much cold as long-suffering. The kind of smile you have when your partner is a lot more enthusiastic—or a lot younger—than you are. She may have been bored with him. Was she capable of killing him?

The details around the couple were fuzzy. I saw what looked like a window, but the drapes were drawn—no luck determining a location. It was probably just his apartment anyway. Most vampires had a place to crash during the day. I could also see a picture in the background.

"Can you zoom in on that portrait in the upper-left quadrant?" I asked.

Rebecca touched the screen with a light-pen, drawing a border around the area, then hit a button. A new window popped up with a 10X magnification of the area in question. I still couldn't tell what the picture was of, since the shadows were partially obscuring it. But it was definitely in a glass frame, which had reflected the flash in a blur of fuzzy white light.

"Could this photograph have been taken with a timer?"

Becka shook her head. "The angle's wrong, and you can tell by the way that they're posing."

"So there's someone else in the room—the shutterbug."

Rebecca nodded. "You want me to keep enhancing that area around the framed picture—see if I can get a reflection? It may very well have been captured in the glass, and in that case, we can separate the images."

"You can definitely try."

"Or—wait a minute." Rebecca traced the area around the woman's face with the light-pen, and another 10X magnification appeared in a separate window. Her eyes were a dark shade of blue—incredibly striking. I could see why the vamp had been smitten.

"You know what they say about the eyes being the window to the soul?" Rebecca smiled at me.

"I'm getting it." I nodded, feeling a small rush of excitement. "Vampires have curved corneas—just like a cat's, they glow in certain lights."

"And they provide an excellent mirror surface for an image," Rebecca supplied. "As reflective as glass."

"If that woman is a vampire as well, do you think you can extract a reflection from her eyes? Something that'll tell us who, or what, she's looking at?"

"I can try. It'll take some time, though."

"Thanks, Becka. I definitely owe you lunch."

She laughed. "Lunch won't fix my aching metacarpals nor will it repair the permanent eyestrain—"

"Lunch, and a cappuccino."

Her smile was sly. "Make it a caramel macchiato, and we'll call it even."

"You're the best." I smiled as I walked out of the computer lab.

It was the last time that I'd smile for the rest of the day.

After hours of fruitlessly searching through just about every database that we had access to at the MCD, I'd come to the following conclusion about Mia and Cassandra Polanski: They were two of the dullest people on the face of the planet. No hits in CODIS or AFIS, so they'd never been printed or had their DNA recorded on file. Most women who'd gone for a Paptest had their DNA on file, but Cassandra didn't even have that. No hits for D-CODIS either, so if she was a demon, as I suspected, then she was also unregistered. Mia was homeschooled, so I couldn't even pull up a report card. She was born May 4, 1992, in Kelowna, British Columbia. Her parents were Anthony Taylor and Christine Polanski, unmarried, and so she retained her mother's maiden name—also the surname of her maternal aunt, Cassandra Polanski. In 1998, both parents went missing. We had access to the missing persons report from the Elder RCMP, but it was a cold case.

"And *fuck* you, too, BC Family Services." Derrick slammed the phone down, then sighed and ran a hand through his hair. "This is putting me in a bad mood."

"The federal government has a way of doing that." I switched off the computer screen. "I'm not having any luck either. Cassandra's never even had a parking ticket. There's nothing in these files that would justify a search."

Derrick put his head on the desk. "I can't find *anything* out about Mia's adoption. All of the papers are 'on file' in some basement library somewhere in Ottawa, but I've talked to seven secretaries already, and I'm still nowhere close to getting the actual papers. They just keep referring me to surlier clerks and assistants."

I stared forlornly at my empty coffee mug. Garfield's smiling face mocked me. "Well, what's our angle with Mia? Do we think she's a mage, or a proto-mage?"

"You're better at mystical-assay than I am, and you didn't sense anything."

"Yeah, but my mage-dar could be broken. Anyway—just because I don't sense it doesn't mean that it's not there. It could be latent still."

"At thirteen?"

"It happens." I frowned. "Never. Oh, wait—there've been cases, I think, where someone's powers didn't manifest until they were in their late teens. Something to do with a retro-virus in the blood."

"Did you read that in *Magic Weekly*?"

"Could you not be a bitch for, like, two seconds?"

Derrick smiled. "Look, Tess, I'm just trying to be realis-tic. Chances are, Mia isn't a proto-mage at all. She's proba-bly just caught in the middle of a mystical turf-war between warlocks and vampires."

"But why would she be in that vampire's head? And what about my dream?"

"We still don't know that it's the same girl—" He saw my expression, and gave a long sigh. "Fine. Let me check."

A window popped up on the screen, and I saw Derrick log into LOOM, the Local Occult Occupational Mainframe. He tapped away for a minute or two, then gestured to the computer screen, which displayed some records that he'd pulled from a private medical database.

"Okay—there *have* been cases where exposure has pro-duced a latent effect, and the subject's powers haven't mani-fested until late puberty." He blinked. "Two cases. One in 1912, and the other in 1942. Both subjects had neurological disorders."

"Well"—I paced back and forth—"maybe Mia is the exception."

Derrick frowned suddenly. "Not necessarily."

"What do you mean?"

"I just thought of something." He typed something else, and a new database popped up. This was the standard occult mainframe, with thousands of documented cases of just about any preternatural activity on file.

He typed in "vampirism," and a screen full of hits appeared.

"Why are you looking up stuff on vampires?"

"Just give me a second."

Derrick clicked his way through dozens of different articles, until he suddenly smiled and pointed at something. "*There*. Read that."

I leaned forward. It was an article on the vampiric siring process. The first paragraph was a detailed description of blood chemistry. But the second was a list of possible mutations, with one in particular highlighted.

> *Retrograde or Interstitial Vampirism: In some cases, the effects of the siring process can be delayed—perhaps indefinitely—due to immunological resistance within the host. Certain blood types, particularly B positive and AB positive, have been known to counteract vampiric viral plasmids. Very powerful vampires—magnate class or higher—are rumored to have the ability to psychically control the siring process, delaying or accelerating it as they see fit. This has never been tested, but can be inferred from patients who enter spontaneous remission, or whose symptoms appear to manifest themselves with unusual slowness.*

"You think the vampires did something to Mia?" I asked. "Found some way to control her powers?"

"It might explain why that vamp had her address."

"Like he was going to—what—activate her powers or something? That seems kind of far-fetched, Derrick."

He gave me a flat look. "We work for an occult government agency, Tess."

I sighed. "Go ahead."

"Vampires are demons, right? They may put on aristo-cratic airs, but they share the same genetic material as goblins and kobolds. And *us*. So why couldn't a demon—a really powerful demon—hypothetically be able to control the rate of exposure in an infected person?"

I frowned. "I guess it's possible. But what would the point be?"

"To camouflage her? Make her like a sleeper agent, just waiting to be activated?"

I rolled my eyes.

"Tess, come on—it makes about as much sense as anything that you've come up with so far. Right?"

He did have a point. Everything we knew about the higher-tier demons, we'd learned from vampires. They were like the demonic upper class. Some were allies. Most weren't. That didn't mean we were fighting in the streets, but we weren't exactly hosting joint Christmas parties either.

"So," I said, "you think that Mia is somehow being controlled?"

"It would explain why her aunt is an overprotective demon."

"But she wasn't a vampire."

"Maybe the vampires are working against her. Or maybe they're working *with* her, like an unholy coalition—"

"Or maybe this is all circumstantial," I interrupted him, "and we really don't have a whit of evidence to go on."

He frowned at me. "Well, Selena said she would call in a few favors with some demon high-rollers in town, see if they've heard of anyone fitting Cassandra's description. If she's powerful enough to have a mage-mark glowing outside of her house, somebody must know her."

"But someone could have just as easily left that mark for us to find, Derrick. Maybe they're just using this poor family as a distraction—"

"From what? Some vampire death-orgy that *nobody* has heard of? As far as we know, the vamps are enjoying their longest truce with us in history. You're going to stir enough shit up when you go talk to their necro flunky."

I closed my eyes. "I'm tired of this. It's nearly four o'clock, and we've been following dead ends since seven this morning. I'm bitchy, and hungry, and I need to eat something that actually contains one of the four food groups—excluding gummy bears."

Derrick shrugged. "I think they have, like, bone meal or something. Maybe that's got iron in it?"

I stood up. "Let's hit that sandwich place across from my apartment. I haven't taken a single break today, and Marcus is in a meeting for the next few hours. Nobody's going to care."

He smiled. "I think that's a capital idea. Can we get the roasted eggplant?"

"Yeah, but you have to order it. I hate that girl with the hoop earrings who keeps shouting 'real hip-hop!' at me every time I order a ciabatta."

As we crossed the parking lot, I zeroed in on Derrick's car—a rusted old Ford Festiva with about 200,000 clicks on its exhausted odometer. Derrick called it the Excelsior, because, like me, he was a dork.

What I didn't expect to see was a familiar teenager with long black hair, clutching her knapsack like a shield as she leaned against the car door. In typical andro style, Mia was wearing a pair of old khakis, Duff skate shoes, and a faded jean jacket. She looked nervous as hell—and as soon as I saw her, my stomach did a flip.

Really, in retrospect, I should have just turned around and walked in the opposite direction. It would have made everything so much simpler.

"Um—hi, Mia." Derrick gave her an odd look. "Any particular reason why you've set up camp beside my car?"

She flushed. "Sorry—I—ah—recognized it from when you were parked outside our house. I got your address from that card—" She looked at me, and I saw the uncertainty flash across her eyes. "I think I need to talk to you guys. There's some stuff that you should know—my aunt doesn't know I'm here. She's at work right now, and I have to meet up with her before suppertime."

"Mia," I said, already hating myself as I switched to professional mode, "if you want to make a statement about your case, we can go back to the department—I'll set up an interview with my boss, Selena—"

"I want to talk to *you*," she blurted out. Her eyes scraped the ground. "For some reason, I think I trust you."

Derrick looked at me. I could already tell that he was reading my mind, and his expression darkened.

"Tess," he said, "you know that it's against code. She's involved in an active case—we can't just take her to lunch."

I suddenly flashed back to being an undergraduate—I was taking a philosophy class to fulfill the breadth requirements for my Crim degree, and we had to cover a unit called French Post-Structuralist Critics. A particular quotation from Jacques Derrida shimmered into being, dancing like a riddle before me.

All passion is a passion for code.

I looked at Mia, then felt my muscles tense. This was about to get messy.

"I don't care much about codes," I said. "All they mean is what we want them to, and right now I'm more concerned with people. Come on, Mia. Let's go someplace and talk." I grinned at her. "Have you had lunch yet?"

7

My apartment was one of those concrete block-monsters in the West End, just a short walk off Davie Street. I think it was built in the sixties, which meant that it leaked like a son of a bitch and had an elevator that I liked to call "capricious" (when I wasn't swearing incoherently at it). The lobby was floored in faux marble, which made visitors think that they were entering a nice hotel—until the elevator doors opened, and they smelled the distinct odor of pot and cabbage rolls. My suite was on the eighth floor, giving me an incredible view of English Bay, as well as a direct line of vision into my crazy neighbor's apartment across the street. Sometimes he walked around in nothing but a pair of black socks—the first time Derrick saw that particular display, he put his breakfast croissant down with a sour face, saying: "I just lost my appetite. Forever."

At first, I was a bit worried about dragging a thirteen-year-old girl down Davie Street, especially since she came from a small town. Some vestige of bizarre, wrong-headed moralism made me want to cover her eyes or something, as if she'd never seen drag queens and leather boys before. But when she grinned and said, "I *love* the PumpJack—the college bears always help me with my math homework!" I realized that Mia was no stranger to the city nor to this enclave of queer culture. Derrick's jaw dropped, but he didn't say anything. We stopped by Jubilatka, the polish bakery, to pick up three cherry-cheese croissants the size of my head. So much for eggplant.

I unlocked the door to my suite, and was immediately assailed by that oddly fragrant mixture of ancient hardwood, Pine-Sol, and stale coffee. Mia took everything in without a word—the sagging chesterfield that my parents had happily pawned off, the IKEA bookshelves filled to overflowing, the deep grooves in the floor caused by innumerable pieces of furniture being moved, jostled, and scraped over thirty years, the bay windows overlooking a cherry tree that was in full blossom. The place was messy, but never *dirty*. That was my mantra.

"Have a seat," I told Mia.

She did so—and proceeded to sink about four inches into the old sofa cushions, as if the couch itself were swallowing her up.

I winced. "Sorry. It's pretty old—comfy, though."

"Um—yeah—" She grabbed on to the armrest as if it were a life preserver. "I'll bet it is. Thanks."

I sat down next to her, and Derrick took the rocking chair in the corner—another odd piece that I'd rescued from a garage sale on Jervis Street. I rather suspected that its previous owner had been crazy, since she offered the chair to me for "either two bucks or a cigarette if you've got one." Sometimes I was certain that an entirely different economy existed in secret areas of the West End, a crazy night market where you could buy or trade just about anything. My favorite piece of furniture was a cart on wheels that I'd rescued from some urban professional's garbage in Yaletown. It was currently trembling underneath the weight of a deluxe spice rack and my wandering Jew plant.

Derrick gave me a pointed look. "Tess—do you think we should maybe record this? We might have to enter the tape in as evidence later."

Mia looked alarmed. "You want to *tape* me?"

I shook my head. "No. It's all right, we don't have to."

"Tess—"

"No." I tried not to look at Derrick. If I saw his "what the hell" look, I'd lose my resolve, and I felt like I owed it to Mia to at least hear her out. Nobody else seemed to be listening to her, and Cassandra was being downright hostile about the investigation. If the necromancer didn't tell us anything, then we'd be stuck at a dead end—I was willing to break a few rules if it meant getting a new lead.

"We're in this already," I said. "It might be a violation of protocol, but right now, Mia's statement is all we've got."

"It won't be admissible—"

"We're not going to court, Derrick, and you know it."

"Fine," Derrick said, looking away. "I trust you. And we're already here, so there's no going back now."

"I don't want to get you guys in trouble—" Mia began.

I raised my hand. "Don't worry about it, sweetheart." God, why was I channeling my mom all of a sudden? Next I'd be offering her Peek Freans. "Right now, our priority is keeping you and your aunt safe—but to do that, we need to know everything. Even if it's odd, or embarrassing, or it doesn't make any sense at all, we need to know everything that you've seen or heard since yesterday."

"Well—I mean, it's not much." Mia fidgeted for a bit in her seat, and I could almost feel the truth inside of her bubbling up to the surface. It wasn't quite empathy, but something else—a connection all the same. Maybe Derrick was right about her being a mage-potential. If her talent was blocked, but still latent, we might be able to feel it as a kind of residual trace.

"Anything will help," Derrick said patiently, "no matter how far-fetched it seems. Not much phases us, Mia. Honest. Whatever it is, we can deal with it."

She nodded. "Okay. Well, when I said that I hadn't seen that guy—I sort of lied." She winced. "Is that really bad? I mean, will I get in trouble—"

I shook my head. "It's fine, as long as you tell us the truth.

Lots of people who've witnessed something—unusual—lie about it at first. Sometimes they're not even sure what they've seen, which is why we have to count on the physical evidence rather than on eyewitness testimony."

"I thought you didn't have any physical evidence."

I gave her a level look. "Not yet. But we will soon."

"Right. Okay." Mia gulped. "Well, like I said, it's not much. The night before last, I was coming home late from the library—usually, Aunt Cassie gives me a ride home, but this time I decided to walk. I thought I heard her talking to someone in the living room"—she shook her head—"I don't know why I didn't just walk in the house, but something told me not to. So I looked in the window instead, and I saw her talking with—*him*. That blond guy."

"Were they arguing?"

She nodded. "Aunt Cassie looked *pissed*, and the blond guy just kept waving his hands around. It wasn't like he was threatening her—more like he just wanted to convince her of something, you know? But whatever it was, she wasn't buying it. He stormed out of the house and walked away. I didn't see him get into a car or anything—it was kind of weird. Like, I turned around for a second, and when I looked back, he was just gone. Maybe he ran away or something?"

Derrick and I exchanged a look. I knew how fast vampires could move, especially when they were feeling particularly motivated.

"Anyway," Mia continued, "I walked into the living room and asked my aunt about it, but all she said was that he was an old friend. He didn't *look* old, though. I mean, Aunt Cassie is old, like, at least *forty*—"

God, I remembered when forty seemed unimaginable. To be thirteen again.

"But he looked young, no older than twenty, maybe even eighteen or something. He had a baby face."

"And your aunt never said anything after that?" Derrick asked.

"No. She didn't want to talk about it. When you guys showed up, I figured that she'd make a statement or something—but then she just clammed up. So I thought I should say something. I mean, if this guy's dangerous, I don't want him coming around our house again. Even if my aunt's too polite to say anything, or too old-fashioned or whatever, I'm not going to risk our lives over it!"

"Good," I said. "That's exactly the right attitude to have. Too many crimes go unreported because nobody wants to say anything."

What I didn't tell her was that, every day, people got killed because of what they *did* say—because they had the courage to stand up to their attackers, but they couldn't protect themselves from eventual retribution. That wasn't going to happen to Mia. If I could prevent it, I would—however crazy things got. I don't know why I suddenly cared so much, but as I looked at her, all I could see was a younger version of myself. Sly and sarcastic, but also scared, alone.

Who was I trying to save exactly?

"Tess." Derrick gave me a warning look. "We have to get back to the lab soon—and we should really have Mia talk to Selena, or even Marcus—"

"Marcus will just get all persnickety and ask her to fill out forms."

"No, no, it's okay." Mia stood up. "I'll talk to someone else—I trust you guys. I can give a statement, or whatever you want me to do."

"She's going to have to eventually," Derrick added.

Why was he suddenly being Mr. Textbook? Normally, Derrick was all about breaking the rules. I once saw him use a gas chromatograph to analyze the chemical content of his Pizza Pocket.

"I can do it," Mia insisted. "Really, and my aunt doesn't even have to know. I think you *should* search the house—maybe that guy's crazy, maybe he left something behind. A fingerprint or something, who knows? I'd sleep better knowing that we were safe—or as safe as we can ever be."

"Okay." I resisted the urge to groan as I sat up. These day shifts were killing me, and all I wanted to do was climb under the covers and sleep for a week. "Let me just get you some water first. Or I've got orange juice, I think." I wandered into the kitchen, careful to avoid the spot on the floor where the old linoleum was peeling. All I wanted to do was postpone the inevitable meeting with Marcus, which I hoped wouldn't evolve into some kind of disciplinary hearing.

I opened up the fridge. "Okay. I've got orange juice, cola, and something blue—Derrick, what kind of juice could be blue—"

That was when my door blew off its hinges.

I grabbed my athame from my jeans pocket, and ran back into the living room. Already, my own panic was fueling it—making the steel warm against my hand. The athame had always been the mage's weapon of choice. A dagger with a symbiotic connection to its wielder, joined in a pact of power, blood, and promise. The process for creating the weapon was ancient—a guarded secret. But it was one of the rare things that a demon feared. Especially if an angry mage was holding it.

Fuck, I hadn't sensed *anything*. What was wrong with me? What made me think that I could just drag Mia over here, and nothing would happen?

In that instant, I realized how stupidly tired I was. Tired of the misery and murder that demons, warlocks, and supposedly "normal" people caused, tired of all the heartache, and tired to death of fighting them. It was my job to make the world safe for kids like Mia, but now, she was the one in danger. A good kid—an orphan, schooled in loss, knowing intimately what it was like to have her parents ripped away from her.

I'd had enough of it. Something was going to pay.

Right now.

What I didn't count on was the demon in the middle of my living room, stepping over the wreckage of my shattered front door and carrying a Browning Hi-Power semiautomatic.

Derrick was standing in front of Mia, one hand held out, as if he could shield her from a spray of bullets. The demon was tall—most demons were—and built like an Italian bodyguard. He was bald, with pale skin and dark, almost black, eyes. I knew he was powerful because I could feel his genetic imprint even standing this far away. It was like the stink of sulfur, assaulting, making my eyes water.

"What do you want?" I asked, silently drawing as much power as I safely could, channeling it through the athame. I wanted to take this thing out without injuring Mia or Derrick, but I wasn't sure that I'd be able to.

The demon extended his other hand, and long, gray claws emerged from the flesh of his fingers with an eerie grating sound, like a Ginsu blade being drawn. It made me shiver. His other hand remained normal, still cradling the automatic.

"What do you think?" He smiled, revealing two separate rows of fangs and a flexible mandible.

Mia screamed. Finally. The demon turned to her, continuing to smile, and his mouth separated into two pieces, both armed with six-inch teeth. He had the grin of a homicidal shark.

Great. A Vailoid demon. They were about as easy to kill as an armored tank. And I had no backup at all. I'd tangled with a Vailoid once before, but that was years ago. *When you were still young,* the voice in my head reminded me. I'd been eighteen then—barely—and practically vibrating with power. And I'd had help. Now all I had was my own, significantly diminished power, a telepath who probably couldn't even pierce the demon's psychic defenses, and a girl who just might be more dangerous than all of us put together. If she really was a proto-mage.

Well, Dad, I thought, as usual, you were right. I should have gone into real estate.

Derrick and I exchanged a look. We both knew that we were up shit creek, but what else could we do?

I raised the athame. "Let's do this."

The Vailoid demon laughed—a horrific, burbling sound.

Then he pointed the gun at me and fired.

8

I remember, quite distinctly, the first time I had to use my powers to kill.

I was fourteen.

I'd already run through endless combat scenarios, and practiced all of my combat techniques until every muscle in my body ached. But that was under controlled conditions. This was in a dark alley at 2 a.m., and there weren't any safeguards in place. Just me and a vampire. A very hungry vampire.

He was young—newly dead, just like the one we found on Granville—and that was probably what saved my life. When vampires are first raised, they're disoriented. Hungry beyond all reason, not thinking at all, but just operating on pure animal instinct. From his red-rimmed eyes and trembling hands, I could tell that he'd just risen from the grave, and he was desperately looking for a blood fix. The vampiric hunger, they say, is an incredibly powerful thing. Much more powerful than meth, or crack, or heroin addiction. I never wanted to find out what that sort of hunger might feel like.

"Don't suppose you'd consider not eating me?" I had to ask. Even at fourteen, I'd always been a sarcastic little thing.

The vampire moved in a blur, and suddenly he was behind me, one arm wrapped around my chest. His grip was like iron—no way I could break it. Vampires are considered the demon upper class for a reason. They have a lot of the vestigial power of the higher-tier demons, including strength and speed, but they're also extremely adaptable. And contrary to the obvious, they actually *like* humans. They find us fascinating. And tasty.

He grabbed my neck with his free hand, angling it sharply upward so that I gulped, straining to breathe. I could feel his rancid, hot breath on my skin, a trail of saliva dripping from his mouth.

I knew what was coming next. I had to let him bite me. It was the only way to ensure that he was completely distracted, which would allow me to fight back. Otherwise, he'd sense the magic building, and pop my head off like a dandelion.

His teeth sank into my neck. It hurt far worse than I'd imagined. Luckily, he was more intent on feeding than on hurting me, so he didn't tear at the flesh or rip into the collarbone. He just sucked, and the feeling was horrific, indescribable. Like having your soul sucked out, one swallow at a time. I remember that I gasped, even though I hadn't meant to. I remember that my eyelids fluttered, and that I felt a nauseating mixture of pain, fear, and desire. It was the desire that still scares me, even to this day.

I got through the pain, though. I found the rage beneath, and poured that, along with my willpower, into the magical attack. When my fingers touched the pale, cold flesh of his face, they left searing red prints. He cried out in unexpected pain, lurching backward and putting a hand to his face.

Then his entire body burst into flame.

And fire, it seemed, would always possess my life. Someone would always be burning—a human, a vampire, a friend—always someone. Fire, like magic, was insatiable. It wouldn't give up until it destroyed everything, even its creator.

Especially its creator.

A lot happens in your brain when someone points a gun at you. I managed to think about all of this, to remember all of it, in less than a second. Watching Mia triggered the memory, since she was about the same age now as I was when I first had to kill something with my powers. And in that instant, I felt a flash of grief as I realized how her life was going to change. How she'd probably have to experience everything that I had. How she'd have to kill, violently, in order to survive. Just like an animal. Sometimes it felt like that's all we were. Just brilliant, logical animals, killing other animals to survive. Just creatures fighting to occupy the top of the food chain.

I'd never seen a demon with a gun before, so at first it took me by surprise. Demons don't normally have to rely on guns, since bullets don't do much to stop them, and they're perfectly capable of killing a human with their own bare hands. But I didn't pause for long. As soon as he raised the gun, I squeezed the hilt of the athame, and released the power that I'd been building up. I felt a hot rush of energy, then whirled around and leapt behind my desk, just as the Vailoid demon squeezed the trigger.

With a standard .45 caliber bullet, the Browning had a velocity of about 1,500 feet per second. I'd seen powerful vampires clocked at over twice that speed, dodging bullets like they were lawn darts. I felt my shoulder slam into the hard linoleum behind the desk, and then, a fraction of a second later, I heard two bullets thud into the desk. I didn't have a stopwatch, but I think, with the magical nitro boost, I'd cleared 2,000 feet per second.

I instantly felt nauseous.

"Mia, go into the bedroom, and stay there," I heard Derrick say. His voice was oddly flat, and calm, as if somebody else was speaking through him. "Don't open the door until we say so."

I dared a glance over the desk. Mia kept looking at Derrick, then at the Vailoid demon, then back at Derrick.

"I—" She didn't quite know how to finish the sentence.

"Mia, go. To the bedroom." I heard the snap of power in his voice. Telepaths called it Vox—a psychic modulation of their voice that allowed them to issue subliminal commands. I'd rarely heard Derrick resort to it, but I knew that he was using it now. I could feel the power in my gut.

Mia blinked at him for a moment, then turned around and walked calmly toward my bedroom. The demon didn't stop her. Clearly, he was here to retrieve her, which meant that she wasn't in any immediate danger. Derrick and I were the ones that were seriously screwed.

Praying that Derrick wouldn't try anything too stupid, I crawled around the side of the desk until I was shielded by a bookcase. It wouldn't provide much cover, but it was better than waving my arms in the open. I held the athame close to my chest, allowing it to draw more power.

"What's a demon doing with a nine?" I asked. "Kind of tacky, don't you think?"

"It's the millennium." I could hear the shiver of pleasure in his voice. "And we're nothing if not adaptable. You know, you move pretty quick for a human."

"Yeah? I'm real bendy, too."

The demon laughed.

I sucked in my breath. Hostage negotiation had never been my thing. Normally, I wasn't the one hiding behind a bookcase. "Why don't you put the gun down, and we can settle this by talking?" Great. I sounded like Magnum P.I.

"I could do that." The Vailoid paused. "Or I could blow a hole in your friend's skull, here. At this range, they couldn't even use dental records to ID him."

I felt bile in my throat. That wasn't going to happen.

The athame began to glow with a pale orange light. *Fire,* I thought. I can be a spark, too. Not enough to burn the place down (I wanted to keep my damage deposit), but enough to drop the Vailoid. I held the athame tighter.

"You've got about three seconds to quit hiding like a little girl," the demon said, "before I chop your friend in half. How does that sound?"

I kept drawing materia, silently. I could feel geothermic

energy from the earth pouring into me, through the soles of my shoes, up my legs, coursing through every inch of my body.

"One," he said playfully.

I held the athame in the air, concentrating on it. This was a familiar combat technique, but I hadn't used it in a while. Timing was everything.

"Twwwooooo." He drew the word out, like a child playing hide and seek. I could feel every muscle tingling. Now or never.

"Three," I said, whirling out from behind the bookcase. The demon raised his gun, and I threw the athame, aiming for his chest.

The blade shimmered like a roman candle as it flew through the air, elongating and blazing outward, until it was the size of a spear. It plunged through the demon's shoulder, and he cried out—more with surprise than pain—dropping the 9mm. Then the athame flared with light, and flames licked along the demon's body.

My aim was off, but at least he'd dropped the gun.

The Vailoid grabbed the spear with both hands, wrenching it out of his shoulder with a low cry of anger. He threw it to the floor, and the athame shrank to its usual proportions, molten light cooling until it was just a normal blade again. The flames trembled and vanished. Still, I could see the wound in his shoulder, leaking out jet-black blood. The smell was horrible—like a tar factory exploding.

The demon came barreling toward me like a logging truck. I kicked the bookcase and gave it an extra push of willpower. It flew through the air, but he flung it aside with one arm, and it crashed into the wall.

Shit. Got to remember that Vailoid strength.

I mentally ran through everything I knew about this type of demon. Strong, smart, ruthless. Generally bounty-hunters, specializing in contract jobs. They work for the highest bidder, and if the price is right, they'll assassinate their own cousin. In fact, they might even do that for free.

To kill a demon, you have to destroy the body completely.

None of this stake-through-the-heart bullshit that you see in vampire movies. Demons were hard as fuck to kill, and unless you did it properly, they didn't stay dead.

"He told me not to harm the girl." The demon smiled. "But nobody said anything about two mages, which means I can do what I want to you and your friend. And I've been giving serious thought to how I'm going to kill you both. How I'll make it last."

"He?" A cold tremor passed through me. The vampire must have had friends—very powerful friends. "What's Mia gotten herself into? And since when do Vailoids work for newly sired vamps?"

"Vampires?" He laughed—as if he knew something that I didn't. "If you don't have a clue, then I'm not about to tell you." The demon paused. "I mean, maybe I'll tell you once I've torn out your ribcage. But then you won't exactly be able to do anything with the information."

"You're very poetic for a Vailoid."

He smiled, and his jaw separated, revealing both sets of fangs.

I kicked the demon in the chest, pouring all of my willpower into the blow. There was a *crack* of compressed air as the energy exploded, then the demon flew backward, crashing into a wall of bookshelves and toppling them over. Oh well. I kind of wanted to move anyway.

I turned, and saw that Derrick was leaning against the desk. A thin trickle of blood dripped from his nose. Shit. Not good. He must have been lending me energy, or concentrating on keeping Mia from moving—it was taking all of his resolve.

"Get out of here," I said. "Go protect Mia. I'll deal with this thing."

"I don't want to leave you alone—"

"Just go," I snapped. "Derrick, you're burned out. You won't be able to help me. Just go and watch Mia."

I could see my athame on the ground—I might be able to get to it in time. The demon was a bit slow getting to its feet. Maybe the wound was starting to bother it.

Shit. Just do it, Tess.

I ran for the blade, dropping to my knees to avoid the demon as he swiped his claws at me. I managed to touch the hilt, but then the demon's other hand locked around my throat. He swept me into the air, and I gasped, seeing bright spots. This was not good. This definitely qualified as a panic situation.

He snarled and backhanded me across the face, and I fell to the floor. It felt like getting hit with a cinderblock, and I spit out blood, feeling the sharp sting where my lip was cut. I was going to look like roadkill tomorrow morning. Crouching, I pressed one hand to the ground, drawing power. The demon lunged, and I thrust upward with my other hand. A column of fire exploded from my palm.

The demon screamed, stumbling backward and clutching his face. Demons could heal fire damage, but it took a lot longer. And it pissed them off.

He leapt at me. I didn't have a chance to raise any sort of defense, and he hit me full on, pinning me to the ground. Three hundred pounds of demonic muscle. I couldn't breathe. My ribs were creaking, and I could feel his breath on my face. It reeked like sulfur, ash, and something rotting.

He wrapped his hand around my throat again. I tried to push him away with the force of my will, but it's hard to concentrate when someone's methodically strangling you. I managed to make him shift position, but that was it. I could feel one claw digging into my side—playfully. He wouldn't draw blood until he was ready. He wanted to savor it, savor my terror, like a wonderful meal.

I kneed him, as hard as I could, in what I hoped was the anatomical equivalent of his privates. I guessed right. He groaned in surprise, shifting his weight just enough for me to get some leverage. I jammed my fingers into his throat. His grip loosened slightly, and I brought my other knee up, smashing him in the face.

He howled, and before I had the chance to move, his claws raked across my right arm and shoulder. They burned for an instant, then the arm went numb. Great. It was either venom, or shock. Praying for the latter, I managed to grab the athame with my left hand. My right hand was pinned against his chest, but I channeled power into the athame, and it flared red-hot. I smelled the acrid stench of burning skin, and the demon cried out angrily, giving me just enough leverage to slice deeper with the blade. Howling, he grabbed my bad arm and wrenched it upward. I screamed—I couldn't help it. He was holding my arm now, and he could pull it out of its socket, or tear it right off. Maybe he really was going to follow through on his threat.

Still holding me by the arm, he closed his fingers around my throat again.

"This time," he said sweetly, "I won't let go."

I dug the blade deeper into his side, but I didn't have the strength to do a lot more damage with only one hand—and my left hand, at that. He squeezed my throat harder. The spots appeared, then little flickers of darkness at the corners of my eyes. If I blacked out, it was all over. I lunged, trying to kick his feet out from under him, but he was braced against the desk. I couldn't move him, and my strength was fading.

Shit. Oh shit.

"I just want you to know," the demon said, "that this won't end here. The fun starts when you wake up. First, I'll make you watch while I carve up your friend. I'll make the girl watch, too. She's got to learn sooner or later, right? About our world. About how things work out here, in the wild."

"I'm taking you with me," I snarled, "you piece of—"

"Now, now, princess—save those fighting words for later. I want you alive and full of spunk, so that you can watch me—"

I heard a loud *crack* that made my ears ring, and the demon's grip slackened. Another explosion, and something warm and horrible splashed across my face. The demon stumbled backward, screaming angrily.

I wiped the blood off my face and looked up. Derrick was standing behind the desk, pointing a Glock .40 at the demon's head. The gun that I kept underneath my bed—the gun that I *should* have grabbed as soon as we entered the apartment, but I hadn't even thought about it. As an OSI, I had a permit to carry concealed, although I usually just kept the Glock at home for emergencies. It was equipped with Hydra-Shok bullets—the kind that blossomed like mushrooms, exploding outward to do the most damage possible.

I looked up at the demon, and realized that about one-third of his head was missing. I didn't want to see what my clothes looked like.

I grabbed the athame with both hands and drove it upward, using all of the strength that I had left. The blade sliced through the demon's abdomen with a spray of blood, spilling out intestines all over my lap. I recoiled from the sharp stink of acid, bile, and excrement, but kept slicing, until the blade popped out of the creature's ruined throat. It was still screaming, but the sound had become more like a gurgle.

Once the head was gone, the body was more or less complacent. It was still alive, one remaining hand clenching convulsively, its claws trembling—but it couldn't attack me anymore. Holding my breath and grimacing, I reached into the chest cavity and pulled the heart free. I told myself that I was reaching into a warm bowl of spaghetti, since that's almost what it felt like. The worst part was that the stench would cling to my fingers for days.

God, this was why I never dated.

The heart was soft and surprisingly heavy, like a lump of ground beef in my hand, slick with blood. I let it drop to the floor.

"Don't touch the body," I told Derrick. "Fuck. Oh fuck. Marcus is going to have *kittens* when he sees this."

He stared at me. "Come on, Tess. That thing tried to kill us. Marcus is a bastard, but he can't possibly think that you had something to do with this."

"Didn't I? We led him straight to Mia. She wouldn't have been here if it weren't for our meddling."

"No, she'd probably be dead." His look was surprisingly calm. "If she'd been at home, alone—you know what would have happened, Tess. You saved her life." He smiled weakly. "You pretty much saved my life, too."

"You held your own."

He chuckled. "I got a nosebleed, and barely slowed him down."

"We worked together. Like we always do." I sighed.

"Well, we've got to call it in. We won't know how it's all going to turn out until you talk to Selena."

I tried to catch my breath for a minute or two, not saying anything. Derrick was silent as well. My right arm was burning now—a good sign, since the numbing had only been temporary, and not some kind of poison. It would definitely need stitches, although the bleeding was shallow, thankfully.

Finally, I turned to him and smiled. "Shit. I can't believe you fired the Glock. And you actually *hit* him."

"I almost dislocated my shoulder." Derrick touched his arm and winced. "Plus, my ears are still ringing. You're banged up a lot worse, though. We'll definitely need to go to a clinic."

"We'd better check on Mia," I said. "You go in first. I don't want her to see me yet—she might freak out."

"Sure. I'll be right back." He paused. "Um—what about—" He gestured to the Vailoid demon's body.

"Just, um"—I sighed—"tell her to close her eyes. And make sure that she doesn't step in it."

"Gotcha." He went back to the bedroom.

I definitely needed time to process. And a shower. And possibly chocolate.

I surveyed the remains of our lunch—shredded cherry-cheese croissants. I couldn't tell cherry from demon blood.

"Derrick?" I called weakly. "Derrick? Are there any cookies left?"

9

After the HAZMAT guys confirmed that the demon's blood wasn't a biohazard, Tasha bagged the body and took it back to the morgue. The photographers snapped more pictures of the bloody patch of hardwood floor where he'd been lying. They took samples of the blood, along with the other fluids that the demon had been kind enough to leave behind. Then they swabbed the blood on my hands for further testing.

They sprayed Derrick's hands for gunshot residue, even though he'd freely admitted that he fired the weapon. Whenever you fire a gun, the primer creates a residue of lead, barium, and other trace elements, all expelled in a cloud that can travel up to three feet away. You'd be surprised how many criminals don't know that, or don't think about other evidence, like the expelled casing shells.

An OSI-1 whose name I couldn't remember—although I recalled seeing her in the office a few times—swabbed Derrick's hands and clothing. The swabs would be taken back to the crime lab and subjected to an Atomic Absorption Test. We had a machine called a spectra-photometer that could detect the amount of GSR—mostly lead particulates—that were present.

They tested my hands as well, and I'd have to give them a sample of my clothing for the AA test. It seemed like such a violation, even though I knew that people at a crime scene have to go through this kind of testing all the time. My Glock .40 was printed, the serial number recorded, and then it was confiscated as evidence.

The same OSI who'd processed Derrick's GSR kit was now spraying a pool of blood near the floor with an aerosol solution. There was a footprint smeared in the blood. I knew it was mine, but they had to make sure—and although everybody was being very polite and listening to me, I knew that I was also being treated like any other potential suspect. They were just here to process the evidence, not to take my side, or assign blame. She sprayed a fine mist on the footprint— Leucocrystal Violet, a spray dye used to enhance prints in blood—then signaled one of the photographers to take pictures of it. After the pictures were taken, she used a rubber-gelatin lifter to extract the print.

I watched Selena leading Mia out of the bathroom. She wrapped a blanket around the girl's shoulders, gave her a cup of water, and then headed toward me. Great. I'd been trying to avoid this conversation since yesterday, but everything was going to come out now. Selena looked calm, but that could be a bad sign. Maybe she was trying to figure out the most creative way to have me arrested.

"Hey." She touched my shoulder. It was a surprising gesture. Selena hardly ever made physical contact with anyone, and it took me off guard.

"Hi," I said weakly. If I concentrated very hard, I wouldn't throw up all over her expensive leather jacket.

Her eyes narrowed. "Are you okay? Really?"

I winced. "I'll need some stitches, and some extra-strength painkillers. But other than that, I'm fine. I got lucky."

"I'll say. A homicidal Vailoid demon is nothing to sneeze at. You did good. Your training has really paid off."

I stared at her. Was she actually complimenting me? I was embroiled in a murder investigation, being stalked by the same demons that I was supposed to be trailing, and now she was giving me a good recommendation?

"Selena," I said slowly. "I know this looks bad, okay? Mia Polanski, here, in my apartment. But—"

She raised a hand. "I wouldn't say anything else, if I were you. This has been a rough day. You're still in shock, and you're probably suffering from a massive hangover, too, considering the power that you threw around. We can save the real questions for when you're feeling better." She smiled—it was small, but conspicuous. "Right now, all I care about is making sure that you, Derrick, and the girl are safe."

The front door opened, and Marcus walked in.

I was afraid that he might show up, but it still surprised me to see him here. As regional director, he didn't have to be present at every single crime scene. He could always just read the report later. But it stood to reason that he'd want to be here to yell at me in person.

Marcus saw me, and for a moment, he looked startled. I didn't blame him. Who would have thought that Derrick and I could take down a Vailoid demon—and one armed with a semiautomatic, to boot? I was surprised to be alive, and I *liked* me.

He walked over, and the momentary look of shock was replaced by anger. His cold eyes seemed to swallow me up.

"What the hell is going on here, Corday? You were supposed to interview the Polanski girl at her home. Now she shows up at your"—he gave the apartment a look of profound distaste, as if he'd just entered a mud and wattle hut—"*domicile*, and suddenly we've got a dead demon on our hands."

"Back off a little, Marcus." Selena glared at him. "The poor girl almost got killed today. Give her a chance to catch her breath."

He seemed about to say something, but then the anger dissipated. He gave me a look up and down. "You okay? Hurt, or just shook up?"

Concern from Marcus felt odd—like the bitchy shoe manager at Holt Renfrew suddenly asking you how your day was. But I saw something close to empathy in his eyes. I started to wonder how much I really knew about my boss.

"Just shook," I said, wincing. "Might need a few stitches. All in all, a pretty standard lunch hour, I'd say."

He nodded. "Don't mind the cleanup crew. They don't mean to treat you like a suspect, but there are—"

"Protocols." I smiled weakly. "I know, Marcus. They're just doing their jobs."

"You'll have to go to the clinic. Her, too." He glanced at Mia. "As they say in the break room—this is going to be a bit of a clusterfuck."

"Marcus!" I don't think I'd ever heard him swear before. "I'm going to have to include your objectionable language in my report."

He smiled wanly. "Don't relax too much. We've got a lot of damage control to do here. The suits are going to want to know specifically what our chief witness in a vampire homicide case is doing at the head OSI's apartment in the middle—"

"It was my idea to come here."

Mia was suddenly beside me—I hadn't heard her move at all. Her eyes were clear and sharp. She had no problem meeting Marcus's gaze.

"We've already taken a statement from you, Miss Polanski," Marcus said. "We've also called your aunt—she'll be coming to pick you up from the clinic, once you've been properly examined."

"I know that." Mia didn't smile. "I just wanted to give my statement again, since you don't seem to know what really happened."

Marcus's face paled for a moment. God. She was contradicting him, baiting him. I hoped Mia knew what she was doing.

"Well then," he said, "why don't you explain it to me? Why do you think that . . ." He hesitated over the word "demon." "Why do you think that killer was after you? And how did you happen to be in Miss Corday's place of residence to-day?"

"I came looking for Tess and Derrick," Mia said. "I remembered them from the other day, and I wanted to talk to them. Tess tried to take me to your office, but I didn't want to go. I—threatened to run—"

Lie number one. I didn't know precisely why she was lying for me, but I wasn't about to bring it up now.

"And what were you doing in the city to begin with? Shouldn't you be in school at this time of day?"

"I'm homeschooled. And I got a ride in with my aunt—she's at work right now, but she's picking me up at six."

"We'll confirm all of these details with her. Just to make sure."

"Whatever," Mia said. "I feel like crap. Someone said we were all going to get checked out at a clinic or something. Can we go there now?"

"Of course." He smiled. "In a few moments. We have a facility nearby. In the meantime, why don't you gather up all your belongings?"

"All right," she said numbly. She didn't even look at me.

Once she'd disappeared back into my bedroom, Selena touched my arm.

"You need anything?" she asked. "Water? Coffee?"

"Tequila?" I asked weakly.

She smiled. "I'll see what I can do."

"Before you go anywhere, Selena," Marcus said, "I want to make sure that we're all clear on the protocol here. Tess will have to be reassigned to another case."

I stared open-mouthed at him. "What? You can't do that!"

"It's policy," he said simply. "Until we've established that you used your powers against the demon in self-defense—"

"He was trying to kill me, Marcus!"

He raised his hand to keep me from interrupting. "Until you're cleared, officially, and we've established that you don't have any kind of previous relationship with the victim, Mia Polanski, I have no choice but to assign you to a different case."

"That hardly seems fair, Marcus," Selena began.

"It's not fair." He gave me a sympathetic look. "We've all been under the magnifying glass at one time or another. Once you're clear, you can go back to working the case. Until then, it's a conflict of interest."

I suppressed the urge to throw something—or kill something. He was right. "You can still check out the vampires—interview Lucian, and report anything that you find out from him. But after that, you're off this case until the paperwork comes through clean. Got it?"

I exhaled. "Fuck. Yes."

"Good." Marcus smiled. "So everyone understands what's going on. Now, Selena, why don't you take these three to the clinic and get them patched up? Call me when the aunt arrives."

He turned on his heel and walked away.

"Sometimes it's like talking to a procedure manual," I said.

"Yeah." Selena fixed me with a level look. "But this could have ended up a lot worse, and you know it."

I could barely meet her eyes.

"Get your things, and take the girl to the clinic," she said. "I'll see what I can do about getting you cleared as soon as possible."

I sighed in relief. "You're fantastic."

"Huh." She grabbed her cell phone and walked away. "Just don't forget it."

10

I was sitting on a very cold gurney in CORE Clinic 21B, wincing from the pain in my newly stitched arm and shoulder. Twelve stitches—not bad for tussling with a Vailoid demon. Derrick was sitting in the chair next to me. He'd overextended himself by trying to attack the demon's mind but hadn't done any permanent damage. They gave him an IV drip to replace some of the fluids he'd lost.

Mia was sitting on the floor. We'd offered her a chair, but I think she felt safer there. She wasn't in shock. She was just very quiet. I was actually a little surprised when she agreed to come with us so easily. She just got into the car and sat silently in the back, her eyes glassy as she stared out the window. She hadn't said a word since we'd arrived at the clinic—not even when we had to walk through a XXX video store to get there. The CORE hid their facilities well, and nobody was about to look for a secret clinic at the back of the Pleasure Box—fine purveyor of adult films, books, and magazines, on Fourth Avenue and Vine.

I still didn't quite understand why she'd lied for me, but I was afraid to ask her. Maybe she didn't even know herself.

She didn't even crack a smile when Derrick pointed out the butt plugs, and that made even me smile, split lip and all. We might as well have been in a grocery store, or a church, for all she knew.

Evelyn, my favorite nurse—and the one who'd just stitched me up—came in bearing a cup full of pills. "Here you go, sugar," she said, handing them to me. "Something for when the Demerol wears off."

"Sweet Jesus, thank you." I swallowed the pills greedily. "Will they make me drowsy? I may have to stay awake tonight."

Her eyes narrowed. "I don't care what you're mixed up in, Tess. If you don't get a good rest and take care of yourself tonight, I'll come over and kick your ass myself."

"I'd listen to her," Derrick offered, still slurping on a juice box. "She could take you, Tess."

"That's right, you listen to him," she said. "He knows what I'm capable of."

Derrick nodded. "I once saw her slap a senior CORE instructor for trying to talk on her cell phone when she was supposed to be resting."

I sighed. "Honestly, Evelyn—I'll try. I just might be getting a rude awakening sometime tonight, and I don't want to be all useless and groggy when it happens."

"What did you do, Tess?"

I looked at Mia, then back at Evelyn. "It's complicated."

"So complicated that a Vailoid demon tried to rip you apart?" Evelyn saw how immobile my expression was, and sighed. "Fine," she said simply. "But if it gets any worse, I want you to call someone. Promise?"

"I promise. Really."

Evelyn shook her head in disgust. Then she turned to Mia.

"What about you, sweetie? You want anything? Some tea or hot chocolate? We could fix you something to eat, too."

Mia looked up. "No thank you," she said calmly, and I almost jumped. "I don't need anything right now."

"Okay, then—but if you think of something, just flag one of us down." Evelyn turned to me. "And if I see you again later tonight, I'm going to kick every inch of your butt, Tess Corday. Understand?"

I swallowed. "Yes, Evelyn."

She smiled beatifically at Derrick. "See you later, hon."

"Bye, Evelyn!" Derrick grinned back, like a sibling who knows that both parents love him best.

Then she turned and walked out, closing the curtain behind her. We had what passed for privacy at the clinic, despite the fact that it sounded like we were in the middle of a crowded theater.

"So," Derrick said after a bout of silence, "are we going to rent a movie? 'Cause I'm voting for *Shall We Dance*. It's a feel-good story about overcoming adversity and learning to embrace a more beautiful you."

Mia giggled.

"Finally." Derrick smiled. "I thought it would take all night to make one of you act normal again."

"Normal. Sure." Mia looked at him. "I just watched some psychotic—thing—with a detachable jaw and fangs try to kill both of you. I don't think movies and popcorn are going to make me feel normal tonight."

I sighed. "She's right—this isn't a joke. Mia, you saw some pretty intense stuff today, and nobody blames you for being scared. Or for thinking that some of it might not have been real—"

"Don't talk to me like I'm a little kid." Her glare was icy. "I'm not stupid, Tess. I saw what I saw." She looked away. "I can't *not* know anymore. Wish I could, though." Her voice fell. "Wish I'd never met either of you."

I wish I'd never met you.

Eve was getting up, stumbling, trying to run away. I'd only shown her something small—the tiniest bit of light that I conjured up, just a pale green glow that clung to my hands like shimmering moss—but it terrified her. I could still remember the look in her eyes, that expression somewhere between fear and disgust. As if I'd just stripped naked before her, and she didn't want anything to do with my body, my powers.

It's just light, I kept saying. *Eve, you don't have to be frightened. It's just a bit of light—it won't hurt you—I won't hurt you—please—*

But she was already running toward her house. Trying to get away from me as fast as possible, with fragments of that spectral light clinging to her shadow, following her, as if out of benign curiosity.

I stared at my hands.

"You don't have to be afraid," I said softly.

Mia stared at me. "Hello? I got attacked by a walking shark! Don't I get to freak out about that?"

I blinked to clear my vision. Derrick was staring at me strangely, but he didn't say anything. God—why were these memories coming back now? And why did Mia have to look *so* much like—*her*?

"I didn't—I mean—" I sighed. "You've got to understand, Mia, that we *are* trying to protect you. We had no idea that demon would come charging in there. We just wanted to talk to you."

"Bullshit."

That caught me by surprise.

"You could have warned me. 'Yeah, Mia, by the way, you might not want to come back to my apartment—since there's a psycho monster with *detachable fangs* that wants to kill you—' "

"A demon," I corrected.

Mia looked at me. "What?"

"It was a demon. A Vailoid demon. They're mercenaries, mostly—working for money or whatever else they might need." I tried not to sound too dramatic, but I knew that I was scaring her, regardless. "It came for Derrick and me. Someone sent that demon to kidnap you—it wouldn't have hurt you, but it had orders to kill us. It nearly did."

Mia stared at the floor for a moment. Then she asked: "Who sent it?"

"I don't know." It was pretty much the truth. "I have some ideas—but nothing concrete. We're working on some leads."

Mia narrowed her eyes. "At least tell me the gist of what's going on. You said that thing was a demon. Like—what—is that a fallen angel or something? Or a vampire? Do those things really exist?"

"I don't know anything about fallen angels, but vampires—yeah, they exist." I cracked my knuckles. "Vampires are demons, too. They don't all have long flowy capes and talk European-like, though. In fact, they pretty much look like us."

Mia blinked. "That *thing*—what did you call it?"

"A Vailoid."

"The Vailoid, yeah—he didn't look like a human. Or he did at first—but he had those crazy fangs." She shuddered. "So some demons look like that, and others are, like, totally human? Like you or me?"

"Right," I said. "Depends on the demon. Some are better at blending in. Some are so good that you'd never be able to tell until it was too late."

Mia digested this soberly for a moment.

"They're not all bad," Derrick said. "I mean, Tess and I—"

"We aren't always fighting them," I said hastily, giving him a sharp look. "Some are actually on our side. A lot of them coexist peacefully with humans, and hardly ever cause us any trouble."

I didn't need Mia to know that her power—if she indeed had power—came from a demonic source. That definitely qualified as too much info for one night, and she was already handling the rest of this pretty well. There was no sense in blowing her mind, or giving her a reason to bolt.

"What about those people who were at the apartment?" she asked. "All the photographers, and the others? They looked like cops, but they weren't."

"They're part of the organization that we work for," Derrick said, obviously picking his words carefully. "They're investigating what happened."

"Organization?" She looked quizzically at me. "I thought you worked for the Vancouver Crime Lab."

"Sort of," he said, trying to smile. "We work for *a* crime lab. But we're not precisely connected to the VPD."

He looked at me, as if to say: *Should I tell her everything?*

I shrugged. At this point, we were already in like bandits.

"So you're not cops," she said coolly.

I sighed. Yet another conversation I'd been dreading.

"We are—sort of," I said. "We deal with things that the cops can't. Cases that are—out of their purview."

Derrick raised an eyebrow but said nothing. For a while, we were all silent.

"So—where do they come from?" Mia asked after a moment.

I was distracted. "Who?"

"Demons." Her look was strange.

I struggled for an answer. "We don't know exactly." When she looked skeptical, I spread my hands. "Honest. We really aren't sure. The records are fuzzy, but we're pretty certain that demons have existed for as long as humans have. Possibly, they were here before us. Although 'here' probably looked a lot different back then."

"Demons are a lot like us," Derrick added. "They come in all shapes and sizes—they all think differently, act differently. They have different jobs and different backgrounds—"

"Jobs?" Mia asked in surprise.

He nodded. "Most demons have to work—unless they're independently wealthy. It's the same with us—we get paid a pretty modest salary for what we do."

"And what exactly *is* that?"

"Demons create chaos," Derrick said. "We contain it. Like *The X-Files*, only without the tubular bells."

She rolled her eyes. "That's all you're going to tell me?"

"I think if we talk any more about this, we're just going to confuse you," I said. "You've seen and heard enough for one night."

"Tess, you said yourself—I need to know this stuff. If one

of those badass things comes looking for me, I'll need to know how to protect myself."

"If a demon comes looking for you, what you need to do is *run*," Derrick said. "Run very fast, and try to find us. Under no circumstances should you try to take one of those things on."

She folded her arms. "So I'm just supposed to run away like a little baby? Like a screaming girl?"

"Yes," I said firmly. "There's no shame in it. And you *are* a—" I stopped short of saying "baby," seeing the dangerous gleam in her eye. "You're a thirteen-year-old girl, Mia, and you don't know what you're up against. Derrick and I have been trained for this sort of thing. We know how to protect you."

"Like you did a bang-up job today," she mumbled.

I frowned. "We tried our best. And this time, we won. I'll admit, it got pretty hairy there for a bit—"

"That thing kicked the shit out of you, Tess."

"Language!" I snapped. I'm not sure why I kept channeling my mother whenever I was around Mia, but I couldn't help it.

"Oh, please—I can watch you decapitate a demon with two mouths, but I'm not allowed to swear?"

"You weren't supposed to see that."

"I watched from the office." Her eyes took on a strange cast—as if some light had abandoned them, and there was just a terrifying blankness beneath. "I saw all of it. Everything. I wanted to tear my eyes out, but I couldn't. And if there was some way to erase all of it—to erase you, Derrick, the demon, all of the"—she swallowed—"all of the blood, and the fire—I'd do it. I'd do it in a second."

I stared at her levelly.

"But there isn't—is there?"

"No," Derrick said. "I'm sorry, sweetheart, but there isn't."

"Don't worry. It's perfectly natural to be confused, to not want to talk about this whole thing." The words came out before I could stop them. God, I sounded like a teen pregnancy pamphlet.

Mia managed to glare at me, and I remembered that no thirteen-year-old girl wants to be told that she's "perfectly natural." I couldn't think of anything to say that might make her feel better, though. I was at a loss.

"For now," I said, "I think we should all just go home. I'll leave my cell phone on, and if *anything* happens—no matter what—call me, and I'll come get you."

"Are you sure that's wise?" Derrick asked. "Maybe Mia could stay at the lab—just for the night. Selena might okay it—"

"My aunt won't let me." Her face was a mask of resolve again. "It's cool, though. That guy said that she was coming to pick me up."

"Marcus? Yes, I'm sure he called her a while ago."

"He doesn't seem to like you," Mia observed.

"You picked up on that?" Derrick asked. "It's so subtle." She managed to smile weakly.

"Maybe we can talk tomorrow," I said.

Mia looked at me sharply. "I thought you weren't supposed to see me again—it's a conflict of interest, remember?"

I stared at her in surprise for a moment. "You heard that?"

"I'm good at eavesdropping," she said unemphatically. "That Marcus guy said you weren't supposed to come near me."

"Well—" I swallowed. How quickly could I throw away my career? "I'm not sure that I can follow those instructions exactly."

"Tess—" Derrick began.

I turned on him. "Oh, like you're just going to sit idly by. We both have to keep working this, and you know it."

"Even if it costs us our jobs? Or worse?"

I shrugged. "There are more important things."

I almost believed it.

Mia gave me an odd look. Almost like she was seeing me for the first time. I knew then that I didn't need to ask her why she'd lied. It didn't matter. She trusted me, and I trusted her. It was a beginning.

For a while, we were all silent. Then Mia cleared her throat.

"So . . . demons." She looked at me. It wasn't really a statement or a question. I'm not sure what it was. "Huh," she said.

"Huh," I replied.

At that moment, the door to the examination room opened, and Selena walked in. Directly behind her was Cassandra.

I froze as soon as I saw her. My heart was pounding—but she barely even looked at me. She went straight to Mia and hugged her.

"Are you all right, sweetheart?"

Surprisingly, Mia accepted the embrace. I realized that this was going to be even more complicated than it seemed. This was a girl who loved her aunt—her only surviving parental guardian. I couldn't just accuse the woman of murder right in front of her, ripping her life to shreds.

"Miss Polanski," Selena said, "your niece is fine, but she was involved in a very serious incident. Tess and her partner, Derrick, managed to subdue the attacker, and Mia was unharmed. But we're still conducting an investigation."

"Of course." Her look was grim. "You need to find out who did this. What sort of monster would attack three innocent people in broad daylight?"

"We're trying to figure that out, ma'am," Selena said. "Can you tell us where you were around four thirty p.m. today?"

Cassandra blinked. "Why, that was barely an hour ago. I was at work. That Marcus person—"

"Marcus Tremblay?"

"Yes." She frowned. "He had a very unpleasant phone manner."

Even though I was a bit wary of Cassandra right now, I still had to smile.

Selena didn't. "That's him," she said simply.

"Well, he phoned me at work, to see if I could come pick Mia up. So of course I got here as soon as I could."

"And where do you work?"

"SemTec Laboratories on Georgia and West Pender."

"She's a chemist," Mia said. It sounded so normal.

"Yes." Cassandra smiled. "That's right. Boring stuff, I'm afraid."

Then the most surprising thing happened. Cassandra walked over to me, and wrapped me in a tight embrace.

"Thank you," she said simply. "Thank you for protecting Mia."

"You—you're welcome, "I stammered. "Miss Polanski—"

Something passed between us—I couldn't quite put it into words, but it was a mixture of warning and gratitude. *You've done me a favor, and I've done you one. But come no closer.*

Cassandra stepped back, smiling. "Everyone here is so efficient. I'll have to send you all a gift basket."

"Aunt *Cassie*." Mia glared at her.

"I'm sorry, dear. I don't mean to embarrass you in front of all the forensics experts." She laid a hand on Mia's back. "Now let's go home, before anything else happens to you."

Watching them go, I wondered how safe "home" was.

I wondered how safe any of us were.

11

The first time Derrick and I met, I was wearing a spiked dog collar and dancing on Katie Green's sofa. I'd smoked some amazing pot about an hour before, and by the time I heard the first strains of Depeche Mode on the CD player, I was pretty much gone. As an undergrad doing a social-sciences degree at the University of British Columbia, I felt the need to go through a "dark" period, which included experimenting with a lot of drugs and listening to *Violator* with all the lights off in my apartment. Yes, I had a plasma globe. Yes, I painted triptychs with names like "Raven Mother Blesses Her Children." To my credit, I've gotten a lot better—although if I'm minding my own business and suddenly hear "Judy Is a Punk," my body will actually explode unless I start dancing. Really.

I was a few minutes away from putting a lamp shade on my head when Derrick walked into the living room. He was wearing a blue silk shirt, black dress pants, and loafers. He had one blond streak in his hair. He was Duckie from *Pretty in Pink*. I could have died. I had no idea that, years later, Derrick would angrily start crying at the precise moment when Duckie started crying, legs pulled up to his chest, somehow occupying the same fucked-up space as John Cryer as he mourned for Molly Ringwold. Except that Derrick was mourning for Tim, his asshole of an ex who was now dating a blond eighteen-year-old with a lip piercing. "It's like I kiss a boy," he told me once, "and they just become evil. Like I'm gay kryptonite."

I fed him chocolate macaroons, and we finished watching the movie. Afterward, I convinced him to prank call Tim and pretend to be a herpes clinic. It was healing.

Derrick looked up at me and smiled. "Having fun?"

"God, I love this album." I half sat, half flopped onto the couch, my leather skirt riding up perilously around my thighs. "Don't you love this album?"

"Sure." He sat down next to me. "Cool party, huh?"

I rolled my eyes. "Blah, blah. Katie Green is such a thundercunt."

"You think so?"

"Fuck *yeah*. She totally slept with Brad Hewitt when he was going out with Stacey Lomar. And I heard she's like a total clepto. She steals cosmetics and shit all the time from Eaton's."

The first was a rumor. The second was entirely fictionalized, and I had no idea why I said it. I just found the image of Katie Green stealing Venom lip gloss to be incredibly funny. Her parents were both lawyers, and they'd bought her a Mercedes S-Class for her sixteenth birthday.

"Wow." Derrick was polite enough to look surprised. "I totally didn't know that about her. That's so harsh."

"It *is* harsh." I leaned back in the sofa. I remember that it suddenly seemed very big—like I was in a boat with green cushions, sailing on a green crayon sea. "What did you say your name was again? Dylan? Like Dylan Thomas?"

"Derrick, actually."

"Isn't the word 'milkwood' amazing? Don't you wonder about it? Like, sometimes I lie in bed at night and wonder what it would be like to be *under milkwood*. Floating on a sea of milk, like the fucking Lady of Shallot."

He didn't say anything, but I think I saw his pupils dilate.

"It's awesome to meet you, Derrick." I grinned blearily at him. "So did you want to go upstairs?"

His cheeks went red. "Like—to one of the bedrooms?"

"Um, *yes*, to one of the bedrooms." I put my hand on his knee.

"S-s-sure." He smiled. "Sure, what the hell. Let's go."

"I should warn you, though. I'm having a bit of trouble walking in these boots." I was wearing a pair of knee-high stilettos that I'd bought from Cabbages 'n Kinx, and to say that I had "trouble" walking in them was an understatement. I looked like a female praying mantis climbing up the stairs.

"That's okay. You can lean on me."

"What a gentleman." I grabbed his arm. "A diamond in the rough."

Derrick led me up the stairs to a room belonging to Katie's younger sister. There was an enormous poster of Boyz II Men above her bed, and a signed picture of Mariah Carey right beside it. The comforter was pink and ruffled. None of this deterred us. We made out for about twenty minutes before Derrick told me he was gay. By that time, the pot was starting to wear off, but I was just paranoid enough to think that I might be gay as well. Derrick assured me that I was probably straight, and flattered me by saying what a great kisser I was—much better than the other three girls that he'd kissed in his entire lifetime, including his grade-seven lab partner, Erika Holtz. "She had braces," he explained, "and not the clear plastic kind. This was some serious hardware. If you had an elastic band, you could play percussion on them."

An hour later, we were eating chocolate-coconut pie at a nearby Denny's while I secretly rolled another joint beneath the table. We walked along English Bay—back then, the trendy Coal Harbor neighborhood had barely been developed; it was still just an explosion of cranes, cinderblocks, and half-finished buildings. We picked our way among the rubble, like explorers walking on the surface of the moon. Now there's a glowing paintbrush in the middle of the water, and a scroll of neon light that fluoresces in different mellow colors, welcoming you to the waterfront in Sannitch, a dialect of Coast Salish territory: xʷə́w'e sə́y'siʔ, x̌ʷən'eŋ' ɫeʔə steʔəw'. "Don't be afraid. Be like the light."

In the pinhole blackness of that warm night by the water, we walked along Sunset Beach, stoned from my little glass pipe. I remember how Derrick used to stare at it, curious at how the brownish vapor collected in its soft heart; how it looked like a moth fluttering. We walked underneath Granville bridge and the cars went galumphing over our heads, *bump bump* of the careless wheels, or a time code or the flash of a pulse, the blooming of blood along plains of vesicle. Kept walking past the waterfront homes where dogs barked richly, past the stone steps dipped in water, all the way to "Be Like the Light," and then we both got lost in the blank waters for a while. Derrick talked about coming out to his parents, how his mother had told him that he could be anything but a Republican, and I snickered and spit on my fingertips from laughing.

Derrick didn't say as much, but I think it was one of the first times that he'd ever been truly high. Magic is different. The rushing of the power, the howling of it through every chamber of your body, like hungry vapor—it's different. They say that there's a 60 percent incidence of drug and alcohol abuse among mages and telepaths. I didn't doubt it. Sometimes you had to turn to other powers, other spells. Things you could control. Maybe even necromancers smoked weed. I amended that. Necromancers *definitely* smoked weed. Given the historical association between cannabis and the Arabic assassin guilds, dealing in death centuries ago, necromancers may very well have invented 420.

"Shh," Derrick whispered all of a sudden. "Quiet. Let's try to be quiet like sea turtles, okay?"

I stared at him. "You are gone, Siegel."

His eyes were red-rimmed, but he laughed. "No—no—shh—just try it. Just try, okay? *Sea turtles.*"

"Sea turtles," I said flatly.

I think I may have fallen a little in love with him then, as much as a straight-but-not-narrow girl can be in love with a fragile gay boy. Fragile, but not weak. Years later, I would watch him ruthlessly interrogate a demon informant, plucking thoughts from his brain like you might randomly play guitar strings, his expression never changing.

Derrick put his hand on top of mine, and his fingers were red from the cold. I thought *sea turtles*. I thought it mightily, as a child might dream of a swimming pool or a lick of ice cream in secret.

"*Wheeyaa*." Derrick laughed and leaned over the railing. "Doesn't it feel like we're going over the edge, like we're moving on the face of the water and something's holding us up?"

What was it, though? I thought later. *What held?*

What didn't yield into plant fiber and the silken hair on leaves, decomp, cell death, and heartache? What said *no lean out just lean out I've got you*. Or was it only a rustle of gears, the pistons in my body, in Derrick's body, firing, failing, and the coping silence after.

I said fuck it. I made Derrick my friend. I thought about sea turtles.

I was remembering all of this because Derrick had decided to stay the night at my place—something we hadn't done in ages. The crime tape was finally gone, and aside from a few holes in the wall, it almost looked more like a domicile than a war zone. Marcus had kindly footed the bill for a new door—I guess he felt bad. Derrick reasoned that if something ugly crawled through the window, it would be better to have two people here. Frankly, I think he was just scared of sleeping alone, but so was I, so it worked out well.

"Should we put on some music?" Derrick asked.

I rolled my eyes. "This isn't a slumber party. Before we break out the episodes of AbFab, we should probably attempt to devise some sort of strategy for surviving the next couple of days."

My claim for seriousness was undermined slightly by the fact that I was wearing Garfield pajamas and holding my Laura Ashley comforter.

"Right," Derrick said. "A plan for survival. That sounds like something useful." He handed me a steaming mug of tea. "First, I'd start with 'running.' That seems like an all-purpose solution for evading death, if you ask me."

"Can we please just do this?" He knew how easily distracted I was, especially at night, when all I wanted to do was curl up on the couch and eat ice cream.

"Fine, fine." He gestured to the nearby chair, and I sat down next to him. "Let's go over what we know about all of these demonic incidents."

"Are we calling them 'incidents' now? I was thinking more along the lines of 'that wacky time yesterday when we almost died.'"

It was bad enough that Marcus had been present for such a humiliating moment—my apartment getting dusted for fingerprints, Selena taking my statement like I was just another vic. And now I was off the case—whatever that meant. How do you abandon a case when your life is right in the middle of it? Can you be reassigned a new life? And is there a carbon-copy remnant of your old one, left behind, tucked away in some fat and dour secretary's desk while she eats her tuna sandwich? I didn't want to envisage drops of mayonnaise spilling on my old life.

"Let's just try to come at this logically," Derrick said, trying to maintain his patience. "We know that Cassandra works at SemTec Laboratories. Her job has something to do with organic chemistry, although I'm fuzzy on the details. She said that it's 'boring,' but somehow I doubt that's true. She's hiding something."

"Everyone's hiding something," I mumbled.

SemTec Laboratories, we'd discovered, was a small, unassuming office in a corporate building on West Georgia, in the heart of the downtown core. It was the city's financial district, and rent was high, so whatever SemTec Labs *did*, they must have been making money.

"Whatever she's doing," I said, sipping my tea, "it can't be good. Demons and chemistry—especially anything having to do with genetics—make me nervous. You might as well just give her a loaded gun."

"Like the one the Vailoid demon was carrying? It's already been done today."

"I was being ironic."

"Yeah, so was I."

"Okay. We've got a dead vamp, who was obviously looking for Mia—"

"Well, we don't know that for sure. He had her address in his pocket, but who gave it to him? Hell, it could have been *Mia*." He shrugged. "I know she's just a kid, but we still can't rule her out entirely as a suspect."

"That demon tried to kill her."

"Well, that's what it looked like anyway. Maybe he was there to kill us, and Mia just happened to be there."

I rubbed my forehead. "We're trying to narrow this down, not blow it up, hon."

"But we've got to be realistic, too. We don't know who sent the Vailoid demon, at least not for sure."

"Cassandra's a suspect—she lied to us when we asked her about the vampire, and I have a feeling that she's still lying to us."

"But that doesn't mean that she tried to kill us. You saw how happy she was that Mia ended up safe and sound. She was really worried about her. I felt it—I don't think she could fake something like that."

I turned the mug around in my hands. "Okay—I don't want to admit it, but you're right. I just wish we could eliminate some possibilities. Nothing fits. The Vailoid bounty hunter, Cassandra working at a lab, Mia—it's all like some poorly plotted horror novel where nothing makes sense."

"At least there are no aliens so far."

"Thank God for that." I wrapped both my hands around the mug, letting it warm me up. I'd been freezing all night— probably a side effect of the painkillers. "Realistically, the vampires are the only angle we've got left. Everything depends upon my meeting with Lucian tomorrow."

"You know what still bothers me, though? Why the gun?" Derrick raised his hands. "The Vailoid could have torn us apart. Why was he carrying a piece—something that could potentially be traced? Seems reckless and unnecessary."

"The gun could have been the cover."

"What do you mean?"

"Well, he shoots us all, execution style—and then what happens?"

Derrick's eyes widened. "It would look like a robbery," he said.

"That's the sort of thing the VPD would investigate—not the CORE. So nobody'd ever know that a demon had done it."

"Huh."

We were silent for a while.

"So we can't finger Cassandra as a suspect," he said, "but we can't eliminate her either. Same with Mia."

"I don't think Mia's capable of anything like this," I replied. "But I do think that Cassandra is."

"Why—just because she's a demon?"

I looked at him flatly.

"Tess, come on. We both know that's hardly fair. You and I are part-demon as well. And we've met plenty of good demons—"

"There are no 'good demons'!" I glared at him. "You know that. You feel it in your gut, just like I do. We're different, Derrick, because we have human DNA. Human blood. It makes us different from them. But the pure demons—they're nothing but killing machines with fancy cars and Swiss bank accounts."

"I wasn't aware that everything had suddenly become black-and-white."

My eyes widened. "When did you go all softcore liberal on me? These are *demons*. We fight them—remember? We protect humanity from them."

Derrick's expression was maddeningly patient. "We don't fight all of them. Some of them are on our side. Some of them are valuable allies."

"Yeah—but we never stop watching our backs when they're around, do we?" I rose. "It's peachy keen to work with reformed vampires, but you never stop thinking that they're about to bite you. It's okay to consult with goblins and kobolds, but you wouldn't invite them into your house. Would you?" I scowled. "And do *not* say that some of your best friends are goblins."

"I just don't think it's that simple, Tess."

"And that's why you don't work in the field." It slipped out before I could stop it.

Derrick returned my look. "Oh. So a telepath doesn't count? I get my paycheck from the CORE, I investigate mystical crime scenes, just like you, but—what—I'm not a *real* investigator? I don't rate?"

"I didn't mean—"

"And why's that?" he continued. "Because I appreciate gray areas? Because I'm willing to entertain the idea that not all demons are bad?"

"Because you hesitate," I said. It was too late now—the Pandora's box was open. All we could do was follow the argument through. "Because, when it comes down to the crucial moment—when you're in a dark alley, and you've got a demon following you, hunting you—there's always going to be that second where you think, 'Wait a minute, what if they're just like me?' And that second will get you killed, Derrick."

"I've seen you hesitate plenty of times."

"Only when there's another option. But I'm always ready to make the decision. I'm always ready to strike first, and sort out the morality later."

He rolled his eyes. "And that sounds like a healthy attitude."

"It's an attitude that's saved both our lives," I snapped, "on many occasions. And don't you dare tell me that the demon who raped my mother was just 'misunderstood.'" I could feel that familiar anger suffusing me. "He left her to die in a *parking lot*, Derrick. It was sheer luck that my father came along when he did. You know that's why they never talk about how they met." I laughed heartlessly. "Although it's kind of romantic, in a twisted way. He really swooped in and saved the day, rescuing some poor woman, taking her to the hospital, and then they just—fell in love. But they'll never know the truth about my real 'father,' and Mom refuses to think about it anymore."

Derrick flushed slightly, but said nothing. He'd hit me where it hurt, and so I struck right back.

"They're *not human*." I exhaled. "No matter how sweet and cute they look, no matter how nicely they talk, no matter what they're wearing—it's all just an illusion. They'd kill us in a second if we weren't useful to them."

Derrick shrugged—a gesture halfway between discomfort and reconciliation. "Maybe," he said simply. "But I have to believe that you're wrong—at least on some level. If I don't, then . . ." He trailed off.

"Then we really are screwed," I finished. "Outnumbered, surrounded by lethal monsters who want to suck out our souls, and trapped in a battle that we're eventually going to lose."

His look was bleak. "That pretty much covers it, yeah."

"Well, I hope I'm wrong, too," I said. "For what it's worth."

We were silent for a while.

"What about Mia?" Derrick asked finally. "Do you think she's a demon? I can't read anything from her, but like we said, it does seem possible to hide a genetic signature. If you're powerful enough."

"We'll have to ask some questions." I drained the mug and put it down. "Selena's already set up the meeting with the necromancer, so I might as well ask him about some other things as well—I mean, as long as I've got his ear, right?"

Derrick eyed me warily. "That sounds a lot like conducting your own investigation—which Marcus expressly told you not to do, especially when we're still waiting on that paperwork to clear both of us for killing Mr. Happy Shark."

"Well, Marcus Tremblay can expressly bite me right now,

if he's so inclined. This is my life—our lives—that are at stake. These demons aren't just after Mia. You and I are both targets now. And if we don't keep working on this case, then that's all that'll be *left* of us in a few weeks—a case file, with three autopsy reports." My look was grim. "I won't let it come to that."

"So you're going to use CORE resources to blow open this case, even though both your superiors have warned you not to? Selena is going to bat for you, remember? She's trying to put a rush on those papers. And even Marcus seemed to care about you, which is kind of like science fiction, but hey, I guess it happens." He gave me a maddening Derrick look. "These people have their asses on the line for you—for both of us—and you could be screwing them over by doing this."

I smiled. "Then I guess I'll just have to make sure I don't get caught."

Derrick sighed. "So what are you going to say to this Lucian character? Won't he get suspicious when you ask him about the siring process? And how much is he really going to know about it as a necro, an outsider? Probably just what the vamps tell him."

"We've got to take our chances," I replied. "Your hunch about Mia and the blood thing is the best that we've got so far. And even if they don't tell us anything on purpose, they might let something slip by accident. Hopefully, they'll be able to ID the dead vampire, and then we can take a look at his digs."

He stared at me. "You're going to go to his *home*? And do what?"

"See what we can find, of course."

"And you're going to steal a couple evidence kits, an ALS light source, a few print lifters—what, just like that?"

"I'll give them back," I said patronizingly.

"You'll have to sign them out first."

"Well, I'll take them to the vampire interview. Then if I get any info about the vic's place of residence, I can swing by there afterward. I'll still have the kits. It won't be a big deal."

"Still seems like a big risk."

"Yeah?" I gestured around. "Seems like a bigger risk to sit on our butts waiting for the next demon to come crashing through. I'd much rather come at this proactively. At least then I'll see my death head-on as it's running toward me."

12

I was meeting Lucian Agrado at a club called Moonbase, which was apparently vampire owned and operated. He was like the freaking Andy Warhol of the immortal-ugly community—everyone wanted to hang with him. I couldn't tell if he was the friendly "human" face for a vampiric hunting ground, or if his role as necro-liaison was something entirely different. The CORE had long heard rumors about vampires and necromancers running in the same circles, but their political alliances were still a mystery to us. If they'd decided to join forces, even casually, we could be humped.

I'd never been to an undead club before—unless you counted The Odyssey with its twink zombies gyrating in unison to progressive trance—so I didn't know what to expect. Goth kids drinking wine and dancing to Vovoid? Cabaret singers with fangs? Maybe a Liza drag-queen twirling a wooden stake. Why did necromancers always frequent clubs? Why couldn't they run a nice café, or a friendly neighborhood pub? Maybe British vampires ran pubs. Maybe it was just like Coronation Street, only with a much higher mortality rate.

The club was on the corner of Granville and Nelson, just before the bridge. It was across the street from a very old strip joint, which occasionally ejected drunk fortysomething guys onto the oily pavement like something unsavory and undigested. It was still early, so there wasn't much of a crowd outside—just a few kids smoking, a panhandler, and an enormous bouncer wearing a yellow muscle-T that said FRANKIE SAYS RELAX. Apparently even the denizens of hell go crazy for Urban Outfitters. He was way too pale to be human, and he was also wearing sunglasses at night.

The building itself was actually quite nondescript—a clean, beige façade, with pillars supporting the entrance, and an ornate, wrought-iron set of gates for the front door. The gates were currently open, but the bouncer was standing between them. I could hear the faint thump of music inside, although it was impossible to tell what kind. Obviously, Moonbase started early. It made sense, I guess. If you're a vampire, you can get your rocks off before 11 p.m., and still have the rest of the night to do with as you please. Rent a video, crochet a scarf, or whatever vampires do with their spare time.

I approached the bouncer. I was wearing my "all about confidence" outfit—black, knee-high Fluevogs (flats, in case I had to run), Kenneth Cole skirt that I had rocked on many an occasion, gray blouse, and long leather pope jacket that I pretended made me look like Anita Blake. The jacket covered most of the cuts and bruises that were still healing from last night, and I'd tried to make my face look like less of a train wreck with some heavy-duty concealer.

I waved to the vampire bouncer. He stared at me without taking off his sunglasses. I stood close enough so that he could sense my genetic signature, but far enough away so that my neck was out of biting-distance. I used a similar move on blind dates—it usually worked.

"I'm Tess Corday," I said. "I have a meeting with Lucian Agrado at nine forty-five."

He stared at me for a while longer, then pulled a cell phone out of his pocket and dialed. He grunted something into the phone, then put it away.

"You're cleared. Go past the dance floor and climb the set of stairs that lead to the sound booth. Walk down the hallway and enter the first open door that you come to. Wait there." His expression didn't change, but I could sense an appalling eagerness from him, a hunger. He very much wanted me to challenge him, so that he'd have an excuse to tear through my carotid. I wasn't going to give it to him.

"First room with an open door," I repeated dutifully.

"Do *not* go anywhere else. Don't open any of the other doors, and don't go into the sound booth. Don't talk to anyone on your way there. If you deviate from these instructions, we won't be able to protect you. Do you understand?"

"What—you mean, I can't take pictures and post them on Facebook?"

He stared at me.

"Don't worry." I smiled. "No sneaking around. I promise."

"By agreeing to meet with you," the bouncer continued, "the liaison and the vampire community are doing you a favor. But if you don't follow his instructions completely, your life will be forfeit. The truce will not matter."

"Yeah—I heard you the first time." My eyes narrowed. "Hey, what exactly do you mean by a 'favor'?"

"You'll see." He smiled—just slightly—then stepped aside. "Welcome to Moonbase, Miss Corday. Have a pleasant night."

"Sure. You, too." I couldn't resist. "Don't eat too much."

He raised an eyebrow, but said nothing.

Some vampires had no sense of humor.

With a feeling of dread that only increased by the second, I walked through the wrought-iron gates and into the club. Something told me that this might just be the stupidest thing I'd ever done. But there was no turning back now.

You don't keep a necromancer waiting.

When the doors opened, I was immediately as-saulted by a wave of trance music. But it wasn't just music.

These beats took the term "progressive trance" to a whole new level. There was dark materia—we called it necroid materia, although nobody at the CORE could precisely confirm its existence—threaded into the tracks, dubbed into the pounding base, the epic keyboard highs and thrumming lows. I was immune to it because I kept pumping low-level earth materia into my aura, kind of like a metaphysical screen door between me and the big dark, but a lot of the dancers, it seemed, were not. They were gyrating wildly, sweating, their hands in the air, and you could tell that it wasn't just G or Ecstasy. The music itself was actually hypnotic, calling to them on a cellular level, convincing them to relax, give up their inhibitions, surrender to their instincts. I could feel it pulsing in the back of my brain.

Now, if they'd been playing INXS, I might have been screwed.

The dance floor was about twice the size of most clubs that I'd been to, surrounded by shimmering lights. Nearly naked men and women danced on raised platforms, wearing thong underwear and knee-high boots. They were human, in very good shape, and I found myself blushing slightly as I stared at them. Strippers were pretty normal at gay bars, but seeing them in a "mixed" crowd bar was a bit unexpected.

As I looked around, I began to see them. Not just vampires—all sorts of demons, some that I couldn't even name. All dancing with each other. Over in one corner, I saw two male vampires making out, showing just a bit of fang, while a woman stared at them, enthralled. Just across from them, a shirtless goblin was dancing with three other women, and appearing to have the time of his life. Near the bar, a vampire was giving amyl nitrate to a young boy— barely sixteen—whose eyes were as big as saucers. On the stairway, a man—human?—was being bitten by a female vampire wearing a red kimono. The blood from his neck pooled around her lips; his eyes were closed, and he was groaning. It seemed consensual. I shuddered.

The song changed. Joy Division, "Love Will Tear Us Apart." It was mashed up with the dubbed materia beats, and something—those dark gaps, the echo and distortion—made it seem even more haunting. As Ian Curtis let his charred and melancholy voice soar above the demonic crowd, I saw two butch female vampires dancing together, hand in hand. One was dark-haired and wearing a Tegan and Sara shirt, the other was taller, with a shaved head and a utility-kilt studded with pockets and buttons. The dark-haired girl wiped the sweat from her lover's shaved head, then leaned in and whispered something. It might have been "I love you." I saw her fangs—small and slick, almost like deciduous baby teeth about to burst out. The other girl laughed and touched her face.

I remembered the bouncer's warning. *Don't stop. Don't talk to anyone. Just follow the directions and wait for Lucian.*

I headed for the stairs. A curtain parted to my left as I passed, and I saw—just for a moment—a glimpse of a woman tied to a revolving cross. Her hands and feet were bound with leather straps, and two other women—vampires, I think, although I couldn't be certain—were whipping her back and shoulders. I felt my stomach tighten, but then I realized that the woman's face was ecstatic—her eyes were practically rolling back in her head. She wasn't in pain at all. The two other women seemed to be enjoying themselves just as much. They were both wearing leather bodices and skirts that appeared to be made of chain mail. One of the women had a cat-o'-nine-tails whip, and the other had a bullwhip. The woman with the bullwhip saw me, and smiled. It wasn't a warm smile.

My mind flashed back to the photograph in the dead vampire's pocket, and I recognized the woman instantly. She was the one with the cold smile that the John Doe had his arm around.

I filed it away and kept walking.

The second floor of Moonbase was a series of different rooms, all partitioned by red and black velvet curtains. One room was full of couches—most of them occupied by people doing all sorts of interesting things. I was all for free love, but interspecies sex seemed a bit risky to me, especially when certain demons had well-known anatomical incompatibilities with humans. But then again, maybe some people liked that. I kept walking and tried not to stare.

Another room was just a bare floor with tables and leather mats. People were reclining on the cushions and doing a wide spectrum of drugs—sniffing poppers, injecting heroin, smoking crack or crystal, doing shots of GHB, and ingesting substances that I'd never even seen before. I noticed one guy in the corner, drooling slightly, comatose, just staring at nothing in particular. Stuck in a K-Hole. A few young vampires were just sitting together, passing a joint around, laughing. I heard a few stray words that sounded like "Bazin" and "mise-en-scene," and it occurred to me that they might be film students at UBC. It looked so normal, except for every few seconds when someone would grin, showing fang.

I kept walking, past the DJ booth—all slick with tinted windows, so that all I could see was a dim blue glow coming from the inside. Then I came to the hallway that the bouncer had been talking about.

I could hear his warning in my head: *Walk down the hallway and enter the first open door that you come to. Wait there.*

There were doors evenly spaced along the hallway, each one closed. As I walked slowly past, I could hear indistinct sounds coming from the sealed rooms. Laughter. Muffled screaming. A bizarre sort of dripping. A regular metallic clang, like something being banged into shape.

I kept walking, telling myself that I didn't want to know what was going on behind any of those doors. Just then, a vampire burst out of the room to my left. His face and shirt were drenched in blood. His clear gray eyes flashed at me for a moment, but he just stood there, not saying anything. Just stared at me. My guard trembled a bit. I was immune to basic vampire mind tricks, mesmerism and metempsychosis, but older, more powerful ones could still affect me. This vampire was medium range in terms of power—not enough to really freak me out, but certainly enough to worry the edges of my psychic guard. If I lost concentration, or panicked, even for a minute, he could find a way in. Tear right through my mental screen door like a killer bee.

Slowly, keeping my expression neutral, I walked past him. You never run from anything immortal. *The Last Unicorn* was right as shit about that one. The vampire made no move to stop me—just kept staring, his face entirely expressionless, as if it was made of sculpted wire or blown into a mandala, entirely still. The undead can look at you that way, and it scares the pants off you. They'll seem warm and human one minute, then bam, you remember that you're dealing with something as old as the dinosaurs.

This one was curious, but not belligerent. He wouldn't give me any trouble as long as I didn't challenge him. So I kept walking, keeping my breathing even, my stride regular. I didn't look back.

I sensed him leave, and my heart hiccupped back into its normal sinus rhythm.

Finally, I came to an open door. The room beyond it was small, but comfortable. There was beige carpeting on the floor, a sofa in one corner, and a chair adjacent to it. They looked surprisingly . . . comfy. Judging from the décor, this wasn't a room where the vampires did any killing. You'd never be able to get bloodstains out of that carpet. Microfiber, maybe.

I sat down on the chair, feeling like I was in a doctor's office.

There was a table next to the chair that I hadn't noticed at first—one of those tiny stainless steel jobs that blend into any room. Sitting on the table was a pitcher full of ice water with lemons, and two empty glasses. Huh. Vampire hospitality.

"You look surprised. Were you expecting two goblets of blood?"

There was no way I could hide the panic in my eyes when I looked up. Normally, I should have been able to sense a necromancer—especially a relatively powerful one—who was near me. Like all demons, they had a peculiar genetic signature that I could feel in my blood. It was sort of like the feeling you get when someone walks over your grave. Like mages, necromancers were only part-demon, a hybrid of sorts. But the similarities ended there.

Lucian smiled and leaned against the door frame. "I startled you. I'm sorry." He clearly wasn't. The way his lip curled slightly, you could tell how pleased he was that I hadn't felt him coming.

The liaison to the vampire community did not look at all like I'd expected he might. That was probably because he was wearing jeans and a black tank top—the kind of shirt that you might go running in. He had a dark complexion— black hair, brown eyes, and dark skin. Chicano ancestry, maybe? Lucian's arms were golden, lightly muscled, and tattooed. I noticed a snake devouring its own tail on his left shoulder, a bracelet of black and blue thorns around his bicep, and some symbols that I couldn't quite make out on both of his wrists.

His hands were in his pockets, and his black boots casually tapped against the floor like a nervous teenager, but I knew better. He wasn't scared—not a bit. I, however, was just a shade above terrified. I was alone in a room with a necro, and he was powerful enough to sneak up on me.

Welcome to the party.

13

"You did startle me," I said. **"But I'm all right now."**

It sounded like we were in *Jane Eyre*. If he took me any-where near an attic, I was bolting right then and there.

There was no sense in lying. If he was as powerful as I suspected, he could probably smell a lie. And I didn't want to do anything to provoke him. I knew from experience that his playful exterior, that boyish grin, those warm brown eyes, were all just a transparent curtain that could be pulled away at a moment's notice.

Was he reading my mind? Sensing my fear? Could necro-mancers do that? Probably. I didn't try to hide it—there was no use. I didn't look him in the eyes. I looked very carefully at a space just above his left shoulder.

Lucian smiled. "So—would you like a drink?"

"Is it poisoned?" The question came out before I could stop it. Shit.

But Lucian only laughed. It was a warm, eerily inviting sound. A human laugh. He could play human very well, and I almost wanted to buy it. But I'd met too many of his kind, and I knew that it could dissolve any second. You can't commune with the dead for that long without absorbing some of their traits, their mannerisms, along with their power. The more you bend the rules of life and death, the more ... different ... you become. Not like a vampire, but not like a human either. Necromancers were their own breed. There was nothing worse than looking for a person in there, but finding something else, something immeasurably ancient, terrible, hungry. Like finding a forbidden hallway underneath the foundations of your living room.

"It's just water," he said. "Go ahead."

I was particularly fascinated by his hair. It was coal black, and gelled into little tufts and spikes. Almost a faux-hawk. You expected death-dealers like him to wear lacey tunics and have shoulder-length hair, but they often surprised you.

"I could get you some wine," Lucian continued. "Or beer."

It was the suggestion of beer that made me laugh. Somehow, the thought of a creature who could raise the dead offering me a Molson was too much to take. I snorted a little, and Lucian smiled. It wasn't an entirely innocent smile—more of a curious one.

"Did I say something funny?"

"No. Sorry." I looked away. "I've just never been offered a brewski by a necromancer before. It seemed funny."

Lucian cocked his head. "I'm not what you were expecting, am I, Miss Corday?"

There were so many answers to that question. What had I been expecting? Someone wearing a cape? Some languid, pretty thing lounging on a canopy bed, covered in red silk sheets? Or an honest monster, maybe. A monster that actually looked the part. Lucian looked like someone you might pass on the street. A buddy who might lend you his Tragically Hip CD, or some mellow friend of your brother's. He didn't look like a death-dealer capable of ripping the immortal soul out of my body, the same as you might rip an annoying tag off a sweater. But I knew that he could. His power was like a heat-haze on my skin.

My own power was responding to it. I could feel the

magic welling up in me, rising from that secret place, wherever it slept. I'd felt it to a lesser extent when I was in the presence of more powerful demons, but this was different. Lucian's power seemed to tease my own, to brush up against it, tongue it like a sore, beckon it. There was a glimmer of darkness between us, just a scrap of empty space that separated me from him, but any moment it seemed like our collective powers might leap the gap.

I risked a glance into Lucian's eyes, and saw that he understood all this—he was amused by it, maybe even a little pleased. It was no surprise to him. But he could feel my anxiety, and he was enjoying that. It made me want to scream. But all I did was pour myself a glass of water and sip on it—calmly.

"You know," he said, "I hear the most popular theory about my kind these days is that we're hatched from eggs rather than born."

I chuckled. "Is that how necromancers come into the world?" I said "necromancers," but I meant "you." *Were did you come from? Who are you? Are you less human than me, more demon, or what?*

He grinned. "'I was from my mother's womb untimely ripped.'"

"Macbeth. Classy." I sipped on the water. It was too cold.

"I tend to surprise most people," he continued. "I've never been very conventional. Would you mind if I sat down?"

"Go ahead." I tried to sound unconcerned. He merely smiled, and sank comfortably onto the couch. He was close enough now that I could feel a thread of power between us, some dark tendril of energy that connected us in a way that scared the hell out of me. Not too close, though. It wasn't overwhelming—just unnerving. And he knew that. All of his movements were careful and calculating. He could read my body from every angle, but all I could sense from him was a feeling of pleasure, an almost tightly coiled delight.

"You're an investigator for the CORE," he said matter-of-factly. "An OSI. What level, if you don't mind me asking?"

"Level one," I said evenly.

"Hmm." He smiled. "You seem more experienced than that. Confident. I'd think someone like you would have risen quite quickly through the CORE ranks."

"I'm barely twenty-four," I muttered.

"Most level ones are teenagers. Girls. Women your age tend to occupy higher positions within the CORE"—his eyes flashed—"or am I wrong?"

"I like my job," I said simply. "It's rewarding."

"Still—you should have moved up by now. Especially someone with your level of power." He smiled as he said "power," and I felt his will nudge my own just a little, a friendly sort of touch. Clearly, he wanted to see some of my power firsthand, but that wasn't going to happen.

"My job is my business," I said. "I haven't asked why you like snorting necroid materia like nose candy, or why you do PR for vampires. Bad career counselor, maybe?"

Lucian smiled again, but this one was genuine. "Something like that. The story might intrigue you, actually."

"Thanks for the offer, but I think that we should get down to business." This time I smiled, ever so slightly. "The night is still young for you. I don't want to keep you from whatever it is you'd normally be doing."

Raising the dead? Perverting nature? Reading Aleister Crowley?

Lucian shrugged. "Your choice. I don't often get to converse with CORE officials who are willing to look me in the eye."

The subliminal suggestion made me look up, and for a moment, his eyes seemed entirely black—two perfect globes of jet staring back at me. I almost made a sound, but managed to hold it in. His eyes grew larger, and the warmth between us flickered, died, became ice-cold, as if the room had suddenly been plunged into winter.

Lucian smiled, and everything went back to normal. The room was temperate again. His eyes were their usual shade of deep brown. Something residual hung on the air, like a flake of tobacco you would peel from your tongue. Dark materia.

I forced myself to smile as well. "I just thought you must have better things to do than talk to me," I said.

"On the contrary, Tess. I think I could talk to you all night." He flashed white teeth. His fangs were purely metaphysical.

Trying to keep the tremor out of my hands, I handed him a color reproduction of the photo from the vampire's pocket.

"We found this male vampire's body in an alley on Granville," I said, "four nights ago. We've been trying to determine his identity. We don't know who the woman is, but I noticed her in the club—um—with a bullwhip?"

Lucian glanced at the picture coldly. "Four nights ago? And you're only just contacting us now?"

"We had a lot of processing to do," I said. "And there've been some—incidents—that have kept us busy." Like demons attacking me.

"You should have come to us immediately," he said. His tone wasn't exactly angry—there was something else. Irritation? Guilt, even?

"We've always cooperated with the vampire community in the past," I said slowly. "We have reason to believe that this vampire was connected somehow to another case. A teenage girl who was attacked by Vailoid demons."

"Vailoids." His eyes darkened. "Mercenaries. They'd carve up their own mother if the price was high enough." He looked at me strangely. "You say they attacked a little girl? Where would the profit be in that?"

"Well, we're not sure. But this vampire had that little girl's address in his pocket—on a note, written in vampiric script."

"And you think he was after the girl as well."

"That would be speculation. All we know is that he was connected to her somehow. Maybe the same demons who attacked"—I almost said her name, but stopped myself—"*her* were the same demons who attacked this vampire." I looked at Lucian closely. "Can you tell me who both of them are? Were they—involved?"

"Yes," he said. His expression was almost—vacant. As if

someone had completely drained any feeling from his eyes. Demon trick. "I know them. And yes, they were 'involved,' as you say. His name is Sebastian, and hers is Sabine."

"Did you know Sebastian well?"

"No. He belonged to Sabine, though, and I do know her somewhat better."

I blinked. *"Belonged?"*

Lucian smiled slightly. "Sebastian was a thrall—a submissive vampire who serves a much older, dominant vampire. He was newly born, you see. I think he was only turned a few decades ago."

"That's what we thought," I said. "He seemed like a new vamp. Inexperienced. Could definitely have gotten himself into a whole world of trouble."

"Yes. The newly born need to be closely protected at first, by a loving sire." His smile widened. "Someone to watch over them. To comfort them, and teach them, while they make the first transition into their new life."

Or unlife, as the case may be.

"Yeah," I said, glancing at the picture, "she looks like a real Professor Higgins."

Lucian merely smiled. I don't know if he got the reference.

"So you're saying that she was also the one who created Sebastian? His sire?"

Lucian nodded. "Yes. Sabine was his sire, and his mistress."

"Any chance I could speak with her?"

"I can summon her," Lucian said, "but I have to warn you—Sabine isn't as friendly as I am." The word "friendly," when he pronounced it, had a sensory flavor that made me distinctly uncomfortable.

"She doesn't like humans, you mean."

"Well, strictly speaking, Tess, neither of us is really human."

I cocked my head. "Touché. All right, she doesn't like the living, then."

"She is . . . complicated." He chuckled softly. "Dangerous."

"More dangerous than you?"

He licked his lips. "I suppose that's a matter of opinion. She does have a quick temper."

"But you're always in control." I smiled back. I was getting the hang of this game—the push and pull of dominance and submission. I wasn't about to tip my hand, but I needed him to realize that I wasn't a victim either.

He seemed pleased by the response. "I am more composed than she is," he said simply. "Less quick to anger. Though you wouldn't want to see me when I'm angry."

"No," I said. "I don't think I would."

Lucian leaned back. "You think Sabine had something to do with this." It wasn't a question. His expression remained neutral.

I shrugged. "I don't know that for sure. But she does fit the bill—someone who the victim trusts, even idolizes. His mistress. He was carrying a picture of her in his pocket, after all."

Lucian looked doubtful. "Sabine is powerful, yes, but no vampire has the ability to inflict such an injury—they can cloud the mind, but not cut *into* it like a surgeon. That is telekinesis."

"What about necromancers?" I tried to sound casual.

Lucian's expression didn't change. "No. A necromancer couldn't do this."

I didn't get the impression that he was lying. Odd. I pushed further.

"I thought that some vampires were telekinetic."

"Some of the oldest and most powerful ones, yes—but even their abilities are limited. Bending light and shadow, levitation, manipulating objects from a distance—nothing so precise as what you've described."

"There are a few demons who might be capable of it," I said. "Rygel demons are often telekinetic, but they're native to South America. And they're secretors, so they'd leave behind some type of bodily fluid. There are some shamanic half-breeds who have the power to heal with surgical precision. They can also use that power to inflict damage, which is why they're sometimes hired as assassins. But that's extremely rare—I don't think there's been a case in over ten years at least."

"The majority of the world's most powerful telepaths," Lucian said evenly, "are human. I don't have to remind you of that."

"But why would a human kill a young, newly sired vampire, then leave him in an alley for us to find? It doesn't make a lot of sense."

"Death never does." He rose. "I'll get Sabine."

14

My cell phone rang. I glanced at the call display and saw that it was my mom. Jesus Christ. Could she possibly have better timing? I switched the phone to vibrate and put it back in my pocket. Now didn't seem like the time to chat about *Canadian Idol*.

Lucian returned a few moments later. The girl with the bullwhip was right behind him. She was the one I'd locked eyes with earlier, when I first walked into the club. She'd gotten rid of her chain-mail outfit and replaced it with a tight-fitting red dress and stiletto boots. It wasn't BCBG either, but Armani. She was either loaded, or she'd recently bitten someone who worked at Leone. It was clear that she recognized me, too, since she was smiling. She glanced at me, then back at Lucian, and I saw a hint of fang—that was deliberate as well.

"Is she lost?" Sabine asked, in a mock-concerned voice.

"Miss Corday is an investigator for the CORE," Lucian said politely. "She found Sebastian's body."

Sabine shook her head. "Poor Sebastian. He was just a baby, you know."

"Actually," I said, trying to keep my voice firm, "I don't know much about him. That's why I was hoping you'd be able to answer a few questions."

She sat down on the floor in front of me. It was an odd position—I was higher up than her, but she knew exactly who was in charge. She was mocking me. Reminding me where we both stood on the food chain.

"Anything to help the CORE," Sabine said, smiling. "Your investigations are always crucial."

She didn't give a rat's ass about our investigations. She was probably close to four hundred years old, maybe five hundred, and—to her—we were just little bugs crawling around the surface of a corpse.

"Did Sebastian have any enemies?" I asked. "Anyone who saw him as a threat?"

"Does a newborn infant have enemies?" She gave me a patronizing look. "Sebastian didn't know anyone—except me—and nobody knew him. The child didn't have enemies. He didn't have friends." She smiled. "He just had me."

"Because you were his mistress. You took care of him."

"I made him." She rolled her eyes. "He was nothing before I met him. A worthless musician who didn't have two dimes to rub together. Playing shitty bars and collecting table scraps. I gave him the power that he'd always dreamed of."

I seemed to remember that Sebastian had long, graceful fingers. The fingers of a guitar player, or perhaps a pianist. I briefly imagined him busking outside of The Commodore, playing keyboard at night while the cabs shot by him like golden daggers, and drunken students narrowly avoided kicking over his hat full of tips. It didn't make me sad. It made me angry.

"You sired him," I said, "which means that you could just as easily destroy him—if you felt that was necessary."

Sabine made a sound deep in her throat. It was like a dog's growl, only much lower. My eyes widened, and Lucian laid a hand on her shoulder.

"Easy," he said. "She doesn't understand your kind, remember."

I noticed he didn't say "our kind." I guess a part of him was still human—he remembered that he wasn't a vampire, at least. But what was the space between human and vampire? Where did that leave him? Riding a difficult hyphen.

"Obviously not," she spat. When she looked at me, her eyes were black with contempt. "To be sired is a holy gift—an act beyond measure. Among our kind, the most loathsome crime is infanticide, for one to murder one's own creation. To destroy my own kin would make me a defiler of the worst sort. An outcast."

"So you didn't kill him," I said affably.

"I couldn't! Such a thing is beyond my comprehension!"

I shrugged. "But you don't seem too distraught that he's dead. You don't seem too surprised either."

Her eyes narrowed. "You know nothing of what I feel. Just because I don't wear every grotesque emotion on my face, like a human, doesn't mean that I don't feel it just as keenly below the surface."

"You've got a great poker face, then."

She put her hand on my knee. The touch was light, but it felt like a ton of bricks. She could tear my leg off before I had the chance to breathe.

"I loved Sebastian," she said. "Perhaps you don't believe that, since he was my inferior—my servant. But I've loved all of them. Everyone that I've sired."

I shuddered to think how many of Sabine's "children" might be out in the world, maiming and killing for her.

"If he was so weak," I said, "he doesn't seem like a suitable mate for you. I get the impression that you like"—I smiled thinly, careful to avoid looking into her eyes—"power. Right?"

Sabine laughed softly. "Obviously, Miss Corday, you know very little about the mechanics of sexuality."

I blinked. "Enlighten me, then."

She licked her lips. "The submissive is always the one

with the power—always the one in control. I enjoyed giving power to Sebastian, just as I enjoyed taking it away. And besides—power is a tricky thing. That, at least, you must understand. Sometimes you find it in the unlikeliest places."

"Even in a human?" I kept my look level.

Sabine shrugged affably. "Humans can be interesting— under the right circumstances." Her eyes fell on Lucian, and he didn't look away.

"Sabine has many outside interests," he supplied.

"Well," I said coldly, "I'll just try not to follow that suggestion to its logical conclusion, if you don't mind."

"Sebastian was gentle, yes," Sabine continued. "His sensitivity made him a good companion, but a poor vampire. I had to protect him at all times, or else he would have been killed by someone more powerful."

"By one of your enemies?" I asked.

She looked at me archly. "I do have several. And yes, to insult me, they might have killed one of my servants. Since Sebastian was the weakest one, he would have been the likeliest target. But Lucian tells me that he wasn't killed by one of our kind."

"We're not sure of that yet."

"Well, what are you sure of?"

I exhaled. I didn't trust Sabine under any circumstances, but I couldn't tell if she was lying or not. I got the impression that everything she said was lies mixed with truth—the hardest kind to decipher. Like political rhetoric.

"All we know," I said, "is that something very powerful killed Sebastian, and then left his body for us to find. His murder is also connected somehow to the attempted murder of a teenage girl who we've been watching. We found her address in Sebastian's shirt pocket."

She raised an eyebrow. "Why would he care about a human girl?"

"I don't know. I thought you might be able to answer that question."

Sabine smiled. "Sebastian's loyalty was rare for a vampire, even a young one. He served me and only me."

"Sexually, you mean."

She nodded. "Nobody else touched him."

"Our serology department didn't find any traces of semen or vaginal fluid on Sebastian's body, so it wasn't likely that he'd engaged in any sexual encounters for at least forty-eight hours prior to his death."

"Sometimes," she said, "I liked to make him wait. Fasting, you might call it." Her eyes swept across my body, and I was startled momentarily by the strength of her hunger. Vampires were known for their erotic flexibility, but Sabine seemed especially voracious. "It makes the prize sweeter."

Lucian was also looking at me, although his expression wasn't one of hunger. I couldn't quite read it.

"I'm sure it does," I said, trying to sound neutral. "Did Sebastian have a residence of some kind? An apartment where he slept during the day?"

She made an unpleasant expression. "A putrid little hole in the Downtown Eastside. The only thing he could afford, the poor lamb."

"You've been there?"

"Sometimes I visited him."

I could only imagine what a nocturnal visit from Sabine might entail.

"We didn't find any keys on him."

Sabine reached into a hidden pocket of her dress—very well hidden, since it was practically skintight—and handed me a generic-looking key.

"I have my own," she said. "Go ahead and search his place. I hope you find some answers there."

"Technically, we need a warrant—"

She laughed. "You don't need anything to do your job. I've seen your kind do all sorts of things without permission. It's all just worthless paperwork anyway, and my people don't respect something that's written on a piece of paper."

"But you do respect power," I said levelly.

Her eyes held mine for a moment, and they seemed to gleam with their own inner light. I didn't look away, although I could feel my insides constricting.

Sabine smiled. "You may not have power, but you do have courage, child. And I respect that. So go ahead. Tell me if you find anything."

I took the key. Our fingers touched momentarily, and I felt a current of electricity pass between us—a dark flow of power. She was tasting me, just as Lucian had. Only, where Lucian's mind had been playful, hers was like a cover of black earth, an immense darkness slipping over me. Her power was old, with sharp edges. Almost animal. I breathed in slowly to keep from being sick. Sometimes you could forget how different vampires were, until they did something like that—and then you remembered that you were dealing with a velociraptor in the body of Scarlett Johansson.

"Thank you, Sabine," I said, weakly inclining my head.

"Like I said"—she laughed—"anything for the CORE." She rose, crossing to the doorway, then put her hand lightly on Lucian's chest.

"Coming?"

"Soon," was all he said.

She brushed her lips against his cheek, then left the room. *Huh—an interspecies romance. He must be v-sexual, after all.*

"Well," I said, "she's certainly a cool glass of water."

Lucian chuckled, resuming his spot on the couch beside me. "Yes—Sabine can be tricky. As you've seen, she respects power."

"But you don't think she's capable of murdering Sebastian."

Lucian looked at me thoughtfully. "To tell you the truth, I don't know everything that Sabine is capable of. But it seems unlikely that she would kill her own servant—especially someone as weak as Sebastian. It makes more sense that someone would kill Sebastian to get to *her*. To send her a message."

"You're right." I sighed. "But what's the message? And why did *we* get it, instead of Sabine? We were the ones who found Sebastian's body. Did the killer simply miscalculate—figure that Sabine would find him before we did? Or was it deliberate?"

"You ask a lot of questions," Lucian said, smiling good-naturedly.

I looked at him, and felt queasy. It was time to ask my second question, off the record. I was just afraid what the price of the answer would be.

"I do," I said, "and I have one more. But first, I need to clarify something."

His expression was inviting. "What's that?"

"This question pertains to Sebastian's case," I said, "but it's also somewhat personal. It's complicated—"

"And your superiors don't know what you're about to ask me." He smiled.

I felt a chill. "Not exactly—no. So I guess you could consider it a kind of personal favor. What I need to know is, if you answer, will I be indentured to you somehow? Will I owe you something?"

"You will simply owe me the courtesy of answering one of my questions—either tonight, or some other night."

I didn't trust that it could be that simple.

"Just a question?" I asked. "That's it? You ask, I answer, and then the two of us are square?"

"Exactly."

My eyes narrowed. "Do you promise not to ask something that will get me in trouble with the CORE?"

His smile widened. "Scout's honor. Or to be more accurate—necro's honor?"

I was momentarily surprised by his easy use of the epithet. Or maybe I was really surprised by my own easy use of it, a term just as debilitating as any other. It was like hearing Derrick say "fag" in relation to himself. It always made me want to jump up, to throw my own body between him and the slur, even though he'd spoken it in the first place, invoking that curious commerce of marginality and its reversals. Talking street. In the same way, unexpectedly, I wanted to protect Lucian from his own term, to shield him from some kind of necrophobia, even if I didn't understand why.

"Fine," I said. "I agree to those terms."

"You agreed the moment you walked through those doors," Lucian said. "I mean—if we're going to get technical."

His playfulness made me uneasy. Like other demons on the dark side, necromancers could be needlessly cruel; they could be bizarre, sadistic, and unpredictable. But they rarely had this sort of playful, boyish charm. It was like talking to a petulant teenager. James Dean with a penchant for the occult. All he needed was the red vinyl coat from *Rebel* (as Derrick always reminded me, it was something that he stole on the spur of the moment from a paramedic on set, knowing that he would be filmed in color and wanting to glow; another queer boy with his own style of magic).

"Fair enough," I said.

"Good." He lay down on the couch, putting his feet on the armrest, mere inches away from me. I stared very intently at the soles of his boots. They were deeply grooved—the kind of boots made for hiking. Did necromancers do much hiking? Must have been night hiking. In graveyards.

The fear was making my mind wander.

"My question involves the siring process," I said. "It's about blood, specifically."

"I'm not a vampire," he said, with what might have been defensiveness.

"Nobody's debating that," I replied. "But you're close to them. Nobody's asking you to divulge anything classified."

"Oh, but it's always secrets, isn't it?" He smiled. "Everything's a secret with our kind. We deal in secrets."

"We deal in different things entirely," I said, before I could help myself.

His eyes betrayed something close to pleasure. "You loathe me, don't you, Tess? Everything about me—you find it abhorrent."

"I just—don't understand it. That's all."

Lucian was silent for a moment. Then he said something odd.

"Stillbirths."

I blinked. "What?"

"That's where we come from. My 'kind,' if you want to call us that. We aren't hatched from eggs, or torn out of pregnant bodies like Macduff."

I was silent. He wasn't actually asking a question. He was giving me something, a secret, a piece of himself. It was unexpected and confusing. I just listened.

"There are nurses," he continued. "Connected. Women in the know. Not every stillbirth has the mark. It isn't the same as SIDS or being born premature and dying soon after; a shriveled, white little thing, like torn silk or"—he stuttered and laughed softly"—or a marshmallow, lying in an incubator, struggling to breathe, all tied up in tubes with some poor mother tickling his feet to keep him alive." His eyes had gone soft, elsewhere. They shone weirdly.

"But some are marked. Born dead alive. Dying to live and living to die. And after the doctor breaks the bad news, and the crying and wailing starts, and the bloody spandex gloves get tossed in the trash along with the wadded-up cotton and what's left of life—after that, sometimes a nurse will slip into the room when nobody's looking. And she'll reach into that tiny white body bag, and she'll unzip it, carefully. She'll take the small thing, bruised and purple, into her arms, and she'll wrap it in cloth of black and gold, and brush oil against its cold brow. And then she'll take it away."

His expression returned. But I imagined that a part of him was still following that dead, swaddled child along forlorn paths, along dark Homeric ways. Following, perhaps, the same route that he'd traveled as a helpless babe. I wondered what waited for him at the end of that journey. Maybe a dark city of glittering emerald, opal, and jet, languishing beneath eternal sunset. A velvet parlor, filled with spider demons and goddesses with snow-pale shoulders wearing black masks, wrapping him endlessly in ties of purple and vermillion. Or a vast room filled with crying children, where a single light-bulb swung back and forth like a pendulum on its chain, casting just enough light to see the shadow things that waited in all four corners, waited with open mouths. I shivered. I wanted to know more, even as I understood that this was a pact between us, a legend meant only for my ears. The CORE would never hear about it.

It was my secret to sleep with, and my new terror in the dark.

"Well," he said at last. "Ask your question."

I ignored the jibe. "Is it possible," I asked, "for demonic viral plasmids—blood pathogens—to be suppressed within a human body? Suppressed through psychic power? Or by some other means?"

Lucian pondered this for a moment. I couldn't tell if he was actually unsure of the answer, or just playing with me. He had that singularly annoying look that some very intelligent people have—the smug knowledge that they're one step ahead of you, no matter what you happen to be talking about.

"That's a very interesting question," he said neutrally. "I think, though, that it would be easier to show you."

Now *this* I hadn't been expecting.

Lucian rose. "Follow me, please, Miss Corday."

Shit. I had no other choice. I had to go with him. But what exactly was I walking into? Something told me that, whatever Lucian was about to show me, I wasn't going to like it.

And I thought I was going to get home early tonight. Now, I'd probably be lucky if I got home at all.

15

My foot struck something, and I almost yelped. But it was just a discarded box that someone had pushed against the wall. Lucian grinned at me.

"Jumpy, Miss Corday?"

"It's been a long night," I said. "I'm just looking forward to going home and curling up with a Jane Austen novel." I tried to sound slightly diffident about the possibility—not like someone who was desperately hoping to survive the night.

"Jane Austen?" Lucian raised an eyebrow. "I would have expected you to read something a bit more exciting—like true crime novels."

"I have enough excitement in my life already. Sometimes it's nice to just sit back and read about ladies fussing over men and embroidery."

His eyes gleamed coldly. "Surely, Austen's work is also a pioneering aspect of the feminist movement. Her women are interested in more than embroidery."

"Of course," I said simply. "Or maybe I just like horses and intrigue."

"Intrigue—that I believe." Lucian smiled again. "You're old enough to be wary but still young enough to enjoy the danger."

"Yeah, it's a magical time in my life," I snapped. I wanted to curb the sarcasm, but I really was getting tired of this. I wanted to go home. This place was sinking into my bones, making me shudder, and I didn't like it. I didn't want to know what sorts of powers were curled up just beyond my vision, watching me, waiting.

Lucian chuckled. "Fair enough. But take it from someone who knows—someone a lot older than you, Tess. You've got to enjoy this time while you still have it. One day, you'll wake up, and the danger will still be there—but you won't want it anymore. You won't want much of anything."

Lucian stopped in front of a reinforced steel door. I expected to feel some kind of magical defense glowing around it. I didn't expect to see a numeric keypad, a magnetic card scanner, and small luminescent panel in the center of the door.

He typed a code onto the keypad, then withdrew a small metallic square from around his neck and swiped it through the card scanner. I heard a chime, and the panel began to glow a soft shade of blue.

"Surprised?" Lucian asked. "You were expecting maybe an army of skeleton warriors guarding the door?"

I shrugged. "I know that vampires are hip with technology."

"Some of them are very good computer engineers, too. You'd be surprised how many work for Microsoft."

"Actually, that doesn't surprise me at all. I'll bet a lot of necromancers work for 7-Eleven as well."

"We prefer Kinko's, actually."

He grinned, then placed his hand on the panel, fingers splayed. A light passed over his fingertips, making them glow red from the inside. It seemed like a lot of security, especially considering the fact that this room was already in the heart of a heavily guarded vampire complex. Who were they protecting it from? Other vampires?

If Lucian read my thoughts, he merely smiled, beckoning me in as the door slid open. This was how the spider beckoned in the fly.

I swallowed my fear and stepped into the room.

It wasn't a warehouse or a storage room like I expected. It was a small laboratory. I saw several microscopes in one corner—high-quality ones, too: a scanning electron microscope, or SEM; a compound microscope that was actually two scopes joined by an optical bridge; and a spectrograph for measuring light wavelengths. Our microscopy techs would be jealous. I saw what looked like an ultracentrifuge for spinning blood plasma, petri dishes, and other predictable instruments.

There was a bank of computers against one wall, their monitors displaying scans of some sort. I looked closer. One of them was an ultrasound, although I couldn't decipher the numbers in the corner. The screen next to it looked like a CT scan of a human chest wall, with different layers showing the lungs, ribcage, and musculature. One screen was filled with symbols that I couldn't understand. Vampiric script. The language of the old demons who'd walked the earth thousands of years ago, destroying human empires and killing as they saw fit. The same script that we'd seen on the note in Sebastian's pocket. Modern vampires seldom used it, except for literature and legal contracts, or secret rituals.

"Follow me," Lucian said, crossing the lab. There was another door in the far corner, nondescript except for the number "7" painted on it in black. I only had a second to ponder that before a wave of mystical energy struck me like a blow in the face, making me stumble and step back. The door was juiced with enough power to incinerate anyone, human or vampire, who touched it. That kind of defense didn't come lightly—it required blood sacrifice, or worse.

"Unless I'm mistaken," I replied, "that sort of power is designed to keep something *inside* as well."

Lucian grinned. "You're not mistaken." He passed his hand across the door, and I felt the threads of power separate, felt the space around us give a peculiar twinge as it came undone. Lucian grasped the knob and turned.

The room beyond was small, and most of its space was occupied by monitoring equipment—an EKG, blood pressure gauge, and several different screens outputting various bio readings and information. In the center of the room was a steel gurney, and lying on it was a figure. I didn't want to look too closely, but Lucian beckoned me forward with a reassuring glance—as reassuring as he could manage anyway.

"Don't worry. He's asleep—he won't mind you taking a closer peek."

I stepped forward. The figure on the gurney was a young man, probably about fifteen or sixteen, judging from the barest hint of stubble on his cheeks. He was stripped to the waist, and his pale chest was covered with electrodes. An IV was pumping something into him, although I couldn't tell what. Probably just saline solution from the look of it, or some kind of nutritional supplement.

"Touch him," Lucian said.

I gave him a look. "What?"

"Go ahead. Touch him." Lucian looked at me curiously. "What do you sense from him?"

It was an odd question. Tentatively, I reached over and put my hand on the boy's chest. Teenager would have been a more accurate description, but he looked so small and vulnerable lying there, pale and silent, that I thought of him as more of a boy. He had short brown hair with blond highlights that fell across his eyes, which were closed. I wondered what color they were.

"Well?" Lucian leaned forward.

I could feel *something* from him, but the feeling was—incomplete somehow. Like I was only getting part of an audio signal, just one channel instead of two, or something that was garbled. His skin was cool, but not cold. There was a faint warmth somewhere, a vibration beneath my fingertips, like a quiet engine humming away beneath all the bone, muscle, and flesh. And somewhere even deeper, a tang of ancient power. A fierce oldness, like dank earth, dust, copper, doom.

"He feels . . . almost like a vampire," I said at last.

"Almost?" Lucian was smiling at me. His infuriatingly amused look made me want to hit him—hard.

"I can't explain it any other way. It's like, there's a hint of vampiric essence, but something else, too. Something—I don't know"—I frowned—"I've never felt anything quite like it before. I don't know what it means."

"Would you like to?"

Such a question. I tried to keep my look neutral. "I'm not sure, to be honest."

Lucian idly studied one of the monitors. "His name is Patrick."

"Patrick?" I studied the firm jawline, the hint of developing muscle in his arms, evident beneath all the electrodes, tubes, and bandages. He looked like a Patrick, if that made any sense at all.

"Yes." Lucian leaned against the gurney. "He's a very special case. A project, you might call it."

"That doesn't make me feel any better."

He chuckled. "Would you like to know more?"

This was pissing me off—the baiting game that he was playing. Suddenly, I didn't care anymore. I turned around and scowled at him.

"Just tell me, or kill me—whatever. Do what you're going to do, but don't play games, Lucian."

"Games?" He was behind me. I hadn't seen—or felt—him move, but his breath was on the back of my neck. His fingertips grazed my shoulder. I shuddered.

"Games are all we have, you and I." His voice curled along the length of my skin, like smoke. I could smell it. I wanted to scream from the weight of it, but I stood my ground. I closed my eyes briefly, then swallowed, concentrating on the earth beneath my feet. The power of the earth—the ancient steadiness of it. My senses linked me to it, all that geothermal energy slumbering just underneath me. I felt it flow through the soles of my boots, through the tendons of my legs, into my blood.

Mages and necromancers drew power from the same place—just through very different methods. We might even be equals in a fight. I doubted it, though. He was older, more experienced.

Less human?

"Is this the part where Sabine jumps out of a closet and slits my throat?" I asked. "So that you can both get off on watching me die?"

Lucian took a step back, smiling. "Sabine doesn't know that we're here. If she knew, then your life would be forfeit."

I glared at him. "So you deliberately endangered my life by showing me this?"

"You want answers, don't you?"

"Tell me—what you need to tell me," I said slowly.

Lucian chuckled, but he was already standing on the other end of the room. I heard the laughter in my ear, regardless. I resisted the urge to run.

"You're strong," he said simply. "Maybe stronger than you even realize. I find that refreshing, Tess."

I stared at a space above his shoulder, but said nothing. Damage control. Don't do anything else to piss him off—just let him spin his story, and then get out of here. See another day. It sounded like a plan.

"Patrick is a special case," he repeated. "A pureblood. He's a potential successor to the magnate of the city."

As far as I knew, the magnate controlled—well, just about everything within Vancouver's city limits. If normal vampires were scary as hell, then the magnate was a walking nightmare with fangs.

"Potential?" I asked.

"There are others like him—children sired by the magnate. We won't know who'll be chosen until the time of succession is at hand."

"And what happens to the ones who aren't chosen?"

Lucian merely looked at me.

"Gotcha." I frowned.

Lucian returned his attention to the boy on the gurney. "Patrick," he said, "was sired at ten years old. He is now sixteen."

"I don't get it." This, at least, was true.

"The siring process began when Patrick was ten, but it still isn't finished." He smiled. "The boy has been—gestating—for six years now. When the time comes, if he truly is chosen, then he will be given the grace of the magnate. He will ascend and absorb a part of the old magnate—just as the magnate once absorbed a part of *their* sire, and so on, for the last ten thousand years. In that moment, he will gain access to the history of the bloodline. The collective memory of vampire civilization."

I took a moment to process this. "So—right now, he's—what—*absorbing* power? Sucking up memories?"

Lucian nodded. "If he's chosen, then the memories will be unlocked. If not, then they will vanish with him." He cocked his head. "The boy will have many abilities—*if* he is chosen. The process fortifies his body; much like you might age a bottle of wine, he is being aged, infused with the power and experience of a creature thousands of years older than him."

"How does it work, then?" I asked. "How do they slow the process?" I stared at him suddenly. "Are *you* part of it? Is that why you work for them? Some kind of truce so that you can combine your powers?"

Lucian kept his expression to himself. "They find my powers useful, yes—and I find their company useful."

"Their protection, you mean."

"It's complicated, Tess."

He gestured to one of the monitors. I saw what looked like a single helix revolving on the screen, elegant in its simplicity.

"RNA," I said.

He nodded. "Vampirism is a retrovirus. It starts out as RNA, and then uses reverse transcription to turn itself into DNA. The same as AIDS."

"I get that," I said, a trifle annoyed.

"Then it's amazing that you haven't figured out the connection yet," Lucian replied, giving me an amused look. "AIDS can't be stopped, but it can be slowed. Drugs like AZT worked for a while on humans, before the side effects became evident. Before you discovered that your drug companies were selling a 'cure' at least half as destructive as the disease itself, profiting from the sick and the dying. Vampirism is just a retrovirus, like any other. It can't be stopped, or reversed, but it can be slowed to a crawl."

"With drugs?"

"They help, yes. But most of it comes from power." He tapped his head. "You know what kind I'm talking about."

"The sire can slow the process. So I've heard."

"Only the most powerful of our kind can do it—for just this purpose. And nobody in the city has more power than the magnate."

I frowned. "So he—what—telepathically broadcasts his mojo to all of these sleeping kids? I don't get it."

Lucian blinked. "Mojo?"

"It's a technical term."

"Ah." He nodded. "It's not telepathic. The magnate leaves a mark on the potentials, and the mark changes their body chemistry. Slows everything down. Here, I'll show you."

Lucian pushed down the blanket covering Patrick's lower half, and I saw a curious mark just above his left hip. It was vampiric script, and I didn't need to touch it to know that it was infused with power. I could feel the energy rippling from it—the kind of power that I didn't want anywhere near me. I took a step backward.

He smiled. "Are you afraid of the mark, Tess?"

"I'm cautious," I said. "They're not the same thing."

"Of course not." Lucian pushed the blanket up. "So now you know. The siring process can be delayed, if the sire himself is powerful enough."

"Could someone other than the magnate do it?"

His eyes gleamed. "Possibly. But without the magnate's permission, and the approval of the council, such an experiment would be—inadvisable."

"I still don't have all of my answers," I said. "Vampirism isn't the same as magic. The two follow similar biological processes, but they still aren't the same. I don't understand how a mage—" I blinked, realizing that I'd been about to tell Lucian everything. Was he compelling me? Or was I just incredibly stupid?

He looked at me expectantly.

"I don't understand," I said, concentrating on every word, "how someone who isn't a vampire might do this."

"Is that your mystery?" Lucian looked mildly interested. His eyes were like a cat's—you could never tell when he was truly engaged by something. "Has one of your kind done something like this?" He swallowed. "Or someone like me, perhaps?"

It was my turn to be aloof. "It's complicated."

"But it has to do with this girl, no? The same girl that you think Sebastian was looking for before he was killed?"

I sighed. "Yes."

Lucian regarded me amiably. If he could sense my moral conundrum, he said nothing about it. After communing so long with the forces of death, was his brain very different from mine? Did he perceive the world in a way that I could never understand, a universe filled with bizarre smells, flashes of color, sensations, rich tastes, and insatiable desires? At the moment, his frustration seemed all too human.

"What are you thinking?" he asked.

I swallowed. "That I'd like to leave now."

He laughed—a rich and terrifying sound. It wasn't the sort of thing that needed an accompanying statement. The laughter itself was his reply. And I couldn't think of anything to say, so I just stared at the wall uncomfortably. As much as I wanted to learn more about this mysterious boy, and the siring process, I didn't want to overextend my hand. I was barely holding a pair of deuces anyway, and Lucian was the House. The House always wins.

I looked once more at Patrick. He seemed so small and vulnerable lying there. Who knew if he'd make the cut—if he'd earn the honor of being the new vampire monarch. If he failed, he died. It was pretty simple. The very thought of it made me weak with anger, but I was powerless to do anything. These were vampires, and this was their culture. Patrick had been a human child once, but he wasn't anymore. His life, as he'd once known it—playing with the family dog, eating ice cream, riding his bike through the neighborhood streets—that was all over. I couldn't do anything for him, but I didn't want to leave him either.

You can't see her.

I remembered my mother's voice—her hand holding me back as I tried to grab the hospital curtain.

Honey, she's—

And then I remembered my mother crying. I'd never seen her cry before, and it frightened me. It wasn't sobbing—just a strange convulsion of her face, almost graceful. Almost beautiful. The tears slid down her cheeks, but her grip remained on my shoulder. I knew that she could hold me—she just couldn't protect me. Not anymore.

Eve has—she's been very badly—hurt—

Burned.

Burned beyond recognition, beyond humanity. I wouldn't recognize her. Nothing but a calcined body, the shadow of the girl I used to play with, a cruel darkness that now lay dying (or dead) on some cold hospital gurney, her blackened digits—their nerves forever eradicated—being snapped off with shears like unwieldy branches. They pruned her annihilated body like a sapling in winter, and she never knew that she was losing fingers and toes while she slept on, darkly and dreamlessly.

You shouldn't see her. You wouldn't want to.

I suddenly hated Lucian—hated vampires and the necromancers who acted as their smiling daylight faces, not for being killers, but simply for following their own demonic natures. I hated that there were demons in the world, and mages to deal with them, and others—like Lucian—in between. Sometimes I just wanted things to be black-and-white. But that was never going to happen.

All I could do was protect Mia, before—like Patrick—she became a lost cause.

16

I had to sit in the front seat of my car, gripping the wheel, for about fifteen minutes until I'd calmed down enough to actually drive somewhere. The adrenaline was still pumping through my system, and I was torn between the desire to smash the windshield or throw up all over the upholstery. Maybe I'd just do both.

Lucian was hiding something—a big something. He was a politician, after all, and it was his job to protect the interests of the vampire community. But how was Mia implicated? She was the key, but what the hell was the lock? I could feel a world-class headache coming on. I was also hungry, which was odd, since my stomach should have been turning itself inside out. There was certainly no way that I'd be getting to sleep anytime soon. My body was still vibrating. I checked my watch: 10:30 p.m. God, I'd been in there for only an hour. It had felt like an eternity.

It also didn't help that Lucian Agrado—a skilled necromancer, and possibly one of the most dangerous creatures I'd ever met in my life—happened to look like a hot, thirtysomething Latino guy. Sure, he was deeply into the dark arts, but I was also a red-blooded city girl whose last memory of getting laid involved a value-priced bottle of Ruffino Chianti and an investment banker named Rog.

Great—sorry, Mia, can't save you now, Mama's too busy getting her freak on with a death-dealer. God. Could I be more selfish?

My cell phone rang, scaring me half to death.

I flipped it open. "This better not be a demon."

Derrick cleared his throat on the other end. "I do happen to be *part*-demon. Will that work for you?"

"This isn't a nine hundred number, hon. What's going on?"

"How did the meeting go?"

I swallowed around the bile in my throat. "Words come to mind—like abject terror. I almost lost it a few times, but I managed to get through the evening."

"Well, I hate to add to your stress-mountain, but we've got a bit of an interesting situation right now."

I closed my eyes. "Interesting means bad, right?"

"I'm not sure yet. I'll let Mia explain."

My heart seized. "What? She's with you?"

The phone crackled for a moment, then I heard Mia's voice. "Tess?"

"Mia, what's wrong? Are you hurt? What's going on?" Lord—I sounded like a hyperactive mom. I sounded like *my* mom.

"I'm fine, Tess. Don't have a stroke."

I suppose I deserved that. "Okay. I'm good. Just tell me what's up. What are you doing in the city this late at night?" I frowned. "On a school night?"

Mia chuckled. "Yeah—'cause I'm allowed to watch demon carnage, but you wouldn't want me to screw up my social studies report on John A. MacDonald."

She wasn't panicking—that was a good thing. I allowed myself to relax a bit. "Just tell me what's going on, okay?"

I heard Derrick say something inaudible in the background. It sounded almost like "cherry sundae."

My eyes widened. "Are you at *Denny's*?"

"Yeah," Mia replied. "I was going to meet Derrick at the

partment, but he thought it might not be safe. So we're
t the Denny's on Thurlow and Davie."

"But what are you *doing*—"

"I had a dentist's appointment, and my aunt drove me
nto the city on her way to work." Mia paused. "I know I
hould have called you earlier, but I was still a bit freaked
ut from yesterday. So I just sort of walked around—"

"Excuse me?" I was trying to keep the righteous mom
nger out of my voice. "You almost got killed by a demon
esterday, and now you're—what—shopping? Doing a bit
f sightseeing downtown?"

"Chill out. I've been careful. I spent most of the day at
he library." I knew that she was smiling on the other end of
he phone. "You know—big public place, lots of books and
ecurity guards?"

"You still should have called us, Mia."

"Well, excuse me if I'm still a *bit* wigged out by my near-
leath experience yesterday! Maybe I didn't exactly want to
ush back to the place where I watched you decapitate a
lemon!"

I sighed. "Okay, you're right. And it doesn't matter. The
mportant thing is that you're still safe. Where's your aunt?
'm surprised that she was even willing to let you out of her
ight after what happened. I thought you'd be under house
rrest."

"Well, that was originally the plan, but I refused to stay
ut."

"Mia, that's not smart—"

"I'm not going to sit in my room and read *Tiger Beat*
vhile people are getting attacked by monsters."

I swallowed. "Okay, fine. So Cassandra took you into the
ity and dropped you off at the library. What then?"

"She was supposed to pick me up after work, but she
never showed up. I waited outside the building for, like, al-
nost two hours. Then I got a bit freaked out—I didn't want
o go in there. So I called Derrick."

Thank God I'd written down our personal numbers on
hat card.

"Good. That was the right move." I started the car. "I'm coming to meet you guys at the restaurant, okay? Then we'll go back to the lab together and see what's happened to your aunt."

"Cool." She was trying to keep the tremor out of her voice, but I heard it anyway. "I'm glad you guys are here."

"Don't worry, Mia. We'll figure this out. I promise."

"Okay."

"Can you put Derrick back on?"

"Yeah, sure."

A second later, I heard Derrick's voice. "Red Leader."

I rolled my eyes. "Okay, how are you really? Is the restaurant safe?"

"Of course. It's Retro-Queer night at Celebrities. Any demon comes within a mile of this place, they'll get their ass kicked by an army of 1950s drag queens wearing curlers. And some drag-demons, too, which is always refreshing to see."

"Fine. I'll be there in ten minutes. Order me—"

"I know, I know. A hot chocolate and a piece of pineapple cheesecake with extra graham-cracker crust. And if they don't have pineapple—"

"Derrick." I was breathing fast. I'd been worrying all day long, and now it was building into volcanic anxiety. "I don't know what to do."

"Neither do I. Just get over here."

"Selena can only watch our backs for so long. If Marcus sees us all together again, you and I will lose our jobs—or worse. And Mia will end up in a foster home. It already looks like we're compromising this case."

"You said it last night—what choice do we have?"

I closed my eyes. "Let's try to keep this very quiet. Just surveillance. If this lab ends up being a crime scene, we can't get near it. We'll just let the CORE do its business, call it in, and take Mia home."

"Right." I could feel that Derrick was rolling his eyes. "Because our lives always go that smoothly."

I clicked off the cell phone, and put the car into gear. If I

urried, I might be able to make it to the restaurant in time
or one last dessert before my life was officially ruined.

emTec Laboratories was on the fourteenth floor
f an office building on West Georgia, all shimmering glass
nd concrete. It reminded me of the HSBC building with the
evolving steel pendulum that *whooshed* over your head.
errick had called it the corporate phallus once, which was
retty funny until one of the security guards heard us. We
ft shortly after. I did my banking with a credit union now.

Standing outside the main entrance, shivering a bit in my
appropriate spring jacket, I felt like my brain was about to
xplode. I had so many questions, and none of them seemed
ven remotely answerable. I'd thought that Cassandra was
ssigned to protect Mia—to be her bodyguard and jailor at
e same time—but why would she just up and vanish like
is? If Mia was her precious cargo, why abandon her?

"What time does your aunt usually pick you up?" I asked.

"Six thirty—sometimes seven, if work runs late." Mia
as wearing a black Misfits hoody, an old pair of men's
ans, and combat boots. It's not like I wanted to see her in
icy Couture or something, but it would have been comfort-
g if she acted even slightly like a thirteen-year-old girl for
nce.

"And she didn't phone you or anything?"

She shook her head. "I even called the house, but no-
ody's home."

"Or nobody's picking up," Derrick added.

Mia turned to him. "What—you think she's tied up in the
itchen or something? Like she's being held hostage?"

"Way to be calming, Derrick," I murmured.

"I just don't think we should rule anything out."

"Well," Mia said, "I checked the parking lot, and her car's
till there. So she must still be in the building."

"Is there some way you can sense her presence?" Derrick
sked.

"Not unless she's standing in front of me." I sighed. "We

already know that she can disguise her—" I glanced quick
at Mia. This didn't seem like the right time for the "He
your aunt's a big hell-demon" speech. I swallowed. "I mea
it would just be confusing anyway. I couldn't tell if it was a
tually her."

Mia frowned at me, but said nothing.

"This doesn't make any sense." I was grinding my tee
again. A bad habit from childhood. "No part of me wants
go in that building."

"Are you kidding?" Mia grabbed my shoulder. "If n
aunt's in trouble, then we've got to help her. What if one
those Thyroid demons—"

"Vailoid," I corrected.

"*Whatever*. What if they've captured her?"

"Somehow, I don't think that's the case."

"Tess." Her eyes narrowed. "You're not telling me som
thing. The last time somebody didn't tell me something, yc
had to shoot a guy with detachable fangs—remember?"

"We're still trying to fix the drywall," Derrick said.

I made a face. "Let's just say it's complicated, okay? Ca
sandra is definitely involved in—whatever you're involve
in."

"Thanks, Nostradamus—could you fuzzy that up a bit?"

"Okay, *look*." It was my turn to glare at her. "We're goir
to go in there, and we're going to help your aunt. I just don
want you to be surprised if—"

"If what?"

I swallowed. "Just be ready for anything, okay?"

"Fine." Her gaze was level. "Let's do it, then."

"Listen to MacGyver-mini over here," Derrick said.

I stared at the door. "She's right. It's now or never. Are w
ready?"

Derrick drew out a Colt .38 revolver, the "detective sp
cial," which Selena had signed out for him. I assumed tha
she'd chosen the .38 Special because, despite having onl
six shots, it was small and accurate. All I had was m
athame, but I figured that if it couldn't protect me, neithe
could bullets.

"Holy crap." Mia stared uncomfortably at the gun. "Are we going to save my aunt or blow her up?"

"This is for the demons," Derrick said. "Not for her. Mia's right. It's time to do this." Holding the revolver with the barrel pointed up, he gently cocked the hammer back, chambering the first bullet.

"You are so butch right now," I said.

"Shut up. You know I can't hit the broad side of a barn with this thing."

"I could try—" Mia began.

"*Oh* no," I said. "No touching guns for you."

"Oh, like he's some kind of arms expert."

"I trust Derrick not to blow my head off. Maybe my arm, but not my head."

Derrick glared at me. "Can we just go in now?"

I nodded. "Yeah. We're as ready as we'll ever be, I guess."

The front door was locked, and had a magnetic card reader. That didn't pose too much of a problem, though. I laid the athame against the reader, and channeled a brief spike of earth materia from the ground. It passed through my body with a sharp jolt, and the athame flared green for a moment. Tendrils of electricity crawled across the mechanical components of the door. The light on the reader flicked from red to green, and I opened the door with a satisfied smile.

"You gotta teach me how to do that," Mia said.

"It only works on some electronic locks. And I'm not about to teach you how to break and enter, sweetheart."

"I guess you guys have way tighter security at HQ, or whatever you call it."

"You mean at the lab?" I grinned. "Actually, we use a similar keycard system, only it's a mystical hybrid thing." I reached into my purse. "The electronic keys look pretty much like your standard swipe card, but they're attuned to your body's biometric readings—" I frowned. "Where the hell did I put my keycard?"

Derrick gave me a look. "Did you stick it in your other fanny pack?"

"Very funny." I practically dumped my entire purse out in the parking lot before I was ready to accept the inevitable.

It's gone.

"Okay, I'm not panicking about this," I said, keeping my smile. "I must have just—left it on the nightstand or something. I mean, it's only a biometric reader that's keyed to my DNA, right? I'm sure they can just order a new one—"

Mia's eyes had gotten very wide. "Holy crap, Tess. You're screwed!"

"I am *not*—" Finally, I snapped my purse shut and closed my eyes. "It's fine. Everything's fine. And shut up, Derrick."

"I didn't say anything."

I put my hand on the door. "You were thinking it—and it was bitchy."

The lobby of the building was completely empty. Not even a security guard. It didn't add up—the building had thirty floors, but no security guards? Unless they were all taking a coffee break, which didn't seem likely.

"This can't be good," Derrick said.

"Let's not panic yet. Mia, do you know where your aunt's office is?"

She shook her head. "I've never been past the lobby. All I know is that the lab is on the fourteenth floor."

"Great." I walked up to the elevator and pushed the button. The doors opened with a soft hum.

Derrick stared into the empty elevator. "This doesn't seem right, Tess. It's too easy so far."

I exhaled as we stepped into the elevator. The doors closed behind us, and Derrick pushed the button for the fourteenth floor. The elevator began to climb silently. It was one of those brand-new ones that didn't even seem to be moving. Not like the elevator in Derrick's apartment, which felt like you were riding up Splash Mountain.

The doors chimed, then opened. It was definitely a lab—a lot like the one I'd seen at Moonbase, only much bigger. There were stainless steel tables filled with diagnostic equipment, shelves of test tubes and petri dishes, and a whole bank of computers against one wall. There was also a laptop sitting on a table in the far corner, and something was flickering across its screen. It looked quite a bit like our serology lab. It also bore a discomforting resemblance to the chamber that Lucian had shown me, where they were keeping Patrick, the magnate potential.

I walked over to the table for a closer look, but I couldn't make much sense of what was happening on the monitor. There was a timer in one corner, which had reached zero. The words "polymerase chain reaction" were flashing across the screen, and underneath that was a double helix with parts of each strand numbered and labeled. There was a gauge of some kind in the right corner that read "hematocrit volume," and next to that the number "0.87."

There was also a microscope next to the laptop. I reached into my pocket and slipped on a pair of plastic gloves. Then I took the glass slide from underneath the microscope stage. There was a splash of blood on the slide—a sample. "DNA testing," I said. "PCR—the short tandem relay test. Not as thorough as some of the other tests, but quicker. Derrick, come look at this."

He peered at the computer screen. "They're doing some sort of ABO typing as well. Hematocrit has to do with blood chemistry, but I don't know much more."

"DNA testing?" Mia stared at me. "Aunt Cassandra said that she spent most of her time developing artificial sweeteners."

"That's not what this lab is for," I said. "This is a serology facility—they analyze blood here, and other bodily fluids." I tried to peer down the hallway that led past the tables, but the light was dim. Great. At least when the demons started crunching my bones, I wouldn't have to watch.

Something crawled across my neck. I resisted the urge to cry out, and willed myself to stand still, listening. It was a genetic signature of some kind. I didn't know who it belonged to, though. Could be another mage. Could be a fire-spewing demon.

"You feel it, too?" Derrick asked.

I nodded. "Cassandra."

"Maybe."

"It's got to be," I said. "Nothing else makes sense."

"What—she's alone in this building, waiting for us? In what dimension does that make sense?"

There was a sudden crash. It sounded like breaking glass.

"Aunt Cassie?" Mia rushed past us.

"Mia, no!" I drew my athame. "Shit!"

I saw Mia disappear into an office at the end of the corridor. The door was ajar—no, wait. The door was ripped off its hinges.

"Come on," I said grimly.

Mia was standing just inside the office—not saying anything or even moving a muscle, just staring. She had the right to be surprised. The office looked like a combat zone. The window in the far wall was shattered, and the ground was littered with papers. Some of the papers were splashed with blood. A filing cabinet in the far corner had been overturned, and a gutted computer was lying on the floor, its monitor smashed.

The only intact piece of furniture in the room was a steel desk, and a body was draped across it. Not a human body. It was bent at a horrible angle—its back must have been broken—and blood was quietly pooling around it. I saw a rib protruding, glistening white, and turned to Derrick.

"Get her out of here."

"Aunt Cassie!" Mia dodged me and ran forward. "Are you—" Her eyes got very wide as she got closer to the demon's body, and she put a hand on her mouth. Derrick tried to grab her, but she was already on her knees, retching.

I took a closer look at the body. Black eyes and detachable jaws, although one row of fangs had been ripped clear off. Vailoid demon. Jesus. Someone had done this to a Vailoid? I leaned forward, then froze.

There was another body lying behind the desk. A middle-aged woman wearing a denim dress that was covered in blood. Cassandra. Oh God.

"Derrick!" I didn't turn. "Get Mia *out* of here. Now!"

"What? What did you see?" Mia lunged forward, but Derrick managed to grab her this time.

"You don't want to look, sweetie," he said.

"No! Get off me! I have to—" She strained against his grip. Derrick wasn't exactly a heavyweight, but he was still twice the size of Mia. "No! I have to see! I—" She sobbed. "Oh God, is it my aunt? Oh God—"

"Let's just get out of here," Derrick said, trying to soothe her. "We'll wait for Tess in the car. I promise you don't want to see this—"

There was a large puncture wound in Cassandra's chest, and her face was covered in blood. Her gray hair was plastered to her forehead, and I saw her glasses, still dangling from that silly chain—smashed.

I didn't get it. Had *she* done this to the Vailoid? Had they both killed each other?

"Shit," Derrick whispered.

"Don't touch anything," I said. I stared at the broken window. Whoever did this was here a minute ago. We'd heard the glass break. They could very well still be in this room. I didn't feel anyone's presence, though. I just felt sick.

I walked over to the window, carefully avoiding the blood. Slipping on a pair of plastic gloves from my purse, I studied the broken glass in the window frame. Our lab techs would have to study it, but I was pretty sure of what they'd find. The stress marks in the fractured glass would be moving outward, which meant that the window had been broken from the inside.

I carefully leaned forward. The window looked onto the parking lot. Lying in a crumpled heap on the pavement below was a second Vailoid demon.

That didn't make sense at all.

"Two Vailoid demons," I said softly. "They both kill Cassandra, and then—what happens? Somebody kills the assassins?"

"Whoever it was," Derrick said, "they moved fast. You

heard the breaking glass. The killer was here no more than a minute ago."

"So why didn't he—or she—attack us? Why throw a demon out the window, and then leave the other body for us to find?"

"Ah, Tess—" Derrick glanced at Mia. "Maybe we should figure out the forensics later."

Shit. I was the worst human being imaginable. Mia was staring at her aunt's body, and I was trying to process the crime scene right in front of her.

She wasn't crying. I could feel her standing next to me, but she wasn't crying. Her face was white. There was power—a fierce power—curling off her skin, flowing around her like smoke. This time I could feel it.

Mia wasn't moving. I put my hand on her shoulder. "I know this is horrible, sweetheart, but—"

"Don't talk to me," she hissed.

"I—" I closed my eyes. "Mia, I don't know what to say."

"I just want to go home." Her voice was numb. She didn't even look at Cassandra's body. She walked out of the office.

"Take Mia into the lobby," I told Derrick, "and call it in. Selena might already be on her way, but we don't want to be accused of not following protocol. I'll seal off the lab and try to make sure that nothing else gets contaminated."

"Tess—" he began.

"I know." I closed my eyes. "We are very screwed."

"We had no choice."

"We could have remanded Mia to CORE custody. Could have assigned her a bodyguard. Could have done a million other official things."

He stared at me. "None of which would have really protected her. You know that we did the right thing, Tess."

I shook my head. "It doesn't matter. I'm past the point of caring. Marcus can do whatever he wants, but I won't stop working on this case." I met his eyes. "We aren't just involved, Derrick. This case *is* our lives now. We're right in the middle."

"Our favorite place to be."

He gave me a sad smile, then walked out of the office.

I stared at Cassandra's body. Her secrets were inviolate now. She'd never be able to talk to me. I'd never get my answers.

It just wasn't fair.

As the unmarked black car sped us silently back to the lab—the CORE had its own emergency service—I felt myself slipping in and out of consciousness. Derrick stared out the window, saying nothing, possibly scanning the psychic airwaves for any kind of disturbance that might follow us. Mia was crumpled against my right shoulder, and I held her like you might hold a fragile seedpod, something ancient and weatherworn and indescribably precious. She could break like a brittle amphora; she could blow away in a flood of black petals.

Her breath was warm against my neck, and its regularity assured me that, at last, she was asleep. Not a fulfilling sleep, but the cruel and utter blankness of dead sleep, the slumber of the exhausted. Like falling into a pool of morbid energy that penetrated every cell, blasting memory away.

I kept drifting. I would start to slip away, then jolt awake abruptly, remembering to hold her, remembering that she was there. For now, she was safe and she was in my arms, under my aegis of protection, however useless that might be.

"Just sleep," Derrick finally said.

"Mmhh?"

"It's okay." He kept looking out the window. "The Alex Fraser Bridge is all clogged up—we probably won't reach the lab for a good twenty minutes. She's out like a light, so you might as well get some sleep while you can."

"Could say the same about you."

He shook his head. "Don't be contrary. Just do what I say for once. I'm here, and I'll watch out for the both of you."

I smiled and touched his arm. "Yeah, you always do."

"Yeah." His smile was tight.

That was all I needed. I slipped down, through the skein

of memories and half-felt impressions that Freud called the primary process, into the deeper stained glass of true dreaming. I kept falling, through every layer of hell, into the endless winter that Lucifer himself might have been trapped in, bisected by cruel ice—if he existed at all. If Earth itself wasn't just the underworld. All of it. Everywhere, and all of us at the helm, with no exit in sight.

Then something unexpected came out of the dark.

Lucian Agrado.

He wore the same outfit that I'd seen back at the club, torn jeans and black boots, only he'd discarded the shirt now. His tattoos lay in startling relief against dark skin. They seethed, the Devil's calligraphy, like some curse sent down through the ages by a mad Egyptian sorcerer, and all I could do was stare at them. Vampiric script crawled across his hands and wrists—I couldn't read it. Just above his right shoulder was the ouroboros, the snake devouring its own tail. And below his left clavicle—surprisingly—a white lily. So white against his skin, lighter than any conventional pigment or tincture could possibly achieve.

And I knew, in that moment, what the lily meant. That patch of skin—the place where the shadows had marked him. Necromancers were part-human, like us, but the other part belonged to something else. *A room with a swinging lightbulb, where shadows with mouths waited. A city of black basalt, without light.* He'd been sired and reborn, not like a vamp, but through some other kind of ritual. It was always about power. He belonged to those forces now, the hidden place where necroid materia came from, like a mote in the eye of the visible world—but what had they given him in return? I stared at it, the cruel mark that would never change, but also a last fragment of his mortal life, an impossibility of muscle, cordage, blood.

I imagined him crying out, terrified, dying, as penumbral claws, nails of moonlight, tore through his major subclavian artery, the push of blood, how sweet the sting. And ekphrasis. Love. The flame and the fracture of dying, only to live again—different. To unknot your old life, undo the ancient ligature and fashion something newer, darker, beyond sin and above any sort of terrestrial judgment. Or maybe he didn't remember, after all. Maybe he'd never known anything but those black swaddling bands, the kiss of the dark.

"What are you doing in my dream?" I asked him.

Lucian reached out, smiling, and touched me on the mirror image of that spot—just beneath my right clavicle. His fingers pressed against the vein, and I felt the vapors of power swirl through them, beneath my skin, calling to my blood in a kind of *lingua hema* that no part of me could resist. Thrombocytes, leukocytes, erythrocytes, all stirred beneath that awful touch, the arterial system suddenly aflame, the blood-rich organs—liver, kidneys, spleen—swelling, engorging, fruits about to burst. The pain was indescribable; the joy was evil, ineluctable.

My blood was boiling. I felt something swelling to the surface. The flesh that he touched was bubbling, seething.

I saw the outlines of the lily. I felt it blooming as it moved through each layer of skin, the subdermal structures, the papillae, the tiny hairs on my neck and shoulders that stood right on end.

"What is this?" I stared at him. "Do I belong to you now?"

Lucian shook his head.

"You belong to nothing, Tess. You don't exist."

This close, he was like gravity. His smell was oaken, timeworn, overpowering. I touched his mark, the mirror image of mine, and the pattern rippled beneath my fingers like a charm. He said nothing, but his eyes were wide and sharp. I pressed my lips against the lily. I inhaled it, kissing, and his skin was hot. Feverish. The hairs on his neck and shoulders were darker, more visible, but still soft. Silk. Ashes.

"If I kiss you," I said, "will this all end?"

He smiled. "You're always trying to read the text."

"Fine." I could smell his breath now, see how soft his lips were. Men's lips could be so fucking sexy, mostly because they never paid any attention to them. His cheeks were smooth, but the dark hair on his arms and chest hinted at something more masculine, adult, not the androgynous youth that we always associated with vampires. Sabine had selected him for that very reason—because he was a man. The trail of soft hair, starting just above his navel and vanishing at his waist, made me curious. Hadn't I always wanted this, in one way or another? An affair with a death-dealer, my hypocrite self, my ethical opposite?

And how fucked up was that?

I'd been created by a demon, born from an act of rape, and now I was about to do something completely forbidden.

"I guess I'll try anything—" I said. "Once."

I kissed him, and that was an end. The beginning of an end.

17

I was sitting in a small interrogation chamber deep within the CORE crime lab. It was the same scene that I'd witnessed hundreds of times before—a suspect getting grilled by Selena and another officer, sometimes a telepath—only I was the one in the hot seat this time. And it was a very uncomfortable chair. I was seated at a small table, with both Marcus and Selena staring at me from the other side. They'd already questioned Derrick, but they wouldn't let me see him. There was a sheet of two-way glass on the other side of the room, and I had no idea who was standing beyond it, watching. Maybe two agents poised to arrest me. Maybe something worse.

I was trying to keep my mind on the matter at hand, but I kept flashing back to that dream. God. My subconscious had a really sick sense of humor sometimes. I also hadn't mentioned my gaffe with the lost keycard. I'd convinced myself that it was a minor fuck-up, and I could just convince Becka to encode me a new one. She owed me for recommending a nontoxic hair dye.

Mia had been taken to the small common area where lab

techs and OSIs usually chatted, smoked, and ate dinner. She was being watched at all times. I hadn't seen her in almost an hour, and I could only imagine what might have been going through her mind. Cassandra was gone. Her only living relative, that we knew of, was dead. Now she had absolutely no one to take care of her. Except me.

Selena motioned to the glass of water sitting next to me. "Have some more. You're not exactly at a hundred percent tonight, and we need you to be thinking clearly."

"Yes." Marcus glared at me. "You wouldn't want to leave anything crucial out of your story."

Ignoring him, I took a drink. If they'd put some kind of sedative or truth serum in my glass, it was well hidden.

"All right," Selena said. "Tell us again. Be as specific as possible, and try to remember everything that you can about last night."

I nodded.

"Mia called your cell phone—we pulled the phone records, and confirmed that a call was placed from Derrick Siegel's cell at 10:28 p.m. last night. The call lasted for approximately three minutes. So what did you talk about?"

"I spoke with Derrick first," I said. "He told me that Mia had called him at home, and that she was worried. Her aunt—"

"Cassandra Polanski?"

"Yes, that's her. Mia said that Cassandra was supposed to pick her up after work, but she was two hours late."

"And Mia was nervous about this."

"See"—Marcus flashed me a meaningful look—"this is where I get confused. You were removed from Mia Polanski's case, were you not, Tess?"

I started to protest, but then thought the better of it. "Yes," I said simply.

"You were instructed, by your director, not to speak with Mia Polanski or to come within a mile of her. So when Mia called you, your first instinct should have been to notify one of your superiors—either Selena or myself—and explain what was going on. Isn't that right?"

He was absolutely right. Smug, but right. I'd completely violated protocol, and everything that he was saying was the truth.

"I should have," I said, "you're right, but I felt that Cassandra's life might be in immediate danger. I didn't think there'd be time to notify the proper channels and organize some type of rescue."

"But you *did* think that bringing Mia Polanski, a minor, to a bloody crime scene was somehow the appropriate thing to do?"

"I didn't want to let her out of my sight. And besides"—I exhaled—"she's already been exposed to a bloody crime scene. I'm not saying that it was the best choice of action, but I was trying to protect both Mia and Cassandra."

"If you'd really been interested in protecting Mia, wouldn't it have been more prudent to remand her to CORE custody?"

I could feel a blush creeping up my face. "Like I said—I didn't think that there was time for that."

"Why?"

I closed my eyes. "It was just—a feeling."

"In our line of work," Selena said, leaning forward, "sometimes that's all we've got. You know that, Marcus. She may not have followed procedure, but it does seem like she had the girl's best interests in mind."

Marcus sighed. "I respect that—I do. And I understand why you might have thought that way, Tess." His eyes fixed on mine. "But we have to deal with the context here. To an outside observer, you've miraculously shown up at two crime scenes in as many days. You've continued to work on a case that you were dismissed from, at least until the paperwork was processed. Now it'll take forever to clear you on the Vailoid death, no matter what Selena or I tell the higher-ups."

I swallowed.

"You've also—either deliberately or unconsciously—placed a minor in grave danger by bringing her to a potentially active crime scene. And all of this could have been avoided if you'd simply picked up that little cell phone and called one of us."

"In all fairness," I said, "you were the one who assigned me to interview the necromancer, Marcus. I was on my way back from the club when Mia called. The case was already on my mind."

"And if I'd assigned you to a completely different case, then would you have followed procedure? Would you have told Mia to contact us?" He shook his head. "No, I think you would have done exactly the same thing. You may have been trying to protect the girl, but you did it by violating the rules and precepts that make this organization run smoothly and *ethically*. You put Mia Polanski in danger, and you deliberately ignored the instructions that I gave you."

"Yeah," I said, "but it's not always about following procedure. This isn't just a case to me, Marcus. This is my life. That demon didn't just attack Mia—it attacked Derrick and me, too, and it would have killed us if we gave it the chance."

"*We* can protect the girl," Marcus said. "We have the resources to keep her safe. You're just one person, Tess. You stormed into that building like you were the hero of the day, and you could have just as easily gotten killed."

"Derrick and I are both trained—"

He raised his hand impatiently. "You're an OSI level one, and you haven't even passed your first review."

"He's right," Selena said. "You should have called me— or anyone—for backup. Going in there alone was reckless and stupid, Tess. You weren't thinking clearly."

"Which is exactly why I had you put on temporary leave from this case."

Marcus looked at me, and I was once again surprised by what I saw in his eyes. Concern. Some small part of him— divided from the career-hungry OSI and the authority figure who worshipped the procedure manual—actually cared about my welfare. And not for the first time, I started to wonder how badly I was screwing both Selena and Marcus even as I tried to protect Mia. I was stuck between a rock and a flamethrower. Not a pretty place to be.

"I know what you think of me, Tess," he said. "I know you're convinced that I'm a supercilious prick—"

Selena's eyes widened, but she didn't interrupt him.

"That I'm always riding you, punishing you unfairly. That I'm out to get you. But I'm not."

All I could do was nod.

"I see a lot of potential in you, whether you believe that or not. The potential to be a great occult investigator. But you're also arrogant. You're dismissive of authority, and you don't take instruction well. Plus, your commitment to the job isn't exactly solid. You aren't giving one hundred percent."

"It's hard to be a hundred percent committed," I said, "when the CORE doesn't even pay me enough to cover seventy-five percent of my rent."

"Every investigator begins at the bottom, and every OSI-1 gets the same pay. All I'm saying, Tess, is that you can't divide your loyalties forever. You're going to have to make a choice—soon—and I hope that you make the right one." His eyes darkened. "Because if you aren't fully committed, you won't pass your review."

"I understand that," I said slowly.

"Then let's continue with the explanation." Selena leaned forward again. "You went to SemTec Laboratories, and then what?"

"We wanted to make sure that Cassandra was okay. But Mia had never been to her office before. All she knew was that it was on the fourteenth floor."

"And how did you gain access to the building?"

Shit.

I swallowed. "I used my athame to temporarily disable the security system. That's how I opened the door."

"So breaking and entering, then," Marcus clarified.

"The lobby was empty," I pressed on, trying to ignore the sound of my career going down the toilet. "At the time, I suspected that the entire building might be deserted— everyone seemed to have gone home for the night. So we took the elevator up to the fourteenth floor."

"And what did you see there?"

"Well, it looked like a serology lab of some kind. There was a lot of DNA and ABO-typing equipment."

"Which we've confiscated," Marcus supplied.

"Of course." I ground my teeth. "I wasn't sure what it was all for, but it looked like there was some kind of DNA test in progress. PCR comparison with a blood sample. I logged the slide as evidence."

"We saw that in your report."

"Did you find out who the blood belonged to?" I asked.

"We can't release that information right now."

Damn. He knew something, and he wasn't going to tell me. Neither was Selena. I was officially out of the loop.

"Fine," I said. "Anyway, we examined the lab without touching anything. Then we heard a sound—a crash. It was a window breaking."

"And you went to investigate," Selena replied.

"Not exactly. Mia ran ahead of us to see what was going on. We had no choice but to follow her."

"But if she hadn't done that," Marcus said coyly, "you would have called for backup and notified us. Right?"

I met his gaze evenly. "I don't know."

Marcus started to say something, but Selena interjected. "So what did you see when you entered Cassandra Polanski's office?"

"There was a dead Vailoid demon lying on top of the desk. It looked as if he'd been completely eviscerated. There was also a broken window, and we discovered another Vailoid body in the parking lot below. He'd been pushed out the window."

"Or he jumped," Marcus said. "You can't know for sure, right?"

I stared at him. "Why would he jump?"

"I don't know, Tess. Why would two Vailoid demons attack a middle-aged woman in her office? None of this really makes sense."

"You must know by now that Cassandra wasn't an ordinary woman."

"Tasha is still performing the autopsy on her, as well as

the Vailoids. We don't have detailed information about her physiology or genetic heritage yet, but we're working on it."

"So you saw the two Vailoid demons," Selena pressed. "Then what?"

"Then I noticed Cassandra's body behind the desk. She had what looked like a large chest wound, and her face was heavily bruised and bloodied. I checked for a pulse, but she was dead. The ME confirmed this when she arrived, about twenty minutes later. I told Derrick to take Mia into the lobby and call in the crime scene. Then I tried my best to make sure that nothing was contaminated."

"We found some fibers on one of the demons," Selena said.

I looked at her sharply. "What sort of fibers?"

"We haven't identified them yet. Tasha found them during the gross exam, and she sent them up to Trace. We'll know more soon—but in the meantime, we'll need the clothes that you were wearing that night."

"I'm still wearing them," I said wearily.

"Okay. We'll give you some new clothes, then. We've done the same thing with Derrick and Mia—just to eliminate any chance that the fibers might have come from any of you."

"That's fine. This outfit is getting pretty ripe anyway."

Selena smiled sympathetically. "You can have a shower, too."

"God, you have no idea how much I'd like that."

"Don't get too comfortable yet," Marcus warned. "I don't think you deliberately tried to interfere with this investigation, but you did violate several protocols. I'm going to have to place you in abeyance for the next week or so."

I glared at him. "Are you kidding? You want me to go on extended vacation?"

"It's for your own good, Tess. You've already got two strikes against you, and I don't want you screwing yourself over." That was almost charitable. He might just as easily have said "screwing *us* over." "So as of this afternoon, you're officially on leave. Once you've passed your review, you can resume active duty."

"This is bullshit, Marcus, and you know it."

"Tess—" Selena warned.

"No, she's got a point. I get why you're frustrated." Marcus suddenly looked as tired as I felt. I could see the shadows beneath his eyes, the lines on his face. He was exhausted—probably not sleeping, like me. "But you understand this as well as I do. These are the rules. If I break them for you, then I have to break them for everybody else. And we've already allowed you to get away with too much. From now on, we have to follow procedure to the absolute letter."

"I guess I don't have a choice."

"That's right. You don't." He rose, collecting a manila file folder—my CORE record, complete with all sorts of interesting notes and blemishes—from the table. "You understand, of course, that you won't be permitted to see Mia, or to talk to her. Not on the phone or via e-mail. Any contact with Mia Polanski will violate the terms of your 'leave of absence,' and we'll have to take disciplinary action. Do you understand?"

"I do," I said coldly, "but at least tell me what's going to happen to her."

"Mia will be placed under surveillance. Don't worry—she'll be comfortable, and agents will be monitoring her around the clock. Nothing will get past them."

"Come on, Marcus. That's going to be terrifying for her."

"More terrifying than seeing her aunt's body? Don't you think this poor girl has been through enough, Tess? All we want to do is protect her from further harm."

I gritted my teeth. "At least let me take her home so that she can get some clothes—a few familiar items. Anything to make her feel more comfortable."

"I don't think that's a good idea."

"Give me a break, Marcus. I'm not going to spirit her away to some tropical island. I'll sign out a vehicle and document the mileage. If we're not back in a few hours, you can send the helicopters out looking for us."

"Tess—"

"Just *listen* to me, okay? This girl is scared. She's just lost everything, and she may be a very powerful latent mage."

He looked skeptical. "Our tests haven't confirmed anything yet."

"It doesn't matter. The potential is there, in any case. The last thing you want to do is put her in a car with a couple of strange investigators that she's never met before. Think about it. She's going to freak. She could bolt."

"We'd find her."

"But would you find her before the next Vailoid assassin? Or before she got herself into a whole new whack of trouble?" I tried to look sincere, although I was resisting the urge to strangle him. "This girl is one step away from a total psychotic break. She needs stability. Derrick and I are the only people that she trusts. I promise you—if you just let us take her home and get a few familiar things, the process will go a hell of a lot more smoothly. And we'll be back before you know it!"

Selena raised an eyebrow. "She's got a good point."

Marcus let out a breath. "Fine. We'll do it your way. But you'd better sign out that vehicle properly. And if you drive even one kilometer out of the way, you'll answer to me."

"Thank you, Marcus," I said sweetly. "I promise not to let you down."

He walked out of the interrogation room without another word. I briefly imagined him as a secret smoker, sucking back unfiltered Marlboros in the men's bathroom. I wondered how high his blood pressure was.

"Great day," was all Selena said.

I couldn't keep the shame from creeping into my eyes. I knew that I should have told her everything from the start, but now I was too far past the point of feeling accountable.

"I'm sorry," I said simply. "I should have come to you."

Her expression was wry—almost subtly pleased. "You did what you had to," she said. "You made your choice. We'll just have to see if it was the right one."

She got up smoothly and left the room.

I was alone again.

.18.

She was pressed up against the wall of the reeking alley, her long silver hair thrown carelessly over one shoulder as she pushed the vampire away. He lunged at her, fangs out, but a nimbus of green energy swirled to life around her left hand, and she struck him hard across the face. The air between them skewed, and the vampire spun backward, dropping to one knee on the ground.

"Bitch!" His shaggy hair was matted with blood. He wasn't quite newly minted undead, but he was still relatively inexperienced—maybe only ten, twenty years since the "change," and still feeling the disorientation. He hadn't yet adopted the cold, dispassionate manner of the ancient undead—the terrifying absence of expression that signaled how bored they were with killing you.

"Oh, *please*." The older woman rolled her eyes. "I've been called a lot worse in my time, by things a lot more distressing than you, night child. Don't try to compete." She flashed a quick glance to the opposite corner of the alley, where a younger woman was doing her best to fend off two more vampires. "Tess, how are you doing?"

One of them struck the girl across the face, raking nails across her exposed cheek. She winced, then kicked him in the stomach, channeling enough force into the blow to spin him almost completely around. Then she kneed him in the groin, while disarming the vampire who was lunging at her from behind.

"Oh, just *fine*, Meredith. Things are—" She elbowed the second vampire in the mouth, and he swore, spitting out blood. "Peachy!"

"Good to hear, love." Meredith smoothed her leather jacket, then withdrew the athame from her belt. It was a very old blade—peerlessly crafted, with a pearled hilt and a single piece of flawless rose quartz encrusted on the guard. Runes swirled along the edge of the blade, glowing softly, like small stars.

"Let's finish this, shall we? I've an early morning meeting tomorrow, and I do hate to arrive in a bad mood."

The vampire sprang at her, pushing off the ground with the balls of his feet like a leopard. He flew through the air. For a moment, he seemed to hover in the darkness, the moonlight glinting against his pale skin and red-rimmed eyes. He was hopelessly lost in the hunger—acting stupidly, carelessly. Mages knew that hunger, too, although it was of a different quality. That feeling of being so locked within a spell, so filled with the power, that you could do anything— *be* anything. The thirst for that warm, cleansing fire that burned through your veins, a million times more powerful than the purest heroin. The euphoria of spellcasting.

Meredith skewered him in one smooth movement, reaching up with her athame and cleanly slicing open his chest. The iron whispered across his flesh, within him, *snnnick*, like a garment tearing, and then blood and viscera spilled out of his ruined form as he crumpled to the ground, screaming.

"I'm sorry," Meredith said softly. Her eyes betrayed no expression as she drew the athame across his neck, swift and clean. The blade was sharp enough to partially decapitate him.

The vampire stared at her, confused, as if she'd just said

something strange or funny. His left hand spasmed, and then the light vanished from his eyes. His head slumped forward.

Meredith wiped her blade—not on the vampire's clothes, but on the edge of her own jacket. Even now, she wasn't willing to defile a fallen body.

She turned, about to say something to Tess—

—turned, but didn't see the fourth vampire, the one who'd been crouching in the deep shadows of the alley, waiting. He held a long, heavy chain coiled between his fingers, making little *clinks* as he shifted position amid the garbage and scraps of newspaper. Too quiet for even Meredith to hear.

"Tess, are you—"

He was behind her in an instant. Tess looked up from her melee, about to respond to her teacher's voice, but terror froze her. She saw the chain glimmer, as if suffused with moonlight, as he wrapped it around Meredith's neck.

The older woman's eyes widened, just for a second—

—then he pulled the chain taught with a barely audible *snap*, like a book slamming shut, or an ornament dropping to the floor—the sound of life fleeing from its warm, huddled cell, the whisper of a soul straying—

—and Meredith's head snapped sideways.

The light left her eyes.

Tess screamed.

She raised both of her hands, and power—dark, graceful, obliterating—poured through her, out of her, in all directions, like a flood.

And she was gone.

The timecode on the video screen recorded a date: May 18, 2004.

The DVD ejected. Carefully, a hand reached out and placed it back on the shelf filled with security footage, stacks and stacks of DVDs and VHS cassettes, going back—lord, who knew how far? Sometimes it seemed as if the CORE's records stretched back to the very moment of creation, the parting of darkness and light. Antediluvian.

The flood.

Eyes stared thoughtfully at the blank screen.
"Damn."

So I was smoking. I was smoking in the west park-ing lot behind the lab, in that shady spot where I used to go with Derrick to eat Snickers and complain about men. Only this time, I'd purposely evaded Derrick so that I could be alone.

Alone and smoking. I felt like someone from a lesbian pulp novel. Derrick showed me one called *Lavender Love Rumble* once, and I almost choked on my milkshake from laughing so hard.

Now here I was, furtively tearing open my pack of Dunhills, momentarily savoring the brush of the golden foil as it crumbled between my fingers. You couldn't get Marlboros in Vancouver, which shouldn't have mattered—since technically I wasn't a smoker—but Derrick didn't know that sometimes I snuck a pack or two into my purse when we were visiting Seattle. I enjoyed the oral fixation more than the nicotine high, but like any girl who'd once been a bit heavy in her teens, I knew how to smoke. Derrick had never mastered the art, which led him to believe that he was a failure as a gay man. I explained to him that he only would have been a failure in the 1950s, but he was still pretty inconsolable.

I held the smoke in my lungs, enjoying the papery feel of it, the sudden tug and smooth, velvety shock of the cigarette doing its work. The wind outside picked up a bit, and I cupped one hand around the glowing cherry, using the other to pull my jacket closer around me. Just call me Beebo Brinker.

"Can I bum a smoke, Corday?"

I looked up, half expecting to see one of the lab techs, or maybe even Selena.

Instead, I saw Lucian Agrado.

I took a step back. "What the hell are you doing here?"

He raised his arms in a gesture of détente. "It's a parking lot, Tess. I don't need a keycard to get in."

As soon as he said the word "keycard," my eyes narrowed.

"You son of a bitch."

He stared at me. "What?"

"You *know* what, so don't *what* me, Lucian—" I gestured angrily with the cigarette, wishing I had my athame. "You stole my keycard!"

His lip curled a bit. "Are you accusing me of something?"

"I'm accusing you of being a big skanky pain in my ass. Now give me the keycard before I call security."

Now it was his turn to look mollified. "No need for that. I didn't steal anything, Tess. You dropped your card when we were in Patrick's room." He reached into the pocket of his jacket and withdrew the familiar plastic square.

I snatched it from him. "Oh, I *dropped* it, did I? Maybe I dropped it after you grabbed me from behind—which is cheating, by the way."

"I didn't know that we had rules and an end zone."

"You mean a blueline and hashmarks—this is Vancouver, after all. Even necromancers have to love the Canucks."

"Well, Trevor Linden's been playing for so long—he must have made some type of pact with the dark forces. You've got to stand up and salute that kind of commitment to necromancy."

I laughed—I couldn't help myself. "You know, when you're not holding court at your psychotic vampire club and scaring the hell out of me, you're almost halfway charming." I exhaled. Very Garbo. "Not that I care."

"Right. So can I?"

"What?"

"Bum a smoke." He grinned. "You know, you have to watch out for the early onset of Alzheimer's. I hear it's an epidemic among mages."

I stared at him. God, he was cocky. Wearing his svelte black coat, with blue jeans and those same army surplus boots, like he'd just gotten off work from the night shift at Costco. Like he wasn't a death-dealer.

Like you aren't dreaming about him.

I dutifully handed him a cigarette. He gestured for the lighter, but I just smiled.

"You're the one with all the badass power. Why do you need a lighter?"

"I don't like fire." His eyes darkened as he looked at me. "Neither do you, Tess."

Just for a moment, I felt his mind brush against mine— not an immense, crushing force, like Sabine's ancient consciousness, but a kind of feathery touch. Like the way your lover puts a hand on your back, ever so slightly, and leads you into a room, or the way a man sometimes helps you zip up a dress without saying anything, even though you know he's pleased. I felt it like that, and the surprising tenderness of it, the finger-brush-sway of contact, was a million times worse than Sabine's invasive power. It was an intimate rape, and I recoiled from it.

"You—" All of my shields were up instantly. I was already drawing power to myself, so much that it shimmered around me like a heat-haze, clumsy and visible but nonetheless reassuring. "You do *not* get to say things like that to me, Lucian. It's none of your fucking business what I'm afraid of, so stay the hell out of my mind unless I give you a goddamn written invitation. Are we clear?"

He looked confused. "I just want to know why, Tess. Darkness and fire."

I blinked. "What?"

"It's always darkness and fire with you. That's the image I get whenever I see you"—he glanced at my hand, still touching the cigarette—"whenever we touch. It's like I'm drowning in it, and so are you."

Darkness and fire.

"You can't just crack open my life and expect to read about every little neurosis. You're not entitled to that kind of—access."

"I don't want to do that, Tess." He gave a weird sort of shrug. "I just want to know why you're—like you are."

"And how's that?"

His face was a mystery. "Sad. Powerful. Angry."

I just stared at him. I didn't know what to say.

"Drowning," he said. "And it all comes back to darkness and fire. But I don't know why."

"Because it's none of your business."

"It's not about *business*." His eyes narrowed, but his expression wasn't necessarily angry—just strangely committed. "You're not a job, Tess, you're not *business*. I'm talking about the real you—"

"Okay, crazy stalker man"—I took another step back—"you don't know the first thing about the 'real me.' You're not my friend. The only thing I really know about you is that you scare the hell out of me."

"But I haven't done anything."

"You don't have to—you exist, Lucian. That's enough."

It was his turn to look pissed. "What's that supposed to mean?"

Crap. Let's just annoy the powerful necromancer, shall we?

"Whatever. It doesn't matter."

"Oh no, I get it." He scowled. "It's not me that you're frightened of, it's *my kind*. That's what you meant to say."

I shrugged. "Your words, not mine."

"Well, I might as well oblige, then. Wouldn't want to disappoint you."

Right—this is exactly the type of scenario you were trying to avoid, Tess. You've taunted Jim Stark, and now he's going to turn you into a zombie.

Lucian extended his hand palm-outward. I felt something— a kind of tug, similar to the feeling of the smoke in my lungs. But this was metaphysical. A coil of green energy blossomed between his fingers. It looked almost like a votive candle, only elemental flame wasn't supposed to look like that. And there was no heat. Just a dispassionate coldness, a sharp edge to the power that made me want to turn away. Necroid materia. I strengthened my shields, but ultimately I wasn't sure how to fend off this sort of attack.

We knew so little about each other. Mages and necromancers were opposite sides of the same occult rune, positive and negative forces whose tension basically propelled the universe along. Not in a creepy Zoroastrian way, but in a much more precisely physical and ontological sense. It was basic thermodynamics.

"You're so scared of my power," he said—but I was more scared of his face. It was entirely without feeling. "Don't you want to see it?"

"Let's not do this, Lucian," I said. Crap—where was Selena, or even Marcus? Someone must be feeling these vibes. Why wasn't anyone coming to investigate?

"Haven't you ever thought to ask yourself"—the blossom in his hand swirled, grew, becoming a tongue of impossible flame—"if I was afraid of *your* power? If 'my kind' isn't even more terrified of yours?"

"The truce between your side and ours has held since the Middle Ages, Lucian. Longer than the vampire pact." I kept my movements small, trying to smooth out my defensive energies so that they weren't so blazingly obvious. "Since Busirayne gave up his undead armies. Since Archimago turned to dust in his crypt. Storybook stuff. That's not going to change tonight, with us—is it?"

Sure, I knew the stories. Wild necromancers who raised corpse armies, plundering the ancient graveyards of the Britons, Celts, and Saxons. Templars and Knight-Hospitallers who fought on the other side, their cruciform broadswords gleaming with sunstruck materia and holy power. Who were we? Just two people in a parking lot, with our borrowed power and our forgotten legacies.

"Who are we to do this?" I demanded. "To change things?" I wasn't even sure what I was talking about anymore. Necromancy? Desire? Sex?

"Who are *we*, Lucian?" I asked.

"Close your eyes."

I felt my heart beating faster. He had more power than me—that much was obvious. All I understood about necromantic magic was that it was viral, destructive, trafficking in curses and macrophages. It was about unraveling, obliterating, separating chains of DNA, tearing phosphate from sugar, guanine from adenine. He could rip me to shreds, and what could I do to stop him?

"What—"

"Close your eyes," he repeated.

I don't know why I listened. It wasn't trust, or even fear, but something else. But I did as he asked. I closed my eyes.

When I opened them again, he was gone.

I was silent for a while, trying to get my trembling under control. Finally, I finished my cigarette and went back inside.

I never said anything to Derrick.

The MCD firearms expert was a short, plump guy named Linus, who wore horn-rimmed glasses and always seemed to be chewing on a wad of gum. People who didn't know him very well often thought that he was clinically depressed, but he actually just had an exquisitely deadpan sense of humor. He would sound positively bored as he described the annihilative power of an AK-47, or ask me what I wanted for lunch after immediately demonstrating what a hollow-point bullet could do to a human femur.

At present, he was test firing a gun into a water tank. That way, he could study the rifling marks that the bore of the gun imprinted on the bullet—what were called "lands" and "grooves." I knew very little about ballistics, not just because I was relatively untrained in the area, but because I hated guns. I always had. I'd trust my athame before I trusted a nine any day.

"Hey, Linus," I said, waving to him. "How's tricks?"

He reached into the tank to retrieve the bullet, then looked up and smiled. Not a wide smile, like you might expect from a friend who was happy to see you, but the sort of casual smile that was always tough to read. "Hey, Tess. How's it going?"

"It's been better."

"Yeah, I heard that you and Marcus had a run-in today."

Shit. I guess news traveled fast.

"Oh—yeah?" I tried to keep my voice neutral. "You heard about that already?"

"I'm sure that people in Siberia have heard about it already. You know how incestuous this lab is."

I rolled my eyes. "True. Guess I shouldn't let it bother me."

He raised an eyebrow. "Being forcibly put on leave? I'd sure as hell let that bother me—if I was the one getting screwed over."

I breathed a sigh of relief. At least he was on my side.

"So—any cool weapons coming through the pipeline?"

He looked at me slyly. "I figured you'd want to know about that Browning Hi-Power that we recovered from the Vailoid demon who attacked you."

"I was curious," I admitted. "You don't have to tell me anything if you don't want to. It's your choice."

"I'm not a complete asshole, Tess." He met my gaze, and I was momentarily surprised by the flash of strength and defiance in his watery blue eyes. "I still trust you, and as far as I'm concerned, you're still on the job."

I sighed. "Thanks, Linus. That means a lot."

"So—" He dug through some papers on his desk, and came up with a set of scribbled notes. "The gun was a Browning Mark III, top of the line. Available to civilians, but expensive. Not the kind of piece you'd see an amateur criminal carrying around, that's for sure."

"There was nothing amateur about him."

"Yeah, I figured that." He glanced at his notes. "The thing was loaded with Black Talon hollow points."

"Those are like Glazer-Safety rounds, right? They blossom on impact?"

Linus made a face. "Even worse—they send little bits of shrapnel and sheared-off bone throughout your body. You could get hit in the shoulder, and have a piece of metal embedded in your leg. And they're a bitch to remove—the copper jacket around the bullet shreds apart, and doctors get cut up on the shards."

"So he meant business," I said, feeling more than a little sick.

Linus gave me a grim look. "He had thirteen rounds, and we found another ammo clip that was left behind. He meant to take all three of you out. It's lucky as hell that you managed to get that gun away from him."

"You don't have to tell me that."

"Now, why a Vailoid demon felt the need to carry a gun—that's a mystery I still haven't figured out. I mean, he's got claws that can dice you into tiny pieces. It doesn't seem like he'd need any firepower."

"I think whoever sent him wanted it to look like a robbery, or an execution-style killing," I said. "Something for the cops to handle, but nothing that would arouse the CORE's suspicion."

"Unfortunately, I can't tell you much about the gun. It doesn't match up with anything in the Drugfire or ATF databases."

"Did you manage to lift a clear print off the handle?"

"We found a smudged print, a partial, which is actually pretty lucky—normally you can't get shit off a gun stock. Didn't tell us a whole lot, though. His name's Kor'Vel. Petty criminal—mercenary. He had a rap sheet a mile long, including several murder charges that he'd been 'cleared' on, which seemed like a minor miracle."

I sighed. "It's like an old-demon's network sometimes—everyone always getting pulled out of the fire by someone more powerful."

"I wish I had more to tell you."

"Don't worry about it, Linus. You've told me plenty. And I'm really grateful for"—I tried to keep from blushing—"you know."

"Yeah." He grinned. "I know. It's no problem."

I left the firearms lab and walked toward the morgue, where my next challenge lay. At least one person still trusted me. Now I was going to see exactly how far I could push my luck.

.19.

The autopsy room was cold and nearly silent, except for the faint, relaxing strains of hip-hop that drifted from Tasha's iPod. Aesop Rock—"None Shall Pass." Tasha loved her anarchist rap, and it seemed somehow fitting that she was dissecting murder victims while listening to Rock's riffs on class prejudice and police brutality. Her stereo sat on a counter next to a jar filled with organ slices—a "scrap jar," as it was called. Tasha kept histological samples of victims' organs for our toxicology lab, in case they wanted to test something after the fact. She usually held on to the jars, which were filled with a formalin solution to preserve the organs, for up to a year after the body left the morgue. "They're like human piñatas," she told me once. It gave me chills.

There were three bodies lying on steel tables, and with a horribly queasy feeling I recognized Cassandra as the body in the middle. She was covered by a white sheet, but I could still see the topmost part of the Y-incision at her shoulders. Her eyes were closed, and the blue veins in her skin were darker and thrown into relief—a change that happens in the early stages of decomposition. Her hair was ash-blond against the cold metal, but the roots were still gray. She must have colored it just before she died. For some reason, that thought made me want to cry.

The Vailoid demons on either side of her were in much worse condition. The one on the right was a bloody, pulpy mess—I think he must have been the one I found on the desk with his ribs and chest plate exposed. The other body had the flattened-out appearance of someone who had fallen from a great height, and the right half of his face was crushed. If Cassandra had done that much damage before they killed her, I shuddered to think of how powerful she must have been. The waves of strength that I'd sensed from her earlier had been accurate.

Tasha looked up from her desk—which was on the far side of the autopsy chamber, well away from all the blood—and smiled. She had a proper office away from the morgue, but she preferred to do most of her work here because it was quieter.

"Hey, Tesseract." She waved. "What brings you to the crypt?"

I smiled weakly. "Just wanted to see if you'd finished the post exam for Cassandra Polanski."

She nodded. "Just finished up with the two Vailoids as well. Anything specific you wanted to know?"

"Well"—I sighed—"I suppose you've heard all about my fall from grace by now—it's all over the lab."

She smiled. "I have no idea what you're talking about, Tess. You know me, though. I never read my e-mail."

"Thank you," I said simply.

"No trouble at all. It's nice to see a friendly face anyhow. I was just starting to feel a bit hermetic in here. Hardly any visitors of the living persuasion for most of the day."

I shook my head. "I don't envy you this job, Tasha."

"Ah, it's not so bad. I get my lab technicians to do most of the really unpleasant stuff." She grinned characteristically. "They know to be nice to me, or else they could end up scraping out someone's duodenum and lower bowel."

I made a face.

"So who would you like to hear about first? The woman, or the two Vailoids?"

Suddenly, the mirth was gone. I sighed. "Tell me about Cassandra."

She lowered the sheet covering Cassandra's body, and I saw that her Y-incision was traced carefully around the large chest wound that I'd seen earlier. It looked almost like a shotgun blast at first. The wound track was wide and had a stellate pattern: the star-shaped burst of an entrance wound left by a close-contact gunshot. Normally, you'd see that type of wound only on the head, where the skin was stretched tight—escaping gasses from the gun's blowback got caught in the thin layer between skin and bone, and the result was a gaping entrance wound.

But this wound was in the chest, and there were no powder burns left behind, and no "tattooing," or burst blood vessels, like angry red pockmarks. As I looked closer, I realized that it only looked like a gunshot wound because it was so forceful. It was more likely that something large and sharp had actually *ripped through* Cassandra's chest, making the star-shaped pattern as it was pulled out. It was actually an exit wound—the violent mess left behind when the weapon, whatever it might have been, was torn away.

"We took a sample of the vitreous fluid from her eyes," Tasha said. Her voice was oddly gentle. She must have known what I was feeling. "Judging by the potassium levels, she died about twelve hours ago—shortly before you found her." She gestured to the deep cuts on her body. "These were made by a thin, double-edged blade. I'm guessing the Vailoid demons used their claws. Some of them are up to eight inches deep—they left marks on the bone. Her liver and spleen were both lacerated."

I remembered the Vailoid demon who'd attacked me, how he'd flexed his long claws and smiled. He could have easily carved me up that way.

"She died, rather obviously, of this chest wound," Tasha said, probing the surface of the wound with her gloved fingers. "It looks like a combination of blunt force and something sharp. The weapon cut through the muscle and shattered the chest plate, breaking four of her ribs and leaving bone fragments in the intercostal space. It perforated her right lung, then pierced the pericardium shielding the heart. Her left subclavian artery was completely transected. That artery is below the clavicle, and comes directly off the arch of the aorta. It's a major source of blood for the upper body, including the lateral and posterior neck and shoulder."

"So she hemorrhaged," I said.

Tasha nodded. "Death by exsanguination: massive internal bleeding." She sighed. "I heard that she had a daughter."

"A niece, actually. Her name's Mia. Her parents died, and Cassandra was the only person left to take care of her."

Tasha shook her head. "That's horrible. I hope that little girl never sees what happened to her aunt. Hell of a thing to explain to someone."

"I'll make sure she never sees it," I said coldly.

"Well, this woman put up a hell of a fight—you can tell her that much. No defensive wounds on her palms either, so she wasn't just trying to ward off the blows. She was tearing right through those demons, even as they did the same thing to her. In the end, I imagine they only killed her first because she was outnumbered."

"So what happened to the Vailoids?"

"Well—" She gestured to the demon whose chest had been opened up. "Bachelor Number One didn't have a pleasant exit. Something literally exploded through his thoracic cavity with the force of a bomb."

She lifted the sheet, and I saw a mangled mess of tissue around the Y-incision. It resembled ground beef.

"I barely needed to open him up, since his chest was already a gaping maw. Ribs were completely shattered. The vertebral column was pretty much pulverized, and the thoracic vertebrae were just gone. They're probably decorating the floor of the office where they found his body. The organs were liquefied."

"So instant death," I said. "Like a bunch of C-4 going off in your chest cavity."

"Pretty much. He was dead before he hit the floor. I'm assuming that she hit him with some sort of ultradeadly magic, since he blew up from the inside. There are some necroid energies that can do that, but I wouldn't want to try them."

"Cassandra would have had access to some powerful magic," I said. "Which is why it seems strange that the Vailoid demons were able to sneak up on her in the first place. You'd think she would have seen them coming."

"Only takes a second to lose your concentration."

I nodded. "That's true."

Tasha walked over to the second Vailoid demon. "Now, this guy is even more interesting, if you can believe it."

"He's a bit of a mystery," I said. "He jumped out of a fourteenth-story window *after* he'd killed Cassandra. I assume he'd rather die than be captured."

Tasha looked skeptical. "I'm not entirely sure that he jumped."

"You think he was pushed?"

"Come here and take a look—I haven't sewn the top of his skull back on yet, so we've still got easy access to his brain." She twisted off the skullcap carefully, and it came apart with that characteristic sucking noise.

Tasha peeled back the dura tissue with her gloved hands, gently probing the surface of the Vailoid demon's brain. I could see a large mass of blood in the brain tissue near the base of the cerebellum—some kind of hematoma.

"There's bleeding in the subarachnoid space," Tasha pointed out, "between the arachnoid and the pia mater. The pia mater is the inner covering of the brain, beneath the periosteal and meningeal layers. It's called the 'tender mother,' because it's the innermost covering of the brain." She pointed to a spiderweb-type layer of tissue, which was covered with blood. "This is the arachnoid, which is another protective layer—and separating this part of the brain from the pia mater is a cavity filled with cerebrospinal fluid, called the subarachnoid space. As you can see, there's a lot more blood in here than anything else."

I felt an eerie sense of déjà vu as I stared at the blossom

of red. "This type of hematoma—it's similar to the brain injury of the vampire that we had in here last week. A subarachnoid hematoma. Right?"

"It's exactly the same," Tasha said. "Which is why I said that this body was even more interesting. This demon may have fallen from fourteen stories, but that's not what killed him. He died of massive intracranial bleeding."

"Is there any way that he could have lived for a few moments after the bleeding started?" I asked. "Maybe he lost motor control and fell through the window by accident." It sounded lame even as I said it.

"It's possible, but doubtful. He would have blacked out very quickly. I don't think even the weight of his body falling against the window would have been enough to shatter it." She adjusted the sheet covering his body, and I saw a number of lacerations on his neck and shoulders. "I found glass embedded pretty deep within these cuts. He must have hit that window at a high velocity."

That trace of power that I'd felt, back at SemTec Labs—it hadn't been coming from Cassandra. She would have already been dead. Instead, I'd felt the power of whoever was left behind.

"I also found some fibers in the neck wound, during the gross exam," she added. "I sent them off to Trace about an hour ago."

"What kind of fibers?"

"Indeterminate. Kind of glossy, though. Maybe acrylic?" She glanced at her notes. "We won't know until we look at them under microscopy."

I nodded slowly. "So this mystery person—they killed the remaining Vailoid demon with a massive brain injury, then pushed him out the window, hoping that the fall would cover up the suspicious internal injuries. And maybe they even left a few fibers behind for us to track."

"They needn't have bothered with the staged suicide, though," Tasha said. "Vailoid demons have a much thicker skull than humans. Their occipital protuberance—that bony ridge on the back of the skull that's more pronounced in men—is twice as large, and acts like a spiny sort of armor. Their cranial bones are especially tough, and even a nose-dive onto the concrete, fourteen stories below, shouldn't have shattered the skull."

With a single, sharp tug, she pulled down the flap of skin behind the demon's ears, reflecting the surface of his skull. It was jagged and spiny, not smooth like a human skull. It was also very much intact.

"As you can see, the skull is clean. No fractures. Not only didn't the fall kill him, but his brain damage wasn't caused by any sort of head trauma. It's the same as the vampire. This hematoma was caused by something different. Some kind of psychic force, maybe."

"So we've got a murderous telepath," I said. "Great."

"That's all I can think of."

"Did D-AFIS come up with any info on either of the demons?"

"We matched their prints, yeah. And you won't believe this." Tasha shook her head. "They were cousins. L'askor and D'alashar. They worked together as petty mercenaries— it was a family affair."

"I'll bet they've got a friend named Kor'Vel, too."

"Who's that?"

"The demon who originally attacked me. I imagine that someone's contracted this Vailoid mob family to do their dirty work."

"So you think maybe the vampire got in their way some-how?"

I pulled my jacket tighter, shivering from the cold of the autopsy chamber. "I haven't figured that part out yet."

"Well, someone's going to have to check out his domi-cile." Tasha looked at me meaningfully. "Might be some clues there. I doubt that Marcus has gotten around to dusting the place for prints."

I smiled carefully. "That seems like it would be pushing it. Marcus is already watching me closely. I shouldn't even be here—I should be sitting at home, drinking cheap sherry and watching cartoons, while my career disintegrates."

"Well, Marcus isn't always right. And we can't always follow rules to the letter, now can we?" She shrugged. "Sometimes the only way to crack a case wide open is to bend the rules a bit. If we'd stayed with tradition, we'd never have DNA testing, or even fingerprinting."

"Things change," I said.

"Yeah. And we've got to change with them. You can't let Marcus hold you back. I know I wouldn't."

"And if it means losing my job?"

Tasha smiled. "I guess," she said coyly, "it all depends on how close you're willing to get to the fire."

"How close would *you* be willing to get?"

Her eyes shone. "You know the answer to that."

20

Ben Foster controlled the DNA lab. He was a young, acerbic, blond-haired guy whose natural baby face made it impossible to guess his age. I could see him through the window now, delicately inserting a vial of clear fluid into a long glass tube—the injector port of the gas chromatograph. The GC was a device used for breaking materials into their separate chemical compounds. A rush of inert gas pushes the substance along the glass tube, and then a sensitive detector picks out the chemical compounds by seeing which ones emerge first. As each chemical "crosses the finish line," so to speak, it gets analyzed and included within a detailed material breakdown sheet.

Across the hall was the fiber analysis lab, which was where I needed to be. Cindeé (don't call her Cindy) was the queen of that domain. Unlike Ben, who might just grunt and point to the scanning electron microscope when he wanted you to look at something, Cindeé would talk your ear off. She had curly red hair that was always tied back with something to keep it from shedding, and her outfits had become the stuff of legend within the crime lab. Currently, she was wearing a white lab coat, but underneath that I could see a diaphanous red top, a black skirt, and knee-high boots. I was instantly jealous of her footwear.

"Tess!" Her smile lit up the room as she saw me come in. "Girl, I haven't seen you in ages! My God, I heard about your run-in with those Vailoid demons. Nasty little SOBs, aren't they? Hope you're okay? Are you okay? You *look* good."

This was how Cindeé usually communicated—at a speed slightly more manic and informative than most human beings.

"Well, nothing's tried to kill me in the past couple of hours. So that's definitely an improvement."

"You field agents—you always get to see all the action. Poor me, I'm always stuck in this hermetically sealed laboratory, staring at pubic hairs and pieces of frayed nylon rope all day."

"That would be a bizarre combination," I said, struggling to smile.

"Oh, but you should have seen—earlier today—Sarah Cooper, you know, the OSI-2 that Selena had put on disciplinary leave because she screwed up the chain of custody on that Spanish warlock case? Well, *she* brought in this piece of rope—wanted me to look at the cordage characteristics, maybe crosscheck it with our knots database and see who might have tied it. Well, turns out, the damn thing was enchanted. It strangled this poor man *all by itself*." Her eyes went wide. "Damn near strangled me, too, until I had it neutralized and sent to the contraband lockup. But really, that's the most excitement I've had all day. Until now, that is."

"Why? Because I'm here?"

"Well, I'm assuming you want to hear about those yellow fibers—you know, the ones we found embedded in the left jugular vein of that Vailoid demon?"

I swallowed. "Are you—looking at those right now?"

Cindeé gave me a mischievous look. "Come on now, Tess. Just because you've been removed from the case doesn't mean that you're not curious as hell. I can see it in your eyes. Isn't that why you're paying me this little visit?"

I looked around guiltily. "I could have just been dropping by to say hello. I mean, we haven't seen each other—"

"Cut the theatrics, Madame Butterfly, okay?" She smiled sweetly. "I know you don't give a camel's hump about how I'm doing, or how long it's been since we've seen each other—which is almost two weeks, to be exact, since I switched from day shift. I was having scheduling conflicts with my Bikram yoga class, and thanks for asking." Her smile never wavered. "I know you, Tess. You're all about the evidence. But that's why I like you. There's no pretending, no bullshitting—you're just here to get the job done, and you don't get caught up in the petty politics of this lab. In that way, sweetie, we're a lot alike."

I nodded. "You're right, and I'm sorry. I do need your help. I need to know if you've identified those fibers."

"Oh, I haven't just identified them, sugar. I've pinpointed them down to the polymer—I've got an exact, irrefutable match."

I stared at her. "Really?"

"You bet your ass I do. You see"—she walked over and adjusted the SEM—"these are the Holy Grail as far as fibers are concerned. Hardly anything's natural anymore, and even organic fibers like wool and cotton are usually full of dyes, delustrant particles, and all sorts of other chemical additives that make pinpointing their exact source nearly impossible."

"But you said that these fibers are different," I pressed. "They're unique?"

"No fiber is *totally* unique, Tess. You know that." Her smile was pure honey.

I knew that Cindeé was enjoying this, and I really needed to hear what she was about to tell me next—that's the only reason I didn't scream at her. I just kept smiling, and said, "Uh-huh?"

"Certain fibers," she continued, like an unstoppable train, "have handy little characteristics that make them more recognizable—but even then, only within a larger group. Natural cotton fibers, for instance, have a small cavity inside the core—called a lumen—that we can see with microscopy. Most synthetic polymers have spherulites, which are these teeny-tiny little globes filled with needles that all line up perpendicular to the outer surface. And then"—her smile was triumphant—"there's silk."

My eyes widened. "Is that what the fibers are? Silk?"

"Have a look-see yourself." She gestured to the microscope.

What I saw through the lens resembled a thick yellow rod filled with small, shimmering triangles.

"Those little triangles that you see," Cindeé supplied, "are highly reflective molecules. They're what give silk and satin that characteristic shimmer. Often, you'll see delustrant particles that the manufacturer has added—they dull the fabric slightly, so that it doesn't look so radioactive. But this sample doesn't have any delustrant."

"So it's supposed to be this shiny?"

"Or it was made before delustering fabric was common practice."

"Huh." I looked at her. "You think it's old?"

"Oh yeah. Old and *rare*."

"Silk?"

She grinned. "Not just any silk, Tess."

I rolled my eyes. "I was waiting for this."

"Are you familiar with the *Antheraea assama*—the Muga silkworm?"

I sighed. "Do I look like I'm familiar with it?"

Cindeé's smile widened. "Let me explain, then."

"Of course. I can see you're just dying to."

"Most silk worms are domesticated. They're fed a steady diet of mulberry leaves, and the cocoons that they produce are harvested into silk. They're not actually worms, you see, but caterpillars. It takes about five hundred silkworms to produce less than one kilogram of raw silk."

"Yes, yes, I'm sure the process is very barbaric." I saw the warning look in her eyes, and exhaled. "And . . . you're going to tell me more about it."

"No—I promise to get to the point." She adjusted the

microscope again. "Some of the rarest and most-sought-after types of silk come from the *undomesticated* silk worms—it's called wild silk, and it's usually produced only in very small geographic areas, within tiny villages."

"And this is wild silk."

She smiled. "Only the rarest kind. It's Muga silk—imperial yellow. Because it isn't treated with any synthetic dyes, the silk retains the natural color of the moth's cocoon. *Muga* means brown or amber in the dialect of Assam, India, which is where one hundred percent of the Muga silk is produced—specifically, in an area called the Brahmapautra Valley. You won't find it anywhere else. According to legend, this yellow silk was the kind that could only be worn by the Chinese emperor—it was a symbol of royalty."

I shook my head. "So you're telling me that whoever killed these Vailoid demons—he, or she, just happened to be wearing something made of an exotic silk that can only be found in some tiny part of India?"

"In Assam—yes."

"Jesus."

"You're telling me. Normally, silk doesn't transfer well—unlike wool, it isn't prone to shedding. But over time, worn areas of fabric can shed, even if the weave is relatively tight. And Muga silk is especially resistant. An article of clothing made from it might last fifty, maybe even seventy-five years, before it began to disintegrate."

I nodded. "And if those fibers were over fifty years old, that would explain the lack of delustrant particles. They wouldn't have been added back then. Especially not in some village in Assam."

"Whoever you're looking for, then," Cindeé said, "is fond of old things and world travel. Someone who's been all over the globe—a collector, maybe?"

"And did you find these fibers on both of the Vailoid demons?"

Cindeé shook her head. "No—just the second one, the one who took the swan dive out the fourteenth-story window."

Obviously. The demon that the killer dealt with personally. He must have been some kind of loose end. Or perhaps it was merely a crime of opportunity. The killer heard us, panicked, saw the window, and killed the second Vailoid demon so that there'd be no chance of us interrogating him. But Tasha had said that a psionic blast of that magnitude would have to depend on proximity. The killer would have been very close to the demon. Close enough for some fibers to rub off.

"Still," I said, "we should have found these fibers on the vampire's body, too. If this is the same killer, that is."

"Maybe he got sloppy," Cindeé said. "Selena mentioned that the place where you found the vampire was swept clean—practically gleaming. The killer covered his, or her, tracks. But maybe, with this crime scene, there just wasn't time. Things got panicky, and some fibers were transferred by accident. Happens all the time."

"So we're lucky," I said. "We've got some evidence that we didn't have before. But we're still facing a veritable jigsaw puzzle that doesn't make any sense. Vailoid demons, vampires, a teenage girl, blood, DNA—and the only person who I really thought might be a suspect was killed last night."

"You mean the aunt? Cassandra Polanski?"

I nodded. "So where does that leave us?"

"It leaves you pretty much humped. And it leaves *me* with a huge backlog of work to get through. I'll be drowning in cuticles and medullas for the rest of the night, while you're out looking for our mystery killer."

I smiled. "You've helped me narrow it down, at least. I owe you a million, Cindeé. Thanks for this."

"Aw, who's counting?" She shrugged. "You just take care of yourself. Don't go doing anything stupid."

As I ran back down the hallway, I heard her yell after me: "And watch out for Chinese emperors! They're suspect number one!"

21

Mia stared out the window, not speaking, as Highway 1 rolled by. She seemed to be two different people. One person was angry and irritable, and the other was completely closed off, silent. I kept trying to encourage the first personality, since anger was better than nothing. But I knew that her grief wasn't something negotiable.

Antoine de Saint-Exupéry was right when he wrote *The Little Prince*. "It is such a secret place—the land of tears."

"You know, Mia," I said, "maybe after we pick up the stuff from your aunt's house, we could all have a sleepover. You, Derrick, and I. The CORE has a nice little apartment picked out for you—someplace you'll be safe and protected. We could stay up and watch videos or something—"

"Oh, can we braid each other's hair and talk about boys?" I could feel her eyes burning into me from the backseat. "Maybe you're forgetting that someone murdered my guardian today. Or were you gonna get around to the whole therapy thing after we make s'mores?"

"We could invite Lucian," Derrick chimed in. "I'm sure

he'd be up for a sleepover, since according to Tess, he's like an Aztec god."

My cheeks went red. "Derrick, I told you about that dream in confidence—"

Mia wasn't paying attention. I could have talked about my imaginary sexcapades for hours, and it wouldn't register with her. She was just—elsewhere.

"Everything's going to be okay—" I began.

"It's not."

"Yeah—it's going to be. You can stay with me for now. Derrick and I will take care of you until we can figure out something more permanent."

"I'm not a baby. I don't need someone to take care of me."

I turned around to look at her. "Mia, I'm not your babysitter. I'm your protector now. I'm the one who's going to look out for you."

"That was my aunt's job, and she's dead. I don't need another mom." She wouldn't meet my gaze. She just kept staring out the window.

"Leave it, Tess," Derrick said. "We've all got to process this. You can't just swoop in and fix everything."

"I wasn't swooping! I never said—"

He stared at me levelly.

I sighed. "Fine. This has been"—I breathed in deeply—"a very bad day. Let's just concentrate on picking up your stuff."

"We're too late," Mia said coldly. "My house is probably getting turned over by demons right now. They're stealing my Britney CDs and trying on all of my clothes."

"Yes," Derrick said tartly, "your house is being ransacked by gay homosexual demons, even as we speak."

I closed me eyes and said nothing. Then an idea came to me.

"There might be a way to tell," I said. "But I'll need your help, Mia."

"Oh, great. Like I haven't been tortured enough tonight."

"*Look*, young lady—" I glared at her. "And I realize that I'm turning into my mother as I say this, but I want you to listen to me. These last two days have been terrible for all of us—for you, most of all. I can't imagine what you're feeling right now, and I'm not going to pretend that it's all going to be fine. Because it won't. We both know that—all of our lives have changed tonight, and nothing's ever going to be like it was again."

Mia scowled at me, but said nothing.

"Right now," I continued, "my priority is protecting you. But I need your cooperation for that. I can't look out for you if you keep firing sarcastic remarks back at me. I can't do this without your help. So can we please just try to get through the next couple of hours? Then you can feel however you like—you can even hate me. You probably already do."

She sighed. "I don't hate you, Tess."

"So will you let us help you?"

She nodded. "I'm just—" Her eyes were bright with pain for a moment—then the veil returned. "I'm just really tired," she whispered. "And I want to go home, but—nobody's there anymore."

"We're here," Derrick said. "You've got us."

"Okay." She nodded slowly. "Okay—what do you want me to do?"

"It's called scrying."

"I think I'm a little young for that, Tess. Fifteen will get you twenty, remember?"

I rolled my eyes. "It's a form of long-range vision."

"What, like with a crystal ball?"

"We don't need a crystal ball, or any other Roma stereotype. Just our eyes—and a bit of a materia boost." I looked at her. "Which is where you come in."

"What's materia?"

"Like heroin for mages," Derrick said, not taking his eyes off the road.

"Don't listen to him. Materia is like a natural conductor. And you"—I smiled awkwardly—"well, think of yourself as a big lithium battery—"

"*Oh* no. I'm not going to be your Energizer Bunny." She frowned. "Okay, that came out wrong. But you know what I mean!"

"It won't hurt, Mia. You have a lot of untapped power, and I just need to borrow some of it for a few seconds."

"Is that wise?" Derrick asked.

"Well, at this point, could it really hurt?"

He shrugged. "I guess not."

"Look," Mia said, "you still haven't explained any of this magic crap to me yet. I don't know what the hell's going on."

"I know this is all confusing, but I promise it will only take a second. Then once we get back home"—I paused—"I mean, once we get back to the lab, I can tell you whatever you want to know. The whole history of magic, with footnotes. Whatever. Your choice."

Of course, I didn't know that for sure. Once we got back to the lab, I might never see Mia again. But I had to at least try to reassure her.

Mia sighed. "Well—I guess. As long as it won't hurt."

"Will it hurt?" Derrick asked.

"*No*. Of course not."

A little, I mouthed to him.

"I saw that!" Mia glared at me.

"Sorry." I undid my seatbelt. "Derrick, please don't crash the car. I don't want to go flying through the windshield."

"Okay, okay. I'll be careful."

I returned my attention to Mia. "I need you to hold my hand."

"But I'm already going steady with someone else." She grinned.

"Just do it, please."

She took my hand. Her fingers were surprisingly warm.

"Okay—now, just close your eyes, and think about your aunt's house."

"Are we going to teleport there?"

"Sorry, but no. Mages can't teleport. Some demons can, but you don't really want to meet anything that's capable of that."

"Magic seems pretty crappy if you can't teleport."

"Yeah, well, things are tough all over. Can you just close your eyes, please, and concentrate with me?"

"All right. Geez." She closed her eyes. "Do you want me to think about anything specific? Like, the bathroom, or something?"

I sighed. "Just think about the house as a whole. What it looks like, inside and out. Think about the yard, and the street that it's on, and the places around it."

"Sure. Done."

She was so brazenly confident. I wanted to tell her to be more careful, but after the night that she'd been through, she didn't need another lecture. Thirteen years old, both parents dead, and now her legal guardian was dead, too. The past week had just been one nightmare after another for her. And I wasn't even sure how to protect her. I mean, aside from throwing myself into the path of the next demon army, what was I supposed to do? What *could* I do?

I cleared my mind and tried to think about Mia's house. I'd seen it only once, but many of the details stuck—the drab paint job, the colossal living room window, the nicely manicured lawn. All I had to do was picture my parents' house in reverse, and everything became clear.

Now for the tricky part. Scrying was an acquired skill—some people were fantastic at it, but I wasn't one of them. My abilities in that area had always been passable at best. You've got to have a calm inner eye for this sort of work, and my inner eye has a nervous tic. Or maybe pinkeye.

I could see Mia's house in my mind, and feel her hand. Now it was time to connect the circuit. I only hoped that the result wouldn't be too explosive. I wasn't sure how much power Mia had locked away, or even what type of power it was.

I concentrated on my own power. I could feel it like a glowing core—a kernel of force inside my body. I couldn't draw materia from the earth—we were driving too fast for that—so this was all going to come from me. And the car. Surprisingly, Derrick's Festiva still had a few nonplastic parts that I could siphon organic materia from.

Slowly, carefully, I willed that power to travel up my arm, down my wrist, into my fingers, which were interlaced with Mia's. The sensation was like having pins and needles throughout your body, sharp and intense. But I kept it under control. Focusing it this tightly was always tricky, but the important part was to keep concentrating. If I let the power go now, it would explode in all directions, like an insane fire-cracker.

With the power humming in my fingertips, I squeezed Mia's hand, and *pulled* with my willpower. I wanted to draw some of her essence up through the connection, like water through a straw—but not too much.

Still, the result was intense. Mia gasped, and I felt a jolt of electricity pass through my arm. My own power flared up in a starburst. It was like someone had thrown a pile of kindling onto a bonfire, and now it was blazing up, wild and almost out of control. I struggled to keep a rein on it, pushing in mentally from all sides, focusing my concentration into a vessel that could contain the energy. It continued to smolder, but it was safe. For the next minute or so, maybe. I didn't want to gamble on my ability to control it for any longer than that. So I'd have to make this quick.

I let all of my senses fall over the image of Mia's house like a blanket. My consciousness permeated every atom in the walls, every drop of water sitting in the sink, every mote of dust and flicker of light against the windows. I smelled the grass, the dirt, the flecks of paint peeling from the front door. I heard the low whine of the fridge, the hum of the nearby computer. I smelled the years of accumulated detritus in the carpets, and over that, the tang of air freshener, clean laundry, and disinfectant.

With my heightened senses, I swept through every room in the house. My mind was a camera, and I was drifting through the building, searching. The feeling brought vertigo with it, but I kept that at bay. I needed to concentrate on genetic signatures of any kind—life signs, human or demon.

I didn't sense anything. I went over the house once again, but there didn't seem to be anyone there. Maybe the demons had come and gone, but if that was the case, I would have picked up on their residual traces. Everyone leaves a psychic footprint, and demons have a much bigger shoe size. I didn't feel anything like that. Either they were completely cloaked, or we might actually have beaten them to the house. I was really praying for the latter.

"Tess?"

I snapped back into focus, and the connection between Mia and me vanished. The air between our fingertips crackled momentarily with lost energy, then it was gone. Mia was staring at me like I'd just grown a second head.

"What was that?" she whispered.

"Like I said." I tried to keep my breathing under control, although it was very tempting to start hyperventilating right now. "It was scrying. I might be wrong, but it looks like the house is empty."

"I felt something—" Mia was looking uncertainly at me. "I think I saw what you saw. The house—everything floating. And I could feel—*you*. Or something like you, connected to me."

"I was borrowing your power. You must have felt the connection between us. That's normal, though."

She shook her head. "Nothing about that was normal."

"Okay, kids." Derrick was slowing down. "I'm getting off at this exit. We should be at Mia's house in a few minutes."

We drove through the familiar streets until we came to Mia's block. It was eerily quiet, just as it had been when we first visited. The house was still there, intact, and I gave silent thanks for that. The windows were dark.

We walked up to the front door—it was just the same as I remembered it, with the big brass knocker. Mia took out her key.

"So should we just—go in?"

I nodded. "I'll go first."

I pushed open the door. The house was warm inside, and smelled faintly of vanilla. Must be the air freshener.

"Our bedrooms are upstairs," Mia said.

We walked through the foyer and into the living room.

Everything seemed fine. There was a large flat-screen television against one wall, a computer desk in the corner, and a comfy-looking sofa with matching throw pillows. Cassandra may have been some kind of higher demon, but she was no slouch in the home furnishing department. This place was actually cozy. It made my apartment look like a skanky hotel room.

"Whoa," Derrick said suddenly. "Do you feel that?"

I stayed very still, trying to listen to my senses. Just barely, like a twinge of something almost imperceptible, I could feel something hanging in the air—something dark and powerful. An echo of a past event.

"Someone died here," Derrick said.

I looked at him sharply. "Are you certain?"

"No, but it sure feels like it."

"Someone died in my house?" Mia demanded. "When?"

"I'm not sure." Derrick walked slowly around the living room, idly touching things as he passed. "Give me a few minutes here."

"Is he feeling the force or something?" Mia asked.

"Shh." I gestured for her to take a step back. "Just let Derrick do his thing. Sometimes he can get a glimpse of things that have happened in the past. Certain events, like violent deaths, leave a kind of psychic residue—it's like throwing a rock into a pond. There are always ripples left behind. Derrick can pick up on them."

"She was here," he said suddenly.

I looked up. He was pointing at a space directly in front of the couch.

"Who was here?"

"Cassandra." Derrick's eyes were open, but unfocused. His pupils were dilated—like they'd been when he was trying to paralyze the Vailoid demon. Wherever his gift came from, he was drawing on it full-force right now.

"Of course she was here," Mia said. "It's her house."

"She was standing right here," Derrick continued. "And he was standing on the other side of the coffee table—facing her."

"He?"

Derrick walked over to the spot on the floor. "It's cold here," he said. "Like ice. Something happened. A violent power was unleashed—right here, in this spot."

He always sounded cryptic when he was profiling. "What kind of power?" I asked. "Are you talking about magic? Did Cassandra use some type of magic to stop an intruder—someone trying to kill her?"

"No." Derrick's voice had gotten soft. "He was only a boy." His eyes widened. "He was so frightened. He didn't know what to do. Didn't realize how powerful she was—what she was capable of. He only wanted to warn her—"

Only a boy.

The vampire's face flashed before me—the blond hair, the manic grin. The golden invincibility of youth. Even the undead could be children at heart.

"Sebastian," I said. "He was here. In Cassandra's house."

"Who's Sebastian?" Mia asked.

"The vampire who was looking for you—the one with your address. He must have come here—to what . . . ?" I frowned. "Derrick, you said that he only wanted to warn her. But what was he warning her about? Did he know that Mia was in danger? Was he trying to explain that to Cassandra?"

But Derrick was already staring at me, looking confused. The power had passed through him, like electricity through a lightning rod. He was tapped out.

"Here, hon." I guided him to an overstuffed chair by the couch. "Sit down. I know that profiling always takes a lot out of you."

He was slightly out of breath. "I'll be fine. The images were—confusing. I'm not sure if anything that I said made sense."

"It did." I folded my arms. "We're back to our very first premise—that Cassandra killed Sebastian. We don't know why yet, or even how, but we at least know that it happened here. Then she transported him to the alley, posed him—or maybe she got someone else to do it. That's why his aura was so faint, and the crime scene was so clean." I gestured to the living room. "*This* was the real crime scene. This is where Sebastian's life was actually snuffed out."

"But we still can't explain the vampire's injuries," Derrick said. "Cassandra didn't have the power to inflict that kind of neurological damage, right? I mean, if she did, don't you think she would have made short work of those Vailoid demons?"

"We don't even know what kind of demon—" The word came out before I could stop it. I stared at Mia in horror.

She didn't react. Her eyes scraped the ground, but she said nothing.

"Mia—" I began.

"Don't bother." She shook her head. "I kind of figured anyway. I mean, nothing else in my life is true, or real. Why should my aunt be any different?"

"She loved you, Mia."

"She wasn't even human."

"Neither are we," Derrick said softly.

Mia stared at him.

"He's right," I said. "Technically, Derrick and I are part-demon, too. A lot of people are." *You probably are,* I thought, but this time I kept myself from saying it. I could hear Derrick's speech about morality, about shades of gray. "Not all demons are evil," I said slowly. "It's complicated."

She didn't say anything.

"I'm—ah—going to go check out the kitchen," Derrick said. "You two can chill out in here for a while."

He disappeared into the next room.

Mia sat down slowly on the couch.

"Are you all right?" I cursed myself. "Sorry. Dumb question."

She shrugged. "You know, I've lived in this house for as long as I can remember. Seems like—God—forever, I guess."

"I know the feeling," I said.

"Yeah. Sure." Mia lay down on the couch, drawing her knees up to her chest. "You probably just think I'm a whiny brat with nothing to complain about."

"Are you kidding?" I shook my head. "Mia, you've got to

be the strongest person I've ever met. I mean, you've been through so much already, and you're still just taking it as it comes. I totally respect you for that."

She laughed softly. "I don't feel like I'm taking anything in a good way right now. Seems more like I'm freaking."

"That's perfectly natural."

"You my counselor now?"

"Mia." I raised my hands. "I don't know how to make this better. There's probably nothing I can say that will help, but I really am trying."

"I know." She looked away. "You and Derrick are both great. I don't even know why you're helping me so much. It's not like I deserve it."

"What are you talking about?"

"Oh, come on." She was staring at the wall—unable to look me in the eye. "The minute I showed up in that parking lot, all hell broke loose. Your lives have pretty much been shit—"

"Language," I said, although I knew it was useless.

She sighed. "Okay, your lives have been *extra-spicy* since I appeared. I mean, have you even slept at all for the past couple of days?"

God, she didn't know the half of it. I hadn't even told her about the vampires yet, or explained the fact that her powers—her *immense* powers, if I was right—were probably being held in abeyance by some kind of mystical retrovirus. Something told me that I wasn't going to be sleeping at all for the next week.

"I can manage," I said, shrugging. "It's you I'm worried about. You're a teenager, and your body—"

"Oh, lord, not the 'your body is a wonderland' speech. I know all about puberty, Tess."

"I'm sorry." It sounded like the stupidest condolence possible. Grief was a gaping hole in your life that no flowers or sympathy cards could fill. It was a mass of bloody scar tissue that people noticed, but politely declined to mention.

"It's no big deal anymore," Mia replied. "I'm used to death."

"Nobody ever gets used to it."

Finally, she looked me in the eyes. "I loved my aunt," she said. "She could be a real bitch—and yeah, I know, that's shitty language. But she could."

"I'll bet," I said.

"Yeah, she could drive me crazy. But she was the only parent I had left, and now she's gone. Completely gone." Her voice cracked. "And that's fucking stupid, and I don't understand it, and it sucks. She's never going to piss me off by calling me on my cell phone again. She's never going to come into my room without knocking, or make me potato salad, or warn me about boys. And she'll never sit on this couch again watching Home and Garden Television."

I smiled.

"It sucks." Mia seemed to collapse into herself. "It sucks that we die. And I hate it, and I even hate myself a little, but I can't just sit here and freak out. Even if I wanted to, we don't have the time, because crazy people are after us."

"Crazy demons," Derrick corrected, walking out of the kitchen. "Everything seems fine in there. Untouched. And if there were any demons here, I'm sure they've heard us all talking now, so there's no use trying to be stealthy."

"We might as well check out the bedrooms, then," I said.

I went upstairs, with Mia close behind. My mind was racing. I kept forming explanations for her, then deleting them and starting all over again.

We came to a hallway with three evenly spaced doors. The carpeting was soft under my shoes—a comforting shade of beige—and the stairs even had one of those plastic runners. This was definitely an older woman's house.

Together, we walked into Cassandra's room. It was fairly spacious, with a big, four-poster bed in the middle, resplendent with pillows, shams, and a down quilt.

"Now, here's a woman who knows how to make a bed," I said.

"Knew," Mia corrected softly.

I looked at her. "Sorry."

There was a Tiffany lamp on the nightstand, and an oak

dresser in the far corner. Everything was clean and tasteful. No dust anywhere. Cassandra had obviously been a Type A personality.

I got down on my hands and knees and looked under the bed—not an easy feat, since my ribs still ached from that last encounter with the Vailoid demon. But there was nothing there. Just darkness and dust.

"Mia, why don't you grab whatever you can carry from your room? Then we'll get out of here before the company arrives."

"Okay. I'm grabbing my flatiron, then."

Then she walked away, leaving me alone in Cassandra's bedroom.

I surveyed it once more—the comfortable furnishings, the cozy bed, the walk-in closet full of sensible shoes. Everything about Cassandra's life had seemed dull on the surface, but who knew what she was really up to? Why would a powerful demon sacrifice her life to save a human girl? I felt like I was shaking a box full of bones and rubies, trying to make something fit, trying to augur something. There was blood. There was magic. And now there was an empty house.

Mia walked back into the bedroom, and I tried to refocus. She had a knapsack slung over her shoulder—it was bulging.

"I've got everything I need," she said. "If I forgot something, we can always come back."

I didn't say anything.

"Tess—we can come back, right?"

"Of course." I tried to keep the fear out of my eyes. "But for now, I think it's time to go. We'll stop by the all-night grocery and pick up some stuff on our way back to the lab. Mia, do you have any dietary restrictions that I should know about?"

Derrick stared at me, openmouthed.

"What? It's a valid question. And no, I am *not* channeling my mother."

"I'm fine, Tess," she said, smiling slightly. "Whatever you get is fine. I'm not all that hungry anyway."

"All right. Let's go, then."

I felt a bit more relaxed now. Mia lagged behind, but I didn't tell her to keep up. She was going to have to say good-bye to this house in her own way. I couldn't rush her through that, and I couldn't do it for her.

We came to the living room again. "Is there anything you'd like to take from here?" I asked.

Mia shook her head. "It's all just stuff, right?"

Sometimes the clarity of a teenager was amazing. I nodded. "Yeah, I guess it is."

"Oh, wait—my green tank top." Mia reached into the couch cushions and pulled up a wrinkled shirt—a very small shirt, I noticed critically.

Then I saw it.

"Tess?" Derrick saw me staring intensely at the couch.

"Nobody move," I said. I reached into my purse, where I always kept a few forensic supplies, for occasions exactly like this. I pulled out a tape-lift and knelt in front of the couch. Lying on the black cushion, like a gleaming gold coin, was a single yellow thread. It gleamed against the dark upholstery.

I lifted the fiber and examined it beneath the tape. Visually, it matched the fiber that we'd recovered from the Vailoid demon's neck wound. I was willing to bet that it was Muga silk—just as Cindeé had described.

But where had it come from?

My mind was racing. Had it been there the whole time, and I just hadn't noticed it until now? Or had it rubbed off Mia's clothing? And if that was the case, then what was *she* doing carrying the fiber around? Where had it originated?

"Tess, it looks like your brain is about to explode." Derrick put a hand on my shoulder. I realized then that I hadn't told him about the silk fiber. I'd forgotten about it until this very moment.

I was about to answer when my cell phone rang.

Shit. I didn't want to take the call, but it might be Selena. I flipped open the phone and said, in that much-too-loud voice that usually comes out when you answer a cell phone: "Yes? Hello?"

I was surprised to hear the voice of Ben Foster, our DNA lab tech, on the other end of the line. He was the last person I'd expect to be calling me. "Tess? This is Ben calling from Serology."

"Hi, Ben—what's going on?"

"Well, we just got the results back from that blood sample—you know, the one you recovered from SemTec Laboratories?"

My heart skipped a beat. "Yes, I know the one."

"I would have told Selena first, but I can't seem to find her anywhere—and Marcus is away on assignment. He hasn't been answering his phone all day. The paperwork that I have might be old, but it lists you as the secondary investigator on this case." There was a pause. "Is that still accurate?"

I breathed a silent prayer to whatever deity might be listening. I had no idea how my name had gotten recorded as the secondary for that case, since I'd been breaking about twelve CORE rules just entering the lab in the first place. But somehow I was on a piece of paper somewhere. By a sheer clerical error, I was still in the loop.

"No—ah—that's right," I said. "You can tell me the results."

"You're not going to like them."

I exhaled. "Just tell me, Ben."

"Well, we compared that sample to the DNA that we took from Mia Polanski, and it's a match."

I frowned. "So the blood on the slide was Mia's?"

"That's not all. We detected an unusually elevated hematocrit volume. Nearly 0.9. The normal hematocrit volume for a healthy human is somewhere around 0.52. You see, hematocrit is the proportion of blood volume that's occupied by red blood cells. Usually, we just look at hemoglobin and mean cell volume, but—"

"Ben, that's not important!" I snapped. "Just tell me what it means. Why is the red blood cell count so high?"

"I was about to explain it," he sniffed.

I closed my eyes. "I'm sorry. Please continue."

"When we saw the hematocrit count, we did an ABO typing, along with a detailed RFLP analysis of Mia's DNA. That's why it took so long for me to get back to you—we had to probe her DNA using the old electrophoresis method, which is slower, but produces a more detailed result. With the Restriction Fragment Length Polymerase Test, you have to lay out the sample on an electrically conducive gel tract—"

"*Ben.*"

He sighed. I was completely disrupting the satisfaction he'd normally derive from explaining a complex technical procedure. "Her blood type was AB positive, but the RH factor was all messed up. So we tested for viral plasmids."

I could feel a sense of dread slowly moving through my chest and into my throat. I swallowed. "What kinds of plasmids?"

"We tested for the vampiric retrovirus." I heard him take a breath. "The test came back positive, Tess. Mia has been infected."

I held the phone and stared straight ahead. I didn't know what to say. Every muscle in my body felt paralyzed.

"Tess?" Mia smiled at me strangely. "Is something wrong?"

22

She sat on the edge of a steel counter, staring straight ahead while a nurse carefully swabbed the inside of her mouth. When the older woman was finished, she clicked the plastic cap closed around the swab—to protect it from contamination—then said quietly, "All right, sweetheart, I'm just going to take some hair samples now. It's uncomfortable, but it'll be over soon. You just lie back, okay?"

Mia did as she was told, lying back on the cold examining table while the nurse slipped on a pair of plastic gloves. I could see it all happening through the exam room window, and I turned away, before Mia could meet my eyes.

"How long have we known?" I asked.

Selena was absently moving a stir stick around in her Styrofoam coffee cup. She'd been stirring it for the last five minutes. She looked up at me, as if I'd only just magically appeared in the room that very moment, and her dark eyes seemed even more weary than usual.

"Ben logged the results shortly after he called you," she said. "He discovered that her red blood cell count was unusually high, so he did further testing, and the vampiric viral plasmids showed up. I don't understand the science any better than you, but obviously, Mia Polanski is an unusual case. She hasn't shown any outward signs of vampiric transition, but her blood is clearly V+. We're going to collect another sample to make sure that the first wasn't contaminated, but I'm pretty certain that the results will be the same."

I remembered the article that Derrick and I had read earlier on Interstitial Vampirism—halting the siring process.

> In some cases, the effects of the siring process can be delayed—perhaps indefinitely—due to immunological resistance within the host. Certain blood types, particularly B positive and AB positive, have been known to counteract vampiric viral plasmids.

Mia's blood was AB positive. And since she obviously had latent mage powers, that might explain why the transformation had been arrested. If Mia already had demonic viral plasmids—from some other source—in her bloodstream, the first contagion might very well be holding off the second. A microscopic battle between mages and vampires, being waged in the immune system of a thirteen-year-old girl.

"So far, her body is fighting off the viral plasmids," Selena was saying. "She seems to be producing natural antibodies. But we don't know how long, immunologically speaking, she'll be able to suppress the virus. We're going to have to do some more tests . . ."

But it still didn't explain who had infected Mia, or why. It couldn't have simply been a random act. I needed to talk to Lucian again. But if he *knew* about this—the urge to kill him was suddenly very powerful. Not that I'd survive, but I might at least be able to take him out in the process.

"Tess?" Selena was staring at me. "Where did you go?"

I shook my head. "Sorry. It's been a crazy couple of days, and my mind isn't exactly running on all four cylinders right now."

"Of course it isn't." She looked at me carefully. "So I'll repeat the question. Is there anything about this situation with Mia Polanski that you haven't told me? Anything that we might be missing?"

I felt my stomach constrict. Oh shit. I didn't think I could lie to her again. In fact, I didn't want to lie anymore.

So I told her.

My hesitant friendship with Mia. How she seemed connected with Eve somehow—a strange and painful link to my past—and how I wasn't even sure *who* I was trying to protect anymore. I even told her that I wanted to go to Sebastian's apartment, just to look around—to see if there was even the smallest clue that might link everyone in this insane tapestry together.

She was silent for a while. Then she folded her hands and looked at me.

"All right—which lecture do you want first? The ethical one, the legal one, or the one where I just plain break my foot off in your ass."

"It's your choice," I said, keeping my voice low. "I know that I screwed up. I know that I should have told you everything in the beginning—but honestly, Selena, everything I did was to protect Mia. I was looking out for her, not for me. And I know that Marcus would say the exact opposite—that if I'd really been concerned about her, I should have used CORE resources to protect her. But Marcus is a machine. I'm not like that." I exhaled. "I have to trust my instincts. Like you said, sometimes that's all we've got. And my instincts told me to act quickly and quietly. So that's what I did."

"And your instincts didn't tell you to notify your supervisor?" She raised an eyebrow. "They didn't suggest that, just maybe, I might have been able to help you? Or was I the enemy, too?"

I shook my head. "You were never the enemy. I just didn't want to drag you into this. If I lose my job—and I probably will—I don't want to take anyone else with me. Derrick's already implicated, but I can probably get him off on a technicality. The review committee might believe that I coerced him, that I took advantage of his trust. Which I pretty much did, so it wouldn't be a huge stretch."

"I know that kid," Selena said, "and he may be a pushover, but he's not an idiot. If he followed you, he did it because he thought you were right. It wasn't just blind trust, or loyalty. He did what you asked for exactly the same reason that I chose to look the other way"—her eyes darkened—"even when I knew that you were openly defying me. Even when I was pretty sure that you didn't trust me, which, coming from you, was pretty fucking ironic."

I looked down. "You're right."

Selena shrugged. "Yeah. But blind faith isn't always a positive quality in an agent, Tess."

I looked at her. "Selena, you're being too forgiving here. I screwed up, big time. I conducted my own private investigation of Mia and her family, without sanction from the CORE, and I continued to work on Mia's case long after Marcus had me pulled off it and put me on leave. I shouldn't even be in the lab right now. I should be sitting in my apartment, watching reruns of *Golden Girls*, or whatever else normal people do when they're given a paid vacation."

"Technically," Selena replied, "you're only getting half pay."

"Great." I rolled my eyes.

Selena leaned forward, resting her chin on her hands.

"Here's what I know," she said. "I know that you acted in Mia's best interests, even if you potentially endangered her in the process. I know that you refused to stop working on a case that you were personally involved with—and it's standard procedure to pull any agent from a case like that, but at the same time, any agent will fight that order kicking and screaming. It's their life, after all. You're no different." She idly tapped the desktop with her knuckles. "I know that you disobeyed Marcus and myself by continuing to work on this case, and you withheld information about your prior relationship with Mia. But as far as the evidence is concerned, I can't see any tampering with the chain of custody. You haven't done anything to actually obstruct the investigation. And your prior connection with Mia may not have been relevant at the outset, though it's certainly relevant now."

I said nothing.

"If it were up to Marcus," Selena continued, "we wouldn't even be having this conversation. You'd be out on your ass—no question about it. And you'd probably be under CORE surveillance for the rest of your life."

I kept my mouth shut.

"Lucky for you," she said, "it's not up to Marcus."

I finally allowed myself to breathe. "Okay." It didn't seem like the necessary answer, but I wasn't sure what Selena wanted me to say.

"That isn't to say that you aren't in trouble," she clarified. "You're most definitely on my shit list, and you know from experience that that is not a good place to be. If you thought Marcus was riding you, his methods pale in comparison to my own personal scrutiny."

I swallowed. "Okay," I said again. It was all I could say.

"I only watch two kinds of people—those who I don't trust, and those who I'm impressed with. In your case, it's a bit of both. So you're not off the hook, but I'm not about to reward you for being an asshole either. For now, let's just say that we're starting from square one. Complete and total honesty."

I nodded. "Of course. I've told you everything now. And I intend to tell you everything from here on in"—I sighed—"which won't be much, since I'm officially off this case. So I won't have anything to report, I suppose."

"You may not be on active duty," Selena said, "but that doesn't mean that I can't enlist your expertise as a consultant. Although if you go anywhere *near* that vampire's apartment, I will personally beat you down. Understand?"

"I read you, loud and clear." I said. Then I smiled crookedly. "You actually think I have expertise?"

Selena just smiled. "Now that I know what *you* know—" She reached into a drawer and pulled out a manila file folder, which she set on the desk. "Here's everything that *we* know. Pretty much."

She opened the folder, and a sheaf of pictures fell out—Cassandra, Mia, the crime scene photographs, Sebastian, and various other bits of evidence, all labeled and numbered by Selena's exacting hand.

"Mia Polanski was born May 4, 1992, in Kelowna, British Columbia. Her parents were Anthony Taylor and Christine Polanski, unmarried, and so she retained her mother's maiden name—also the surname of her maternal aunt, Cassandra Polanski. Anthony and Christine moved to Elder in 1994—I guess Kelowna was too big for them." She scanned farther down the file. "In 1998, both parents went missing. We have the missing persons report from the Elder RCMP."

"Let me guess," I said. "It was Cassandra who filed the report."

Selena nodded. "Cassandra was Mia's godmother and legal guardian—all the papers are accounted for, and they check out. Anthony and Christine were never found. The last place they were seen . . ." She squinted, trying to decode the RCMP officer's squiggly handwriting. "Looks like Anthony had a job at a computer repair shop, and he clocked out like normal around five thirty p.m. on Tuesday, May 2, 1998. Christine was the assistant coordinator for a nonprofit women's shelter, which has since been torn down and replaced by a video rental shop." Her eyes were flinty. "Government cutbacks."

"And she was seen at work as well?"

"She clocked out at the same time as Anthony—around five thirty p.m., according to her boss. They both shared a car, so one of them must have picked the other up. Then they just vanished."

"Obviously, it doesn't add up," I said. "And it strikes me as suspicious that all of this would happen so close to Mia's birthday. No mother that I can think of would abandon her only child when she was two days away from her sixth birthday."

"Oh, but it gets stranger." Selena flipped a page in the file. "After Cassandra died, we pulled all of her records. If anything, we just needed someone to claim the body, so that she could be interred. But it was the oddest thing." She looked at me. "The woman doesn't seem to exist before 1998."

I shook my head, angry at myself now for not being even

more suspicious of Cassandra and her demon heritage. "The year that Mia's parents go missing."

"We got quite the runaround from all of those paper pushers. Documents got lost. They were updating their record systems. A new birth certificate was in the process of being printed. Some records were destroyed in a flood." She looked disgusted. "The bottom line is that Cassandra Polanski wasn't on anyone's radar before 1998. And guess when her guardianship papers for Mia were signed."

I sighed. "The same year that her parents disappeared."

"She officially became Mia's legal guardian in February of 1999—government bureaucracy, of course—but Christine Polanski had already named Cassandra as Mia's godmother prior to that, in a document that was signed by both parties and dated April 15, 1998."

She handed me the document, and I saw Cassandra's signature, along with the faint, scrawled autograph of Christine Polanski—Mia's biological mother.

"So she signed this about two weeks before Mia's parents went missing?"

"You got it."

"Identity theft is easy—and even easier for a demon, especially since we're not even sure what kind of demon Cassandra was. She could very well have been some kind of shape-shifter, impersonating all sorts of people in order to secure a claim on Mia."

"Actually," Selena said, "Tasha just called me from the morgue. The histopath samples have come back from the lab, and they've been able to determine Cassandra's demonic heredity. She's waiting for us with the results."

I practically jumped out of the chair. "Then let's go."

"Easy, cowboy." Selena followed me out of the office. "You're *consulting* on this case, remember? You're not the primary. However closely this might concern you, I still can't offer you complete access. You're just going to have to trust me."

"That's what I should have done a long time ago. And I promise it's what I'm doing now."

We walked down the congested hallway until we reached the elevator that only went down. It had only one destination, after all—the morgue. Tasha called it the Carnival Cruise of the Damned. Currently, she was typing up something on her computer—she saw us enter, but didn't smile.

"Thanks for taking another look at her body," Selena said.

"Well—" She stepped away from the computer and slipped on a pair of blue plastic gloves. "When Tess brought in that trace evidence from the victim's house, I hoped that we might have missed something the first time."

"But I get the impression from your tone of voice that we didn't," I said.

She shook her head. "I've been over every inch of Cassandra Polanski's body with every form of ALS that we have. We didn't miss anything the first time. There aren't any stray fibers, and there certainly aren't any fibers as remarkable and unique as the silk thread that you found in her house."

"So it must have been transferred by someone else," Selena said. "Maybe someone who visited after the fact? Or from the vampire's body?"

"But we didn't find any fibers on Sebastian's body."

"We didn't find *anything* at that crime scene," I reminded her. "It was swept clean. Maybe, like you suggested the first time, Tasha, our killer got messy. Left something behind by accident."

"Do we know for certain that Cassandra killed Sebastian?"

Tasha smiled. I knew that I wouldn't like what I was about to hear.

"Oh yes. But it didn't happen the way you originally thought. We finally got some results back from Serology, and we were able to determine what demon bloodline Cassandra came from." She flicked on the X-ray screen, and I saw two images of what looked like Cassandra's skull appear. "I also called a few forensic osteologists—bone specialists—and did a little research of my own. I was sure that I recognized something about Cassandra's cranial X-rays when I saw them the first time, but it took me a while to figure it out."

"And are you ever going to tell us?" Selena asked mildly.

In response, Tasha pointed to a peculiar ridge on the topmost part of Cassandra's skull—from where I was standing, it looked like little more than a dark smudge. "Do you see this bony outgrowth—right next to the sagittal suture on the frontal plate? At first I thought it was part of the epiphysis—the cartilage and tissue where the bones connect—but it's actually a naturally growing arch that's meant to protect a hidden nerve canal. Like a secret pocket inside of her skull."

Selena stared at the ME blankly. "She had pockets in her skull?"

"Well, strictly speaking, we all do. We have bony arches and fissures that protect our optic nerve canals, and the delicate sphenoid and ethmoid bones that line our nasal cavities—the skull isn't just a hunk of solid bones. It's a system of connective tissue, fissures that grow and harden as we get older, cavities and lacunae where delicate optic and neural equipment gets tucked away."

She kept smiling. "But Cassandra, it seemed, had a secret hideaway that even I didn't know about, until I realized where to look for it. You see—" She pointed to the second X-ray, which was a magnification of the bony ridge. It looked almost like a miniature vent, like the kind you'd see in the surface of volcanic rock. "This cavity protects a delicate mesh of nerve fibers that hook directly into the optic nerve. As far as I can tell, this is what would allow Cassandra to use her unique powers—without laying a hand on anyone. Her eye movements would trigger the nerve cluster, and the effect would be instantaneous. She could literally stare you to death."

My eyes widened. "You're saying she was a telepath?"

"Not just any telepath. Cassandra was a Krell demon. It's a rare shamanic half-breed, capable of performing telepathic surgery."

I remembered my conversation with Lucian, when I'd suggested that only a few rare types of demon would be able to inflict the kind of substantial neurological damage that was evident in Sebastian's brain. My hunch had been correct from the start.

"If Cassandra was a telepath," I said, "and one powerful enough to kill, then we've been going about this all wrong. We've got the order of death wrong. All of this must have started long before we first suspected."

"All I know," Tasha said, "is that Cassandra was more than capable of killing someone without even laying a finger on them. But she didn't possess any superhuman strength or speed. Aside from her telekinetic abilities, she would have been no stronger than any of us."

"Certainly not strong enough to tear a Vailoid demon apart," Selena said.

I looked at her. "I think we should take this to the simulation room—see if we can reenact these events, but this time in the right order."

"It's already prepped and waiting for us."

23

The simulation room was the ninth wonder of the CORE crime lab. While most conventional crime labs had 3-D modeling software that allowed them to re-create crime scenes, inputting the correct angles, body positions, ballistics, and every other exacting detail that was involved in violence, we could go a step further. This room was a virtual reality environment, and with the right details, and the right biometric peripherals, we could literally build an interactive crime scene from the ground up.

Part of it was technological, but the most important part was mystical—a simple illusion charm, or glamour, that had been taken apart and multiplied a million times in complexity, until it became an ingenious algorithm for building whole interactive worlds. With the help of the electronic equipment, the materia channels allowed us to bend, tweak, and manipulate every detail of our constructed worlds, and its verisimilitude was unparalleled. I'm not talking about boxy, hexagonal graphics and clunky interfaces. I'm talking about the freaking *Star Trek* holodeck. That real. Sometimes it even scared me a little. It was uncomfortably close to re-living the actual crime.

Selena opened the door with her keycard, and we stepped into the sealed chamber, which was kept at arm's length from the rest of the lab for good reason. We didn't want in-experienced lab techs taking the sim-room for a joyride, only to discover that the graphical interface was just a little *too* lifelike. If you weren't careful, you could actually get the life scared out of you.

The room itself was spheroid, with a domed roof and smooth, egg-shaped walls that were covered in reflective white paneling. The panels were made of delicate fiber-optic nerves, which was where the room got its nickname—The Nerve. Rebecca got really twitchy if you touched any of them. In fact, this room was so expensive that most people were afraid to breathe in here.

On the far side of the room, a set of stairs led up to a raised metal platform. The mezzanine floor was filled by a bank of computers, all humming busily, and sitting at the hub computer was Rebecca Simmons. Her hair was still blue, which was probably a record, since she normally changed its color every few days. She waved as we walked in. I could see that she was in the middle of eating some-thing, although from this distance I couldn't quite tell what it was.

"Hey, Becka," I called. "Any luck on manipulating that photo of Sebastian and Sabine yet? I'm still gambling that we might be able to see a reflection from those pretty blue eyes of hers."

Rebecca managed to look chagrined. "I'm still working on it. We've managed to peel away the two images, but it'll still take some work to enhance the reflection. I'll definitely let you know as soon as I find something, though."

"Thanks. At this point, any clue will help."

"Which is why we're here," Selena said, climbing the stairs. "Have you got the simulation program booted up?"

"Just finished debugging it five minutes ago." Rebecca

smiled. "I put in the new data that you asked for, and it's ready to go whenever you are."

As I followed Selena up the stairs, I saw what Rebecca had been eating—there was a plastic bag full of sunflower seeds on the metal desk next to the hub computer. I noticed a few discarded seeds littering the floor.

Selena looked at the bag, and her eyes narrowed. "Aren't you the one who's always getting mad at us for touching the equipment, Becka? Why don't you just get a salad bar installed in here?"

She blushed. "Sorry—I'm bloody *starving*. Marcus had me doing network maintenance for most of the morning, and then two hub computers in the serology lab went down. I've just spent the last thirty minutes debugging this sim program, and after that, I have to figure out why Ben keeps getting Viagra spam e-mail on his laptop." She rolled her eyes. "I've barely eaten all day."

Selena sighed. "Just try not to get any crumbs on the fiber-optic plates. I don't know how we'd explain that to Marcus."

"Next time, I'll bring a bib." She smiled. "So are you ready?"

"Sure." Selena gestured for me to follow her, and we climbed down the stairs again, positioning ourselves in the center of the chamber. "Fire it up."

"All right. I'm activating the image matrix now." She pressed several buttons, and a low hum began to emanate from the wall panels. "Hope nobody's using the microwave, because this baby takes a lot of power."

"It'll be a tragedy if Ben's burrito comes out only half-defrosted," I said.

"I wish *Ben* could be half-defrosted," Selena replied. "Would do him good."

Rebecca hit the lights, and for a moment, the room was almost completely dark—save for the glow of the computer screens. Then a soft, pale blue light began to emanate from the fiber-optic panels. The light grew more intense, until it culminated in a bright flash that left me rubbing spots from my eyes.

When I could see again, I was standing in Cassandra's living room.

The Nerve was incredible. It had replicated Cassandra's house exactly, down to the exact shade of her chocolate brown carpet and black couch. There was a coffee table next to the couch, and standing on either side of it were two figures. I recognized them as Sebastian and Cassandra.

I resisted the urge to walk up to Sebastian and peer into his eyes. I knew that the 3-D digitization was perfect, down to the very last pore and stray hair. Cassandra, too, was completely lifelike. They both stared straight ahead, standing on either side of the table, saying nothing. Audio wasn't a part of the simulation. Most of the time, it wasn't needed anyway.

"All right," Selena said. "We're assuming that, at some point in the evening—shortly before he died—Sebastian paid Cassandra Polanski a visit at her house. We can only imagine what they talked about."

"Mia." I swallowed. "Sebastian must have known something. Maybe he knew that Mia was already infected with the vampiric retrovirus. Hell, maybe *he* was the one who turned her. Either way, Cassandra didn't like what he had to tell her."

"Continue with the simulation, Becka," Selena said.

Before my eyes, Cassandra took a step forward and gestured with her right hand in Sebastian's direction. Sebastian crumpled soundlessly to the floor—dead.

Cassandra reached down and picked up Sebastian's body. She struggled briefly with the weight, then swung him over her left shoulder.

"Wait," Selena said. "That's not right."

"That's the data you gave me," Rebecca protested.

"Yeah, but I forgot about something. We found a partial print on the bottom portion of Sebastian's thigh. It was the only mark that we could find on his body, and that was only after we fumed it. The print was too smudged for us to match with anything, but now that we know more, I'd bet that it was Cassandra's. For that print to have gotten on his thigh—"

"She carried him differently," Rebecca interjected. "I see where you're going. Just let me make a minor change to the program. It might flicker a bit, since I don't have time to properly debug it."

The image of Cassandra and Sebastian shimmered for a moment, and then they were standing in their original positions again. I saw Cassandra gesture once more, saw Sebastian fall for the second time. But then, as Cassandra picked his body up, she held him close to her chest this time—with one arm wrapped around his legs.

"She cradled him," I said quietly. "Like a parent carrying a small child. She didn't want to hurt him. She must have felt incredibly guilty."

"She still murdered him," Selena said.

"Yes, but we don't know what they talked about. Maybe Sebastian threatened her. Maybe he threatened Mia's life—"

"A weak little bird like him? You said that he was a submissive. He was basically that Sabine woman's trained bitch. No way he would have blazed in there and started threatening a powerful demon like Cassandra. It doesn't make sense."

"We might never know."

"I'm loading the second part of the program now," Rebecca said.

There was another flash of light, and when it cleared, we were standing back in the alley on Granville Street. We watched Cassandra carry Sebastian's body into the alley, then carefully lay him down on the ground.

"She posed him," Selena said. "She wanted us to find him that way—wanted us to investigate."

Cassandra laid out Sebastian's body, folding his arms across his chest, as if he were merely sleeping. Wearing gloves, she removed his wallet and slipped it inside her own jacket.

"Of course, we're just extrapolating here," Selena continued.

"We don't know what Sebastian was originally carrying, or what Cassandra took from him. If he had a wallet, we never found it. But she must have put on gloves after the fact, since we found that one partial print on his thigh."

"What about the note? And the photo?"

Selena shrugged. "Maybe she planted them both. Maybe she saw them and decided to leave them there. Or maybe she was flustered and missed them. Either way, she wanted us to find the kid's body. She was leading us to something."

"You think she wanted to be caught?"

"No. I think she wanted us to catch someone else. But the plan ended up backfiring, because they got to her before we could get to them."

"Running part three of the program now," Rebecca said.

When the third flash of light cleared, we were standing in Cassandra's office. There were four figures before us. Cassandra was standing in front of the desk. The first Vailoid demon was positioned directly in front of her, and the second one was standing by the window. There was also a fourth figure, who was just a dark outline, standing in the corner of the room.

"That fourth figure is our mystery player," Selena said. "The person who took out the second Vailoid demon. Possibly the person who hired them in the first place to kill both Cassandra and Mia. We still don't know for sure exactly what Cassandra was doing at SemTec Laboratories, but she did test Mia's DNA. Her prints were all over the equipment. So she must have known that the girl was infected. She probably found out shortly before the Vailoid demons arrived."

"I'm running the final part of the program now," Rebecca said.

As I watched, the first Vailoid demon approached Cassandra. She gestured again with her right hand, and the demon began clutching its head. Then, horribly, it reached out and plunged its hand into Cassandra's chest. Normally, the simroom could re-create precise blood splatter, but Rebecca had been kind enough to remove that function from this particular program. Both Cassandra and the demon fell to the ground at the same time. As the second demon walked over to finish off Cassandra, the first demon began crawling in vain toward the window.

I felt like some kind of deity, watching this silent, terrifying masque play out before me. Cassandra was lying on the ground, still. The demon that she'd mortally injured was lying next to the window, eyes staring straight ahead.

Then the fourth figure—the figure without a face—advanced upon the second demon. As the demon turned, the figure did the exact same thing that the first Vailoid demon had done to Cassandra. It plunged a hand into the demon's chest. But it was a lot more creative about it. The figure reached its *other* hand into the gaping chest cavity, and pulled outward, shearing through the rib cage and literally tearing open the Vailoid's chest completely. Then it threw the demon's ruined body across the desk, where it lay there, bleeding and still.

"Tasha had originally thought that some sort of magical force ripped through the demon's chest," Selena said. "But she took another look at the X-rays, and found claw marks on the rib cage that she'd missed before. Whatever did this to the demon must have used its bare hands."

The fourth figure then grabbed the first demon's body and threw it out the window. Glass shattered in all directions, and the demon abruptly vanished in a spray of pixels. There was no need to map its trajectory through the air. We knew what happened after it hit the ground.

What we didn't know was how the fourth figure escaped. There was no data for that—so the figure just remained there, voiceless and faceless, staring at us.

I shivered.

"We originally thought that whoever killed Sebastian must have also killed the second Vailoid demon," I said, "and that he, or she, then threw the body out the window to cover up the brain trauma and make it look like the fall killed it. But we had the identities switched around. It was *Cassandra* who killed Sebastian, and then Cassandra again who killed the first demon—using her telekinesis both times. Then this mystery figure killed the second demon, but left its body on the desk for us to find."

"It wanted us to think that Cassandra was a lot more dangerous," Selena said. "That she was capable of tearing a demon apart with her bare hands. But she was actually desperate, and using her powers to defend herself. Her only premeditated murder was Sebastian, and even that might have been impulsive. If he threatened Mia, or hinted that she might have been infected—maybe Cassandra freaked out and killed him, thinking that she was protecting the kid."

"But she's obviously got a more ominous role in this," I added, "if we consider all of the coincidences surrounding Mia's parents and their disappearance, the custody papers that get conveniently signed only two weeks before Mom and Dad both vanish, the complete lack of material on Cassandra before 1998—I'm starting to think that this was all some kind of deal that went sour."

Selena nodded. "You mean that Cassandra knew the person who killed her—that they were working together."

"In some capacity, yes. I think they must have hatched some sort of deal to get rid of Mia's parents, and Cassandra was the one who would look after Mia until she reached a certain age. Why her birthday was important, and what they planned on doing with her—that, I don't know. But something went wrong, and Cassandra obviously wanted to protect Mia from her partner, or partners. She failed."

We both stared at Cassandra's lifeless body. I flashed back to that night at the office, when I first saw her lying there by the desk, bleeding. The look on Mia's face. The sound of her world crumbling to dust.

"You can shut down the program now, Becka," I said.

Rebecca pushed a few buttons, and the image vanished. We were left in the white-walled sim chamber, listening to the contented hum of the computers.

"This all just brings us back to our first mystery," Selena said. "What sort of killer is brilliant, connected, powerful enough to tear apart a demon with its bare hands, but conscientious enough to mix up the evidence—"

"Aware of the vampire community," I continued, "knowl-edgeable enough to seek out a rare type of healer-demon, like Cassandra, who normally wouldn't live anywhere near this area—"

"Obsessed with a teenage girl"—Selena shook her head—"and fond of rare yellow silk?"

Rebecca chuckled softly. "You OSIs and your mysteries," she said.

24

The pillows were on fire. They looked like pink creampuffs, slowly melting as the flames consumed them. Everything in Eve's bedroom was pink—it had been, after all, her favorite color. I'd always liked gray myself. Even as a little kid, I always wanted to wear gray hooded sweatshirts and formless gray slacks, like I had already become an old maid. Lucy Snowe from Bronte's *Villette*, fighting with my outraged sense of adolescent Protestantism while swaying to the Catholic sexiness of French professors. But Eve liked pink. She had a pink ruffled bedspread, pink pillows, and pink shoes—now seething with smoke against what used to be her soft beige carpet. Pink gumballs were cooking in her very own gumball dispenser, which had become a wreck of molten plastic and cheap metal. I remembered the taste of them—almost too sweet, like you could barely stand it.

I dragged myself along the carpet. I could feel the edges of my heat shield beginning to waver, and the power was dragging on me, threatening to slack off like an abandoned rope. At thirteen, all of my magic was an exercise in torsion, my will against the universe, but there's only so long that you can keep that kind of intensity up. I hadn't learned about focus yet. All I knew was how to channel my will, and right now, every ounce of it was pouring into the shield. In a few moments, I'd be bone-dry, and then the flames would rush in.

I almost wanted to let them.

"Eve!"

I pushed aside a broken lamp and crawled behind the bed. The window was blackened—I couldn't see the outside world anymore. There was only this—the hell of flames, the flush of killing heat on my skin. Maybe the earth was gone. Maybe I really was in hell, and my eternal punishment would be to remain in this room, always, looking for a hidden girl. Looking for a—

It was some kind of gas leak, I think. They weren't clear.

—her blackened body—

Maybe someone left one of the elements on. Such a tragedy. Nobody else was there—the poor thing was all alone. She was a latchkey kid, after all.

—frozen in a boxer's pose, hands clenched to her chest—

If only someone had been with her.

—muscle and bone fused, tendons boiled until they were soft, pliable—

A girl her age should have been out playing with friends. What would she be doing home in the middle of the day? So odd.

—and a filigree of light around her, a pattern, maybe smoke—

The firemen came too late. She was already—

—was it her soul? That tracery of silver, that snowflake? Was it?

You can't see her. You don't want to see her.

Honey, she's already—

But it wasn't my mother standing in the hospital. It was Lucian. He was surrounded by black flames, what Milton called "darkness visible," fire licking at his skin without leaving a mark.

"Tess, she's already gone." His eyes were two black "lunettes," sucking all the light from the room. They were worse than the fire, worse than all the dying. That unsigned space, that *nonlife*, the grave where a soul turned endlessly, polished and hewn to icy marble. We both surveyed each other across the frozen bier of the dead or dying universe, like unfamiliar lovers on a hotel bed.

"You're gone." He raised his hand, and a black moth unfolded itself in his palm, fluttering, ecstatic against his flesh. I could see the powder on its wings.

There are over 60,000 distinct species of blowfly in the world. How can a person not love entomology? Each fly is like a small black equation in the air, lighting upon a blade of grass or a dead body without discrimination. Even if you die in secret, in silence, in the darkest of sealed chambers, a blowfly will find you in minutes. So you're never alone. Not really.

The CORE's special entomology lab—which dealt with both terrestrial insect varieties and mystical hybrids of the sort that you didn't really want to meet—was overflowing with genus charts and diagrams of succession. Bugs on pushpins and cards, hundreds of individual families with all of their blood feuds and hereditary disputes: Calliphorae, Diptera, horned beetle, blood scarab. Leigh Mussell, the director, had one butterfly on her desk with its wing covers gently scraped away, so that you could see the delicate veins underneath, like a hidden city. Even maggots have veins, teeth, a circulatory system, taking in shallow pockets of air through tiny spiracles in their flesh. Under the SEM, they look like gorgeous silken islands, or neural sulci. I was at a scene once where they had climbed up the trees in search of a safe place to pupate. It was literally raining maggots. Poor Derrick had to run back to the car to get us umbrellas.

People follow laws of succession as well. They arrive at scenes sometimes, when they're told, do their business, and leave. They abandon a dark shape, the empty room where love used to shelter, a hollowed-out comma of delicate space.

Lucian stroked the wings of the moth with his fingertips, so careful that he didn't brush away any of the precious dust—actually tiny scales that felt like the most delicate of talcum powders against your skin. He extended his other hand. If I'd been able to put that gesture, frozen in time, underneath a scanning electron microscope, I would have seen thousands of electrons splitting their shells, protons changing their spin and flavor, blazing into new atomic valences.

"Who are you?" I grabbed at his wrist, but the black flames swept over me. They felt like a thousand wings dusting my mouth and eyes, the voices of the dead. And whatever came after. I stared at the hairs on his wrists. What would it be like to fuse my hands to his, epiphysis, bone spur, metacarpal, surrendering like wax? I thought of the carelessness with which men washed their hands. The warm water passing over his palms as he washed them, unthinking, hand over hand in automatic motions. To be inside those hands, in the column of warm water. To be the fine hairs on those wrists, the dermal papillae just beneath the skin, erytheic, blushing.

I pulled away. "You necromancers are so fucked up, you think you can control life and death like a game of poker—but the universe doesn't work that way! There are always consequences—you can't play with those kinds of forces. Everything you do leads you closer to—"

He stared at me. "To what, Tess?"

His eyes were loud. I could hear them; the shadows they made, the flutter of their gaze, like the many-tongued angels that guarded the ark, a skein of wings and open fingers and grazing mouths.

I realized then that I didn't know. I didn't know anything. It was a two-way mirror—I couldn't see into the void, but it was watching me. It could see everything. Just biding its time. And I didn't know if light and redemption and—hell, even forgiveness—waited for me on the other side, or something else entirely.

"Everything has consequences," he said. "Especially this."

"But what *is* this?" I glared at him. "What are we doing here?"

He was silent.

Suddenly, all I could feel was anger. Lucian and his shadowy competence, his *ease*, walking into my dreams like some careless sheik and handing me fucking riddles. I imagined him as a cocky teenager. Guys like him, laughing and prancing on the soccer field in their shorts, which flared against the warm air like bits of brightly colored foil or winking eyes. I liked legs. I was fascinated by the curve of a man's leg, how it could be muscular and covered in a soft sheen of dark hair—I knew how it could feel, like spider silk, or the satiny edge of that old baby blanket that you used to drag around the house. Mom says I constantly referred to my blanket as "the stem," since it was really just a frayed piece of sky blue silk that curled around my arm, and I couldn't pronounce "satin." Never good with words and their consequences.

I think myelin must feel that way—the silvery connective substance blanketing our nerves that allows them to communicate through synaptic conduction. Our thoughts, our moods, everything that comes out of us is regulated and made possible by that shimmery floss, diaphanous, subtle as a bee's wings on your tongue or the silken remnant left behind by a beetle pupating, what Leigh would have called "frass."

Yes. Lucian would have been out on that field with the other boys, a few bright points of sweat collecting in his shaggy black hair (shaggy then), the muscles in his legs and thighs tensing like golden puzzle pieces when he kicked the ball. And the simple pleasure afterward, hot and uncomplicated; the kind of happiness that made you run around the room on coiled springs because you were utterly consumed. The small and elegant ecstasies of fresh Cheerios floating in a bowl of milk, Triaminic cough syrup with its brandywine flavor, orange shag carpeting, your best friend's pool. His eyes would have crinkled up when he smiled. If I were a boy, I would have run out to him with cherry Popsicles, and he would have laughed and put his arm around me, easily, just like that. If I were a boy, I would have been just as complicated.

I realized that the dark fire around his body looked like a chemical reagent burning. Luminol on video is one of the most beautiful things I've ever witnessed, sparkling with the blue of a flame's core, like God moving over the face of the waters.

"Please." My voice broke. "God, please, don't let me be like her. Not like Eve. Don't let me be—"

"Where is she?"

I blinked. "What?"

The fire around him seemed to die, but an aura remained. The moth perched on his fingertips became a scrap of carbon paper. Or a flake of calcined material; the thinnest tissue layer of bone, like Donne's "gold to airy thinness beat." Metaphors were crashing around in my head. Why couldn't I think like a scientist? What was wrong with me? What was wrong with him?

"Where do you think she is?" he asked. "Your Eve."

Derrick had to study ASL years ago as part of his linguistics training for the Telepath Division—he had to know how to communicate with disabled witnesses, especially in high-pressure situations when emotions were clouding their thoughts. I knew that the sign for "dead" was a flipping of the hands, a soft reversal. You start with your hands open, fingers pointing ahead and arms held side by side, and then the right and left hands reverse their positions in a wave-like motion, a smooth slithering from one signifier to another. Dead left. In the mirror world of the dead, every action is completely reversed. Or maybe it's like the spirit realm in *Gilgamesh*, with everyone drinking tea from cracked cups, eating stale bread and wandering left, right, left on dark, unvarnished promenades of black oak.

Derrick also taught me "asshole": spinning your index finger around your clenched fist with the nub of your thumb just barely visible, imitating the organ it describes. It really gets your point across.

Lucian's question hung on the air. Eve. Where was Eve?

A wave going from left to right, positive to negative. Like a true photon, she was both waveform and particle, a solid

point and a clear white spectrum. She went out—somewhere.
And sometimes I imagined her exploding in tiny twinklings
of different-colored Christmas lights, like the rainbow blur
you'd see if you lay beneath the Christmas tree and squinted
hard. The garlands tickling my ears. I imagined her flying
apart in streamers, or flaring up in cold eyelets of fire, sun on
stained glass, the brilliant surface of my treasured LiteBrite.
Oh, those black cardboard frames with their dozens of holes,
like sine graphs! They always reminded me of the chocolate
side of the Oreo cookie; I wanted to cram them all into my
mouth and chew on raw physics. Sweet as a strange quark
melting in my mouth.

"All I know," I told him, "is that we went to the same
place. I feel dead, too."

Lucian didn't move, but he seemed to be closer now.
Somehow everywhere—a necromantic trick of distance. His
fingers with their smooth nails (not bitten down, like mine)
were almost touching my back. His right leg almost inter-
sected mine. Our ankles formed a strange narration. I thought
of Planck's Principle: the law which states that, as distances
grow infinitesimally closer and closer, eventually the whole
nature of space and time changes at the subatomic level. Our
bodies already shared leptons, muons, and other quarks and
quantum particles. Certainly, at a molecular level, we were
already lovers. So why was I so scared?

"If the universe stopped expanding for even a second,"
Lucian said without moving his mouth, "the sky would be
pure light from blossoming stars. That's what I feel like
sometimes. With you. Stabbed by light. I can't bear it."

People didn't talk this way. You didn't hear this in bars.
But we weren't people. We were both something different,
strange, and slantwise.

I tried to imagine a conventionality: a not-fucked-up moment with Lucian. *Necromancer Knows Best*. Lucian making
a spinach salad for dinner. Those long, slim fingers covered
in brimstone, grease, and innocent blood as he chopped up
bacon and hardboiled eggs. Little half-moons of yolk would
peel from the egg as he guided the knife. Maybe his other

hand would be resting on the bottle of dressing. What would he like? Something with ginger, garlic, and cardamom. Suddenly, all I wanted to do was cook for him: sharp yellow curries, laksa swimming in coconut milk, alu gobi with spicy cauliflower and crisp golden papadam resting on the edge of the bowl. I wanted to pour mandarin orange slices into his hands, get drunk with him, rub slow, soft circles on his back while he threw up after drinking too much Santa Clara red.

"Do you—like red wine?" I asked him. It was the stupidest question imaginable. I had become a chalk outline of myself—an empty test tube.

He frowned. "I don't understand."

"What about fireworks?" I pressed on. "I remember watching fireworks with Derrick on Canada Day. You know, *The Lord of the Rings* begins with fireworks. He's always telling me that. We're both loser types. I don't care. But people forget about that—Tolkien and the fireworks. Whenever someone says it's not a thrilling read, I remind them of the fireworks. That night, they were burning papyrus spread against the black sky. One looked like a strand of RNA. I thought: If God was going to destroy the world with holy fire, this is what it would look like. Gleaming slippers and cones of white-hot color, vortices of amethyst and bloodstone, and one like a cosmic rain. Maybe that's what microwave background radiation looks like. Lucian, I don't know what the fuck I'm talking about, haven't you figured that out yet?"

"Burning papyrus," he said simply. "You've got a funny face."

"What?"

He kissed me. His tongue caved in my mouth. A hot cinnamon shell. I made a noise and leaned into him. His other hand was on my waist. Tentative—almost chaste. I guided it down. His stomach was sucking in and out, almost palsied. I pressed my fingers against his chest, twining them in the soft, black hair, so mysterious and comforting at the same time, like a kitten's warm back as she slept within the crook of your knee. He wrapped both of his arms around me, and we moved backward. I felt the steel edge of the hospital gurney—or was it Tasha's autopsy table? He lifted me onto the slick, antiseptic surface, and I shivered violently in the matrix between blushing skin and dead, ferric chill.

Can you screw death? Or is it exclusively a top?

I wanted everything about him that was normal, but normal was a fantasy. What would we be like together? At night, after work, once we'd both had a few beers and weren't thinking about the world anymore—How was the crime lab, sweetie? How was the death-dealing, love?—would he consent to my body in gray sweats and an old UBC T-shirt? Could I lay my head against his stomach, fold into him? Would he stroke my hair absently, call me "baby," rub his bare feet against mine in slow, reassuring circles?

Or would I comfort him instead, wrapping thin arms around him, rocking him a little, chin propped against his dark hair as I pretended to watch TV with the sound off? I imagined the static settling on our bodies. Snow falling softly on our bloody deeds and hiding them in mile-long drifts.

"Tess."

Lucian was kissing my neck—dragging his tongue along the sensitive skin, burrowing his heat into my clavicle. I opened my eyes, and could see, just barely, the outline of a girl standing behind him.

"Eve?"

"No." She smiled. Her pink dress was charred and hung in rags, fouled and black from soot. She was bleeding from a thousand cuts. "I'm gone. My name is gone. My life is gone. So that's what you can call me now."

I tried to scream, but Lucian's hand was against my mouth. His palm smelled like wood shavings and adiopocere. Grave wax. I choked and gagged.

"Gone!"

I was tangled up in my down comforter, one foot dangling over the couch, shaking uncontrollably. I didn't remember falling asleep. Derrick must have thrown the quilt over me. We'd been talking, and—

"Honey?" Derrick emerged from the kitchen, staring

oddly at me. "You can bet I *felt* that before I heard you cry out. What's wrong? Nightmares?"

I stared at him, and my eyes filled with tears.

"Fucking Christ," I whispered. "She's gone."

He knelt down beside me. "Who's gone? Mia? Tess, we haven't given up on her yet. There's still lots to do—"

"No, not *her*. Eve."

He blinked. "Who's Eve?"

I started to cry. Fuck, I *hated* crying. I hated how spastic and childish it made me feel, like I had no control over my own body. Derrick was probably the only person in the world—besides my mother—who I could actually cry in front of.

He didn't say anything. He just wrapped his arms around me. They were skinny arms, but they worked, all the same. I cried stupidly into his chest, holding on to him like I was about to explode into pieces, and he was the only thing keeping me in this world. Sometimes I actually felt that way.

When it was over, he settled me back down on the couch, got me a glass of water, tucked the quilt in around me, and then sat down on the floor.

"Let's hear it," he said simply.

Between gulps, chokes, and ragged indrawn breaths, I told him. Not about Lucian—that was too fucked up, even in dream world. Just about Eve.

"She was my best friend. At thirteen, she was my *only* friend. One day, I decided to show her a trick—a magic trick—just a bit of ghostlight, but that was enough to freak her out. She ran away, and I ran after her."

Derrick nodded. I was sure that he'd probably done something similar—maybe offered to read a friend's mind or something—with similar results.

"I knocked on her door, but she wouldn't let me in. So I waited for—I don't know, it felt like hours. Then I smelled smoke. I banged on the door again, and this time, I could hear her screaming." I swallowed. "So I used my power to break it down." A mirthless chuckle. "Don't know how the firemen explained *that* one. I summoned a fire shield, and then I crawled through her house. But I couldn't find her. So I went upstairs. To her room. Upstairs—"

Derrick didn't nod—he didn't even move. He just looked at me, and I could tell that we were deeply in sync. He wasn't reading my mind so much as traveling like a needle across the surface of my thoughts, following them as he listened to me. I could tell from his expression that he saw what I saw, *felt* it.

"She was in her room. Behind the bed—her arms—they call it the 'pugilistic pose,' when the arms and legs curl up. Like a doll. Like she was just sleeping."

"And you saw everything," he said.

"I couldn't save her, Derrick. And I can't save Mia either. These powers, these things that are after her—they're bigger than all of us, and they've got a million times more resources than we do. How are we supposed to fight them?"

"The same way we always do." He grinned sheepishly. "Luck and irony."

"But what's the point?" I stared at him. "What's the point of all this fucking magic, of all this power, if it doesn't *work* in the end? Things are supposed to turn out okay! We're supposed to *win* every once in a while! But it never seems to happen. And I just—don't know what the point is anymore. Of anything. If it can't save her—if *I* can't save her. What am I supposed to do?"

We stared at each other in silence for a while. I sipped on my water.

"And Mia—she reminds you of this girl?"

I closed my eyes. "They could be sisters."

"Right," was all he said.

Right.

I don't remember what we talked about after that.

25.

I sat in my kitchen with a loaded gun, feeling the cold weight of it in my hand. Selena had finally given me back the Browning Pro .40, and I wasn't going anywhere without it. I'd spent the last hour or so obsessively ejecting the magazine, just to reassure myself that it was actually loaded. You'd be surprised how many people sleep with a gun underneath their pillow, but forget to load it the night before. This one was loaded with Hydra-Shok bullets, hollow point with a tip full of silver nitrate.

I was scared.

We'd traded places, and Derrick was now the one sleeping on my couch. He'd insisted on staying the night, although I wasn't sure how he might actually protect me. Like me, he felt helpless, and he was just trying to assert some kind of routine. I watched him move slightly underneath the spare blanket, then sigh once before returning to deep sleep. Derrick never snored. He slept so deeply and so quietly that I often found myself listening closely, just to be sure that he was still breathing. I was the exact opposite. I snored like a banshee, tossed and turned, slept fitfully, and woke up about a million times a night. Sleeping was one of my least favorite activities. And I never remembered my dreams. Usually. Until this week.

Most days, I still felt like a confused teenager. Like Mia.

That was where all of this had started.

Mia was the one who'd made me start questioning everything. She was the one who made me ask myself: *What the hell am I doing?* The desire to protect her was so powerful, so surprisingly maternal and unexpected, that it made me doubt everything about my life until now. Maybe I really did want to help people. Maybe I really was a good person, and not such a self-indulgent screwup.

Currently, Mia was sitting in a heavily guarded suite at the Wal Centre, probably watching a plasma screen television and wishing that she was home. Or anywhere else. If only she was here, I could protect her.

I got up and walked to the bedroom, taking the gun with me. The idea of a mage with a gun seemed bizarre to a lot of people. Mages were supposed to be loving pacifists who wore robes and respected the earth. See, those are witches. Magic isn't about charms, illusions, or summoning spirits. It's about materia, shearing forces, gravity, life and death, darkness and light. It's hard work, and you usually die young. Or live wrong—like some alien, twisted oak, consumed by the power that you desire. The magic fucks you and leaves you broke, like a stripped car burning in some parking lot somewhere, circled by curious dogs and night dwellers. Or you just explode.

Up until now, I thought I'd made peace with that fact. But I wasn't really prepared to die. All I could think about was how lonely I felt sometimes, how I hadn't slept with a guy in almost six months, how Derrick and I ate clodhopper ice cream and watched *Trading Spaces* every Friday night, how my mom laughed sweetly whenever I told her that I enjoyed living alone, how crazy-in-love I'd been with my first boyfriend, when I was only nineteen, back when I still had the capacity to feel perfectly happy.

I shut the door and sat down on the bed. I was bone tired,

ready to collapse, but I couldn't sleep. I was terrified of that dark interval between night and morning. I didn't want to lose control, not even for a second. If necessary, I'd stay in this position all night, holding the gun like a teddy bear.

"You look tense."

I resisted the urge to scream. I was up like a shot, my feet spaced apart, my right arm holding the gun extended. The safety was already off, and it was comforting to know that a silver bullet was chambered and ready to fly. Still, I felt naked and defenseless, like a little girl holding a wooden sword. I had only one shot. What if I missed? What if the action jammed, or the firing pin didn't work, or the primer didn't light up, or—

"What are you doing here?" I asked, forcing my voice to remain calm.

Lucian smiled. He was wearing a white T-shirt and blue jeans. He looked disconcertingly like Stanley Kowalski in *A Streetcar Named Desire*.

"Answer me," I said, "or I swear to God I'll put a bullet in your brain. Then you can try to bring yourself back to life."

Why was this man stumbling through my dreams, through the most shaded, intimate parts of my consciousness, with his heavy boots and blue jeans and bullshit teenage smirk? What gave him the right?

Lucian raised his hands in a mock-friendly gesture. "Come on, Tess. Think about it. If I'd come here to harm you—do you honestly think you'd be pointing that gun at me right now?"

I exhaled. "No. Probably not."

"Right. So I'm not here to hurt you."

"You're here to talk."

He nodded.

"You almost killed me in the parking lot."

"You were never in any danger," he said cryptically. His tone was still light.

"Well, let's chat, then." I kept the gun level. "I'm comfortable where I am. If you want a Dr Pepper, there's some in the fridge."

"I'm a lot more conversant when I'm not being threatened by a loaded firearm," he said. "Would you mind putting it down?"

"Yes."

Lucian sighed. "Fine. We'll do it your way. Like I said, I only came here to talk—I wanted to check up on you. I was worried."

I used my left hand to draw my athame. It was reassuringly warm against my palm. Between the two weapons, I might be able to fend him off—or at least leave a mark before he ripped my throat out.

"You snuck into my apartment at 2 a.m. to tell me that you're worried about me? Try again. Why are you here?"

"Actually, it's more like midafternoon to me. I'm a night owl."

"I don't care about your screwed-up biological clock, Lucian! You'd better give me an answer, or else this is going to get really ugly." It was an effort to keep my hands from shaking, but I'd always been a champion bluffer. "I may not be able to take you out, but I can sure as hell cause you a lot of pain before I die. And even necromancers understand pain—right?"

He shook his head. "You're misreading me, Tess. I only came here to talk. But I'll go if you want."

I rolled my eyes. "Oh, the 'I'll go' routine is supposed to work on me? What is this, *The Hills*? Come on. Just tell me what's going on."

"You know, you can be very difficult to talk to sometimes."

"Yeah. I have emotional problems, too."

Lucian sighed. "I came because—I heard about what happened to the girl. Mia. The one you're trying to protect."

"Oh, you *heard* that, did you? Like your friends weren't the ones who infected her. Like Sabine didn't hold her down."

"Tess, I swear—I've never even met her. Maybe Sabine knows her, but she guards her secrets, and I can't exactly force them out of her." His expression was surprisingly rueful. "In case you haven't noticed, she could eat me like a hashbrown patty. The only reason she tolerates me is because of our agreement."

"And what agreement would that be?" I scowled. "Oh wait, don't tell me—it's complicated. God, I don't even need to be talking to you, I just need an annoying 8-Ball that gives me shitty, half-assed answers all the time."

Even so—the thing about the hashbrown patty was kind of funny. He almost had a sense of humor.

Lucian sighed. "I'm here to help, Tess. Honest. After you came to visit me, I became very interested in this case of yours. I want to figure out what happened to Sebastian, just like you do."

I tightened my grip on the gun. "I don't believe you. I don't believe you're capable of caring about another life— even one of your vampire playmates. You're in this because you've got something riding on it, but I don't know what that is yet."

"You see conspiracies everywhere, but I'm only trying to help you. I came here tonight to warn you."

My eyes narrowed. "No shit."

"Is it so hard for you to believe that I want to help you? Just like you're trying to help Mia?"

"I'm a human protecting another—that makes sense. You're a death-dealer. All you care about is the game—the power."

He took a step forward. "Aren't you forgetting something?"

"Oh, what—that I'm a demon, too?" I rolled my eyes. "We are nothing alike, Lucian. My mother was raped by a demon, and so my genetics got messed up—I inherited the magic gene." I thought about his story—about that tiny, half-dead (undead?) baby being swaddled in black and gold, his cold brow anointed with myrrh, whisked away to some court of shadows. Where was his choice?

Were we really so different?

"You must think I'm a monster." His eyes were almost black—but they weren't those terrifying orbs that I'd seen

earlier. They were the color of damp earth. A brown so dark
that it was almost colorless. Like the soil of a grave.

"I don't think. I know."

He shook his head. "You don't understand the first thing
about necromancers—or about vampires. You see us as in-
discriminate killers, cold-blooded predators, and sexual
sadists. But what would the human race look like, if we only
judged you by your serial killers, your rapists, your pe-
dophiles?" He stared at me. "Every species has violent indi-
viduals. Some demons kill for pleasure, and some live in
perfect synergy with humans. You can't judge all vampires
when you've only met a few terrible ones. And you can't
judge a necromancer when you don't know the first thing
about us. You can't even admit that we might share the same
power."

He was uncomfortably close now. I couldn't tell if he was
playing with me, or just being polite. If he wanted to disarm
me, he could do it easily. I knew how fast he could move.
Right now, he was being slow—almost careful. But I didn't
know why. Staring at this strange half-demon, I suddenly realized that I knew as little about him as he knew about me.
Our lives were a coil of dark secrets. We were both perfect
strangers, facing each other, and maybe neither of us knew
what would happen next.

"I've killed." He said it offhand, like one might say, "I
play the flute." "Many times. When it was necessary."

"But never just for the fun of it?"

"Desire and death are always closer than they seem."

"Is that supposed to turn me on?"

"What do I have to do to earn your trust?"

"Well, you could start by getting the hell out of—"

He was behind me in an instant—pressed up against me.
His right hand was on top of mine, pressing down on the
gun. His left hand was wrapped around my waist. I still had
the athame, but I lacked the leverage to do much damage
with it. I might be able to slash him, but that was it.

It felt like the dream. His hand on my waist. His tongue—
Focus!

I could feel his breath on my neck. His lips were an inch away, and I could smell his body. Not sweat—but a dark, spicy kind of tang, a hint of something metallic, a whiff of earth, cloves, leather, and leaves. A hundred impossible smells mingling with each other. I'd expected him to be cold, but his hand was surprisingly warm against mine. I felt a flush creeping up my neck. Lucian seemed to sense it, and his breathing quickened.

"Do you trust me now?" he whispered.

I could see the dark hair on his arms, the burnished gold skin, and beneath that, the veins thrown into startled relief. There's a stage just before decomposition that we call "marbling," when hemolysis begins to break down the red blood cells in the body, causing them to spill out hemoglobin like punctured balloons. It makes the veins appear dark and appalling against the skin, almost writhing as they slowly begin to disintegrate, being broken down by bacteria inside the body. Lucian's veins reminded me of that. Somehow, he was both dead and alive. Necromancers absorbed death, and their bodies told the story of every ritual, every spell. Like the track marks of an addict.

His hand applied a gentle pressure to my arm, slowly pushing the gun down. If he wanted to, he could rip my arm right out of its socket. But it was clear that he didn't want to hurt me. He'd been telling the truth about that, at least.

"You know," he said, as if by way of conversation, "vampires are about as different from us as we are from *real* humans—the normal ones, I mean."

The lucky ones, I thought momentarily.

"When a vampire is turned," he continued, still slowly forcing my arm down, "his body changes. Blood pressure drops. Heartbeat slows. Temperature falls. But he doesn't die. When humans die, their cells break down. The process is called autolysis—correct?"

"You're suddenly a biology major?"

He smiled. The Browning was in his right hand now. He casually let it fall onto the bed, a few inches away and completely useless. "A vampire's body goes through a similar process. The cells 'die,' in a sense—they undergo a partial kind of autolysis, but then they are transformed. The vampire sees, smells, and tastes everything in a completely different way. He uses different parts of his brain, and understands his body in a way that a human never could. But he isn't dead. Far from it."

"And what happens to necromancers?" I swallowed. "Lucian, what happened to that baby, swaddled in black? Where did he go?"

He smiled slightly at my recognition. "There are rituals," he said. "Secret rites. Complications. The same as with your kind. Less paperwork."

I turned around, and was suddenly surprised that I could. He wasn't holding on to me anymore. I still had the athame in my left hand, and the gun was within reach—although I didn't think that I could move fast enough.

Lucian was just standing there, staring at me with this mild expression, like we'd only been talking about politics or the rainforest.

"What did you come here to warn me about?" I asked coldly. "Try condensing it to five words or less."

"You know that your life is in danger, Tess. You know that you're getting close to something very old and powerful—something that you don't have the resources to fight. You must feel that."

"And I suppose you understand exactly what's going on."

"I understand that Mia is connected to the vampires. Someone has chosen her, left a mark on her. Whoever that vampire is, they won't let you stand in their way. I just want to make sure you know what you're dealing with. That you're fully prepared."

"There's a lot you aren't telling me."

He shrugged. "There's a lot I don't know."

"Bullshit. You're their liaison, and it's your job to know every little thing that goes on there, every step that your buddies take. You must know who infected Mia, but for some reason, you want to protect them."

"The only person I want to protect is you."

"Oh, quit it with the puppy dog eyes. I don't buy your false concern for a minute, Lucian. You've got an agenda here, just like I do."

His expression was mellow. "Of course I do. But part of that agenda happens to be keeping you safe, and protecting the life of an innocent girl—a girl who's been violated and threatened, probably by someone close to me. They aren't just my employers, Tess. Some of them are my friends, my companions." His eyes darkened. "You could even call them my family. Don't you think that betrayal makes me furious? Ashamed? Don't you think I want to see the vampire who did this punished?"

My arm was aching from keeping the knife raised. I tried to ignore it. "I have no idea what your motivations are. I don't pretend to. But when you skulk in here, in the middle of the night, telling me that you have to warn me and then throwing out some cryptic horse shit—yeah, I'm a bit skeptical, Lucian. Can you blame me?"

"No. I understand—"

He reached out his hand, and my body acted before my mind could. I slashed downward with the athame, and the blade sliced through his palm. There was no castoff spray of blood, though. It was the oddest thing. I saw a red line form against Lucian's flesh, but the blood just hung there, frozen. It didn't drip.

Lucian looked genuinely surprised. He stared at his palm, as if in wonder.

"I'm sorry," I said. "You moved, and I just reacted on reflex. It was stupid. I'll go get you a bandage—"

"No need." He held his palm out. As I watched, the cut slowly closed up, as if a zipper was being drawn across the flesh. A thin trail of blood remained on the surface of his palm, but the cut itself was gone. Lucian looked at the blood. I couldn't tell what he was thinking.

I knew that necromancers could heal, but not that fast. It was uncanny.

I don't know why I reached out to touch his palm. Maybe I just had to feel it for myself. Maybe it was a compassionate reflex—some need to wipe away the blood. When my fingers touched his, I felt a shock. It was similar to what I'd felt back at the club, when our powers mingled with each other. It wasn't just my hand touching his. Some darkness inside me was brushing against his own. I felt the hairs on the back of my arms and neck standing straight up. His blood was wet against my fingertips.

I looked up, and his eyes were fixed on mine. They looked human. It may have been a trick of the light, or just a necro mind trick, but they seemed once again like the eyes of a young man in his early thirties, still flickering with some kind of promise. I saw that there was a faint scar on his chin—possibly from some childhood accident. It would never heal. Like vampires, the most powerful necromancers could defy death. Maybe his hair would never grow, his body would never change. The normal fusions of muscle and bone, the tectonic shifting and wearing down of a human body, would never take place. He would stay like this, just like this, forever.

It seemed almost cruel. And yet I could understand the desire for it. A writer once said that people desire immortality only because they know that it could never happen. If they really understood it, they'd never wish for it.

If I could see into Lucian's mind, would I even understand it? Would his thoughts, his emotions, make any sense to me? Or would it be like reading a foreign language, or trying to watch television with the sound turned off? Some frightful, silent play, where nothing made sense, where the actors seemed inseparable from their parts, where there was nothing but penumbra, dance, and blood.

I could see his mark now—the lily. The touchstone of my dreams. Just below the collar of his shirt. I reached up, brushed the fabric aside. It blazed white against his skin, just as I remembered it. I wanted to touch my own neck, to make sure that I wasn't marked as well. Because I could feel it. Still. I could feel it moving beneath my skin, and it terrified me.

Lucian gave me an odd look. "How did you know about that?"

I swallowed. "It was in my dream—you—and that mark. I touched it." I stroked the skin without meaning to, and Lucian's breath quickened. It was hot, like I remembered, almost feverishly so.

"What is this thing that connects us?" I asked. "What is it, Lucian? Because it scares the shit out of me. *You* scare the shit out of me. But I'm dreaming about you, thinking about you—it's driving me crazy!"

Lucian was silent for a moment. Then:

"I'll ask my question now."

He touched my face and kissed me.

I felt like I was back in that alley again, all those years ago, being attacked by the vampire. The heat of his breath, the terrible pain of his fangs sinking into my flesh, and the disorienting rush of desire rising up all at once, as if my whole body was freezing and on fire at the same time. It felt like that again, only this time, I was more frightened—not of the vampire, but of myself. In the alley, I'd known that it was only a ploy. That vampire was going to die as soon as I could raise the power, and my body was just the distraction. Now, I wasn't so sure. A voice inside me screamed: *You're letting this happen! You're letting him do this!* He wasn't a vampire, but he wasn't human either. And what did that mean? What had he become? What was I becoming?

Before I could stop myself, I felt the power flowing up the hilt of the blade, into the athame, through my arm. Lucian's blood burned against my fingers. I pushed him away with my left hand, and struck him across the face with my right.

I channeled a lot of power into that punch, and he actually staggered backward a bit. He stared at me with a ridiculous expression of surprise.

Then he was kissing me again. And that was good. Sweet Jesus, that was good. His weight pushed me down on the bed. I shifted, rolling onto my knees so that I could straddle him, my palms pressed against his chest. His eyes were half-closed, and he smiled, but didn't say anything. Lucian didn't suffer from the particular weakness that some men have, that desire to talk with your mouth when you should be talking with other body parts. I didn't want composition. I wanted to burn.

The door was still partway open, but I didn't care. If Derrick got up for some ice cream, he was going to get an obscene surprise. But I liked that sliver of warm space, that connection to the rest of the apartment, to my life. It kept me from drowning.

I pulled off my shirt and threw it—I don't know, somewhere, that random place where clothes go when you fling them unthinkingly at some corner of the room. It takes forever to find them in the morning, but in the moment, you feel like you actually know where they'll land, that you can divine those coordinates. Like you pretend to know whose bed your body might land in, whose mouth might be pressing on yours. It's all really a fucked-up lottery. Or one of those equations like pi that goes on forever.

I reached my hands up his shirt, pressing my thumbs into his chest, kneading, as I licked his neck. He gasped softly, leaning into my tongue, and I realized that our positions were now reversed. This was no dream. And if I was going to hell, at least I'd fucking be on top for once.

Lucian reached his arms above his head, and I pulled the shirt off. The tattoos flared—black leaves against his skin, crow's feathers and mottled islands slowly coming together through tectonic upheaval. I kissed the ouroboros, and felt his tail moving against my lips. I tongued the lily, fast, then slowly, and he made a muffled sound as he grabbed my hair.

I reached down to unfasten his belt—as tricky as undoing a bra sometimes, although girls will never admit it. He didn't say anything, but his grip on me tightened. His body felt so malleable—not like the bad dates who pawed you all over and then fell into a tedious, uninspired rhythm. Lucian moved with the unhurried grace of someone who'd enjoyed sex with a lot of different partners, who knew how to surrender to the ebb and flow and about-turn of what was always strange, unpredictable, didactic, sometimes even funny. He didn't have to lead because we were both under thrall, both in control of each other. Like Paul's gospel. *My body*

*belongs to you, and your body belongs to me. But please, be
kind, even in the dark, because it's still my body.*

I slipped off his socks. His toes were golden and small.
Almost petite. I kissed the pad of his foot. He arched his
back. Were necromancers ticklish?

I tugged his pants halfway down, still holding on to the
belt. He shifted position—not an invitation, but more of a
suggestion. A careful lover can tell the difference. I pressed
my mouth against the soft fabric of his briefs, tasting the
heat, inhaling; there was that powerful, sweetbitter smell,
dank and incredible. I trailed two fingers along the edge of
the waistband, and he shivered. I felt his stomach muscles
clench. I dragged my tongue upward, licking small circles
around the column of fine, black hairs on his abdomen while
I cupped him with my other hand.

I've got you, I wanted to say. *I've got you and I'm not letting go.* But talking would have only confused matters. Our
bodies knew perfectly well what to do.

He wrapped his arms tighter around me, and I sat astride
him, rocking slowly, letting him get closer and closer. He
didn't push forward. I let him feel the contours of my body,
the silken edges, and he breathed harder into my ear and bit
down, tenderly, his legs tightening around my waist, but he
still didn't push. I reached down farther, slipping past the
black cotton until my fingers closed around him. Slick. I
rubbed some of it between my thumb and forefinger, then
stroked him along the ridge of flesh that was most sensitive,
applying pressure so that I could feel him breathe in sharply.

I spread his legs and worked him gently with my fingers.
His ankles were dark and beautiful, like Athena, olivine and
sandaled as she rode the currents of the air. I moved my
tongue, and his feet went back and forth against the sheets. I
could feel the pressure building, but he didn't want it to be
over yet. He pulled me on top of him, and his tongue was all
over, like a Bedouin, dragging along every slant and surface
of my body. He kissed my wrists, my fingertips, my thighs,
swirling hot circles so close to my center but never going
farther. I rocked with every movement of his mouth. The

feeling of him pressed against me, of his legs around me, of all the curious muscles in his arms moving in unison like an eternal golden braid, and the smell and the feel of his baby fine hair, his spit—I was gone.

Gone.

I'm gone. My name is gone.

Eve was bleeding. Mia's face was in my mind, her eyes stained with tears, her mouth open in a silent scream.

Fuck. *Fuck!*

"No—" I tried to push him away, but he wasn't holding me, so all I did was push myself halfway off the bed. "I can't—fuck—Lucian, we can't—"

We were both out of breath. He stared at me, his face slick with sweat, his eyes opaque as the surface of the moon.

Then he dressed, quietly and efficiently, and walked out of the room. I didn't hear the door close behind him, but I knew that he was gone.

I threw my shirt back on and walked into the living room. I was shaking.

Derrick groaned, shifting in his blankets. He looked up at me, blinking sleepily. "Hey. Did I hear something?"

"No, hon. I was just talking to myself. Go back to sleep."

"S'good . . . have to fight the giant Jell-O monster anyway . . . and all the squirrels on bicycles . . . where did they learn that?"

He was already asleep again.

I stood in the darkness of the window, staring out at the massive silhouette of the Wal Centre in the distance. A pale red light was blinking on its roof. The lights of the city surrounded it, all of those skyscrapers, where people worked their normal jobs and ate lunch and felt like they were safe.

Derrick's quiet breathing filled the room.

I sat down at the kitchen table again, exactly where I'd started, holding the gun in my hand. Feeling its cold weight.

I knew what I had to do.

26

Light glimmered against the tall bank buildings and corporate skyscrapers as I drove along West Hastings Street. It was a very long thoroughfare, encompassing some of Vancouver's wealthiest and poorest areas at the same time. The Downtown Eastside, stretching from the infamous Main and Hastings intersection—the site of a prominent needle exchange program at the Carnegie Library—to the gritty area around Cordova Street known as Pigeon Park, was still Canada's poorest postal code. It was a focal point for Vancouver's homeless community, and an area of contention for the RCMP, who often walked an uneasy line between letting the neighbors live autonomously and trying to enforce some semblance of civic law within the area. People went missing all the time within that maze of alleys and Dumpsters, fire escapes and squalid tenement buildings, and their disappearances were often given little media attention. People didn't want to hear about sex-trade workers and the drug-addicted homeless who died under mysterious and often suspicious circumstances. They wanted to hear about the fireworks at English Bay, or the Dragon Boat Festival, or the unveiling of new transit services from one rich suburb to another.

I kept driving, past the Price Waterhouse Coopers Building, with its black marble fountain and gleaming silver dome. It was supposed to be an accounting firm, but it looked more like a Las Vegas resort. Right next to that, there was a tiny ESL college, where students puffed on their cigarettes and spoke in broken English. Across the street, Luce, a once-hot club, had shut down. It would be replaced soon enough. Clubs were a revolving affair in the downtown core. I turned onto Richards, and the street sloped sharply downward, as if I were descending into some lower ring of a parallel dimension—which, possibly, I was.

It was almost 2:30 a.m., but the Pink Martini was still in full swing, its neon sign glowing like an unbelievable kitsch lantern against the night. I slowed down, wary of drunken and drugged-out pedestrians wandering across the street, along with the silent homeless pushing their shopping carts full of discarded bottles and pop cans. Vancouver wasn't exactly the city that never slept, but you could always find some sort of community that was active, regardless of the hour. This was how people lived, I realized. In odd shifts. In mysterious communities and enclaves, some blurring into each other, some never touching at all.

I parked at the edge of Gastown—a tourist trap area, full of gift shops and heritage sites that existed uncomfortably alongside the city's most impoverished neighborhood. Gastown had no middle-class apartments. The buildings were either million-dollar lofts owned by the megaprosperous, or squalid three-story walkups and second-story suites above shops with barred windows. This area was an odd mixture of different races and classes, filled with touristy restaurants—like Monks, where the waiters dressed in cappucine robes—existing alongside dance clubs like Shine and 23 West, pounding house music, fetish clubs, antique stores, specialty booksellers, and upscale computer firms who had managed to survive the dot-com collapse of the late 1990s. Every sort of person wandered along these streets; which seemed to be in a state of semipermanent construction and renovation. As if the neighborhood itself were rapidly decomposing, and the city was unsuccessfully trying to apply patches and Band-Aids everywhere.

I walked past the eclectic row of shops along Cordova—Deluxe Junk, Biz Books, a fetish clothing boutique, and a shop that appeared to sell nothing but designer buttons. I saw a man kneeling in an alley, his hand pressed up against a Dumpster. He was panting. He looked up, and I realized instantly that he was a vampire. The hair on the back of my arms and neck stood up straight. His pupils were almost completely dilated. Had he just fed, or was he just about to?

He took a step forward, but I lifted up my jacket, revealing the athame that I'd tucked inside my belt. The vampire saw it. He looked indecisive for a moment, then turned around and walked back down the alley. A gun might not have deterred him—especially if he was hungry—but he recognized the athame. Vampires knew who mages were, and they weren't willing to violate the truce. Yet.

Most people had no idea that they were mingling with demons all the time. Still, the chances of being killed by a demon weren't statistically greater than the chances of being killed by another human. Or a bus. Most demons tended to confine violence to their own species, and even considered humans to be beneath their notice—too contemptible to actually kill. It didn't make me feel any better.

I was standing in front of a convenience store with Urdu script on the twenty-four-hour sign and yellow awning above. Hidden among those graceful loops and swirls was exactly what I'd been expecting to find—a single character, in vampiric script, which indicated that this was a vampire safehouse. Vampires could take refuge here if they were caught outside just before sunrise, or they could choose to rent the dingy apartments—little more than rooms, really—above the store. Just like Sebastian had done.

I took Sabine's key out of my pocket. It still had the blue evidence tag wrapped around it. Selena could say what she wanted, but I hadn't broken any rules—at least not technically. I'd signed the key out of the evidence room, and documented everything that I was doing. The clerk had given me an odd look, but he'd given me the key anyway.

Of course, nobody would notice for a few days, at least. This case was in the middle of paperwork hell at the moment, and nobody cared about Sebastian's apartment. It wasn't the primary crime scene, and it wasn't even the dump site for the vampire's body. We didn't have much reason to check it out, and any evidence that we found there would be out of context to begin with. Sebastian's prints would be all over the place, and possibly Sabine's, but that didn't prove anything.

I wasn't looking for prints. I was looking for a thread.

The key turned in the lock, and I labored my way up a long, steep flight of stairs that creaked piteously with every step. The upstairs hallway was like a furnace, and it smelled incredibly stale. Storefront apartments were usually like that. The floor, remarkably, was free of vomit and broken beer bottles. Only a few stray cigarette packages were scattered around, along with assorted bits of cardboard, wires, and scraps of debris that I couldn't identify. It wasn't a comfy place to live, but it wasn't the stinking hell-hole that I'd expected it to be either. It rather reminded me of Derrick's first apartment, which had been above an Italian restaurant called Spargo's. His living room always smelled like baking ravioli.

Sebastian's apartment—109—was at the very end of the hallway, right next to the emergency exit and rear stairs. We usually called a place like that murder central. The ideal location for killing someone, since it had an easy escape route, and no neighboring suites on the opposite side.

The same key opened Sebastian's door, and I wrinkled my nose as I was hit by a draft of stale, squalid air. Obviously, the place had been shut up tight for several weeks, with no ventilation. Slipping on a pair of plastic gloves, I fumbled for the light switch. When I could finally see the inside of the apartment, my eyes widened in surprise.

I'd expected something extremely utilitarian—like a student's dorm or a junkie's crack pad. A mattress in the corner, maybe, and shelves made out of cinderblocks. But Sebastian's apartment was actually . . . *comfy.* The floors were hardwood, old but serviceable, with all the nicks and grooves that had accumulated over the decades. There was a window in the corner that overlooked the maze of Gastown streets, some paved, some cobblestone, all snaking crazily and intersecting around old brick buildings and heritage sites. The bed was positioned close to the window, and I saw that the quilt and sheets were rumpled. If I looked closely, I'd probably still be able to see the soft impression of Sebastian's body there.

There was an oak bookcase in the corner—the attached kind that came with the suite—and it was overflowing with books and papers. I took a closer look, and saw a whole shelf devoted to poetry. Emily Dickinson, Dorothy Parker, Sylvia Plath, Christina Rosetti. Either Sebastian had a fondness for female poets, or these books belonged to Sabine. There were also sketchbooks and loose papers with charcoal drawings on them. Mostly landscapes, with a few cityscapes thrown in—I recognized Kitsilano, the area around Main and Twenty-Second Street, and the West End. I tried to picture Sebastian sitting at a café on Main Street, like Soma or Balducci's, sipping on a latte, quietly and patiently drawing in his sketchbook. It baffled me.

There were no pictures on the top of the bookshelf, but there was an empty frame. I looked at it curiously. This must have been where the photograph of Sebastian and Sabine came from.

I opened up my kit and got out some black dusting powder and a brush. Dabbing the brush in the powder, I twirled it lightly between my fingers to fluff the bristles, then carefully applied the powder onto the glass frame and wooden backing. The surface was a mess of prints—probably all Sebastian's. I concentrated on the area around the clasp that undid the frame. The most recent print left there would have to be from the person who removed the photo, and to have done that, they must have touched both the glass front and the wooden clasp. A single, clear print resolved itself.

Still, that didn't mean much. It was probably just Sebastian's print—but there was always the possibility that this mysterious third person could have planted the photo on Sebastian's body. Maybe they'd forgotten to wear gloves this one time. I was gambling on the fact that, whoever this X-factor subject was, they'd been in Sebastian's apartment before. There had to be a connection between the two of them. It was the only thing that made sense.

I lifted the print with a tape-lift and compared it to my copy of Sebastian's prints, which Tasha had inked from his body. Even with just a magnifying glass, and no formal training in ridgeology, I could tell that the two prints didn't match. So who did this belong to? Sabine, perhaps? But why would she remove the picture?

Slipping the frame into an evidence bag, I examined the rest of the suite. There was a miniature kitchen in one corner, and a tiny bathroom with a coffin shower and crumbling tile on the floor. I noticed a wide array of shampoo, hair, and skin products lining the rim of Sebastian's tub. Either he was extremely well groomed, or Sabine stayed here more often than she cared to admit. I looked closely at one bottle. Redken anti-snap formula for silky hair. Even a vampire could be vain.

The floor of the living room was dusty—it obviously hadn't been swept in a while. I peered into Sebastian's closet and saw a neat row of stylish dress shirts and casual pants, along with four pairs of shoes. Loafers, mostly, along with a pair of running shoes. Was he big into exercise? Did he jog along the seawall at night, or through Stanley Park, like countless other neighborhood residents? Maybe I'd passed him during my own evening run. Maybe we'd waved or nodded to each other. A mage and a vampire passing in the night. It seemed so ridiculous.

I knelt down and examined the area around the doorway. There were a few stray pebbles, some sand, and other fine particles at the bottom of the door, along with a torn piece of paper in the corner. Hah. Now we're getting somewhere.

I picked up the scrap of paper with a pair of forceps, holding it to the light. It was obviously water damaged, and had the splotchy appearance of a wet receipt that had gradually dried. Blue ink had run in gaping teardrops along the surface of the paper. Gingerly, I unfolded it, and saw that it was half of a parking receipt. I recognized "Imperial" as a popular company that rented lots in the downtown area. I squinted at the address, and my heart nearly froze. The date and time were clearly stamped on the receipt: August 10, 6:45 p.m.

The night that Sebastian was murdered.

The block number was obscured, but I could just make out the fragmentary words "ville" and "elson." Granville and Nelson.

I could see it clearly in my mind's eye. Our elusive third suspect had walked into the alley on Granville and seen Sebastian's body, perfectly posed, just as Cassandra had left it. Cassandra herself had no reason to come to Sebastian's apartment after she murdered him, and I sincerely doubted that she'd ever been here before to begin with. Sebastian had met Cassandra for the first time when he knocked on the door of her comfortable home in Elder, and his murder had been an act of passion—or revenge. After dumping Sebastian's body, Cassandra would have hurried home. Mia would have been waiting for her, or perhaps she was tucked safely in bed, sleeping. Either way, Cassandra wouldn't have wandered along the streets of Gastown looking for Sebastian's apartment.

But someone else was in that alley, and they saw Sebastian's body. They stepped on that receipt, and the wet paper stuck to the sole of their shoe. I could clearly see grooves impressed into the surface of the paper—a partial footprint. They must have tracked the receipt all the way into Sebastian's apartment, and then, in an act of complete universal randomness, it came unstuck and fell off. They never noticed it. Who would notice a wet clump of paper on the floor?

Someone else had been here. Someone who was trying to tie up loose ends—or perhaps to doctor the crime scene so that we'd be led in a very specific direction.

I reached into my kit and brought out a sheet of magnetic plastic for lifting latent prints off smooth surfaces. I used a roller to smooth down the paper, and static electricity from the plastic and the roller penetrated deep into the surface of the hardwood, reflecting the print that I knew must be there. Carefully, I turned the plastic sheet over, and there it was. A perfect boot print, right next to the door sill.

It was big—probably a size twelve or more. Sebastian's shoes had all been much smaller, a size ten or less, and most of them were loafers. I hadn't seen any boots, and he'd been wearing dress shoes when we found him. I thought of Sabine momentarily, remembering how envious I'd been of her black boots with the stiletto heels—but these were clearly men's boots.

"Who do you belong to?" I murmured.

My cell phone started ringing.

I hated cell phones, and couldn't understand why I even owned one. They only rang when you absolutely didn't want to talk to anybody.

"Hello?"

The voice on the other line was crackly and indistinct. It took me a moment to recognize it as Rebecca's.

"Tess? I—ex—the—"

"Becka?" I held one hand against my ear, in that useless gesture of all cell phone users that doesn't actually do anything to improve the reception. "Becka, is that you? I can hardly hear you. The reception in this apartment is shit."

"Tess—" I could hear what almost sounded like a note of panic in her voice. "Results back from—enhancement—your reflection—"

My eyes widened. "You managed to enhance the reflection from that photo? That's great! Can you tell who it is?"

"You have to—no—I need to—"

"Becka, you're breaking up. I can't understand anything that you're saying."

"Tess—the *photo*—you've got—"

All I could hear was static and the occasional word fragment.

"Look, Becka, I'll call you back as soon as I'm done here. Thanks so much for letting me know about the picture. I definitely owe you that macchiato."

I flipped the phone closed. I was tempted to run immediately back down to the crime lab, but I wanted to finish up here first.

I tucked the magnetic print lift into an evidence bag, putting them both inside my kit. It wasn't much, but it definitely supported our theory that there must have been a third member in this bizarre triangle.

The coffee table was scattered with scrap paper and magazines, and the only other object of furniture that interested me was a bedside table. I slid open the top drawer and found the usual items—a package of condoms (for STD protection rather than birth control, since vampires couldn't procreate, but they could get herpes), a pair of handcuffs, some nylon rope, leather cords, and lubricants of various kinds. Sabine and Sebastian had definitely had a healthy sex life.

Something caught my eye in the far corner, stuffed beneath a wadded-up ball of socks and small packet of weed. I reached in carefully with a pair of forceps, and pulled out something that made me swear softly beneath my breath.

I'd come to Sebastian's apartment looking for a few stray fibers, but I was holding something much more substantial in my hands.

A yellow scarf.

I couldn't imagine Sebastian wearing such a delicate item of clothing. That left only one person.

My stomach began to clench. Not just from the realization that Sabine was intimately connected to both of these murders, but to a much more terrifying feeling of recognition—the shiver of power that I felt in my limbs, and the unmistakable sense of being watched from behind.

Sabine was here.

"You know," a familiar voice said, "I was wondering where I'd left that. I didn't realize that Sebastian was keeping it locked away in his drawer, like some kind of teddy bear. Isn't that positively adorable?"

I turned around slowly. Sabine was standing by the window, regarding me casually. Both my athame and my gun were within reach, but could I get to them in time? Why hadn't I drawn the gun earlier? How could I have been so stupid? I was wandering around a strange apartment at 2 a.m., searching for evidence. It wasn't exactly the safest position to be in. God—had I even locked the door? Had I even been paying attention to the signs that someone might be following me?

My enthusiasm had finally caught up with me, made me careless. This was the moment that I'd had nightmares about. I was alone in a tiny room with a powerful vampire, and she had no qualms about killing me. I was like a six-year-old child facing down a serial killer. And I'd told Lucian to leave me alone, to stop protecting me! I sure as hell could have used his protection right now.

"Hello, Sabine," I said, trying to sound casual, like we'd just bumped into each other at The Gap.

She smiled. "Tess. It's been too long. We really should chat more often."

"I thought you hated humans. Except for Lucian, of course."

"I like them when they're interesting—like Lucian." Her smile widened, and I could see her front-row incisors. I knew what it would feel like to have them tear through my neck. I remembered. "And you're very interesting, Tess. In fact, I've sorely misjudged you. I thought you'd never get this close, what with your incompetent Nancy Drew routine, but you've actually done pretty well."

"Yeah, well, I'm a real firecracker."

She laughed. "I see now why Lucian desires you. He only likes things that intrigue him, and you're a bit of a mystery."

"Look—" I didn't want to make any sudden moves, so I just stayed where I was, with my hands in full view. "I don't want to blunder into the middle of some vampire-necromancer love triangle here. I've got no romantic feelings for Lucian, so if you have some sort of claim over him, be my guest. I won't stand in your way."

Sabine rolled her eyes. "I no longer desire Lucian. We satisfied each other once, but over the years he's grown too complacent—too weak. Always wanting to live and let live, preaching his peaceful coexistence. It makes me want to puke."

"So you'd prefer murder and chaos?"

She shrugged. "I choose power. I always choose power, Tess, and Lucian no longer has the strength that he once did."

"Power, huh?" I felt the anger rising in me, but I kept it at bay. "Is that why you turned Mia? Infected her? Because you wanted her to be some kind of pawn in your insane power struggle?"

As I said the words, they suddenly blazed with a tremendous clarity. Sabine didn't reply—she merely smiled—but she didn't have to say anything. Suddenly, the most elusive piece of the puzzle made sense to me. I understood what Mia's role in all of this was. I knew where it had all begun, and why.

"That's it, isn't it?" I shook my head. "I get it now—the whole twisted thing. Mia's parents vanished almost seven years ago. That must have been around the same time that your overlord, the vampire magnate, announced that he'd be retiring soon. The same time that you began looking for successors."

Sabine's eyes darkened. She didn't look impressed. "You've met Patrick, then. Lucian must have shown you. That spineless bastard. He was ordered not to let anyone near the boy, but he just had to show *you* because he wanted to impress you. To make you think that he wasn't a monster. That he was still human." She growled. It was the same sound I'd heard her make when I accused her of murdering Sebastian. "But he's not. He's a killer, just like me. The only difference between us is that I wear my animal face all day long, and he puts his away, hides it when company comes.

But we're still both the same creature, Tess. Deep down, you must know that. Vampires beget necromancers like humans beget serial killers, on and on, forever and ever."

I ignored what she was saying—it was just to goad me anyway. "You infected Mia all that time ago," I continued, "because you wanted to challenge the magnate's line of succession. Poor Patrick with the tubes and wires was Lucian's pick, but you wanted someone even more malleable. Someone that you could control. You're a powerful vamp, Sabine, and you knew all the dark, dirty secrets for making a new vampling. You knew how to sire someone and make it *last*, even if it was forbidden. But you didn't care. Because you're all about power."

Now it was my turn to smile. It was probably stupid, since she could still destroy me at any moment. But I'd been wondering about this for so long that now, as things were finally coming together, I couldn't help but savor the moment.

"Too bad," I said, "that there was a tiny problem. Mia's body didn't exactly take to the vampiric retrovirus. You couldn't quite make it past her immune system. Maybe you never knew that her parents had been mages. Maybe you just picked her at random and didn't realize. Or maybe you just never bothered to do a simple blood test, which would have told you that Mia was AB positive. That ABO type is extremely resistant to vampiric viral plasmids."

"We knew that her parents were mages," Sabine said, her voice thick with condescension. "That's why Mia was chosen. The combination of demonic blood in her veins—both vampire and mage—would make her doubly powerful. A hybrid that we'd be able to control, once she was fully turned."

"So you killed her parents and gave her a fake aunt. Cassandra."

Sabine sighed, as if I'd just reminded her of a particularly annoying relative. "Yes, Cassandra. We met while I was traveling in Assam. We needed a shamanic half-breed, and Cassandra had some problems with the CORE that she needed to resolve. Together, we struck up an arrangement."

"But Cassandra didn't live up to her part of the bargain, did she? When the crisis moment came, she wasn't willing to give Mia up."

"Her weakness was what killed her."

"That's funny—I thought *you* were the one who killed her, by reaching into her chest and tearing her guts out. Isn't that how it happened?"

Her eyes gleamed. "Yes, that was definitely some of my finer work. But I didn't do it alone, Tess. You must have pieced that together by now."

There was a knock at the door. Sabine turned, and in that instant I managed to draw both my gun and my athame. I clicked off the safety, and Sabine looked at me with mild surprise.

"I suppose that's loaded with silver-tip bullets," she said.

"You bet your skanky undead ass it is."

"Open up," a voice bellowed from the hallway. "Corday? Are you in there?"

"Marcus?" I called back, feeling utterly bewildered. What the hell was he doing here? Had he been checking up on me? Whatever the reason, I didn't care. Two against one were much better odds, and Marcus was a far more powerful mage than I was. His presence, although it had never been comforting before, suddenly made me think that I actually might not die a horrible death tonight.

The door opened, and Marcus stepped into the apartment. He also had a gun, a Glock .45, which was now trained on Sabine.

"Corday, what the hell are you doing here? I *explicitly* said that you'd been removed from this case. Why are you poking around a dead vampire's apartment, and what's *she* doing here?"

"Marcus," I said softly, "please believe me when I say that I've never been so glad to see you." I gestured toward Sabine with my gun. "This is Sebastian's dominatrix girlfriend. She's also our new prime suspect in the murder of Cassandra Polanski."

He raised an eyebrow. "Oh really?"

"You'd better believe it. We found yellow silk fibers on the body of the second Vailoid demon, and those fibers match a yellow scarf that I found in Sebastian's drawer. It's Sabine's scarf. She's already admitted that she killed Cassandra, and that she deliberately infected Mia with the vampiric retrovirus. We seem to have wandered into some kind of bizarre vampire political scandal."

"Huh." His expression was impossible to read. "I don't say this often, but good work, Tess."

I almost blushed. "Thank you, Marcus."

"So"—he stared at Sabine—"you say that *this* lady is the one who killed Cassandra? She tore that woman apart with her bare hands?" He looked more than a little skeptical.

"Absolutely. She's a killer, Marcus."

"Well then"—he grinned—"guess I'll have to be extra careful."

Then the most insane thing happened. Marcus put down his gun. He walked over to Sabine, put his arm around her waist, and kissed her. It was a full, deep kiss, almost violent in its intensity.

I could only stare, utterly shocked. When it was over, they both looked at me, still grinning.

"Uh-oh." Sabine laughed softly. "Who's confused now, Tess?"

I tried to make my mouth form words, but I couldn't. The sense of bewilderment and anger completely paralyzed me. Was this really happening? Had I just seen . . . what I *thought* I'd seen?

All I could think of was the abrupt phone conversation that I'd had earlier with Rebecca. The strange note of panic in her voice, as she kept saying, "The *photo*, Tess, the *photo*." Now I knew, without a doubt, what she'd seen—who had taken that picture.

Marcus Tremblay.

But I couldn't say a word. I was numb. I just stood there, staring at them both like a complete idiot. An idiot who was about to die.

"Here, Tess." Marcus crossed the room and stood close to

me, so close that I could see how cold and gray his eyes were. How completely devoid they were of either emotion or humanity. "Let me make this easy for you."

He struck me sharply across the head with the butt of his gun. The room swam for a moment and then everything went black.

27

When I was a little girl, I always wanted to be dif-ferent. Special. I suppose everyone wants that, but I felt that—somehow, deep inside—I wanted it just a little bit *more* than everyone else. Every night, I would go to bed and wish, with every ounce of my being, that I might wake up transformed. I wanted to be someone who mattered. Some-one who had amazing powers, who could really fix things with the universe. Someone to be loved, trusted, and counted upon.

I never thought in a million years that I'd get my wish—or that it would end up so horribly twisted.

One day, when I was about ten years old, I was walking to school when I noticed two boys beating up on a much smaller kid. I recognized him—Gary Saunders. He was a bit of a loner, like me, a geek who wore glasses and carried his science textbooks wherever he went. He was often the target of older bullies. I'd seen kids picking on him before, but this time was different. These kids were really wailing on him, seriously kicking and punching him, like they meant to hurt him permanently. He was writhing around on the grass, his knapsack lying a few inches away, his glasses sitting askew next to it with one of the lenses broken.

Gary wasn't yelling or crying—he was just sort of whimpering, like a wounded animal who couldn't even summon up the strength to resist—and I think that's what really got to me. That horrible sound. Like a mewling kitten that was being kicked and stepped on, a devastated human being who'd been so drained of spirit that he couldn't even raise a hand to defend himself.

I walked over to the scene and grabbed one of the boys by the back of his T-shirt. He turned around, ready to clock me one—no matter if I was a girl or not—and I was startled by the naked, almost animal hatred in his eyes. He wanted to hurt me. He needed it, like human suffering was his natural food, his bodily sustenance. I didn't understand how someone could get like that. How a young kid could become so gnarled and withered, so angry on the inside, that all he wanted to do was destroy things.

He swung at me, but I didn't move to get out of the way. I just stood there, and a wave of calm rushed over me. I felt a hot warmth, beginning with the soles of my feet, then spreading up through my chest and into my arms, hands, fingertips. It was like someone had poured molten iron into my bloodstream, and it burned, but there was also something sweet and mellowing about it. A clenching and a release at the same time—an impossible heartbeat, systole and diastole at once, opened and closed, with blood, fire, and strength rushing everywhere in all directions.

It's called mystical tachycardia—the initial rush of endorphins and increase in heart rate that precedes a magical event. But at the time, all I knew was that something had just been released inside me. Something was rushing up toward the surface, and for the first time, I didn't want to stop it. I welcomed it. I finally wanted to see what it really looked like.

There was a flash of light, and I felt something like electricity burst out of my fingertips, completing a circuit between my body and his. The boy flew backward with a startled cry. He landed in the grass about ten feet away, gasping. Clearly, the fall had knocked the wind out of him. But where had that force come from? What had actually pushed him, like an invisible hand?

It couldn't have been me—right? I couldn't have done that.

Right?

The other boy took one look at me, then ran away as fast as he could. As soon as the first kid was able to rise, he ran away, too. It was just Gary and I.

"Hey—are you okay?"

I extended my hand to him, but he flinched away from me. His eyes were round with undisguised terror.

"Get away from me! Don't touch me!"

I felt a flush creep up my cheeks. It was the first time I'd ever felt truly ashamed about using my powers, but it wouldn't be the last.

"Gary, don't worry. I'm Tess. I want to help you—"

"No, get away from me, you freak!" He was stumbling backward, groping blindly behind him for something, maybe a weapon of some kind that he could use against me. Tess Corday, the freak. He finally grabbed his knapsack, stumbled to his feet, and ran off.

I bent down in the grass and picked up his glasses. They were broken in several places and smudged with dirt. I remember that I sat there for a long time, just sat there, slowly rubbing the dirt off those glasses.

I sat there for an eternity.

Huh. I don't know what made me think of that.

Why would I think of that now?

I blinked.

When was *now*? Where? Where was I, and why did I hurt all over?

Slowly, I opened my eyes. Everything was a mess of hard angles and sharp lights, glaring and indistinct. I was aware of a pounding pain in my left temple, as well as a feeling of general dizziness and nausea. My mind seemed to be working okay, but my body was a wreck.

As the shapes came into focus, I started to remember. I saw the window overlooking Gastown, the comfortable bed, the old hardwood floors. I saw my gun and athame sitting on the nightstand, about six feet away from me. They might as well have been six miles away. I felt an odd tightness in my wrists, as well as the feeling of something sharp and heavy against my back and shoulder blades. I looked down, and realized what it was.

I was tied to a chair.

A tall, familiar woman was standing over me, smiling. It was Sabine. She reached out and applied something cold and soft to my aching temple. A damp washcloth. I wanted to push her hand away, but it felt so good.

"Sorry about Marcus," she said sweetly. "He has such a temper, you know."

Marcus was sitting on the bed, his hands folded neatly on his lap, as if he was about to watch a really great movie. Lying next to him, her hands tied behind her back with the same rope, was Mia. Her eyes met mine, and I saw real fear in them.

I struggled to speak. Sabine pressed a cup of water to my lips, which I resisted at first—but my throat was dry and constricted, and I'd be less than useless if I couldn't talk. Judging by the dizziness and nausea, they'd already drugged me with something, so they weren't about to do it a second time.

"It's just water," Sabine confirmed.

I took a couple sips, and the liquid moistened my mouth enough so that I could croak out a few words.

"Don't hurt her," I whispered.

"Well, Tess—" Marcus rose, giving me an amiable look. "I think that would be missing the point. This isn't a social call. Both of you have become a bit too much to handle lately, so I'm going to have to do something drastic."

"Mia hasn't done anything to you." I could feel my voice coming back, although my body still felt broken and impossibly weak. "She's just a kid. Let her go, and whatever you want to do, you can do it to me. I'm the real threat."

Marcus rolled his eyes. "I'm afraid you're wrong there,

sweetheart. Mia is the real threat. You're just collateral damage. In fact, up until a few days ago, you weren't on anyone's radar. Nobody cared about you. Nobody thought of you as anything but the perennial screwup who couldn't even make it past OSI-1."

"If you're trying to piss me off, it won't work. I used to be a retail employee, Marcus. Psychological torture is what I live for."

"I'm not torturing you. I don't have to. In case you haven't noticed, you've pretty much screwed the pooch here. You don't have any options left."

Buy some time, I thought. Just keep stalling him, and buy some more time. Like they taught you in that hostage negotiation class in year one.

Crap. Why hadn't I paid closer attention in that class? I'd spent most of my time passing notes to Derrick about how cute the professor was.

"What did you drug me with?" I asked.

"Oh"—Sabine smiled—"sorry about that. We used GHB. Sebastian happened to have some in his fridge. He was a sweet kid, you know, but he had a real problem with those illicit substances."

"I think I'd rather be drunk for this," I said.

"Well, sorry, but Sebastian didn't have any booze that we could find. You'll have to content yourself with dizziness and—if you're really lucky—mild incontinence."

I closed my eyes. "What about Mia?"

"Miss Polanski?" Marcus put a hand on her shoulder, and she recoiled from him, eyes wide. "We decided not to drug her. I wanted her to be lucid for this. Gives the whole situation a certain edge, don't you think?"

"I think you're a pretty sick fuck, Marcus."

"Am I?" He chuckled. "You know, I always just thought of myself as a professional middle manager. Downsizing, cost cutting"—his eyes were dark as they held mine—"retiring employees. Especially problem ones, like you, Corday. People who've outlived their usefulness, and no longer have anything to offer to the CORE."

I searched for a line of questioning that might steer him away from death threats. Come on, Tess—what do you know about Marcus Tremblay? He's arrogant. Most calculated killers are arrogant. So appeal to his vanity.

"How did you get Mia down here?" I asked. "She was holed up in the Wal Centre—heavily guarded."

He shook his head. "Sweet, stupid Tess. Who do you think assigned that guard detail? Who do you think had the key to her room?"

"I should have known."

"Not really." He shrugged. "Nobody expected you to figure it out. After all, you're not exactly the sharpest knife in the drawer. All that training, and still just an OSI-1? That's got to be some kind of record for global incompetence."

"I'm a slow worker," I said from between clenched teeth. "I was concerned with doing my job right—not with getting promotions."

He laughed—it was a sharp, ugly sound. "Oh God, that's a good one! *I was concerned with doing my job right*." His eyes narrowed to hateful slits. "Corday, you couldn't do your job right if your life depended on it. Everyone knows that you're one taco short of a combination plate, honey. You screwed up paperwork, botched evidence, showed up late, clocked out early, got hopelessly confused on your way to the bathroom, and you couldn't even work the photocopier. You were a vapor trail. A walking stain on the crime lab's record. The most idiotic, autistic child could do your job better than you could."

I wanted to say something angry in reply, but some small part of me believed him. I knew that Marcus was a maniac—that he'd killed, probably several times before, and that he was probably going to kill both of us tonight. But he still retained that cold, steel-trap logic of his, and right now, what he was saying held a grain of truth. It was worse than getting pistol-whipped. He was hitting me with what I couldn't control. The truth about my life. About what a colossal screwup I'd always been.

"You're weak," he continued. "You've always been

weak—" And something flickered in his eyes—an ugly, sallow flame. "Just like Meredith. She died stupidly. And you should have died, too—that night in the alley. Don't you think?"

My heart was pounding. "How did you know—"

"I watched it, of course. You know the CORE—we see everything. It's all on tape, kiddo, and I watched it in Technicolor."

"You—" I thought I might throw up. "You just— *watched*—"

He laughed. "It was a fucking showstopper."

Everything went red. "You *sick* son of a—" I tried to move, felt my own power pushing against the restraints, almost breaking them. I didn't see Sabine. One second she was standing off to the side, and the next she had her hand wrapped around my jaw. Her fingers were crushing into me. I couldn't speak or turn my head.

"I'd watch that pretty little tongue," she said, "before I bite it out. The only reason I haven't done it yet is because Marcus likes to hear you blabber on. But all he has to do is say the word, and I'll reach my hand right down your throat. Understand?"

You can't always be a locked tower, Tess. You have to let people in. You have to stop apologizing for being so— human—

Meredith's laugh. Meredith's smile.

She was dead, and Marcus had watched her die. Probably countless others had watched, too—watched, and done nothing. I wanted to bang my head against the floor, to vanish in a storm of blood and pain, until my consciousness finally snapped. They saw everything, they *knew* everything, and I was just—what? One person. A number. A piece of film.

Even as the madness poured through me, my survival instincts kicked in; I willed myself to listen to Sabine's words carefully—not because I was terrified (although I was), but because of the interesting and unexpected truth that they contained. She wanted to torture me—just like she'd tortured Cassandra—but she hadn't yet. Why? Because Marcus didn't want her to. *All he has to do is say the word.*

Sabine was following Marcus's orders. She obviously needed something from him, and right now, he was the one calling the shots. If I could find a way to take out Marcus, Sabine might just fall in line.

Either way, Marcus would be more willing to keep us both alive for longer. Sabine liked the thrill of physical violence, but Marcus was into psychological warfare. He wanted to tear us down mentally before he gutted us physically. If I could keep Marcus talking, then Sabine wouldn't be able to do anything without his consent.

"I understand," I said after Sabine had removed her hand. I swallowed through the pain. She'd come close to dislocating my jaw, and it hadn't taken any effort at all. She was an elder vampire—she could pulverize my skull by flexing her fingers, and do it so fast that I wouldn't be able to react at all.

"Now, Tess." Marcus put a hand on Sabine's shoulder, drawing her away from me. She glared at him for a moment, but stepped aside all the same. "I want you to do something for me. I want you to read this crime scene. Put the pieces together, and tell us exactly what happened."

I stared at him.

"Come on, Corday. You're an OSI, aren't you? All that extensive training, all those hours. You do this for a living. So do it now—for me." He smiled. "Tell me everything, tell it just right, and maybe I'll even let the girl go."

I knew that was impossible. He was just goading me. But I didn't have any other options left. I'd have to play along.

"Don't listen to anything that he says, Tess," Mia said. "He's going to kill both of us, and you know it. He's not going to let me go!"

I looked at her, and saw how grim her expression was. She'd gotten past the fear, and now she was in the same place that I was in. The numbness of defeat. It killed me to see that look on her face. And she was right. Marcus was going to kill both of us. All I could do now was delay the inevitable, and hope for the right moment to make a last stand. If I got him absorbed enough in the details, I might even be able to snag some of Mia's power and use it against him.

"Do you want me to start from the beginning?" I asked coldly.

28.

Marcus grinned. **"Just pick a place, and go from there.** I'm confident in your reconstructive abilities. And besides—it's one hell of a good story."

"Yeah," I said weakly. "It's a real page-turner."

I looked up, and saw that Sabine wasn't listening. She was staring out the window instead. I had to get her involved in this as well. I couldn't afford to have her paying too close attention to the outside world, in case help arrived.

Yeah. Sure. The mystical cavalry.

"I've got to admit," I said carefully, swallowing the bile around my words, "the whole thing was brilliant. You heard about the magnate and the vampire line of succession from Sabine, your undead girlfriend. I'm pretty sure that's a violation of CORE rules, by the way—dating a vamp."

He said nothing. Just kept smiling.

"And you," I said, looking straight at Sabine, "back at the club, you told me that you liked humans, so long as they were interesting. Well, Marcus Tremblay was all kinds of interesting, wasn't he? Smart, rich, powerful—he had complete control over the CORE Mystical Crime Division. With an ally like that, you'd be able to do all sorts of nasty things to the humans that you found *less* interesting—and there'd be no consequences. You must have gotten all lubed up over that idea, huh?"

"Don't pretend to know me, human." Sabine glared at me. "I deal in power, just like Lucian Agrado deals in death. Marcus had the power that I was looking for. It was as simple as that. Desire never played a part."

I looked at Marcus, and saw a flash of annoyance pass across his face. Annoyance, and something deeper.

I'd been right. Marcus was a lot deeper into this relationship, while Sabine was just in it for the swag. The power. And that irked him. If I could get them mad at each other, I could throw them off balance.

"So," I continued, "Sabine tells you about Patrick—the number one draft pick for vampire magnate—and you can tell that she's just itching to have him replaced. Lucian was the one who picked him out, and Sabine has a real problem with Lucian. Maybe it's an intimacy thing, maybe she resents the fact that he still has a heartbeat and doesn't turn into Korean barbeque whenever the sunlight hits him—hell, maybe he just wasn't very good in bed—who knows how her mind works? Whatever the case, she's got a vendetta. And that's where you come in."

I saw a dark shadow pass over Sabine's eyes when I mentioned Lucian's name. I'd been right a second time. I remembered her words. *We satisfied each other once.* I'd assumed at first that Sabine, the powerful immortal, was the one who ended the relationship, but now I was willing to bet that Lucian had done the deed. Sabine still had feelings for him. She was displacing all of that onto Marcus, but he was just a pawn. It must have pissed him off so much. He was a powerful mage, at the height of his game, and he knew that he'd never mean anything to Sabine. She loved her poor submissive thrall, Sebastian, more than she'd ever care about Marcus.

"You and Sabine talked it over and decided that a little change was in order. If Patrick became the magnate, then

Lucian would convince him to take a more active role in cementing the peace between vampires and mages. He was like Desmond Tutu in necromancer's robes. You said it yourself, Sabine. Lucian was a pacifist."

She continued to glare at me.

"But that would shake up everything," I continued, "especially for you, Marcus. You were profiting from the conflict between vampires and mages. It gave you all sorts of high-profile cases to investigate. If the truce between us became something stronger—like an alliance—then you'd suddenly be pushing paper. You wouldn't be the CORE's golden boy anymore, and Internal Affairs would be going over your entire life with a fine-tooth comb. They'd be investigating every office, and you knew that they'd turn up all sorts of other nasty deals that you had in the works. All of the skeletons in your closet. You couldn't let that happen."

I took a breath. "That's around the time you discovered that your beloved Sabine had a younger vamp on the side. Sebastian. He was newly minted undead, all enthusiastic and full of promise. You knew that Sabine would get tired of your relationship eventually, and make Sebastian her exclusive paramour. So that's when you realized that he'd be the perfect victim for your plan involving Mia."

"Sebastian was pathetically stupid," Marcus said. "Loyal, like a puppy. He followed her around everywhere. He was the easiest one to manipulate."

Sabine flashed him a look of undisguised hatred. This was working better than I'd thought it would. Both of them clearly despised each other, even as they desired each other at the same time, only for different reasons. They were using each other ruthlessly, but now the fibers of their sick partnership were beginning to come undone. I could see the fractures. Both of them underestimated each other, and both held the other's dreams and desires in contempt. They'd made no effort to understand one another—it was just business. But that would end up being their most crucial mistake.

"You introduced some poisonous gossip into the mix," I said to Marcus. "You let Sabine drop some of the details about Mia, the line of succession, and what you planned to do with the poor girl. He didn't realize that you'd already infected her long ago."

Mia looked stricken at this, although she must have known by now. She didn't say anything. She just stared straight ahead.

"Poor, noble Sebastian," I went on, "still so young and enthusiastic—he couldn't stomach the thought of a young girl dying, just to prevent a political alliance. So he went looking for Mia—not to kill her, as you made us believe, but to *warn* her. But you and Sabine were one step ahead of him.

"You knew how Cassandra would react when she saw Sebastian. She thought that he'd come to take Mia away from her, and she wasn't about to let that happen. After she killed him, she left his body for us to find. That's when one of you came along, although I'm not sure which one."

"I found him," Sabine said. Her voice was unexpectedly muted. "I saw his body there—saw what that bitch had done to him."

I understood it now.

"You told Marcus," I said, "and then he joined you in the alley." I looked at him. "You posed Sebastian's body—made it look curious. You could have eradicated the body, but you knew that it would be a challenge. His death was so mysterious, so bizarre, that you knew we'd have to investigate it. And for the finishing touch, you put that photograph in his pocket, so that we'd come straight to Sabine. She'd be able to handle us from there. And then you made sure that I was assigned to the case."

"Because I knew you'd screw up," Marcus spat.

I smiled. "Exactly. You'd seen my records, and you wanted me gone. So I was your second victim. You made sure that I'd be occupied with figuring out what happened to Sebastian, and then—well, that's when things got complicated." My smile widened. "You hired the Vailoid demons because they were mercenaries—they'll do anything, if the price is right. You sent them after Mia, but here's where your plan hit its first snag. You didn't expect her to be with me."

I remembered the Vailoid demon's words. *Nobody said anything about two mages.* Marcus hadn't expected us to be with Mia at all. It was designed to be a clean kill, slick and execution style, but Derrick and I became the unexpected variables.

"It didn't make any sense," Marcus admitted. "She wasn't supposed to be at your apartment."

"Of course not. So when your Vailoid demon tracked her, he ended up following her there—into the middle of a very unexpected confrontation with two CORE operatives."

My eyes narrowed. "At first, I couldn't figure out why he had a gun. A Vailoid is more than capable of tearing a human being apart with its bare claws. But now I realize that it was part of your original plan. You were going to have the Vailoid shoot Mia, execution style, and then blame it on a human criminal." I smiled. "Probably me. Then you could blame Cassandra's death on me as well. Since I was supposed to be working Mia's case, I was the one responsible for her death. But that plan didn't quite work, because Derrick and I managed to kill the Vailoid."

Marcus said nothing. I had him there.

"So you sent another group of Vailoid demons after Cassandra. This time, I wouldn't be there, since you'd assigned me to check out the vampire's den—where Sabine could keep an eye on me. Or rip my throat out. Whatever came first. But Mia got spooked and called me. Once again, you'd managed to underestimate our relationship. You couldn't fathom that I might actually care about this girl—that I might jeopardize my job, and my life, in order to keep her safe. That's why you were so surprised when you saw me at SemTec Laboratories. Well, not *saw* me." I gave him a pleasant look. "You *heard* me—us—coming out of the elevator. And I felt the hint of your signature." I glared at Marcus. "You couldn't hide from me forever."

"I wasn't hiding." He chuckled. "You know that by now."

"You'd sent two Vailoid demons to murder Cassandra," I continued, "and she managed to kill one of them. So there was one left. One loose end. You heard us and panicked."

"We didn't panic, sweetheart." Sabine shook her head. "We knew that you'd be coming. You just got there a little too early—that's all. So we did a little slice and dice on the Vailoid demon—"

"And then you threw him out the window," I finished. "That makes sense, since Marcus alone wouldn't be strong enough to lift him. You both figured that his cranial injuries would look consistent with a fall from a fourteenth-story window. But you were a bit rusty on your demonoid biology. You forgot that Vailoid demons have a thick outer carapace on their skulls—a bony covering. Cassandra's psionic blast hit his brain directly, just as it had with Sebastian, but it couldn't smash through his skull. And neither could the pavement. The demon's injuries didn't make sense—and they led us right back to Sebastian's autopsy results."

I continued to smile. "And because you were panicky now, you made another mistake. You didn't have the chance to clean up this crime scene, and you left a fiber. A very unique fiber—the same kind that we found on the body of the *first* Vailoid demon who tried to kill me."

"The scarf," he muttered.

"Oh yes. Sabine's scarf. Made of rare Muga silk, and distinctive as hell. Those fibers put Sabine at both crime scenes, and you knew it." I cocked my head. "You knew that I'd figured it out, so you had to step up your plan."

"You weren't even supposed to be *working* this case," Marcus snarled. "I ordered you to take a leave of absence!"

"But I couldn't just leave Mia. I'm her protector." I smiled. "And the people at the crime lab trust me, Marcus. Some of them trusted me enough to put their own jobs on the line, so that I could continue to use the lab's resources. I never quite ended up where you thought I'd be. I was always tracking you. Finally you decided to end it here, once and for all. You brought us here to get rid of us."

I looked at him coldly. "How about it, boss? Did I get it exactly right?"

"Pretty good. You forgot one thing, though." Marcus

grinned. How could I ever have thought that he was any-where close to human? There was nothing behind his eyes. They were a million times worse than the terrifying black orbs that I'd seen when I stared at Lucian that night. Those had been dark with power, but all I could see in Marcus's expression was an impossible absence. A void where desire should have been. That nothingness was so much worse.

"What's that?" I asked shakily.

"You never asked what happened to Mia's parents."

"What about my parents?" Mia lunged forward suddenly, struggling against her bonds—but she couldn't break the rope. It was probably enchanted. "What did you fucking do to my mom and dad?"

Marcus gave her a slight kick, and she fell off the bed, landing facedown on the floor. I flinched. Mia struggled up to her knees, staring at him with blazing hatred.

"What did you *do* to them?" she repeated.

I could feel her power again. It was gathering.

Oh shit.

"You know where we found you, sweetie?" Sabine smiled indulgently at her. "In a shopping mall. Cassandra sniffed you out—said that you had a lot of potential. Of course, at the time, she didn't realize that you had the wrong sort of blood for the job. We had no idea that you'd be able to resist the vampirism for so long. Other than that single flaw, you were absolutely perfect."

"So you kidnapped her," I said.

"Oh, we did much better than that," Sabine continued. "Cassandra struck up a friendship with Mia's mother. First they were just casual acquaintances, but soon she was babysitting for Mia all of the time. Just before her sixth birthday, when her latent power was beginning to peak, we knew that the time was right. So we convinced the Polanskis to sign a few documents."

"What did you do—hold a gun to their heads?"

"I believe it was a knife to Mia's throat," Marcus said pleasantly. "That was a lot more efficient than threatening either of them. Paternal love, you see. It wins out over common sense every time."

"You killed them," Mia said. Her voice wasn't soft, or broken, like it should have been. It was like a single, clear note, unbearable in its pain and density. A steel cord being snapped. "You killed them," she repeated. She was staring straight at Marcus. Something fiery and impossible had awoken in her eyes.

"But don't you want to know *how*, little girl?" He smirked.

"Fuck you, Marcus!" I snarled.

He was off the bed in a flash. He struck me across the face, but there wasn't any magic behind the blow. Just his naked fist smashing into me, with nothing I could do to stop it. He didn't need magic anymore. He had me. I tasted blood in my mouth, but I wouldn't give him the satisfaction of saying anything.

"I'll tell you," he continued in a storybook voice, as if he hadn't just hit me. As if he'd been merely relating a pleasant anecdote this whole time. "After we convinced them to sign the papers, I borrowed a van from the lab. Signed it out and everything." His smile was maddening. It wasn't just derangement, but pure pleasure. He was absolutely proud of what he'd done. Of how well he'd done his job. "I drove them out into the woods, and I made them beg. I made them get down on their knees and beg." He looked at Mia. "Just like I'm going to make you beg, kitten. And it'll do you about as much good as it did them."

Mia didn't say anything. She'd gone to some other place—some dark and unreachable cavern in her own mind. I hoped that she wasn't listening. I didn't want to be listening. I wanted to shut my ears and scream.

"Sabine rounded up some of her friends," he continued, "made sure that they were good and hungry. And then they fed. They drained every last drop of blood, until the bodies were white—" His eyes suddenly burned, as if some sort of madness were taking hold. Whatever he'd kept at bay for so long was finally coming out. The killer inside him. The invisible monster that I'd never seen until now. "Almost holy, you understand? White like snow. White like a marble sculpture. They were beautiful and perfect. It was almost a shame to burn them."

I turned away. I felt like I might throw up.

"Of course, Tess"—he smiled brightly at me—"*you* know, and *I* know, that it's almost impossible to burn away a body completely—even in a crematorium. There's always some pesky bone fragments, a tooth here and there, a jawbone, some calcined material. They can always be identified somehow. But that night, Sabine and I made sure that the fire was *extra* hot. We eradicated all trace of them. Not even ashes. Not even a scrap of flesh left behind."

He shook his head. "It's been nearly seven years, and I can still remember it like it was yesterday. The burning. How it smelled—"

I remembered the dream. I saw it so clearly in my mind's eye now. *The light.* The fire that Derrick had seen in Sebastian's mind. That's what it had meant. The horror of that light enveloping Mia's parents, the sound and the smell of them disintegrating, like scraps of parchment. Their final thoughts. And Eve—the same smoke, the same fire. Was she calling to me? Or was it just—coincidence? Sebastian must have known, too. Sabine must have let it slip, either on purpose or by accident, and he saw the image just as I did. It struck him to the core, and that was when he decided to act.

The pain of it twisted in every inch of me, and suddenly all I could think about was how it would feel to snap Marcus's neck.

But I never got the chance.

Mia was standing. Her eyes were incredibly wide and bloodshot. I could almost make out what looked like petecchial hemorrhaging—burst blood vessels—around the surrounding conjunctive muscles and eyelids. As if some terrible force was strangling her from the inside out.

She flexed her arms suddenly, and the ropes fell away. Power was flowing like a dark river across her limbs now, warping the air around her body, making her appear bright and somehow far away at the same time. I could feel it humming through every inch of the room, a giant conductor. The waves struck me, hot and sickly sweet, amazing and horrifying at the same time.

"Sit down—" Marcus began.

Mia screamed. It wasn't a normal, human scream. It pierced me down to the marrow, so sharp and so agonizing that it brought tears to my eyes instantly. It was an angry, desolate howl, so full of desperation and rage that it seemed impossibly large for her small, fragile body. It was the sound of a human life coming undone, avulsing, tearing apart cell by cell, until there was nothing left but a wash of naked power.

She raised both of her hands, and a pulse of energy exploded outward from her body. It was invisible to the naked eye, but I could feel the immensity of it, and feel ripples as they passed through the air. The force of the blast knocked me to the ground, chair and all, and I found myself lying on my side. Marcus and Sabine both flew backward—Marcus smashed into the bookshelf, and Sabine bounced off the nightstand, knocking it sideways as she tried to regain her balance.

I watched, as if in slow motion, as my gun and athame fell from the top of the nightstand. The gun slid beneath the bed, but the athame rolled slightly, coming to rest a few inches away from me.

"Grab her!" Sabine leapt across the bed, moving so fast that she was a blur. Marcus shook his head to clear it, then stalked across the room.

I had only a few seconds to react. If I grabbed the athame, I'd be able to melt the ropes and get off maybe one flash of power. But what could I do? I might be able to knock out Marcus with a single blast, but that left Sabine—she'd rip my throat out before I could move. I could set the place on fire, but then I'd still have to get Mia out of here, and Marcus would kill me before he let that happen.

Both of them were a lot more powerful than I was, and both had very little to lose. I realized then that the situation was impossible. There was no one magical technique that could get me out of this, no deus ex machina that would save the day.

There was only one thing to do.

I gave a sharp tug with my will, and the athame leapt into my hands. Concentrating, I channeled a rush of power through the blade and felt the ropes disintegrate in a flash of heat.

Marcus was standing in front of Mia now. He raised his hand, and I saw a nucleus of dark power swirl to life around his fingertips. Electrical materia—the equivalent of indoor lightning. Only very stupid or very powerful mages played with electromagnetism, and I knew that Marcus wasn't stupid. That bolt of energy would cleave through her chest with a concussive force more powerful than any shotgun blast. It would annihilate her.

I held the athame outward and, closing my eyes, willed all of the channeled power inside it to release itself—to obey the form that my mind had given it.

A shaft of energy exploded from the tip of the blade, fluorescing the air around Mia's body just as Marcus released his levin-bolt. The two energy matrices met each other, their forces colliding with a sound like a gun going off. Both Marcus and Mia were flung backward. Mia landed in a crumpled heap on the ground, close to me, and Marcus crashed into the coffee table.

"You tricky little bitch." Sabine grabbed me underneath the arms and lifted me up, until I was dangling about four feet off the ground. "I'm going to snap every one of your little bird bones, and let me tell you, honey, I'll *enjoy* doing it."

"Put her down," Marcus said, his voice slightly hoarse now.

Sabine didn't respond. She just kept looking at me hungrily. It was the same hunger I'd seen at the club, only far more intense. She wanted to rip me apart.

"Sabine. *Now*." Marcus glared at her. "I'll deal with her."

She growled at him. "Don't command me, Marcus!"

"Then don't lose your head!" He put a hand on her shoulder. "Don't lower yourself to human emotion, Sabine. Let me deal with Tess for now. You'll have plenty of time to work on her—later."

I wasn't quite sure what that meant, but I knew that I didn't want to find out.

Sighing, she dropped me, and I landed on the ground with a sickening thud that only increased my nausea.

Marcus looked at me and sighed. "So that's it, huh? Your awesome display of power? A pathetic little shield?"

"It was worth it," I said simply. "And if I had more power, I'd shove eighty thousand volts up your ass, you fucking psycho."

Marcus ignored this. He looked at Mia for a bit, then shook his head. Like a guidance counselor who's finally given up. "Poor kid. She never realized how powerful she was. It's such a shame that she's damaged goods."

"You don't have to hurt her," I said. "You can still fix this, Marcus. You can still walk away—"

"And I'm going to, kitten." He pointed the Glock at my head. "I'm going to walk away from this, easy as you please. Not you, though. You're too much of a liability. Stupid as you are, there's still the chance that you could screw things up again, and I can't have that."

"So you're just going to kill me?" I met his eyes. "Just like that? A bullet to the brain, and you think all your problems will be solved?"

"I didn't say where I was going to shoot you, Tess." He shook his head. "And besides, I can't deny Sabine the pleasure of torturing you. So we've got something extra special planned. You see, Mia never got to see her parents die, and I think that's really unfair. That really deprived her of a formative experience."

He looked at the comatose girl and sighed. "In order to make up for that, I'm going to let you bleed for a while—nothing fatal, mind you. Just a bit of tenderizing. Then we'll be sure to wake Mia up, so that she can watch as Sabine drains the life out of you. Real slow and gentle. It'll be just like an Anne Rice novel, I promise."

"Go to hell, Marcus."

"There are a lot of dimensions that I might end up in, baby, but hell won't be one of them." He smiled. "Now, let's see what these hollow-point bullets can do at close range. You'd be amazed at what the body can survive—what you can live through, despite the pain, when your heart just keeps on pumping. Stubborn thing, really." He leveled the gun at my chest. "It's a flaw of being human."

The apartment window shattered. I turned in surprise, just in time to see a dark shape tumble into the living room. It leapt at Sabine, and she cried out, snarling and slashing with her fingers. Both of them were moving so fast that they became blurs, like two shadows fighting. I watched in a kind of grim fascination as they flowed through the air, bouncing off objects, striking each other, growling—two spectral panthers slashing at one other, fighting on some other bizarre plane of existence.

Finally, one of the figures slowed down enough to appear slightly distinct, and I felt a wave of sudden hope rush through my body.

It was Lucian.

He struck Sabine across the face, and her form seemed to shimmer for a moment—all of her shadows collapsing into themselves—before she tumbled across the floor and struck the far wall. Lucian gestured, and I felt the cold immensity of his will slam into Sabine. His power held her in place, even as she squirmed—I'd always heard that necromancers could chain the undead with their will, but I'd never actually seen it in action. They just stared at each other, the master suddenly surprised that her thrall was demonstrating real power. As usual, she'd critically underestimated a human.

Sabine growled, shaking off his control like a cat might shake off a glancing blow. Then she went for his throat. He rolled backward and kicked her in the face, but she grabbed his ankle and hurled him sideways. He slammed against the wall, crying out as he slid to the floor. That ankle was definitely broken.

Marcus pointed the gun at Lucian, but I kicked him sharply in the kneecap, channeling enough power to break it in several places. He fell to the ground, half grunting, half swearing, and I dove for the bed. I groped blindly underneath until my hands closed around the Browning Pro .40. Thank God.

Lucian managed to raise himself up, hanging on to a light sconce for support. His left foot was bent sharply, but he could still balance on his right foot. I thought of the smallness, the delicacy of those feet. His body, already so marked.

I was going to kill Sabine. For good.

She grabbed the bedpost and wrenched, pulling off a sharpened stake the size of a bat, then advanced on Lucian again. I felt the hairs on the back of my neck stand on end as he channeled necroid materia. Ropes of shadow twined and swirled around his fingertips, like raw dough that was pitch black, its cold, silken scales tightening around him as his will shaped it. Sabine swung the makeshift bat. Lucian flung his hands outward, and the shadow-swarm leapt at her, steaming, visceral. It wrapped its tendrils around her face, and she screamed, but the fleshy vines only pried her mouth open farther and slithered down her throat. Black oil poured from her eyes.

This wasn't any magic I'd ever seen. It was the closest thing to raw evil that I could describe. And Lucian wielded it, calmly, unthinkingly, his eyes narrowed as he poured the coagulated mass of darkness down Sabine's throat.

My God. Who *was* he?

Shuddering and crying out as she raked at her face, Sabine managed to pick up the sharpened stake again. She drove it forward like a spear, and Lucian had to roll to the side, his arms going awry. The night-strings melted back into the air as he lost control of the necroid materia in what I could only imagine was its purest form. Sabine vomited darkness and blood onto the ground. Then she rose, her face covered with self-inflicted cuts, and her expression was more than determined.

Suddenly, Lucian's eyes flicked to me, and I saw something in his expression.

"Tess!"

He was too late. Marcus's fist caught me across the chin,

and I stumbled backward, trying to hold on to the gun. Before I could raise it, Marcus already had the Glock .45 trained on my head. At this range, with what I could only assume were Hydra-Shok bullets, it would blow a crater in my skull. All over, just like that. One squeeze of the trigger.

"You worthless bitch!" There was spittle on the corners of his mouth. He'd completely come undone. There was no going back for him now. "You are *not* walking away tonight. Do you understand?"

I understood.

So much became clear in that instant. I knew that Marcus had never been human—that all of his criticisms, all of his condescending looks, hadn't ever been the result of my actual incompetence. He'd always wanted me dead, no matter what, and breaking me down one piece at a time had simply been the easiest way. In fact, I'd never really listened to him to begin with. Selena had always been my teacher, and it was her opinion that mattered. I understood that Mia's place in this, like mine, was so wildly random. Like Patrick, the poor vampire-chosen lying in his hospital bed, his life erased, we'd been selected because we happened to fit certain types. I was the patsy; Lucian was the diversion; Sabine was the muscle; and Mia was the spark, the energy source that set all of this into motion, but that was *all* she'd ever been to Marcus. Just a battery. Just a living flame, a vessel for power that I could barely imagine, let alone understand.

But I didn't have to understand it to use it.

I didn't have to look over at Mia to see that she hadn't moved—she was still curled in a ball on the floor, eyelids fluttering, struggling to remain conscious.

I'm sorry, I thought. *Mia, I'm so sorry. For this, and for everything else. I wish I could have been a better protector.*

And suddenly Eve was there, and I didn't know who I was sorry to, who I was even looking at. Her shadow burned within Mia's, a transparency laid upon her, features blurring until I couldn't tell one girl from the other.

"Eve—" My eyes filled with tears. "Oh God, I'm sorry—"

Marcus stared at me. "What?"

But Eve only smiled. And for the first time, I didn't feel that icy sadness, those choking tears—I only felt a kind of warmth. A light. It spread through my body like glory, filling me. I stared at the girl who'd haunted me for so long, and she looked—different. Or maybe I looked at her through different eyes.

It's just light, she said, still smiling. *We both know that now. The fire, the magic, the sun, the gleam of a blade, even the glow of love in your friend's eye. It's all the same spectrum. All just light. And you don't have to be afraid of it anymore.*

The tears slid down my face. *I don't?*

No. Because it's beautiful, Tess. The light that we created. The soft flush of the northern lights, the blood-kiss of the Occident, the warmth of the sun on new leaves, the shimmer of a coin tucked inside your pocket, the slumbering glow of a dying hearth. It's all magic, and it's all light. The point of grace where two humans connect, if only for a moment—that shock of brilliance, like a tongue of flame—and yes, it burns, too, but how brightly! And how sweet! And isn't that worth the fire?

I knew then. The light could both heal and harm. The same hand that wove thread and kneaded dough could crack a skull, pound human flesh—the only thing separating a weapon from a tool was the soul behind it. The fire poured across my body, as if someone had tilted forth a chalice of liquid light, but it didn't frighten me.

Eve reached out, and I felt her love slam into me, and it was on fire.

I let my gun drop to the ground. For just an instant, I saw a flash of confusion in Marcus's eyes—*What's she doing?*—and his concentration wavered. A moment was all I needed to reach back with my mind, to follow the tenuous thread that still linked me, as one mage to another, with Mia. Her power was raw and wounded, like a drawer full of broken knives, but I'd drawn upon it once before and I still knew the way. It was a door that opened easily, if painfully, as I pushed on it, and I could see the burning light that lay beyond, a whole desert of searing, impossible strength.

Thought travels more quickly than bullets. Mia wasn't awake, but I didn't need to talk to her conscious mind—in fact, that probably would have just gotten in the way. I reached for the sleeping girl inside her, reached out to touch her insubstantial cheek with my hand, to say once more how sorry I was.

She felt my need, and her reply was simple:

Take it. Take it all.

She opened beneath my touch, a burning orchid, a deadly plant with dark, furious leaves that swarmed over the length of my body, down my throat, into my eyes, suffusing every inch of me. I held in the scream, swollen to bursting with Mia's stolen energy, and tried with every ounce of my will to channel it.

I saw, as if from a distance, Marcus stare at me in disbelief. I knew what he was seeing—not a twenty-four-year-old girl, a perennial screwup, a stick of a thing wearing a bloodied jacket and barely standing. No. He saw me taller, brighter, my eyes glowing with golden light, my hand raised as if it could ward off anything. He saw what was inside me, and I knew that it terrified him, because he was nothing but detritus and shadows inside, nothing but the suggestion of a man, a human stain.

Lucian and Sabine had both stopped now, and were staring at me. He shuddered as he stood on the wounded foot, but his eyes were fixed on me.

"Marcus." My voice was even as I said his name, steady. I was bleeding from half a dozen cuts, bruised all over, but I could barely feel it anymore. "Put the gun down. This is over."

He laughed, but it was a staccato sound, sharp with anxiety. "Because *you* say it's over? Nice try, Tess. You may be running on borrowed power, but it isn't enough. It's never going to be enough." He shook his head. "You could borrow all the power of the ancients, all the massive, searing energy from every star in the sky, and you still wouldn't be anything but a worthless piece of trash. You *know* that."

I gestured, and the gun flew out of his hands. Just like that. All of his shields melted like a burnt sheet of plastic, and suddenly my hands were on him, my mind was touching his, all over him. Marcus flinched, trying to step back, but I didn't let him. Invisible vines curled around his arms and legs, holding him in place.

"What I know," I said, "is that you talk too much."

I drew my athame, focusing the power down to a point, and the blade began to glow with curling golden fire. I could see the tendons in his neck straining as he tried to move, but Mia's power was too much for him. I placed the tip of the blade on his neck, and he cried out as smoke leapt from the contact, as the metal burnt his skin.

"What do you say, Marcus?" I smiled. "You like fire, right? You burned both of Mia's parents, watched them smoke and smolder until there was nothing left. Why shouldn't I do the same thing to you?"

"Because—" He was sputtering now, his lips wet with saliva. Losing control. Finally after all these years, something had surprised him. "You know damn well that you *can't*. There are rules and protocols to follow, procedures for dealing with people—" He smiled. "With people like me. You can't kill me, Tess, and you know it. You'd be ejected from the CORE, and that's worse than death."

"Maybe it would be worth it," Lucian said coldly. Sabine gave him a strange look, but said nothing.

"Hah!" Marcus glared at him. "This coming from a necro—the original betrayer. I don't take ethical advice from traitors, and you're the worst kind of all."

"Maybe." I kept the knife point against his throat. "But it doesn't matter in the end. You're right, Marcus. I won't do it. You're not going to die tonight."

His Adam's apple bobbed up and down as I pressed the knife to it for one moment more, then let it fall.

He chuckled. "I knew you'd see reason."

"No." I looked at him. "This isn't because of you. It isn't because of rules, or protocols, or even ethics. I'd love to kill you, Marcus. Right now, I can't think of anything else that would make me feel better. And nobody would stop me. You know *that*, don't you? Look around—" I gestured to Lucian and Sabine. "They won't do anything to help you. Sabine was never loyal to you, and Lucian doesn't give two shits about you. As for Mia, well, she's probably less discriminating than me, so it's a good thing that you don't have to deal with her."

Marcus was silent.

I sighed. "I'm not saving you, Marcus. I'm saving me. Your life—the blood pumping through your veins, the breath in your lungs—that's the only thing that separates us. Such a fragile thing, really, but it's the only barrier between us, the only thing that keeps me from *becoming* you. If I live, then so do you. I think it's a fair trade, so long as I never see you again."

I turned around, knowing as I did so that Marcus was already moving. I felt him gathering the power, but with Mia's heightened senses, it was like hearing a gunshot rather than a whisper—I'd caught on to it long ago. I smelled the whiff of ozone as the levin-bolt materialized in his hand; I saw Lucian's form shimmer as he tried to interpose himself between us; but just this once, I was faster than him.

I thrust my athame backward, without turning around, and felt its red-hot blade sink into Marcus's chest. It passed through the flesh easily, between the ribs, until its point burst through the pericardium like a window being thrown open, a ray of deadly sunlight flooding a darkened space, the horror of Marcus Tremblay's heart.

Marcus stiffened. I turned. I looked into his wide eyes, and managed to smile, even if every part of me wanted to scream.

"I'm sorry," I told him, watching the spark of recognition die in his eyes, watching his jaw slacken, and *feeling* what was left, what may have been his soul or something else, unfold into a thousand whispers, hovering in the air for a moment before it flickered out.

I withdrew the blade, and Marcus fell to the floor.

The power left me in that moment, and I almost fell myself—but a surprising hand reached out to steady me. Selena? Where had she come from? Her free hand, holding a

Glock .40, was trained squarely on Sabine. Luckily for me, Selena could do two things at once.

I saw Derrick standing in the doorway, looking more than a little frightened, and realized that he must have gone for help.

I looked again at Marcus. I watched the blood as it flowed from him, almost cherry red against the dark wood floor. Blood. That's what this all had been about. Blood. It was so rich and red as it pooled against the wood. I suddenly wanted to cry.

Crouching on the floor, I turned and saw that Mia was looking at me. She was awake now, and her eyes were incredibly wide. I reached over and grabbed her hand.

"It's over," I said. "Look. It's over."

I didn't believe it for a second, and she probably didn't either. But she squeezed my hand tight, all the same.

.29.

Marcus's blood was everywhere—on my jeans, my jacket, my shoes, my hands, possibly even my hair. I must have looked like one of the Furies. Tisiphone in a Gap jean jacket. Mia was staring at me, wide-eyed, and I couldn't tell if she was relieved or terrified. I held her with one arm—she resisted at first, but then she leaned into me. There was no trace of the power left, the wild energies that she'd unleashed only moments before. It had left her like a bad dream, and now she was just a thirteen-year-old girl sitting in a pool of blood, looking like she wanted to wake up.

"Tess?" Selena peered down at me. "Are you okay?"

I nodded. "Just a few bruises and scrapes—nothing major. I think Mia's in power-shock, though. We'll have to get her to the clinic later."

Selena nodded. She surveyed Marcus's body, and for a moment, I thought I saw a glimmer of sadness in her eyes.

"Fucker," was all she said.

I felt something then—a dark and languorous presence, like a sheet suddenly clamped down around my body, saturating my senses. It wasn't entirely unpleasant, but I still felt that twinge of dread that precedes meeting a powerful immortal. Something was nearby, and it was very old and dangerous. Both Sabine and Lucian looked up. Lucian's expression was a mystery, but Sabine was clearly terrified. I hadn't thought that she was even capable of feeling fear.

A woman strode through the open doorway—I say "strode" because that's how she moved, slowly and decorously, like an aristocrat about to enter a cotillion dance. She didn't seem particularly imposing at first. She was short, about five-four at most, and wore plain blue jeans and a leather jacket over a green velvet blouse. The only hint of affectation was an ivory comb, glimmering with opals, that lay in her shock of curly red hair. Some redheads are beautiful, but she had a kind of deadly sensuality that took my breath away, and I'd never in a million years call myself bi.

Her eyes surveyed everyone in the room in the time that it took me to blink, and in that instant, we were all weighed, judged, and dismissed. I felt her mind brush against mine, the barest touch, but I was still floored by the immensity of her power. She could kill everyone in this room without breaking a sweat.

There was no question about it. This woman was the magnate.

Lucian and Sabine both gave a low bow.

The woman walked past Selena, Derrick, and me—we were nothing but air to her, and we could have left in that instant without attracting her notice. But I didn't want to leave, and it was more than curiosity. Her dark glamour was working on me, despite my defenses, and I *wanted* to stay in her presence.

Was this how Sebastian felt when Sabine touched him, kissed him, when she simply entered a room? Was he glad to die for her?

Her eyes passed over Mia for just a moment, and I thought I saw something like sadness—not the pity that some vampires have for humans, but a genuine sorrow. Then she approached Lucian and Sabine, and everyone held their breath.

"My lady." Lucian bowed again. She touched the back of his neck briefly. Then she turned to Sabine.

"I—am sorry, my lady," she managed to stammer, her eyes scraping the floor. "It was wrong—I know I must be punished."

"No, Sabine." Her expression didn't change. "You don't know my mind, so don't presume to know what your fate will be."

Sabine sank lower. "Yes, my lady."

How old was she, I wondered. How long had she ruled the city with an iron hand, the secret emperor who pulled all the strings? Was she kind? Could a killer, a deadly empress, still somehow be merciful?

"Sabine." She spoke to the vampire without looking at her. "You have violated our precepts and endangered our way of life. You unlawfully sought to create a new vampire, a night child, to challenge my successor's claim to the title of magnate."

A night child, I thought. *That's what Mia was. A daughter of dark things, of alleys and corners, locked windows and ancient gates. A cipher.*

Sabine said nothing.

The magnate looked at Marcus's body. There was no hint of lust or hunger in her eyes, despite the fact that human blood was pooling softly all around her feet. She was in utter control of her passions.

"An immortal's life is worth no more than a human's," she said, "and no less. The little bairn"—she looked at Mia—"her parents were killed, but now this one is dead as well. Killed by magic, and beyond resurrection." She sighed. "His death brings no satisfaction, but it does bring balance."

"My lady." Lucian's voice was unexpected—almost like a gunshot in the night. "Might I beg clemency—as an outsider—for Sabine's life?"

I stared at him, dumbstruck.

The magnate looked curious. "You are not one of us, Lucian Agrado. You have no part in our justice."

He kept his eyes on the ground. "I know that, my lady. And I know that Sebastian is gone. But he favored Sabine—loved her. And she, in her way, loved him. It would satisfy his spirit, I think, to know that Sabine yet lived."

The magnate seemed to consider this for a moment. Then, unexpectedly, she turned to Mia. "What say you, child?"

Mia blinked. "Um—*me*?"

The magnate's expression was indulgent. "Yes. Sabine stole something precious from you, and for no better reason than to gain a bit of power. I believe it should be up to you whether she lives or dies. I place her soul in your hands."

Mia looked at Sabine. I couldn't tell what passed between them, but there was no hint of vampiric charm, no immortal hubris. Sabine, at last, lowered her eyes.

Mia squared her shoulders. "I want her to live," she said. "I hope that she has a long, *long* life."

There was no trace of malice in her voice—just a barely checked despair. The magnate nodded, although I couldn't tell if it was a gesture of approval, or merely assent. She turned back to Sabine.

"Your sentence is wrought. Sabine, my daughter." My eyes widened. She'd sired *Sabine*? "You are now apostate to the Nine Houses. I no longer call you family, and as one of my final acts as magnate, I banish you from this eyre. If you return to the city, your punishment will be far worse than death."

I thought I saw Sabine choke. Then she lowered her head, and her voice was even. "I understand. My lady is gracious."

"The child is the one you owe thanks to," she replied. "Her mercy has spared your life, even if I account it no worth at all."

Without waiting for a reply, the magnate turned and walked toward the door.

"Ma'am?"

Mia's voice was timid—in that moment, she truly sounded like a frightened teenage girl, a stick of a thing who'd seen far too much.

The magnate turned to regard her, and she flushed.

"I mean—my lady. Or—your eminence? I'm not sure what I'm supposed to call you, so I'm sorry if I seem—um—disrespectful."

The magnate smiled. It wasn't an overly warm smile, but it wasn't the gesture of most vampires either.

"My name is Caitlin," she said. "Why don't you call me that?"

Lucian's eyes widened at this, but he said nothing.

"Okay—Caitlin." Mia swallowed. "Do you know—I mean"—I could see pain glowing in her eyes—"my parents—do you know where it *was*—where he killed them?" She looked over at Marcus. "He said it was in the woods somewhere. I'd like to go there, if I could. To the place where it happened."

Caitlin glanced at Sabine, and I saw a mixture of anger and utter exhaustion in her look, as if she was finally casting out an impossible child. She placed a hand on Mia's shoulder and sighed.

"I'm sorry, sweetling. That secret, I think, died with the human called Marcus, and I sense that Sabine knows nothing more of what happened that night. I doubt you will ever find the place where your sire and dam died."

Mia nodded. "I understand."

"No." Caitlin smiled. "You do not—you could not. But someday, perhaps. And if you look hard enough, you will find other things." Her eyes darkened, almost imperceptibly. "Many things. That I promise you."

Then she walked out of the room, and her presence went with her.

We were all silent for a while, even Sabine. Derrick grabbed my hand. Slowly, cautiously, I felt slick, bloody fingers curl around my other hand. Mia. She looked at me, and her expression said: *Let's go home.* Even if none of us knew where that was.

Lucian stared at us. I didn't ask him if he was all right. He sensed my fear—he knew that I couldn't erase what I'd seen, the enormity and the violence of his power. But he didn't look away either.

"What happens now?" Mia asked.

It was possibly the most complicated question I'd ever heard. But I knew what the answer was. That riddle, at least, I could solve.

"Now," I said, "you come home. With Derrick and me."

She blinked. "To live with you?"

"We'll figure that out in good time."

Mia looked at Derrick. He smiled.

"Good," she said. "That's good."

The next day, two other things happened that would forever change our lives. Caitlin, the vampire magnate, vanished. And only a few blocks away from where I'd almost died, a teenage boy in a hospital bed suddenly opened his eyes. He stared at his room in complete confusion—at the EKG and other monitors, at all of the tubes and wires hooked up to his body, and finally, at his own hands. At the mark.

Then his screaming began.

About the Author

Jes Battis was born in Vancouver, British Columbia, and currently lives in New York City. He is a writer and academic whose research focuses on popular culture, gay and lesbian youth studies, and disability. His previous publications include *Blood Relations* and *Investigating Farscape*. He has taught English and film studies at Simon Fraser University and Hunter College, and his most recent academic project focuses on the history of gay and lesbian teen writing. Look for his forthcoming book of essays, *A Dragon Wrecked My Prom: Teen Wizards, Mutants, and Heroes,* with Rowman & Littlefield, to be released in 2010.

**Explore the outer reaches
of imagination—don't miss these authors
of dark fantasy and urban noir that take you
to the edge and beyond.**

Patricia Briggs	**Karen Chance**	**Anne Bishop**
Simon R. Green	**Caitlin R. Kiernan**	**Janine Cross**
Jim Butcher	**Rachel Caine**	**Sarah Monette**
Kat Richardson	**Glen Cook**	**Douglas Clegg**